W9-BQS-985

ACT OF VALOUR

Also by Emma Drummond

Scarlet Shadows
The Burning Land
The Rice Dragon
Beyond All Frontiers
Forget the Glory
The Bridge of a Hundred Dragons
A Captive Freedom
Some Far Elusive Dawn
A Question of Honour
A Distant Hero

ACT OF VALOUR

Volume III of the Knightshill Saga

EMMA DRUMMOND

St. Martin's Press New York

 For information, address St. Martin's Press, 175 Fifth Avenue, New York, N.Y. 10010.

Library of Congress Cataloging-in-Publication Data

Drummond, Emma, 1931-
Act of valour / Emma Drummond
p. cm.—(Volume III of the Knightshill saga)
ISBN 0-312-18521-9
1. World War, 1914-1918—England—Fiction.
I. Title. II. Series: Drummond, Emma, 1931- Knightshill saga : v. 3.
PR6054.R785A64 1998
823'.914—dc21 98-14845
CIP

First published in Great Britain by
Simon & Schuster Ltd

First U.S. Edition: August 1998

10 9 8 7 6 5 4 3 2 1

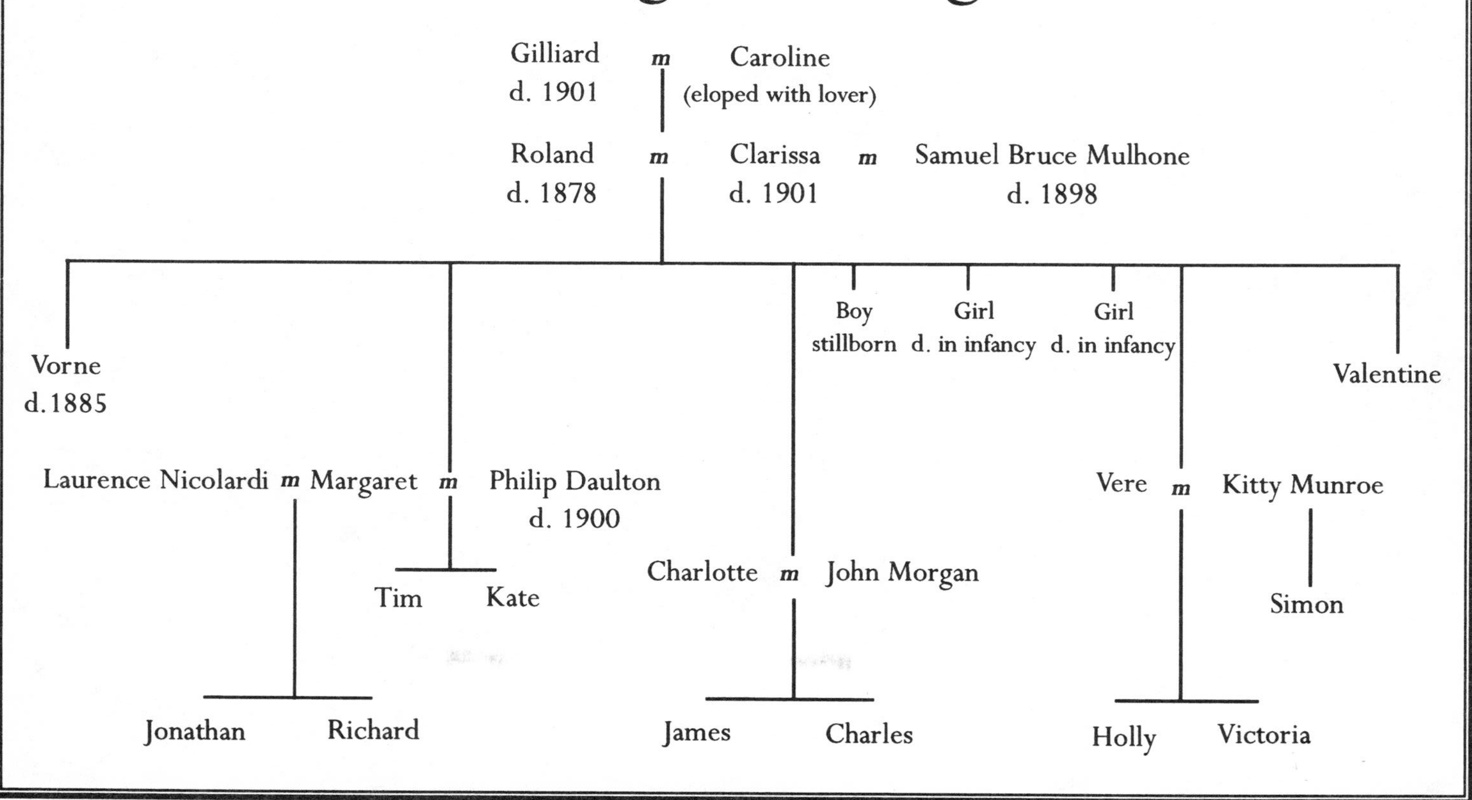

The Ashleighs of Knightshill
Gilliard
d. 1901
m
Caroline
(eloped with lover)
Roland
d. 1878
m
Clarissa
d. 1901
m
Samuel Bruce Mulhone
d. 1898
Vorne
d.1885
Boy
stillborn
Girl
d. in infancy
Girl
d. in infancy
Valentine
Laurence Nicolardi
m
Margaret
m
Philip Daulton
d. 1900
Vere
m
Kitty Munroe
Tim
Kate
Charlotte
m
John Morgan
Simon
Jonathan
Richard
James
Charles
Holly
Victoria

CHAPTER ONE

By the time he was twelve years old, Tim Daulton knew he was going to lead a charmed life. He passed examinations without too much effort, won sporting laurels with the ease of a born athlete, and made friends wherever he went. At fourteen, girls began swarming around him like bees at a honeypot and he discovered one of the pleasures of life was his for the taking. When he reached the age to embark on the military career he had wanted from childhood, there was just one desire left to fulfil. This was taken care of by the family solicitor and so, in that year of 1914, it was Second-Lieutenant Timothy Edward Verity *Ashleigh* who took his place with the West Wiltshire Regiment, eager to emulate his distinguished ancestors.

However, on a morning in late June when it was already hot, military distinction was not uppermost in his mind. A girl wearing a diaphanous négiligé had woken him offering tea on a tray, and he was wondering who she was. Blonde hair, wide, teasing blue eyes, peaches and cream skin? Well, they all had those . . . unless they were the brunettes with dark, fiery glances and intense natures. Molly? Jeanne? Flora? His gaze travelled downwards from her face. Well, they all had those, too. No clues there to her identity . . . but they invited him more than the prospect of tea. As he twisted free of the sheet and grabbed her he told himself her name was unimportant, anyway. She would get a new hat or a little pearl bracelet out of the encounter, and they would both have enjoyed it.

When the girl brought in fresh tea an hour later and told him in pouting manner that he was a lazybones, Tim then remembered he had a train to catch. Jumping from the bed, he snatched the cup from its saucer as he headed for her tiny bathroom. If he missed this fast train there was no other until tomorrow. Only by reaching Yeovil and taking a charabanc mainly used by farmers, then two different horse-drawn vehicles, could he then get home tonight and avoid family censure.

Returning to the girl, whose pout had deepened, he held out the cup to be refilled, then began pulling on his clothes that lay scattered around a room decorated with far too many pink, fluffy things.

'You're not *going*, Bobby!' she complained.

'Have to. Got a train to catch,' "Bobby" replied.

Tim never gave his real name on these sexual jaunts. He could not risk one of his partners turning up at his barracks, or at Knightshill, to claim that she had been 'wronged'. Thrusting his legs into evening trousers, Tim attempted to work out how long it would take him to reach his rooms, wash, shave and change his clothes, then take a cab to the station. It would be cutting it fine, but he would sooner miss that train and arrive late than walk into Knightshill looking like the contents of a horse's nosebag. One glance in the mirror confirmed that description. Bloodshot eyes, thick blond stubble, tangled hair, swollen mouth and a bruise just below his right ear where little whoevershewas had nibbled in her excitement. Good God, if the Elders of Knightshill saw him in this condition they would urge him to change his name back to Daulton.

On reaching barracks Tim narrowly missed an encounter with his CO, Colonel Manners, who was a bachelor married to the army. Needless to say he came down hard on a promiscuous subaltern who enjoyed life to the full. A man did not have to be a monk to be a good soldier, and Manners would never have reason to fault Tim Ashleigh's military performance, he vowed.

Shouting to his batman to fetch hot water and clean clothes, Tim burst into the quarters he shared with John Marshall.

'I thought you had a train to catch,' John murmured, reading a letter in his own room where the door stood open.

'I have.' Tim made for the bathroom. 'Could you lend me a fiver?'

'No.'

Stripping off his outer clothes and dropping them on the floor, Tim called out, 'It's just until I get back from leave.'

'*No.*'

'I haven't enough on me for the train fare.'

'Then you'll have to walk to Wiltshire.'

Cleaning his teeth vigorously, Tim went to the doorway. 'I'd do the same for you.'

John continued reading. 'You wouldn't. You never have any spare money.'

Through the foam in his mouth Tim protested. 'That's rot! I'm as well heeled as you. It's been a particularly heavy month, that's all.'

His friend glanced across at him then, dark eyes full of resignation. 'You're such a high flyer, that's your trouble. Find a few waitresses or chambermaids who'll give it to you for no more than a hair ribbon or a frilly garter. The girls you choose want diamonds on them.'

Their batman arrived with a can of hot water, clean underwear and a starched white shirt. Tim continued his pleading. 'Come on, old chap. Just a fiver until next week. The Elders will give me hell if I don't get there on time. You wouldn't want that, would you?'

John took his notecase from his pocket. 'If I thought it would chasten you, yes.' As he put a five-pound note on his small table, he added without much conviction, 'This is the last time.'

Tim vanished into the bathroom to make himself presentable enough to face his family within the shortest possible time. He had been right in saying he was as wealthy as his friend, who was the son of a distinguished banker. It was simply that Tim found so much more than John to spend it on. Life was there to be lived and he had expensive tastes. He had been brought up to enjoy the best and saw no reason to change. He always repaid John or any other of his friends who helped him out when funds were low, and was meticulous over his Mess bill. Tradesmen seemed happy enough to wait, which was just as well because he never had sufficient left at the end of each month to settle the accounts of his tailor, bootmaker and wine merchant.

Dropping his razor in the bowl of soapy water, he peered at himself in the mirror. He could not do much about the bloodshot eyes, swollen lips and bruises, but he looked more respectable now. 'Ah, you handsome devil,' he told his reflection with a grin, 'only the high flyers are good enough for you.'

He caught the train by sprinting along the platform and jumping aboard the last carriage. Having had no breakfast, he made his way to the restaurant car, then found he could eat no more than coffee and toast. There had been a round of parties this week. A great deal to drink and a different girl each time. Even at twenty-five a man needed a breather to recoup his energy. What he should do was sleep before encountering Ashleighs *en masse*. He found an empty first-class carriage, stretched out, pulled his hat over his eyes and expected to go out like a light. To his annoyance a cavalcade of thoughts kept him awake.

He had been summoned home by his Uncle Vere, who was the head of the family and one of those Tim called the Elders, the others being Aunt Lottie and his own mother. These were the senior generation of Ashleighs who upheld tradition and family values. There was another Elder, of course – the reason for the summons to Knightshill – but he was something of an unknown quantity. Tim had last seen Val Ashleigh more than fifteen years ago, when the latter had been a sixth former at Chartfield. Separated in age by only ten years, Tim had then regarded his uncle more as an older brother, someone he greatly admired and envied, because Val had the Ashleigh name and was destined for a career in the West Wilts. Both these things had then been out of reach for the son of a churchman named Daulton.

Tim was fond of his family and proud to be a member of it, but he had always deeply resented being the child of a female Ashleigh who could not pass her name to him. The Reverend Philip Daulton had been a good father until he suddenly discovered a burning compulsion to bring heathens to Christ. The laughing, gentle papa had then become a tyrant. Overbearing to the point of violence, he had terrified little Kate, bred in Tim defiant hatred, and driven his wife into the arms of another man.

On the morning before they were all to have sailed to an isolated mission in Africa, their mother had driven Tim and his young sister in the trap from Knightshill on the pretext of collecting new shoes, then boarded a train for Southampton to join her lover, Laurence Nicolardi, who had booked cabins on a steamer leaving that evening. They had moved from country to country to avoid being traced, until Philip Daulton's murder at the hands of those he had wished to 'save' enabled the lovers to marry.

Kate had not taken to the peripatetic life and, after a severe attack of fever which had left her unable to speak, Charlotte Ashleigh had agreed to rear the child at Knightshill while the Nicolardis sailed for South America where Laurence would take up a diplomatic post. Tim had gone with his mother and step-father, eager for adventure. He was a great adaptor to circumstance when it gave him all he desired, and he had thrived in the comfort, distinction and variety of embassy life. That period in South America had been instrumental in turning a bright ten year old into a multi-lingual youth at ease in any company and free to follow any star.

Tim liked and respected the man who had given him all his true father would have denied him. He also loved his mother, Margaret, who had become an accomplished hostess known for her impeccable taste and style. When first Jonathan, then Richard, had joined the family, Tim had accepted his half-brothers willingly. They had made little difference to his life at the start. Then he had, one summer, gone home for the school holiday to find everything changed. Jon and Dick appeared to have supplanted him in his mother's affections. She no longer kissed him goodnight or ruffled his hair and called him her splendid boy. What was more, Laurence began shaking his hand in formal fashion. This sign of maturity had taken Tim by surprise. He found it difficult to adjust, especially when his young brothers were still getting the loving attention he missed. Feeling very much a cuckoo in the nest, he had been glad to sail for England and Oxford.

During his wild student days, Tim had made a momentous decision. If he had to be the only member of his family group whose name was not Nicolardi, he would be an Ashleigh rather than a Daulton. When his parents discovered what he had done they had been amused rather than shocked, but the legal deed had brought penalties. Ashleighs were expected to walk the straight and narrow, and must distinguish themselves to a greater extent than any other officer in the regiment. In that respect Tim knew he would not fail. He had won all the top honours at Sandhurst, looked every inch the budding hero in uniform, and was willing to lay down his life for king and country. Good thing the Elders knew nothing of his boudoir activities and list of debts, however. They certainly would not approve of *those*.

Shifting restlessly on the train seats Tim craned his neck to look from the window for evidence of where he was, then lay back covering his face again with his hat. Nowhere near Yeovil yet! Sleep remained elusive as he reflected once more on the reason for his journey. He had envied Val all those years ago, yet *he* was the one who presently had all his youthful uncle had then seemed set to gain, whilst Val . . . ? There was a mystery surrounding the man who was returning to Knightshill today.

He reviewed the facts he knew. When his mother had fled with her children, Val had been at odds with his grandfather over his determination to join the cavalry instead of the family regiment. The next thing Tim had heard was that Val was in a cavalry regiment but as a *trooper* masquerading under his middle names, Martin Havelock. As a boy he had deduced that Great-grandfather was to blame, but the adult Tim sensed a scandal behind it all. Even so, Val appeared to have distinguished himself during the war against the Boers in South Africa, being decorated for bravery and commissioned in the field. Kate had a photograph of the uncle she had idolized as a child, looking proud and handsome in Lancer officer's uniform, so *that* must be true, if nothing else. Tim knew little more save that Val had left the army and gone to work in Australia, where he had been for the past twelve years. Why would a successful military officer do that? The Elders were close-lipped on the subject, which strengthened the theory of a scandal.

Uncle Vere's telegram had revealed only that he expected everyone to be at Knightshill for Val's arrival. Of course they would all obey, and eat the fatted calf prepared for the returning prodigal . . . but Tim intended finally to get to the bottom of the affair. After all, why should he be expected to give up his leave and forego several social engagements for the sake of an Ashleigh who had failed to live up to his obligations?

On that disgruntled thought he must have fallen asleep because he came to his senses with a jerk to the sound of banging doors. One glance from the window showed Tim the small station of Dunstan St Mary and Parsons waiting for him with the pony and trap. Shooting to his feet, Tim pushed open the carriage door as the train began to leave the station. Jumping to the platform, he realized that a young woman standing and gazing at the surrounding hills was about to be struck by the door left swinging on its hinges. He lunged forward to snatch her from danger in the nick of time, then smiled down into her startled face as he explained how some person's carelessness could have caused her serious injury. She was decidedly pretty and looked at him as if he were the answer to all her prayers.

'I'm so thankful I spotted the hazard,' he added, taking her travelling bag with one hand and her left arm with the other. 'Is someone meeting you? I can't leave you here all alone. Railway stations can present all kinds of problems to unescorted ladies.'

'Like unescorted men, for instance?' she asked in innocent tones which did not hide her caustic amusement. Yet she made no attempt to draw away from his hand beneath her elbow.

Tim's interest flared. Not the ingenuous young creature he had thought her to be. 'You're very unkind,' he protested. 'I've just saved your life.'

Her brown eyes were full of laughter. 'I'm truly grateful but, you see, as you and I were the only people to leave the train at this station, it must have been you who left the door swinging so dangerously.'

Tim was further intrigued. 'I could have left you to your fate,' he pointed out, guiding her through the gate in the direction of Parsons and the trap. There was no one else in sight so he had every intention of taking her to her destination before someone turned up to do so.

'And had the deed on your conscience for the rest of your days? You're much too gallant for that, Mr Ashleigh.'

Tim stopped and stared at his companion. 'We've met before?'

She shook her head. 'Mr Parsons is waiting for you, and I've occasionally seen you in the village. Everyone in the district knows the family from Knightshill.' She held out her hand for her bag. 'I hope you enjoy your leave . . . and thank you once again for your prompt action just now.'

Tim kept hold of her luggage. 'You must allow me to make amends for my carelessness by giving you a ride in the trap to your destination.'

'No, no. There's really no need.' She made to take her property, but Tim resolutely held it out of her reach.

'Has someone promised to meet you?'

'No, but . . .'

'Then I *insist* on escorting you.' He took her arm again. 'I'm a very determined man. It's a family trait.'

'So I've heard,' she murmured, as he led her to the trap and handed her bag to the groom watching with interest.

'Parsons, we shall take this young lady to her destination before going home.'

'Whatever you say, sir,' said Parsons with a knowing grin.

Tim helped his passenger into the trap and was treated to a glimpse of lace generously trimming her silk petticoat. Beneath her sensible exterior she was delightfully feminine. He leapt up to sit beside her with interest deepening further. During the drive he would pursue this fortunate encounter as far as he was able. He hoped their destination lay on the far side of the village. Not only would that give him enough time to win her over, he could ride there very swiftly down the bridle-path behind Knightshill. This spell of leave might prove quite enjoyable after all.

He gave her his most irresistable smile. 'Where to?'

She smiled back. 'The Stag's Head, if you please.'

Interest, intrigue, instantly developed into a sensation he could not name as he gazed down at a face covered in feigned innocence. The Stag's Head Inn lay just fifty yards away across the cobbled square. Now he understood Parsons' amusement.

The girl relented, saying gently, 'You were so determined you allowed me no chance to finish what I was saying.' As he continued to study her, for once lost for words, she stood up and made to pass him. 'I'll leave you to go on up to Knightshill, Mr Ashleigh.'

'No, you won't,' he said swiftly. 'I promised to deliver you safely to your destination. Please sit down.' When she did so, no longer quite as assured as before, Tim said over his shoulder, 'Parsons, the Stag's Head.'

As the trap covered the short distance at sedate pace, Tim studied the neat features and dark chignon of this girl who now refused to meet his gaze, although she was clearly aware of being scrutinized very closely. Who was she and why would she be staying in the village inn alone? He judged her to be a year or two younger than he. There was a soft Wiltshire inflection in her speech which suggested local roots, yet this was overridden by tones that could have been carefully taught. Was she an actress, perhaps? No, not in the least like any actress he had ever encountered. She had been pert enough at the start but the bantering exchange between them had ended very abruptly.

'The Stag's Head, sir,' carolled Parsons gaily as he brought the trap to a halt in the inn's yard.

Without a word Tim stepped down and held out an arm. His silent passenger put a white-gloved hand in his and joined him on the cobbles. Then he took her bag from beside Parsons, slid his left hand beneath her elbow, and led her through the entrance to the dim interior smelling of ale and tobacco in addition to the aroma of rabbit stew. Through the open door to the bar he could see a group of farm-hands enjoying their pints of ale, and a big brute of a man slumped in a corner staring moodily at a row of empty glasses on the table before him. Hardly a congenial atmosphere for his companion.

'Thank you, Mr Ashleigh. I'll take up no more of your time.'

Tim stopped and turned to her. 'Are you sure you'll be all right here?'

'Oh, yes.'

'Well . . . I'll ring for the landlord.' He took her luggage across to the desk in the corner and shook the little brass bell on it before turning back to her. 'May I know your name, since you know mine?'

After slight hesitation she said, 'Amy Sturt. *Mrs* Amy Sturt.'

He had not expected that, although he should have guessed, he told himself. There was nothing to do but bow out. 'Goodbye, ma'am. I hope you'll enjoy your stay in Dunstan.'

Back in the trap and bowling through the village towards the lane leading to Knightshill, Tim put curiosity before pride and questioned Parsons. 'How did you know the lady would be staying at the Stag's Head?'

'She's the Moorkins' niece, sir. Lived there for a while when her father died,' he said above the sound of Grace's hooves on cobbles. 'Nellie Moorkin's sister married someone who had a little teashop in Salisbury. Then he took up partnership with a chum of his in London and, 'cording to Moorkin, they worked up a nice little place and did very well. But Miss Amy's mother was lost soon after. Couldn't take the smoke and fog up there. Then her father upped and died two year ago leaving the girl in awkward straits, if you get my meaning.'

'So she came to live at the Stag's Head.'

Parsons told the mare to slow as they neared the turning into the lane which curved upwards quite steeply for the first hundred yards before changing into a gentler, straighter climb.

Tim pursued the subject. 'What happened then?'

'Beg pardon, sir?'

'Who is Sturt?'

'Miss Amy's partner. Things was tricky, you see. Mr Sturt was a bachelor, and they'd all lived over the premises. Well, Miss Amy couldn't stay there, could she? But the money was tied up in the business and Miss Amy, she'd run it. Well, the teashop side. Employed three girls, I heard. Wore uniforms, and all. Real nice place. So Miss Amy accepted Mr Sturt's offer to marry and move back there. It was the best plan all round.'

Tim frowned. 'Then he's the same age as her father?'

'But he's got a tidy sum behind him. The young lady's done well for herself. When he goes, she'll get the lot.'

Tim fell silent. He would not have judged her a gold-digger, but one never knew with women. That's why he loved them and left them. 'Bobby' had all the fun and none of the pitfalls. He remained deep in thought until Knightshill came in sight and he recalled the reason for his visit. Better to concentrate on the enigmatic uncle returning from a far colony than waste time on a girl who had made something of a fool of him today.

Kate kept her eye on the watch pinned to the front of her spotted blouse. She intended to catch the train no matter what Sister had said. Her weekend leave should have begun when she came off duty at midnight, but there were no trains to Salisbury until this morning. The one she wanted to catch departed in forty-five minutes, but Sister had decreed that all off-duty nurses should clear the remaining débris from the fête held yesterday to swell hospital funds. For over an hour and a half Kate had been folding and stacking chairs, then picking up litter from grass burned brown by constant sunshine and lack of rain. When Sister decreed, nurses obeyed even when they had a train to catch. All the same, Kate proposed sneaking away after fifteen more minutes to where her bicycle was hidden behind the gardener's shed. She would have to pedal furiously to reach the station on time, but there was no more than a light wind and it was downhill much of the way.

Stuffing lollipop sticks, toffee papers and cigarette packets into a sack alongside her friend Rosie, Kate murmured, 'Here comes the

Dragon. As soon as she's checked up on us and gone inside again, I'm leaving.'

'You shouldn't be doing this, anyway,' Rosie claimed for the fourth time that morning. 'Because of that emergency, you didn't even have the fun of being here yesterday. It's not fair.'

'Shhh! She's got ears that hear around corners, and she's getting close,' warned Kate, head low over the sack. 'I didn't mind missing the fête. That young boy's life hung in the balance for a while, you know. I'm glad I was there when the fever broke. He trusts me and does all I ask of him. It's half the battle when the patient has faith in you.'

Rosie straightened up, pushing a loose strand of flaxen hair back into the glossy chignon with a sigh. 'Kate, you're twenty-four but behave like a matron. When are you going to start enjoying life?'

Kate glanced up at her. 'I do enjoy it. What I did yesterday instead of frolicking amongst the coconut shies gave me much more satisfaction.'

'I know. That's what worries me, dearie.'

'Then it shouldn't. Come on, this bag's full. Let's make a show of starting on another in case she glances this way.'

They carried the bulging sack across to the place where they would be collected later that day, and took up an empty one from the pile. Rosie continued her theme. 'I had a delicious hour or so with a fellow who spent money as if there was a never-ending supply at his disposal. Paid for me to go on everything, bought me tea, then won a doll for me at the rifle range. He's asked me to meet him by the river on Saturday night.'

Bending to pick up a paper bag containing the remains of a sticky bun, Kate issued a warning. 'Don't go. He sounds altogether too smooth.'

'He is, but I'm on to his game. I also know who he is. Hugo Darville, youngest son of Sir Roderick.'

Kate was alarmed. 'You idiot! Aren't there enough young men for you without getting entangled with *him*? What if he tells his father about you?'

Her friend broke into merry laughter, her expressive face showing no anxiety over the warning. 'I'm not *entangled* with him . . . and if I go tomorrow night I'll be armed with a hypodermic to use at the appropriate moment. As for telling his father about me, I imagine this saucy lad has a long, long list of girls he'd prefer Sir Roderick *not* to know about.'

This in no way reassured Kate. 'That's all the more reason why you should steer clear of him. He doesn't sound very honourable to me. A word from him could get you dismissed from the hospital.'

'So what?' Rosie dropped the sack she had been holding open. 'I don't want to spend my whole life in hospital wards. I want to be married and have children, live in a cottage of our own and laugh a lot. I want hugs and kisses, not bedpans and dressings. Don't you?'

'At the moment all I want is to leave here in five minutes so that I can catch my train,' Kate said under her breath as she hunted lollipop sticks in the grass.

'Daulton, haven't you a train to catch?' asked Sister's voice from nearby.

Kate straightened up turning red. She had not realized the woman was so close. 'Yes, Sister.'

Shrewd eyes studied Kate from brown hair to neat brown shoes. 'I suggest you tidy yourself before going to the station. I cannot have my nurses being seen in such a state.' She began turning away. 'Be sure you are back by noon on Monday, ready for duty at two.'

'Yes, Sister.' Grinning at Rosie, Kate hurried away as fast as she could without actually breaking into a run. Nurses must *never* run, even in the direst emergency.

By the time Kate reached the station she was so hot and breathless she went to the far end of the platform where there was a tree-shaded seat. As she waited, the dedicated nurse slowly turned into a young woman anticipating a momentous occasion. Val was coming home, and the whole family would be at Knightshill together for the first time in a very long while. Dear Aunt Lottie would be in her element.

Once on the train Kate was happy to watch the passing scene from her corner seat. It was stuffy but her request to lower the window a little was refused by a staid woman in black facing her. Perhaps it was as well. The air gave little relief to compensate for the smuts which came in from the engine. Ashleighs normally travelled first-class but Kate was a working girl who used her private allowance for more essential things.

Watching the soft charm of England which spread away into

the distance as the train puffed across a patchwork of fields, over meandering rivers unusually low between their banks, and past market towns where farmers were heading thirstily for a noonday glass of ale, Kate continued the transition she always underwent when going home. Life at Knightshill was as far divorced from that at a hospital as anyone could find, so she had to think herself back to the ways she had known since childhood.

The early days in that great stone mansion had been wonderful, although the passing of time and the romance of extreme youth might be misleading her. Everyone had lived there then, Val returning for school holidays to complete the number. Uncle Vere and Aunt Lottie had been full of fun, Kate's father was the best papa in the world, Mama and he had always been together, and Great-grandfather had looked after them all. Then, when Kate was six, everything had changed. Uncle Vere had run away to the war because a lady had refused to marry him, Val had stopped coming home for holidays, and Papa had stopped loving them.

Kate sighed softly as they passed several vivid fields of mustard. She understood those traumatic events better now, but a child put her own selfish interpretation on them, and they had all added up to rejection of *her*.

The next few years at Knightshill had been miserable and frightening, until Mama had taken them on a train to where a familiar visitor was waiting to go with them on a big ship. As their new father, Laurence Nicolardi had been a great success, but young Kate's heart had remained at Knightshill. The constant travelling from country to country populated by people with dark faces and strange clothes had upset her. When a virile fever struck her down, Kate had related the pain and sickness to the fact of leaving the haven of Knightshill, and retreated within herself.

Kate was brought back to the present as the train stopped at a station with honeysuckle rioting over the fence. A mother with her children got out. A young girl stepped into the carriage, slammed the door, lowered the window as far as it would go and leaned out to hold the hands of a desperate-looking young man in dusty working clothes.

'It won't be long, Joe,' she told him in dramatic tones. 'I'll be back at Christmas.'

The matron hurrumphed disapprovingly, but the girl took no

notice. Kate felt sorry for the pair. Christmas was a long way off and six months was an eternity to those who waited impatiently. Slow, laborious puffs heralded the train's departure and the lovers held on to each other until the platform ended. The girl then collapsed in a corner with her face buried in a handkerchief while she sobbed. A meaningful glance from the matron set Kate on her feet to close the window, then she resumed her scrutiny of the countryside while the girl sobbed on. It was pointless trying to console her. Only time would do that . . . or another handsome face to make her forget the lad left behind.

Kate had never felt that way about any man. She thought of Rosie preparing to flirt with Hugo Darville, careless of her career as a nurse. Her friend had asked if Kate did not want marriage and children. Returning to earlier times at Knightshill Kate recalled the conversation which had decided her future plans. Uncle Vere had brought home from South Africa a bride with a son no older than Kate. They had become firm friends – a deep, committed relationship which allowed them to tell each other things they would not reveal to others. Simon was more like a brother to her than Tim, whom she rarely saw.

On one April day, when she and Simon had run for shelter during a storm up by Leyden's Spinney, he had declared his intention of training as an engineer because he wanted to design flying machines.

'How splendid,' she had said. 'I haven't yet decided what I shall do.'

'Get married and have children, of course,' had been his careless reply. 'You're quite pretty, so I don't suppose you'll have much trouble finding a husband.'

Having given her future very little thought until then, Kate had rejected the picture painted by a dismissive thirteen-year-old. *She* wanted to do something exciting like engineering. It had taken her no time at all to decide that she would be a nurse. Her visits to Sir Peter Heywood during her illness may have added weight to the appeal of this course, but she had not wavered from it from that moment on. Women were kicking against tradition and achieving amazing things thought impossible before. While she had no desire to climb mountains or explore the Amazon, Kate did want to do something useful with her life. In the absence of her mother and stepfather, she had had her way. At twenty-four she still had no desire to find a husband. The girl in the corner had now stopped crying and was blowing her nose with the damp handkerchief and Kate reflected that a woman was better off without men if they caused such misery.

Salisbury at last! The lemonade Kate bought at a station stall as she changed trains was lukewarm and much too sweet. The heat seemed even worse here. It would be a relief to reach Knightshill. Tim was certain to arrive late, or not at all. Her brother could manage to be a brilliant soldier yet never turn up anywhere else on time. She did not understand why. Maybe military excellence put so great a strain on him he went haywire when away from the regiment. Still thinking of Tim as she found a seat in the crowded train for Dunstan St Mary, Kate then thought of the last time she had seen Val.

After the end of the war he had mysteriously vanished into the heart of South Africa. Uncle Vere had gone in search of him, but had returned heavy hearted believing he must be dead. Three years later Val had turned up. Everyone had rejoiced, but he had not seemed in the least like the Val Kate remembered as a most beloved older brother rather than an uncle. He had acted as a stranger, hurting her unbearably by his distant manner. Even his dear face had grown harsh. Then he had slipped away while she slept, without a farewell or an explanation. The photograph of that smiling, handsome young officer which had broken her self-imposed dumbness had been put away in a box and never brought out again.

As she grew older Kate learned that Val was in Australia, yet no one had ever told her why he had left so suddenly, or why he stayed away for so long. Now he was returning without apparent reason, and everyone was summoned home to welcome the heir to Knightshill. Kate was unsure of her feeling about this. Val had a habit of taking himself off, leaving the family to worry and wonder. There was no guarantee he would not do so again.

It suddenly occurred to Kate that there were a great many more people at Knightshill than the exile might be expecting. Cousins James and Charles, as well as her half-brothers Jon and Dick, were on summer vacation from Chartfield, and Uncle Vere's twins were home from their school in Richmond. Six precocious adolescents likely to behave unpredictably when their enigmatic uncle arrived. Together with two generations of adults they would make the number up to fifteen. A formidable family to face after twelve years.

On arrival at Dunstan St Mary Kate was delighted to find not Parsons with the trap, but a young man with bright red hair standing beside his most prized possession. Simon waved and called her name. She ran to fling her arms around him.

'You've brought Jessie. How lovely! When did you arrive?' she asked, stepping back to study his round freckled face. Then, without waiting for his reply, she said, 'You've *heard*!'

He nodded.

'Well?'

'I passed with honours . . . and Sopwith have offered me a place in their design lab.'

It said much for the transition which had taken place during the journey when Nurse Daulton cried, 'Yipee!' and gripped his hands to send them both into a twirling dance of elation before the eyes of fascinated onlookers. Breathless, Kate halted, then impulsively kissed Simon very heartily on the cheek.

'Congratulations. You deserve it all.' Tucking her hand through the crook of his arm to walk across the small yard to his car, Kate asked, 'Is Aunt Kitty absolutely *bursting* with pride?' When he made no reply she glanced up at him and halted. His giveaway expression of suppressed excitement had been replaced by a curious suggestion of shock, and he had turned rather pale. 'What's wrong, Simon? Is Aunt Kitty ill?'

'No . . . no, she's fine,' he replied in a strangely abstract tone. 'Mother's pleased about it, of course. So's Father. He was frightfully keen for me to get into Sopwith, so he probably put in a good word for me.'

'You got in on merit, not Uncle Vere's good words,' she contradicted, concerned about the sudden change in him. 'Are you sure you're feeling all right? You look decidedly odd all of a sudden.'

His colour returned with a rush. 'It's the heat, I expect. Come on, Nurse, you must be ready for a cup of tea after that journey.'

Kate climbed into the front seat of the motorcar and began telling him about the litter collection she had done right up to the last moment. 'Then the Old Dragon relented and gave her gracious permission for me to leave just as I was about to go without it.'

'That woman sounds worse than my old physics master.'

'She's *much* worse.' Kate leaned forward to squeeze the bulb so that the horn blasted out to announce their departure. 'I'm *so* glad you came to meet me. It means we can have a lovely chat about everything before we're swallowed up by the others. Tell me *all* your news.'

Driving from the station yard in the vehicle he allowed no one other than himself to maintain, Simon appeared to be back to normal. He looked the perfect motorist in his pale-brown tweed suit, leather helmet and goggles. Kate sat beside him in the same clothes she had travelled down in, wondering if the helmet and goggles were really necessary or if they were Simon's one and only vanity. She would not dream of asking. He was deadly serious about engine-driven machines and very soon took umbrage at any hint of teasing on the subject, as she had learned over the years. Happiness bubbled within her as Simon elaborated on details of his examination results and the invitation to join the staff of the aircraft designers Sopwith. She was so glad for him.

Within no time at all her professional life slipped to the background and Kate was again a member of a large family of wealth, property and distinction. The gentle rush of air as they chugged through sweet-smelling lanes cooled and soothed her after the scramble of the morning; the sights of rural Wiltshire drove away thoughts of antiseptic wards filled with frightened, suffering people. So completely did the spell of home work, she gazed ahead at Knightshill on its hilly perch above the village and wondered how she could ever have left it.

'You're the last to arrive,' Simon told her after his long account of those things dear to him. 'Tim got here about an hour ago with bruises and bloodshot eyes. Your mama looked distinctly shaken as he explained that he had been hit by an open carriage door at the station. You know how she dotes on him.'

Kate was enjoying the scent of ripening corn and sun-baked earth as she gazed around at the scene they both knew so well. '*He* doesn't think she does. He once told me Jon and Dick are her favourites and he's the cuckoo in the nest.'

'Rot! You only have to see the way she looks at him to know

he's her golden boy.' Simon swung the car's bonnet around a bend with expertise, then added as he manoeuvered handles and sticks, 'If anyone should feel the cuckoo in the nest, it's you.'

'Well, I don't,' she declared, still enjoying the spread of open valley growing further and further distant as they climbed. The railway station was now only a white and black oblong way below at the far end of the village. 'I haven't even *been* in the nest since I was eight or nine.' She sighed, but it was more for nostalgia on returning to this heavenly spot than regret over her circumstances. 'I call Laurence Father because Tim does, and because it pleases everyone, but I know him as little as I know my half-brothers. As for Tim, we've absolutely nothing in common.' She turned to Simon with a warm smile. 'I think of *you* as my brother, rather than him.'

He concentrated on the lane ahead, then eventually said, 'But I'm not, am I?'

'You're not what?' She was now studying the house as they approached the spot where a bend in the lane offered a splendid view of the whole edifice.

'I'm not your brother. I'm no relation whatsoever to you.'

Kate was not really listening. Putting out a hand in his direction she said urgently, 'Stop here for a moment, Simon.'

When the car came to a halt she climbed down to the dusty lane which was often impassable in winter when snow drifted deeply, or when water rushed downwards in a torrent after the thaw. A small gate gave access to a footpath which led to the lower gardens of Knightshill. Today the house, with its famous Great Window centrally placed in the façade, stood as it had for the past three hundred years, the grey stone walls mellowed by the sun and the multi-paned windows glittering from its strong rays. Knightshill suggested invincibility, the very essence of a people who had created a vast empire and successfully defended their own tiny island from any invader. Kate felt inexplicably moved as she stood there.

Movement beside her heralded Simon, goggles dangling from his hand as he studied the house which had become his home fourteen years ago. 'It's pretty impressive, isn't it?'

Kate nodded. Then a moment later murmured, 'I wish I hadn't come.'

He turned to her, the marks around his eyes made by the goggles giving him an owl-like look, and there was a touch of dismay in his voice as he said, 'Wish you hadn't come? *Why*?'

Simon was the person she could say anything to. 'I'm not sure this is a good idea. If I . . . if *I* was returning after twelve years in exile, the last thing I'd want is the whole family on parade. Don't you think it would have been better to let him slip back here in his own fashion?'

Simon shrugged. 'I'm not an Ashleigh so my views can't be counted. Whatever he's done, Val's still heir to all this. Father, your mother and Aunt Lottie are so keyed up over his arrival. Put on a show of unity, Kate. This is their great day.'

'But it's also Val's,' she said in troubled tones. 'Whatever his reason for returning, I doubt if it's to assume the rôle of heir. If it meant that much to him he would never have gone away as he did and abandoned us all, would he?'

'From the little I've been able to garner about him I suspect he had little choice when he made the decision. No man goes off as he did after being acclaimed something of a hero with a medal to prove his courage. Don't forget, I saw him on the day Mother married my step-father in Kimberley. He was happy and as pleased as punch with his new officer rank. When he turned up here three years later, after your Great-grandfather died, I didn't recognize him. Something happened during that time which changed him completely – something the older generation have kept secret all these years.' After a moment or two he gently turned Kate to face him. 'It isn't that you wish *you* hadn't come, is it? You wish *he* wasn't coming.'

CHAPTER TWO

Vere glanced at the clock once more. Simon had gone to the station almost an hour ago. They should have been back by now. Everyone else was here, including Laurence who had managed to get away for a weekend even in the present European crisis. Vere was as proud of Simon as if he were his own son and suspected the poor fellow of being in love with young Kate, but as she regarded him merely as a brother they were unlikely to be dallying for romantic reasons. Maybe Kate had not been on the two forty-five. Simon would surely have returned to say so, in that instance. Could Val have been on that same train? Were they dealing with his baggage? Could his brother be here at any moment?

Vere moved to the window in restless fashion. No, Val was coming from Southampton, so he would hardly be travelling on the Salisbury line. The liner had docked on schedule. Vere's telephone call to the shipping line had confirmed that. Consultation of rail timetables had shown a train departing at three-thirty from the docks – time enough for Val to go through disembarkation procedures – and a connection at Romsey would get him to Dunstan St Mary by five o'clock. Vere planned to send Parsons down with the trap and Ebson with the large carriage for trunks and heavy baggage.

At that point Simon's car came into view across the old moat bridge, with Kate in the passenger seat. Vere breathed a sigh of relief. Despite his step-son's enthusiasm for things mechanical, he himself preferred the grace and quietness of horse-drawn travel when in the country. It was bad enough to endure the noise and clamour of motor vehicles in towns and cities; he was old-fashioned enough to want to keep them from country lanes for as long as he could. They would come, of course. Nothing would stop them now. Young Simon was going to dedicate his life to filling the *skies* with engine-driven machines, too. Whatever would Sir Gilliard have thought of that; a man who had deplored the advent of trains?

Even now, all these years on, thoughts of his grandfather who had ruled the family with a set of standards none of them could ever match, gave Vere a twinge of conscience. His own devastating words had killed an old man as demanding of himself as he was of others; a distinguished general obsessed with continuing the Ashleigh bloodline and determined to re-create the family's dead hero in young Val. Because of it, the boy had been driven to desperate measures at school which had resulted in dismissal. The young nineteen year old had fought back in his bid to earn Sir Gilliard's forgiveness, but he had tried too hard to live up to the impossible burden put on his young shoulders. During an incident in wartime, Val had been the victim of cruel circumstance which had completed his downfall.

Wandering in the realms of memory, Vere thought of those four months he had spent in South Africa at the tail end of the war searching for a young man whose certain golden future had been destroyed by belief in a family hero – an older brother whose feet had not only been of clay, they had trodden in the mirkiest of mires. For three years, the family had believed Val dead until he arrived at Knightshill haggard, penniless, frighteningly changed but still with a tiny flame of courage burning within him.

Vere's brow furrowed. His own words had once more had a devastating effect on a member of his family. This time they had not killed the recipient, but Val had slipped away during the night after hearing the truth about the man for whom he had suffered so much in trying to emulate. His spirit had been finally broken.

Six months after Val's departure a brief letter had arrived from a strangely named place in Australia where he was working on a cattle ranch. Vere and his sisters had written regularly, but only once a year had a reply arrived at Knightshill to prove Val was still at the same address. Those letters had made no comment on family news passed to him. They had been economical with words which merely described the spartan life he led in an isolated, primitive region and were always dated January 22nd, the anniversary of Vorne Ashleigh's supposedly heroic death.

Out of the blue last week Vere had received a cable stating that his brother would be arriving at Southampton on the 20th of June. Vere's enquiries had revealed that only one liner was due in from Australia on that date, and port officials had this morning confirmed its arrival. After twelve years, Val was coming home. Vere's happiness would then be complete, because for all of that time he had felt responsible for driving his heir from his birthright.

There had been great changes at Knightshill since the old general had died. The overwhelming military influence had been diluted, and Vere had introduced elements which his artistic nature appreciated. His career continued in spasmodic fashion with occasional commissions to paint battle canvases, but other interests now filled his life so that something which had once been his lifespring was a secondary factor.

He ran Knightshill in conjunction with John Morgan, his sister Charlotte's husband who had formerly been bailiff of the estate. There was also a vast, prosperous cattle ranch in America left to her four surviving children by their mother. In the intervening fourteen years the property had prospered. They had all done very well from the profits, especially Val who had been bequeathed a double share by the mother who had married a Texan and deserted them all when her youngest child had been a mere infant. Val would find a small fortune awaiting him.

In the midst of these commitments Vere had not completely lost touch with friends he had made as a fighting man in the Sudan, and later as a war artist during the struggle against the Boers when he had met the woman he determined to make mistress of Knightshill. He was invited to a number of military functions, and army men often graced the table at Knightshill. Yet few of them were members of the West Wiltshire Regiment, which still lionized Vorne Ashleigh as one of its great heroes.

Vere turned away from the window to study his sister Margaret's son, who had arrived with a cock-and-bull story about an accident with a carriage door. Tim had joined the family regiment on leaving Sandhurst with the highest accolades, and was as fired with eagerness to live up to Vorne as Val had once been. Margaret, as well as Charlotte, had agreed to keep the truth to themselves for the family's and the regiment's sake, but they all found Tim's enthusiasm for his hero difficult to cope with. Margaret nevertheless adored her first born, a fact she tried too hard to conceal. The young man himself tried too hard to pretend he did not care about his imagined exclusion from the Nicolardi ménage. Mother and son hurt each other unnecessarily.

Watching Tim now as his own twin daughters hung on the young officer's every word – he could never resist pretty faces even when they belonged to his cousins, and fourteen year olds were *very* impressionable – Vere wondered if Margaret believed the reason given for her son's appearance today. That Tim had been with a woman last night was all too obvious, and Vere suspected his nephew of having that same streak of wildness which had developed to such dangerous proportions in Vorne. Tim possessed Vorne's blond good looks and beguiling charm. Sir Gilliard had maintained that the West Wilts would make a man of *anybody*, but Tim was the first Ashleigh member of the regiment since the death of its hero and a subaltern so closely resembling the portrait hanging in the Officers' Mess would surely be treated as heir apparent to the Hero of Khartoum, and indulged. It was worrying.

Simon and Kate entered the room just then and, as he surveyed the crowded room, Vere felt a fresh surge of excitement. The Ashleighs were an attractive, talented crowd. He was proud of them. His twins, Holly and Victoria, were artistic and pretty enough to break hearts wherever they went in coming years. Charlotte's two sons were sturdy and intelligent, James already fascinated with science and Charles hoping to manage the American ranch one day. Then there were the Nicolardi boys. Dark and intense, they were promising classical scholars. Like Tim, their life as a diplomat's children had made them multi-lingual. Yes, the Ashleighs were certainly making their mark in the world.

Thornton came in followed by two maids. They all carried laden trays which took the attention of the youngest generation present, who were forever hungry. While the butler poured tea into numerous cups, and Rose and Ginny handed round plates of sandwiches, Kitty made her way across the thick blue and cream carpet to the window embrasure. Vere made no attempt to meet her, and instead stood watching the woman he adored as much now as when he had pursued her across South Africa at the turn of the century. In a dress of grey silk, with her beautiful titian hair glowing richly in the light from the many windows, his wife looked every inch the mistress of this lovely old house. Vere was a man widely blessed.

'You're looking remarkably like a mother hen surveying her brood,' she teased on reaching him.

'Can a man be a mother hen?'

'I only said you looked like one, darling.'

He smiled. 'It's a brood to be proud of, don't you think?'

She half turned to survey the minor chaos caused by the distribution of tea to fifteen people. 'It's a rather large one when they all gather.'

'When Val joins it, it'll be complete.'

She wore a troubled look as she glanced back at him. 'Are you certain that's what he has in mind? He's been away a very long time. Since he was thrown out of Chartfield, in essence.'

'Exactly. That's why his return is so significant. He clearly feels ready to take his place here now the past is well and truly exorcized.'

'Mmm! What *is* his place?'

'My successor. He'll need time to reacquaint himself with life on the estate, of course, then he'll get to work. He must be an expert on cattle, so he can take charge of that aspect when Lottie and John go on their trip to America in September.'

'And what will Val do with the rest of his time? Our cattle won't be enough to keep him fully occupied.'

He took her hand, saying gently, 'Don't rush things, my dear. He'll have thought out his own plans before he made the decision to come home. I suspect one of them will be to find himself a wife.'

'I see. Have you considered the possibility of his bringing a wife with him . . . and a child or two?'

'Good God, no! Val wouldn't marry a woman from the back of beyond.'

'You did.'

It took him aback, but not for long. Putting his hands on her waist he said fondly, 'What a howling success it's been. This house is bustling with life and laughter, a meeting place for the talented and famous, a real *home*. For years it resembled a military museum.'

'And that's how Val will remember it. Don't expect too much of the lad and start putting too many burdens on his shoulders the minute he gets here.'

'He's no longer a lad, my dear. You've forgotten how time has slipped past. He's thirty-five, and clearly ready to settle down. The place for him to do that is Knightshill. He's the only one who can continue the direct Ashleigh line.'

Kitty frowned. 'That sounds remarkably like Sir Gilliard.'

'Quite possibly, but the difference is that *I* don't expect my heir to marry *any* woman of the right pedigree who will produce sons galore.' He smiled. 'Come on, let's have some tea before all those children devour everything.'

He led his wife across to the noisy group doing justice to sandwiches, scones and cherry cake. There was a babble of conversation for Vere and Kitty had never believed in children being seen but not heard, stipulating only that what they said was worth hearing. Today, they exuded an underlying air of excitement. After all, they had never before had a stranger uncle return from the other side of the world; an uncle who, despite the adults being tight-lipped on the subject, they *knew* was the black sheep of their family.

The landlord appeared before him and began collecting the array of empty glasses on the small table, saying conversationally, 'We do have rooms upstairs, sir. Our charges are very reasonable.'

Val shook his head and got to his feet knowing he was really being asked to leave. He supposed the man must be Lionel Moorkin, unless the Stag's Head had changed hands during the last twelve years or so. It was time he got moving, anyway. He could not put off the inevitable any longer. Taking up the canvas bag which contained two sets of clothes and a stockman's coat, he left the inn and stood for a moment or two in the yard gazing up at the mansion high above Dunstan St Mary. He should never have come.

The cargo ship he had travelled on had docked a day early at Southampton. He had been making his way here as slowly as possible; calling at a number of inns along the route. England was so green, so busy, so small and so full of people. They bothered him as much as the landscape. It was divided into pocket-handkerchief fields giving a patchwork effect with hedges and fences everywhere, and hills rose up to restrict one's view. The sensation of being shut in by the encroaching heights was almost claustrophobic, and it seemed impossible to get away from noisy crowds. After spending three years in South Africa, then twelve in Australia, Val found his homeland difficult to accept. He had been in the Stag's Head for several hours fighting the urge to go back to Southampton and take the first available freighter to Darwin. It was still strong in him as he studied Knightshill.

Realizing he was being watched by Moorkin from the entrance to the inn Val moved across the square towards the lane which would take him to his destination. As he walked past hedgerows filled with wild roses and blackthorn, grassy verges covered in white clover, and buttercup meadows where cows pulled the juicy grass and chewed it noisily, the scents wafting to him on the hot afternoon air seemed sickly sweet. He was more used to the smells of scorched earth, close-packed cattle on the move, and men's sweating bodies.

For twelve years he had lived in a place of endless distances with little between the land and the sky. He had slept in a communal bunkhouse on those nights when he had not bivouacked beneath the stars or cat-napped in the saddle. For twelve years he had worked hard and drunk freely amid men who asked no questions and expected nothing from him but basic loyalty. Stockmen were rough, laconic, pugnacious and, invariably, people who were at ease with isolation. It took a certain brand of toughness to be able to ride for days, often weeks, driving thousands of head of cattle over featureless country in company with other riders who were spaced so far apart there was little communication between them. A man needed particular qualities to eat rough, sleep rough and stay in the saddle for hour after hour beneath the burning sun with only one's thoughts as companions; it demanded expert horsemanship to control sudden stampedes of thirsty or frightened cattle on territory offering no natural barriers to their progress.

Coming to a five-barred gate Val decided to vault it and climb up to the house over Ashleigh land – he supposed it still was – taking in the spread of the valley as he went higher. The open space would diminish the claustrophobic quality of a narrow lane between high hedges. His landing in the meadow was somewhat unsteady and he almost fell, dropping the bag from his shoulder.

He left it on the grass as he leaned back on the gate to survey his boyhood home through narrowed eyes. He had never really looked at it in those days. God, how much he had taken for granted!

Goonawarra had been a nice place, but nothing like this. An Outback homestead could be surprisingly elegant, and old man Collins had built a home for his family which rivalled any in the vast Northern Territories. Val recalled his first sight of it as he had ridden up the long dust track after being told by a tinker travelling the same road that they were hiring hands there. Bang in the middle of nowhere he had found a two-storey house with ornate columns and verandas, surrounded by small cultivated garden patches. There were spotless lace curtains at the windows and tasteful ornaments on the sills. After the tin shacks and dosshouses he had frequented since landing in Australia, Val found Goonawarra easy on the eye.

He had not gone inside the house until much later. Stan Collins had really wanted an experienced stockman, but study of Val's impressive physique, and belief in his claim that he had been a cavalry trooper, persuaded him to give the stranger a trial period of employment. Val's experience in the ranks of the 57th Lancers then stood him in good stead. Those years in South Africa's wild isolation had taught him endurance in the saddle and superb horsemanship which enabled him swiftly to convince his boss that he had got the ideal man. Valentine Martin Havelock had also got the ideal hideaway. He had given his name as Ashleigh, which was immediately shortened to Ash by men who had no time for unnecessary embellishments. His fellows were all known as Buck, Grig, Spat, Clip and so on. Val supposed they had other names, but he never asked and they accepted him on the same terms. His time as a trooper had accustomed him to bedding down in a long room with men who observed no more than the basics of civilized living.

Val shifted from the five-barred gate with a heavy sigh. The sooner he got up to Knightshill and settled the necessary business, the sooner he would be able to return to his monastic life. He began to climb with long strides towards the house which had been owned by thirteen generations of Ashleighs. It had stood for centuries overlooking the valley giving views of any intending attackers, virtually indestructible. Not so poor old Stan Collins' homestead. Fire had raged through it one night three months ago, fanned by the constant wind. The whole place had been devoured by the flames and Stan had perished in the house he had built with such pride.

Val had been in the bunkhouse with a dose of fever, the only hand near enough to attempt rescue. Together with his boss he had brought to safety Mrs Collins and the girls, but Stan had gone back for the contents of the safe. The roof had then collapsed blocking all access. Three times Val had tried to get in through windows to reach someone he was sure was already dead, but the looks on the faces of those three women had driven him to attempt the impossible. He seemed destined to be allied with fire. Twice before he had risked his life in burning buildings. As on those other times, he survived the hazards.

When the other men rode in having seen the blaze from where they were working, they formed a chain with buckets of water to help Mrs Collins, her daughters and the six Aborigines they employed. It was far too late to save anything. Goonawarra burned to the ground. Stan's charred body was buried in the corner of the tiny garden four days later when the priest arrived from town. The men had continued with their work uncertain of the future, but Mrs Collins had asked Val to escort her and the shocked girls to town where Stan's legal man would meet them to discuss the situation.

Drinking in the bar whilst waiting for their discussion to end, Val had faced his own future. His boss's widow had intended to go back to Melbourne where she had relatives. She had not the heart to continue alone without even a house to live in. She and her daughters were presently occupying an outhouse. The men had put in beds and lent them clothes, but stoical though women were in the Outback, these were intent on leaving as soon as possible. Who would take on Goonawarra Station? The new owner would have to build a house before bringing out his family. It would all take time, and what if he brought his own stockmen with him?

Halfway through another glass of beer, Val had walked from the bar and crossed to the hotel where Mrs Collins was having her meeting. In that parlour he had pledged to buy Goonawarra for whatever the lawyer discovered it was truly worth, with an additional sum to allow Mrs Collins to get a little house in Melbourne. The woman had broken down and cried for the first time since the night of the fire. She had not questioned Val's ability to get the money, nor his word that he would not let her down. Even so, the lawyer had drawn up a legal document of intent to purchase with a limit of six months' duration. If Val had not returned by the first day of October to fulfil his pledge, all opportunity to purchase the property would be forfeit. The legal representative had studied Val's signature closely. If he made discreet enquiries about an Englishman called Valentine Ashleigh he would learn nothing disparaging. It was Martin Havelock who had been branded a traitor and kicked out of an honourable regiment.

Val was now near enough to Knightshill to see the blaze of colour in the lower gardens, but it was something of a blur. The climb had taken more out of him than it should have done. It was a very hot day but he was used to temperatures in excess of this. The long voyage cooped up on a freighter must have softened him up. It was almost as if he was starting another bout of fever. Glancing over his shoulder he saw it had been a very steep climb, but a superbly fit man should not be breathing as heavily as this and feeling slightly unsteady. For a moment he was tempted to turn back down that slope rather than go to meet those things he had shut from his life and did not want to let back in. From the village Knightshill had been a long way away. From half-way up the hill it was still a distant place. Once he set foot in the gardens, Val Ashleigh had returned home. It was a bigger step than he had reckoned on.

The twins and James Morgan were quarrelling over the last scone, Charlotte and Kitty were pouring more tea and Vere stood discussing with Laurence the situation in the Balkans. Even so, part of Vere's attention was on the French antique clock on the mantelpiece. It was almost four-thirty. Parsons and Ebson had been instructed to get down to the station in good time to meet the train from Romsey. Should he check that they were preparing to leave?

Tim had eaten more than his share of sandwiches but was happy to forego the sweeter stuff. He would have a hearty dinner, which his aunts said had been especially chosen for the man they were all there to welcome. The fatted calf, as he had guessed. God knew when it would be served. At the whim of the prodigal, probably. The activities of last night were beginning to take their toll and he still smarted from the encounter with Mrs Sturt. He rarely let women make a fool of him. He felt jaded and uncomfortably hot. It was all right for the females who could wear the lightest, coolest clothes and still look dressed. Chaps had to wear waistcoats and jackets, whatever the temperature, for formal occasions, and Uncle Vere had insisted on this being one. The twins had ribbons in their hair and wore pink muslin dresses more suited to a swanky garden party. Surely Aunt Kitty had not told them to dress up to the nines.

His sister still looked like a nurse in her neat-as-a-pin blue skirt and white blouse, with her light-brown hair in a businesslike chignon. Aunt Lottie was beginning to show her age; the flush of excitement on her cheeks clashed with her dark-red gown. Tim judged his mother superb, as always. She put everyone in the shade today in a dress of pale yellow silk-embroidered chiffon, with her lovely golden hair piled high in an intricate arrangement of curls. No one would believe she was older than her sister Charlotte and Vere. To offset his admiration for her Tim was greatly disgruntled because she had criticized his waistcoat, and everyone but the twins had agreed with her opinion. He was damned if he was going to change it for the sake of a cowherd from Australia.

Kate wished the children would keep their voices down. Better still, stop chattering altogether. They were excited, of course. *Everyone* was excited, especially the older generation. The members of her diverse family were normally charming, rational people. Today they were all trying too hard. She had been dismayed to find them dressed as if expecting visiting royalty. Apart from tidying up after the journey, she had chosen not to deck herself out in ribbons and frills. They were not her style, anyway.

Simon caught her eye across the room and raised his eyebrows expressively. She smiled at him. Dear Simon. He, at least, was behaving like his usual self, although the marks around his eyes left by his motoring goggles still gave him an owl-like look. Kate longed to shake her brother who had turned up in a waistcoat that would put a rainbow in the shade, and looking decidedly the worse for wear. He had twice almost dropped off to sleep, although how he could with this conversational babble all around him she could not imagine. Holly and Victoria prodded him each time his eyelids began to droop. They always became giggly whenever Tim was around, and he usually played up to their admiration. This afternoon he was irritated by it. However, the twins were awaiting the arrival of a greater attraction to girls who were much too occupied with thoughts of the opposite sex.

As Kate watched their adolescent antics she wondered if she had been like that at fourteen. Almost certainly not. Perhaps sisters led each other on. Glancing across at Vere talking to her step-father, she saw him glance once more at the clock. Poor man! This was such a special day for him. She prayed it would equal all his hopes.

At that moment she became conscious of movement at the nearby french windows, which stood open to the terrace. A spasm of apprehension clutched her as she saw someone standing there; a tall, heavily built muscular man in drab-coloured trousers and a rough cotton shirt open at the neck with sleeves rolled up beyond his elbows. His heavy boots were covered in dust, and over one shoulder was a stained canvas bag on rope handles. Thick blond stubble on a dark-brown face added to his vagabond appearance, and he gazed at them all with an expression akin to horror.

Conversation slowly petered out as everyone grew aware of the rough intruder. Within five seconds there were fifteen faces all around that room staring in mild shock at the figure in the doorway. A pin could have been heard dropping in the sudden silence, until it was broken by a hearty oath.

'*Christ Almighty*!' The man spun round to face the terrace, took one step out on to it, staggered backwards, then collapsed full length on the blue and cream carpet.

Vere quickly overcame his initial frozen reaction and strode across to where the man lay more or less at Kate's feet. What a thing to happen right now! His anger melted into a sense of deep shock as he neared and saw the intruder's face at close quarters. The features had aged a little, certainly, and been toughened by long exposure to the sun but a man surely knew his own brother even after an absence of twelve years.

'It's . . . it's Val!' he said with difficulty, as Kate went on her knees beside the unconscious figure.

There was a scramble as the children crowded forward only to be pushed aside by Margaret and Charlotte. Tim remained where he was, watching in disgust. If this pathetic tramp was Uncle Vere's precious heir, God help Knightshill and the Ashleigh family!

While Kate's professional side made her do all the right things, the woman beneath the calm nurse was filled with compassion. This was the youthful uncle she had adored as a child. Whatever had happened to bring him down to this? She checked his pulse, her fingers on his wrist, laid her palm on his brow, opened his shirt to examine his brown torso, then laid her ear against his chest to listen carefully. Sitting back on her heels she studied Val with a growing sense of distress. His heartbeat was a trifle fast but not significantly so; his temperature was within safe bounds. He was breathing easily with no evidence of wheezing in his lungs. There was no sign of a rash in the most likely places, and he was far too sturdy to be suffering from malnutrition. There was only one conclusion to draw from her tests.

'What do you think's wrong, dear?' asked Vere in hushed concern as he squatted beside her. 'Shall I call Dr Pope?'

Kate had no option but to tell the truth. 'I'm afraid he's just extremely drunk.'

Val's eyelids fluttered to give Kate a momentary glimpse of vivid blue eyes, before they closed again as he muttered in a slurred baritone, 'Not me, lady. It's another dose of that bloody fever.'

Kate reached up to take a cushion from the chair she had been sitting in, and put it beneath Val's head. She worked on a fever ward and knew the signs well enough. He was simply as drunk as a lord. As she gently pushed his thick fair hair back from his forehead she knew why she had wished he was not coming.

The family ate the welcoming dinner without the guest of honour. He had been put to bed and was still dead to the world. Vere sat with his wife, his sisters and their husbands at one end of the table; the younger members gathered at the other. There was a marked difference in the atmosphere within each group. The older generation were trying to come to terms with the ruin of this significant day, eating and conversing almost automatically. The children were full of excitement. They whispered and stifled giggles whilst casting wary eyes at their parents.

The middle generation, as Tim termed himself, Kate and Simon, were all at odds with each other. Simon's philosophical personality enabled him readily to accept the manner of arrival of someone who had lived for twelve years in fairly primitive conditions, but

Simon was not and never had been an Ashleigh. Tim was full of disparagement for someone whom he had once regarded as an example to follow. It was perfectly clear that Val had gone to the dogs in spectacular fashion. Kate appeared to be in a world of her own.

'Well, I still think he's like someone you see in bioscope dramas,' declared Holly in an emphatic whisper. 'The hero who staggers in after doing impossibly brave deeds.'

'He *smelt!*' said Charles Morgan, wrinkling his nose.

'That was the ale he'd been drinking,' Richard Nicolardi informed him airily. 'It always smells foul. That's why *gentlemen* never touch it.'

'Uncle Val's one of us,' cried Victoria, as starry eyed as her twin. 'That means he *is* a gentleman.'

'Pity he didn't remember the fact before he arrived in that state,' put in Tim through a mouthful of pigeon pie. 'Good thing the Elders hadn't invited half the neighbourhood to meet him tonight! And they criticized *my* appearance! My waistcoat may not be their idea of elegance, but I didn't arrive at the stately home resembling a *tramp*.'

Kate turned on him with hushed passion. 'You're being particularly beastly today. Grow up, Tim!'

He leered at her. 'You're a fine one to talk. The way you've been mooning around since your "nursy" act, one would put you at the same age as the twins. You've always been a bit daffy about him, as I recall . . . and wasn't it one look at his photograph that put an end to your nonsense of pretending to be dumb?'

'She was only *nine years old*,' Simon pointed out with unusual heat.

Tim was unperturbed. 'As you were at the time still living in a *veld* hamlet with your mother acting the local innkeeper, I think you should keep your comments to yourself, old son. This is a strictly Ashleigh affair.'

Simon's colour rose, and the twins tittered. They were fond of their step-brother, but the extraordinary events of the day had over-excited them and led them to indulge in adolescent audacity. Victoria nudged her sister conspiratorially as she said slyly, 'We're *real* Ashleighs, Tim. You're a Daulton pretending to be one.'

Something about the broad smiles on both their faces reminded

Tim of the girl who had put one over him at the railway station, and he lashed out. 'The only way you can stay Ashleighs is to die old maids, and you're both disagreeable enough to succeed.'

Jonathan Nicolardi, the same age as the twins and normally dismissive of his cousins, surprisingly fired up in their defence. 'They were only ragging you, Tim. Kate was right. You do seem like a bear with a sore head today.'

Tim turned on the half-brother eleven years his junior. 'Since when have you reached an age that permits you to offer an opinion on your elders and betters, you little pipsqueak?'

'Leave him alone,' cried Richard Nicolardi.

'Yes, leave him alone,' echoed James Morgan, Richard's close friend as well as cousin.

'I think we should talk about something quite different,' suggested Simon, who was always the most equable person at Knightshill.

'*We* want to talk about Uncle Val,' insisted Holly pugnaciously. 'Is he really going to live here all the time from now on?'

'And will he go around looking like a tattered hero, and drink too much ale, and *swear*?' added Victoria with awe.

Tim had had enough of their juvenile nonsense. 'If he does you'll soon find you have no friends left, and people will stop visiting Knightshill. Tattered or otherwise, real heroes don't let themselves go to the dogs in that disgusting manner. No one has ever said *why* he left the country, but now it's pretty damn certain he *had* to. Doubtless he's come back because they've kicked him out of Australia for the same reasons.'

'Shut up, Tim!' cried Kate in tones which caught the attention of those at the far end of the table.

Laurence frowned in the direction of his step-son. 'I expect admonition of the children, but not of someone who should be setting an example.'

Tim was instantly furious. Throwing down his knife and fork he got to his feet so abruptly his chair went over on to its back. '*I* wasn't the man who staggered in to Knightshill and passed out in the middle of the welcoming committee. What kind of example was *that*?'

Laurence regarded him with a steely eye. 'If you feel unable to sit at the dinner table with your family in civilized manner, I suggest you leave us. You will not be much missed, I assure you.'

Flushing with angry colour Tim made for the door, but he could not leave things as they stood. With his hand on the doorknob, he turned back to his step-father. 'I thought you wanted a son to be proud of, but I'm always found wanting. No matter that I distinguished myself at Oxford and Sandhurst, my waistcoats are too gaudy, my timekeeping deplorable, and my manners uncivilized. I suppose, even if I die a hero, like Uncle Vorne, it still won't be enough because I'm really a Daulton. It apparently doesn't matter how the hell a man behaves if he was *born* an Ashleigh.'

It was quiet for a while following Tim's dramatic departure, the children being particularly subdued by what had happened. It was bad enough when *they* were told off in front of everyone. Tim was counted as a grown-up despite being of their generation, and they all felt uncomfortable about the scene they had just witnessed.

'That was *awful,*' whispered Holly, looking close to tears. 'Poor Tim.'

Jonathan now abandoned his championship of the twins and spoke up for his half-brother in his most superior tones. '*Poor Tim*? It's *your* fault he got such a wigging.'

'It is *not,*' she hissed, turning red.

'No, it's *not,*' Victoria said in support of her twin.

'You went on about him being a Daulton,' said the other Nicolardi boy. 'You know how touchy he is about that and you deliberately said it to make him mad. You *are* to blame. Both of you,' he added, ganging up with his brother against their only girl cousins.

The twins were furious. 'Who was it called him a bear with a sore head?' demanded Holly, tears forgotten.

'Who insisted on going on and on about Uncle Val?' countered James Morgan, coming in on the boys' side.

Victoria would not allow him that. 'And who sided with Richard when Tim called Jon a pipsqueak?'

Kate could stand no more and said in a weary undertone. 'Keep quiet, all of you. Our parents are very upset. You might show them some consideration.'

Jonathan challenged his half-sister who had always lived at Knightshill. 'It was because *you* shouted at Tim that Father's attention was drawn to him. Perhaps you should take your own advice.'

'All right, that's *enough*,' ruled Simon. 'I suggested a change of subject a while ago. Unless you do it now you'll all end up with a wigging because I shall shout at the lot of you.' As none of them looked abashed by his threat, he added swiftly, 'Who wants a ride in my motor tomorrow?'

It was an infallible subject changer. Simon was committed to a full timetable of joyrides by the time the meal ended and the youngest members went upstairs leaving the rest of the family to drink coffee, with brandy for the men. Simon sat beside Kate, who was lost in thought, and mentally reviewed the day. All Tim had said was basically true. The planned welcome had been totally ruined. Val had behaved badly in arriving home too drunk to stand and resembling a wayfarer. It had been an insult to his brother and sisters, and it had set the children agog over an uncle who appeared to be a ruffian of the worst order. He was not certain how Kate felt about it all, and broke into her reverie by offering a penny for her thoughts.

Simon's quiet voice brought Kate back to awareness of where she was. She sighed. 'What a day!'

'Tomorrow will be different. Everyone will be calmer, for a start, and Val will have sobered up.'

'I hope Tim's in a better mood.'

'Poor chap. I'm sure Uncle Laurence will corner him for a few to-the-point words, when it would be better to leave the matter alone. I know your brother has a ridiculous complex about being the child of a man who became violent to you all, while Jon and Dick are the children of a deeply loving relationship, but he does have a point, Kate. He got an excellent degree at Oxford, and passed out from Sandhurst as best cadet of his course, yet Aunt Margaret seems intent on making Tim perfect in *every* way, and your step-father is so crazy about her he goes overboard to gain for her whatever she wants. I think they should both ease up on him.'

Kate studied him in surprise, 'I've never known you to champion Tim before.'

He shrugged diffidently. 'I've just done well in my exams and received plenty of congratulations. It's nice for people to be glad for you . . . but I don't *need* fuss like Tim does to compensate for being the son of a country churchman who went slightly mad over his sense of mission to the heathen.'

'I certainly don't worry about Papa Daulton. Why should he?'

'Because you've had love galore from everyone at Knightshill, who encouraged you to be yourself and follow your own inclinations. There's been no pressure on you, Kate, as there has been on Tim. Have you ever noticed that a person's brilliance is taken for granted, but the smallest imperfection seized upon? Tim's achievements were only what everyone expected, but they're achievements all the same. He needs the fact to be recognized. Why else would he have made that remark about dying heroically not even being enough?'

'Good heavens, you don't miss much, do you?' Kate murmured with a frown.

'No. Tim wasn't the only one deeply unsettled by Val's arrival, was he?' he said gently.

'We all were.'

'Some more than others.' After a brief silence he added, 'Kate, I'm *not* your brother. Not even a substitute for one. I'm your friend and always will be. If you . . . if you ever need someone, you know how to reach me.'

She gazed at him, still frowning. 'I think I'll go to bed. I hope you're right about everything being better tomorrow.' She stood up and lightly touched his shoulder. 'I know you're my friend, but I still feel you're more like a brother to me than Tim. You're also far nicer. Goodnight.'

Kate walked away to bid goodnight to the older generation still talking in heavy tones as they rode out the evening which should have been so triumphant. She did not see the bleak look on Simon's face as she left the room and made for the branched staircase. Reaching the place where the stairs divided she hesitated, then took the flight which led to the corridor where Val's room was situated next to Tim's. She prayed her brother would not come out as she passed. He would not understand that it was her nursing duty to check on a patient.

The room was dim, curtains drawn against the late evening sunshine, but there was enough light to show the dark gleam of polished wood, the sparkling mirrors and the arrangement of carnations from Knightshill's hot houses. Tiptoeing through to the bedroom Kate found everything tidy, the atmosphere cooled by open windows. Val lay face down in the large bed, his brown arms and back bare. A discarded pyjama jacket lay on the floor. All around him were adjuncts of wealth and gracious living; silver-backed brushes on the chest, leather stud box bearing his initials VMHA in gold, several silver-framed photographs of favourite thoroughbred horses and one of the Ashleigh brothers and sisters in their youth. Along one shelf was a row of sporting trophies and certificates adorned with school colours. Across a chair lay a monogrammed silk dressing-gown folded with precision by the valet.

Kate stepped nearer and automatically smoothed the crumpled sheet across his body. 'You poor thing,' she whispered. 'No wonder you needed Dutch courage to face all this again.'

CHAPTER THREE

It was a while before Val could assess where he was as he gazed at a man in black clothes who looked down on him with curious lack of expression.

'Will you be taking breakfast downstairs, sir, or shall I arrange for a tray to be brought up to you?'

Val said nothing as full awareness developed to remind him of what had happened. He was at Knightshill, of course. This was the room he had always occupied when at home. He glanced around it with a growing sense of unease. Everything within these walls was a reminder of a person who no longer existed. The sporting trophies had been won by a boy who had then been branded dishonourable and dismissed from a distinguished public school. The equine photographs were of horses he had ridden across acres owned by the family he had disgraced. Silver-backed hairbrushes; what foppery! A leather stud box with the initials VMHA. Martin Havelock had committed the worst crimes of all, but the army had decided execution was too kind and had tortured him instead.

There was a discreet cough from the manservant. 'About breakfast, sir.'

'Steak, four fried eggs, potatoes, and a pile of beans with plenty of bread and a can of strong tea,' Val directed. 'I'll have it here.'

The man did not bat an eyelid. 'Certainly, sir. At what time would you care to eat your breakfast?'

'As soon as you bring it.'

'Yes, sir.' The man allowed a fleeting sensation of long-suffering to pass across his features before adding, 'Do you wish to ride first, or shall I put out your morning clothes?'

Val sat up, running his hands through his hair. 'Just bring the bloody breakfast.'

'*Yes*, sir.' That heavy emphasis augmented the expression on the man's face as he left the room with a show of dignity.

Val got out of bed. He was wearing silk pyjama trousers unfastened at the waist. They matched the jacket on the floor. He had no idea who had undressed him and put him in bed. The last thing he remembered was standing on the threshold of an elaborately ornate room filled with pale-faced people dressed to the nines, all of whom stared at him in genteel affront. Somewhere in that sea of faces he had seen one remarkably like his own had once been, and instinct had told him his past was nowhere near as dead as he thought. Retreat had seemed imperative. What had happened after that was a blank.

In the bathroom he saw, with a sense of unreality, an entire array of snowy towels, cakes of pure soap, a shelf filled with pots and jars bearing fancy labels, a gleaming white bath long enough for a man to stretch out in, and a lavatory covered by a polished teak lid. As he raised it he recalled, with a continuing sense of unreality, that he had grown to maturity accepting these things without question. As a cavalry trooper he had been forced to use communal facilities and became used to them. Later, in South Africa, wartime had brought primitive conditions for every rank. Ash, the drover, had therefore thought nothing of relieving himself wherever he happened to be at the time, or stripping naked to sluice his sweating body with the billycan of water he had used for shaving alongside men as tough as he. It was with a strange sense of guilt that he closed the lid and flushed this elegant piece of equipment, almost as if he had no right to use it.

Turning away he was startled by the reflection of a ruffian gazing back at him. He ran a hand over his chin. At least three days' stubble on it. Even on a cattle drive he had shaved every day with the help of a piece of cracked mirror and a can of tepid water. Martin Havelock had been proud of his thick blond moustache. Val Ashleigh was still fanatical about removing any reminder of that man. He quickly lathered his face and began scraping the infant beard and moustache from his skin but, halfway through the task, his hands stilled. He had not seen himself so clearly for many years. The two bunkhouse mirrors had been badly spotted and covered in fly spit. Who had cared? They had served their purpose well enough. Steers had not bothered about the looks of the men who manhandled them to the ground for branding, or headed them off from rushing to water.

Studying the lean, tough features of his reflection as he finished shaving, Val knew he no longer belonged in a place like this. It was too fancy and pretentious by far. The business he had come to transact could have been done through legal channels at long distance. What perverse urge had sent him homeward? The need finally to conduct a civilized farewell to people and places that would pay no further part in his life? His Christmas departure while still a senior schoolboy had been taken in the belief that he would be back for the summer vacation. The nocturnal one five years later had been a protest against all he had suffered for mistaken ideals. Had he made this long voyage only in order to put an official seal on the abandonment of his heritage?

Dropping the trousers to the tiled floor, he turned the taps of the bath so that water gushed from them. How long since he had done that? Eager to feel clean he sat in the warm water as it slowly rose over his body, and lathered his skin with a large cake of soap which smelled too strongly of lavender. It must be girls' soap. Despite its perfume, he used it to wash his hair, dunking his head beneath the water until the last of the foam had gone. It was curious to lie full length in water he had just washed himself with. Not liking the sensation, he got out and towelled himself down. On a cattle drive the sun and wind had dried their skin, but then sweat had dampened it again within minutes.

Walking from the bathroom Val looked for his bag in vain. Neither it nor any of his clothes appeared to be in the bedroom or the adjoining sitting-room. A light tap on the door was immediately followed by the entry of the black-suited man carrying a large tray. He stopped dead at the sight of Val in the centre of the room, and the girl coming in behind him let out a squeal as she cannoned into the valet and registered the sight of a naked male at the same time.

'Wait outside!' the servant commanded sharply, then kicked the door shut as the girl backed out, pink in the face. 'There is a *robe* on the chair by the bed, sir,' he added in pointed fashion. 'If I had known you wished to take your bath while breakfast was being prepared, I would have run it for you and laid the garment ready.'

Val strode back to the bathroom and hitched a towel around his waist, saying over his shoulder, 'Where are my things?'

'Mr Ashleigh's man had the foresight to hang a selection of clothes in your wardrobe early this morning.' There was the sound of clattering china before Val heard the man open the door to say, 'I'll take the tray, Ginny. You may return to the kitchen.'

When Val re-entered the sitting-room the table had been set with several covered silver dishes, an array of crested china and an embossed silver tea service all standing on starched white linen. He was still staring at the table when the door opened again to admit a tall, good-looking man in his mid-forties whose light-brown hair was greying at the temples. Dressed in fawn breeches and shirt, with a yellow and brown cravat around his neck, he looked taken aback to find Val wearing only a small towel, but he covered the moment well.

'Thank you, Phipps. I'll ring if you're needed.'

The brothers said nothing for a moment or two after the servant departed; each studying the other gravely to assess his mood. Then Vere held out his hand. 'Welcome home.'

Val gripped it unsmiling. 'It's been a long time.'

'Too long.' An awkward silence followed until Vere indicated the table. 'I thought I'd have breakfast with you, if you have no objection.'

'It's your house.'

'Which will eventually be yours.' Vere forced a smile. 'You must be hungry, old chap. Shall we eat?'

No one had called him 'old chap' for years. It was cobber, mate, mucker, bastard and worse variations going down the scale according to how drunk they got. Val found the phrase rather comical. He indicated the towel at his waist. 'Where are my clothes?'

'I'll lend you some of mine until you're kitted out. There should be a robe in the bathroom, however.'

'So I was told by that bloody stuffed penguin.'

Vere frowned. 'I'll pour tea while you find a shirt and trousers, if you'd rather dress before eating.'

The robe had to suffice after all. None of Vere's things would fit. Even the dressing-gown would barely meet around Val's muscular frame and it was uncomfortably tight across his shoulders. He only put it on because he sensed near-nakedness did not suit his brother's notion of good manners.

'I'd forgotten how big you are,' Vere said, striving for ease between them.

'You've got to be to throw a steer.'

'Yes . . . I suppose so.'

Val lifted the covers from two dishes. 'What, in God's name, is this pap?'

His brother lowered his cup to the saucer and betrayed his tension with a slow sigh. 'Val, I know this must be difficult for you – I suppose I hadn't realized just *how* difficult – but you can't walk in and expect things here to be the way they are in Australia. Phipps is doing his best. He brought you a selection of today's breakfast dishes. Scrambled eggs, kedgeree, devilled kidneys. If it isn't what you asked for, I apologize, but . . .'

Val got to his feet, marched into the bedroom and peeled off the tight silk robe to replace it with a sheet swathed toga-wise across one shoulder. How soon could he get a ship to Darwin? Vere followed him in and they confronted each other again. Val vented his anger because he knew he was in the wrong place.

'I sent a cable telling you I was coming. Didn't you get it?'

'Of course. I had people at the station to meet you and pick up your baggage.'

'What flaming baggage? I've been driving cattle in the bloody Outback.' He walked to the window trying to control himself, then turned back to Vere. 'Right, if you knew I was coming why hold a party on the same day? They all damn nearly passed out from shock when I walked in.'

'Because you resembled a thieving ruffian and stank of the taproom,' Vere snapped back. 'That might be acceptable to cattle, but we're used to civilized behaviour here. Can you believe I was so delighted you were coming home at last I asked every member of the family to be here to welcome you? My God, what an entry you made! If it was your intention to show your contempt for us all you thoroughly succeeded. The children were shocked and nervous, Kitty is still distressed, Margaret and Lottie are deeply upset. As for the servants . . .'

'I don't give a poddy's arse for the servants!' roared Val. 'What the hell did you all expect? I'm a bloody no-hoper, not an Ashleigh gentleman.'

They stood for some moments as if ready to spring at each other's throat, then Vere said in steely fashion, 'But you are, whether you like it or not.'

The fight suddenly left Val and he could think of nothing more to say in his own defence. He had been far too long with men of few words, and those mostly oaths. His brother had always been concise and able to express his thoughts. 'I should have stayed in Goonawarra.'

'I should have listened to Kitty. She was doubtful about involving the entire family.'

There appeared to be a truce. 'Are they all still here?'

'The children are on summer vacation. Simon, Tim and Kate have taken weekend leave. Margaret is staying at Knightshill at present, Laurence has to return to London on Monday. Yes, they're still here.'

'Oh, Christ!'

'Don't worry. You did your damnedest yesterday. They now know what to expect.' Vere's tone softened. 'Come and meet them, Val. Margaret and Lottie, especially. They deserve your consideration.'

'Not with an empty belly,' Val hedged. 'Let's eat.'

'Will that *pap* do?'

Val nodded. 'If it's the best you can offer a bloke.' He walked back to the table, sat and piled as much from each dish as his plate would hold. Unaware of his brother's expression he began to fork it into his mouth with gusto, only now realizing how long it had been since the bread and cheese meal at the Stag's Head.

'This isn't bad once you get used to it,' he commented, wrapping his large brown hand around the delicate cup to swallow the small amount of tea it held, then refilling it from the silver pot. 'Not the same without the flavour of smoke, but there you go.'

'What are we going to do about clothes for you?' Vere mused, ignoring the scrambled egg on his own plate. 'You can't go around resembling Nero or Julius Caesar.'

'Shouldn't that be Brutus?' asked Val, then felt surprised that he had spoken of something out of his past. Ash, the drover, had not once thought of the classics. To cover this unwelcome slip he added, 'Whoever took my stuff away'll have to give it back. It fits me.'

'Where's the rest of your baggage?'

He gave a short laugh. 'There you go again. I brought with me all I own. Christ, Vere, you've been with an army and know how little a bloke needs when he lives in the bloody saddle and sleeps under the stars.'

His brother was quiet, watching him eat but having lost interest in breakfast for himself. When he next spoke it was on a different subject. 'I must ask you to watch your language when you're with the family. I accept that you've been mixing with rough company, but I can't have the women and children upset whenever you speak.'

Anger flared anew as Val tossed his fork on to the crested plate. 'Then I'll keep out of their flaming earshot. As soon as I've settled the business with you, I'll be on my way.'

Vere looked bewildered. 'On your way?'

'Back to Goonawarra. I guess I've got enough piled up here to cover the price of the station and the running costs for the next thirty years. No one gives a tinker's piss what I say over there.'

Wearing his own shirt and trousers hastily dried and ironed by one of the laundrymaids, Val went with Vere to meet his sisters. As they walked through long sunlit corridors, memories Val had banished by burying himself in a harsh life on the far side of the world returned in a rush. He had been fooling himself all this time in the belief that he was a new man. At this moment he again felt as he had twelve years ago, defeated and bitter.

For a house supposedly filled by a large family it was amazing that they encountered none of them, nor even a servant, on the long silent walk. Val wondered if his brother had put that part of Knightshill out of bounds until they had passed through. Maybe Vere felt the sight of him would offend as much as his language. There was constraint between them. The entire Ashleigh family had been led to believe the heir was returning to take up his rightful place. They now had to be told he had come to collect all the money he could lay his hands on, before finally shaking the dust of Knightshill from his heels. His cable had made no mention of taking up permanent residence – it was mere assumption on everyone's part – but Val was being made to feel he had let them down once more. Small wonder he was in a black mood.

The small day-room they entered looked unfamiliar to the man who had last seen it during Sir Gilliard's reign. It was now all pink and ivory, with French tapestries adorning the walls in place of battle canvases. Margaret and Charlotte turned from studying the gardens through windows thrown wide to let in the warm morning air, but they remained where they were as Val halted on the rich pink carpet. No one said anything for a moment or two, and his sisters' expressions seemed to Val to damn him further.

The ice was broken by Margaret, who moved to him with a rustle of silk skirts. 'You should have come home long before this. *We* did nothing to drive you away. It was your own foolish decision to become an exile.'

'You weren't here when I made it,' he retaliated defensively. 'And you'd done the same thing several years earlier.'

'Yes, I had,' she agreed quietly, 'but *you* went off utterly alone. I went with my children and a man I loved.'

'That's why you have no right to comment on what I did. You've no idea what has happened to me since we were last together on my Christmas vacation from Chartfield. Philip was conveniently killed, which meant you could marry Laurence and have a rip-roaring time in South America. Things didn't work out so bloody fine for me.'

'*Val!*' said his brother in admonition, but Margaret held up a silencing hand, saying, 'No, he's entitled to be angry. Val, I *don't* know what you've been through; I suppose none of us does. But it's all over now. You're home where you belong.' There were tears in her eyes as she took his hands. 'Not one of us lived up to Grandfather's inflexible demands, my dear. There's no need for you to feel you let him down.'

As Val gazed at this beautiful woman, he hardly recognized the loving sister he had affectionately called Aunt Meg. An elegant creature such as he had not seen for many years, there appeared to be nothing left of the substitute mother she had once been. He released his hands, saying, 'We're all different people now.'

'*We're* the same; you're the one who has changed,' cried Charlotte coming to stand beside Margaret. There were red anger spots on her cheeks and her eyes were full of accusation, not tears.

'When you turned up here three years after Grandfather's death we were all delighted, even though you had allowed us to believe all that time that you were no longer alive. We welcomed you with thankfulness and joy, Val. We neither questioned nor condemned you; we said nothing about the things you had done. All that mattered to us was that you were alive and had come home. Can you deny that?' When he said nothing, she nodded with satisfaction. 'No, you can't. Yet you went off again in the middle of the night without a word of explanation within three days of your return, and have stayed away for twelve years. Isn't it time we had a little consideration from you, time you started behaving with a little more responsibility? We've had to cover up for you all the time and it hasn't been easy. Now you're here you'll have to live up to the lies we've been forced to tell all and sundry – even our children. What you did yesterday was *disgraceful*.'

Val turned on her. '*You* certainly haven't changed, Lottie. You never approved of anything I did, and you never gave me the flaming benefit of the doubt, either. Isn't there something a bit crook about your attitude? When I came home after being kicked out of Chartfield and then kicked out of my regiment, you welcomed me with "thankfulness and joy". But just because I walked in on your fancy party blind drunk yesterday I'm getting the bloody riot act read out.' He moved away from two sisters who were like strangers. 'I never asked you to lie about me. All you had to say was that I had decided to live in Australia, and that was the truth.'

At the window he turned to confront them, finally understanding why he had come home instead of settling things through lawyers. All this had to be said at last. 'No one knows about that affair at Chartfield. I simply slunk off and joined the 57th as Martin Havelock so there'd be no connection with the family. Wasn't that showing consideration; behaving responsibly? I didn't ask for help from any of you, did I?'

Dragging up the facts from his past brought back the sharpness of defeat, of humiliation which he had lived with for so long. 'You say it wasn't easy to cover up for me. How bloody easy d'you think it was for *me* to join the ranks with sweaty, swearing troopers after nineteen years of the privileged life you're still leading? My God, you've been sitting happily at Knightshill all these years with your husband and children, and you've no more idea of life than a dingo's runt.'

'Val, I think that's *enough*,' ruled Vere.

Val rounded on him. 'You should know better than her. Christ man, you've lived and fought with an army. You should know things are never black and white. A man does what he has to. Sometimes he's wrong and becomes a hero; sometimes he's right and dies because of it. Life isn't as flaming simple as she seems to think.' Really worked up by now, Val walked up to his brother. 'Have you forgotten so soon how that bastard was held up as the example to follow? Vorne Ashleigh was on a pinnacle so high no other man would ever reach it. But he had to try or be counted a failure.' He gave a bitter laugh. '*You* went off to almost certain death in the Sudan because of him. You were lucky and came back after acquitting yourself well, in addition to finding fame as an artist. I imagine the only reason for keeping your mouth shut about what you'd discovered concerning Vorne was because you then knew you were the better man. You felt the world didn't need to know, just so long as you did.' He took a deep breath. 'But why the hell didn't you tell *me* when we met up in Kimberley? Wasn't I bloody entitled to know?'

Vere looked at him with a troubled expression. 'At the time I made the decision to keep the truth to myself, it seemed to be in everyone's best interests. When you came to my wedding in Kimberley you'd just been commissioned and decorated for bravery. Martin Havelock appeared to be riding high. You were doing well. You were proud and happy. I saw no reason to spring such a shock on you. You were going back to active service a few days later. I felt it was hardly the right time to shake your confidence.' He sighed. 'I still believe I made the right decision.'

'*Oh, do you*!'

'What difference would it have made if you'd known about Vorne at that stage?'

Val's mouth twisted with the pain of his memories. 'My arrival yesterday was *disgraceful*. The children were shocked, Kitty distressed, my sisters deeply upset. As for the servants . . .' He quoted Vere in harsh tones. 'My language is unfit for the ears of my family and I smell of the taproom. *That's* the difference your silence at Kimberley has made. I came home from South Africa with my pride and happiness ground into the dust, but ready to try again. *Then* you told me what I should have been told at Kimberley and I left for Australia vowing also to grind into the dust all Grandfather and this family stood for. You now know I succeeded.' He swung round to include his sisters in his next statement. 'I hope to God my arrival made the old devil turn in his grave. I only wish you'd invited the entire West Wiltshire Regiment to the welcome home party. I could've shown them what I think of their bloody Hero of Khartoum.'

When Tim reached the library his step-father was not there. He had not expected him to be. It was common practice to leave the culprit to cool his heels and grow apprehensive over the coming castigation. Tim took a book from the nearest shelf and flipped through its pages. In truth, he was surprised that Laurence had summoned him here this morning for a parental ticking off. It seemed melodramatic in proportion to his 'crime', and unlike his step-father to go to such lengths over it. Everyone had been overwrought yesterday, and this seemed particularly unfair in the face of the disgusting behaviour of the returned prodigal.

Tim could not abandon that name for his young uncle, for that was surely what Val Ashleigh was. Tim had slept only fitfully last night, supremely conscious that the ruffian had been put to bed in the adjacent room which had been unoccupied during his long absence. How could the boy he had once admired and envied have turned into the pathetic creature who had collapsed before their eyes yesterday? Val had had everything he could want for a golden future. Only a fool or a villain could have thrown it away . . . and Ashleighs were no fools. It surely should instead be Val here in the library for a few harsh words of rebuke.

Laurence came in, but Tim took his time in looking up from the pages of the book before closing it and putting it back on the shelf. He watched his step-father approach, the feeling of protest at this interview overriding his affection for the man who had rescued him from life with an oppressive religious fanatic.

'An interesting book, was it?' Laurence asked dryly.

'Just something to pass the time,' he said with a touch of defiance as he glanced at the clock.

'Have I kept you from some pressing engagement?' Laurence knew how to fence with finesse.

'No, sir.'

'Good. Then you have time to listen to a little advice.'

'If it's about what I said at the dinner table, I . . .'

'I said *listen* to a little advice. When you have heard it we can discuss anything you wish to say.'

'There's a lot I wish to say,' Tim said, pushing his luck due to the strength of his feelings on the subject.

'There always is, Tim, which is why I've ensured that you can say it in at least four other languages. However, we shall use English to straighten out a few points regarding your behaviour, so that there's no danger of you misunderstanding.'

'Shouldn't you be saying this to Val? I thought his behaviour outclassed mine in every respect.'

Laurence's approach underwent a lightning change, which Tim should have expected. His step-father was a passionate man who quickly reacted to opposition. 'If you wish to make an enemy of me I can't stop you, but I won't allow you to distress your mother. Kindly refrain from ill-mannered interruptions until I have finished saying what I intend you to hear.'

Tim's resentment grew, but he knew there was no way out of what was coming and clamped his lips together. This dark, fiery man was expert at handling situations at international level and had occasionally had Tim and his own sons on the carpet, but today he appeared to be far more serious than ever before. An outburst during dinner surely did not warrant this.

'You said last evening you thought I wanted a son to be proud of,' Laurence began, putting his right hand in the pocket of his grey trousers in assured manner as he crossed to the empty fireplace covered by an ornate carved screen. 'I have *three* sons, Tim. I hope to be proud of them all. In order to achieve that they do not necessarily have to be the best at everything, pass examinations with maximum marks, be the centre of attention at all times. They will earn my *approval* if they use their opportunities as fully as they are able, and live their lives wisely. But a father needs only to have sons who are men of integrity and compassion to be *proud* of them.

'Your achivements at university and Sandhurst are formidable. You have laid an academic foundation for a distinguished career in the regiment you have wanted to join since childhood. Your mother and I are extremely glad for you, but there's more to becoming a military officer than understanding battle tactics and wearing badges of rank. To lead men you have to earn their respect.' He waved his left hand in an expansive gesture. 'Oh yes, you can bully them, make them obey you through fear, but that kind of leader invariably undermines confidence and they are all unnecessarily lost in the heat of battle.'

Tim stayed silent because he was wondering where Laurence was heading. This did not appear to be connected with his outburst over Val. His step-father was a diplomat and, therefore, a skilled orator. Some of Tim's defiance faded beneath the spell of charmed words.

'When you changed your name to Ashleigh I believe you thought the legal document was enough. It was *not*, Tim. Are you aware that you also took on a heavy obligation? This family created the regiment you have recently joined. You're therefore more than a normal member of it; you're a guardian of its honour, so to speak.'

After a short silence during which Tim struggled against the urge to say something, Laurence appeared to switch focus completely. 'When you arrived yesterday it was apparent to every man present that you had come straight from a woman's bed, despite your pathetic lie concerning a carriage door which insulted your mother's intelligence.' As Tim opened his mouth he was silenced by a frown. 'Yes, it was an insult. A man must seek his pleasure, that is accepted, but I suspect you are becoming dangerously self-indulgent in that direction.' He held up his hand. 'No, allow me to finish before you offer further lies on the subject. I have seen the way you look at the maids here, and how you react to the foolish adolescent attentions of the twins.' He exhaled heavily. 'I trust you are not allowing your basic desires to rule you. A man should know when to stop or he will end up ruining himself. Believe me, I've seen too many young fools throw away a promising future because they become entangled in the silken mesh, especially in lonely outposts.'

Tim had expected a lecture that would allow him to retaliate with Val's greater sins, but he was being hauled over the coals for something which was no man's affair but his own. Laurence was only guessing, anyway. It made him furious. He was no adolescent boy making his first indiscriminate inroads to one of life's greatest pleasures, he was a man of twenty-five with years of experience behind him.

'I can see you resent my advice,' said Laurence.

'This is hardly a lonely outpost,' Tim snapped, 'and I know what I'm doing.'

'I'm sure you do. It's how frequently you are doing it which is my present concern.'

'That territory is no one's business but my own.'

'Surely it's of great importance to your men. An officer who is expending his youth and energy night after night with paid women is likely to grow careless in battle, when lives depend on his being supremely alert.' He crossed to where Tim stood beside the book shelves. 'The demands of our individual professions keep us from meeting very frequently so I'm taking this opportunity to speak on a confidential matter. You are well aware that trouble is brewing in Europe – has been for some while. The major powers are involved in an arms race. They're all watching each other while making secret plans for expansion. The Hapsburgs are greedy; Kaiser Wilhelm, whilst openly flaunting his family fondness for our king, would think nothing of breaking his promises to him. He's a wily, devious man with his eye to strengthening his position in Europe. The Russian monarchy is unstable – four daughters and a Tsarevich unlikely to live to maturity.'

Laurence perched on the arm of a chair and frowned at Tim. 'Something is going to spark conflict sooner or later, I promise you. When it does all those crouching lions will pounce. Diplomacy will not stand a chance, Tim. It will mean war, and I cannot see how we can fail to become involved in a conflict which will be bigger than any we have known.'

All anger and resentment flew as Tim took in the import of that statement. Laurence was telling him the most exciting news he could hope to hear. 'I shan't need girls, sir. I'll be far too busy.'

Laurence studied him for a moment or two, then said, 'It won't be like your mock battles at Sandhurst. The bullets will be killing men . . . and the enemy will have more of them than we have.'

'Troops or bullets,' Tim asked with a laugh.

'Both. Tim, war isn't *fun* for anyone. Ask Vere. He fought in the Sudan and South Africa.'

Tim was not listening. This awful weekend had suddenly become bright with promise. *War*! It was what every soldier needed to prove himself. There were always tiny colonial uprisings to put down with arms, but full-scale conflict against a formidable opponent would give Second-Lieutenant Timothy Edward Verity Ashleigh the opportunity to make his mark and climb on the same pedestal as his Uncle Vorne. He might even topple the hero from that supreme height and take his place.

Laurence was speaking again. 'I know you welcome this piece of balanced judgement on that situation. I suppose military men need battle as much as musicians need compositions to play, but yours is a dangerous profession and you must accept that those who care for you will not share your enthusiasm. Hence my reference to compassion a moment ago. You are your mother's firstborn, which makes her inordinately fond of you. Yes, Jonathan and Richard are our sons through love, but *you* hold a special place in her heart which makes her vulnerable to your carelessness. She's a woman of the world, Tim, astute enough to recognize the signs of undue passion when her son arrives with a swollen mouth and bruises on his throat.'

Tim felt his colour rise and he avoided Laurence's dark eyes. It was all right for men to see marks they almost regarded as emblems of virility, but he felt uncomfortable at the thought of his beautiful, elegant mother understanding such things. He now flushed further on recalling his silly tale about the carriage door hitting him. She must have thought him idiotic as he stood regaling everyone with that nonsense concocted because of the girl who had mocked him at the station.

'She cannot, of course, chastize you on such a subject, and so she instead criticizes your choice of a waistcoat to cover her concern. In her anxiety once hostilities commence she may well be unneccessarily critical of things you regard as of no consequence. Bear with her, Tim. Women have always dreaded war. It takes away the men they love. Don't be unkind enough to show your enthusiasm and eagerness for battle when she is present.' He put his hand on Tim's shoulder. 'Of course I applaud your recent achievements, but how you behave in the coming months will govern my pride in my son. Don't allow your weakness where women are concerned to make you unfit to lead your men. Your first duty is to them. Their lives will be in your hands . . . and so will your own.'

Kate had breakfast in her room, then took out one of the mares for a solitary ride before the day grew too hot. It already promised to be a scorcher as she cantered along the downs above and behind Knightshill, but the breeze lifting her hair and billowing her white shirt gave pleasant relief from the warmth. She had not had much sleep. The events and tensions of yesterday had kept her mind troubled, and she could not forget the man lying in the room next to Tim's. Today he would have to face them all in sober state. She did not want to be there when he did. In fact, she wanted nothing more than to get the train back to Oxfordshire and lose herself in her work.

Simon was heavily committed to taking the children for rides in Jessie for most of the day – certainly all morning – and she felt little desire for Tim's company. She dreaded to think how he would behave today. From the little she knew of him it seemed more than likely that he would deliberately set out to be unpleasant to Val. Tim was the opposite of Simon, who too often hid his feelings. When her brother was around no one was left in doubt of his mood or opinions. Kate supposed it might be a praiseworthy trait in an aspiring army officer, but it would not help the unexpected situation which had arisen this weekend.

The house had been remarkably quiet when she walked through it to the stables; almost as if everyone had been confined to their rooms for some reason. It was a relief to escape for an hour or so, but she could not stay away all day. As she gazed out over the green valleys on either side and the distant smudge of the Dorset hills way ahead, Kate told herself she was being remarkably silly for a professional woman who was competent and cool-headed. Things did not happen that way, except in the flimsy romances Rosie was always reading. A woman did not take one look at a man – especially one who had dropped in a drunken stupor at her feet – and know that she would never love any other. It was too absurd. Then why was she so reluctant to go back and face him again?

It was past mid-morning before Kate rode slowly along the path leading down beside Leyden's Spinney. They all used to skate on the pond on the far side when it froze, but that had been some years ago and, after a boy fell through the ice and drowned there, the skating parties had ceased. Youngsters from the village often trespassed on Ashleigh land to go fishing for tiddlers, but local people thought the pond dangerous and only the most adventurous children defied the ban. Kate was therefore surprised to see a horse tethered at the spinney, and her surprise grew as she recognized the gelding, Boris, from Knightshill's stables. Uncle Vere must be here checking on the depth of the pond during the long drought.

Dropping from the saddle, Kate looped Dilly's reins over a branch and made her way along the path through the spinney. The coolness was welcome after the considerable heat on the open downs, and she thanked her favourite uncle for being there. She would not have to return to the house alone, and he might give her some indication of how he and the two aunts felt about Val today. She hoped they would be more understanding than they had seemed last night.

Not until she was almost beside the pond did Kate become aware that a man was actually swimming in its dark water. She pulled up short, knowing he had not heard her approach because of his vigorous splashing. His milk-fair hair identified him as someone other than Vere, who anyway would never come up here to swim, and Tim was most unlikely to indulge in this carefree activity. As Kate watched, her guess was proven right. Val reached the edge of the pond and climbed out. As a nurse she was no stranger to the mysteries of the male body, but this was different. She watched with a growing sense of helpless admiration as he walked across to pick up the clothes he had left on the ground, rays of sunshine penetrating the foliage to gild his tanned skin glistening with runnels of water. He had no towel with him and put on over his wet body the shirt and trousers he had worn yesterday.

Kate ran back along the path and swiftly mounted her mare, then found she could not ride away. She was still there when, a few moments later, Val appeared along the path. He stopped to stare at her with wariness in eyes as vividly blue as Sir Gilliard's had been.

'I'm Kate,' she managed with commendable calm. 'You won't recognize me after all this time.'

He approached slowly, water dripping from his wet hair to add to the damp patches on the shoulders of his shirt. 'Too right, I don't. You were a little kiddy when I last saw you. *Kate*? I'll be damned.'

'You look different, too.' She was feeling decidedly light-headed as she gazed at a face she thought strong and very striking now he was shaven and sober. 'I wondered who'd left Boris here,' she added, to explain why she should appear to be waiting for him. 'What have you been doing?'

'Swimming in the lake. It's smaller than I remembered.'

'I expect it's that you're bigger.' She had just seen that he was.

'Could be.'

There was a moment of awkwardness which Val was either unwilling or unable to break, so Kate asked, 'Are you going back? It'll soon be time for lunch and we could ride together.'

He hesitated, then nodded and unhitched Boris's bridle. 'I've got to face them all sooner or later.'

They set off at walking pace with Kate supremely aware of his proximity. 'Has it been *very* terrible coming back?'

'Pretty much. None of it seems real,' Val replied searching the valley to their right with a frowning gaze.

'I sometimes feel like that when I come home after a long stretch at the hospital.'

He glanced back at her. 'Are you still ill?'

'No,' she said with a gentle smile. 'I'm a nurse.'

'Good God! However did you manage to escape?' She laughed, then even more so when he added, 'Are you one of those women who march around with banners and knock coppers' hats off?'

'So you've heard about that?'

'Yeah, they're doing it out there, too. I read about it.'

'Don't look so concerned. Things are changing for women – not before time – but because we want to do something useful with our lives doesn't mean we have to belong to the suffragette movement. Uncle Vere would be *horrified* if I chained myself to railings or went on a hunger strike.'

'You'd be letting down the Ashleighs,' he commented, a harsh note entering his voice. 'You must have been bloody persuasive to get permission to become a nurse.'

'Not really. Laurence isn't my father, and he and Mother lived abroad until recently. Aunt Lottie looked after me until Uncle Vere came home with Aunt Kitty and Simon. He and I were in much the same boat with regard to step-fathers, and it seemed so complicated we regarded all three as combined guardians. It worked very well, but when I decided I wanted to take up nursing I had no idea who I should properly consult about it. So I simply went ahead and did it.'

'Good on yer.'

His smile hit her between the eyes and she looked away towards Knightshill's extensive gardens, because she had never before felt this way in a man's company and was afraid it would show in her face. They walked their horses for some time in silence, the sun hot on their backs, then Val said, 'A hell of a lot of people were here yesterday. How about telling me who they are before I go in and prove I'm not a sot who'll cut their throats. Vere says I scared them half to bloody death.'

Kate looked back at him with swift compassion. 'No! It's just that we were expecting you to . . . well, it . . . you took us by surprise. Uncle Vere was convinced you'd be on the five o'clock train. Tea would have been over and we'd all have been sitting there waiting. Oh lord, it would have been awful for you however it happened, wouldn't it?'

'Not half as bad as for the welcoming committee.' He smiled again, allowing her a glimpse of the proud young officer in the photograph she had resurrected last night. 'You're a nice girl, young Kate. You always were a caring little thing.'

'And you were always a wonderful . . .' She refrained from saying 'big brother' because the feeling she had for him now was incestuous in that connection. She had no idea whether an uncle rated the same. Nothing could stop her from asking the ultimate question, however. 'Val, why *did* you go off so suddenly and stay away for so long?'

As she watched his face grow tense Kate knew she had shattered the moment of closeness, and told herself she should have known better. He was like a nervous patient who had to be handled with care and understanding. She had rushed things because they were close to the house now, and he would soon be surrounded by people who regarded him as an object of curiosity. How could she defend him if she had no facts to help her?

'Like you with the nursing, I simply went ahead and did it,' he said tonelessly, then dug in his heels to urge Boris forward at a swiftly gathering pace.

Kate set her mare off after the gelding's flying hooves, but Val was already handing the animal over to Stubbins, the stablelad, when Kate arrived. He showed every sign of walking off as if she were not there, so she called out, 'You asked me to tell you about the family before you went in.'

'Forget it,' he flung over his shoulder. 'I won't be here long enough to get to know them.'

Kate was unaware of Parsons waiting for her to dismount as she watched Val stride away across the gravel and wished yet again that he had never come.

CHAPTER FOUR

Vere had some years ago abandoned the habit of expecting ladies to depart after dinner leaving the men to drink port, smoke cigars and talk on weighty matters, or on those subjects which would offend female ears. Neither he nor John Morgan cared for cigars and discussions of a lewd nature, so they drank in the company of Kitty and Charlotte talking together on various subjects whenever they were all at Knightshill. Only at formal dinner parties was the old tradition maintained. On this particular night two days after Val's arrival, the younger ones had gone off to their rooms and the remaining ten members of the family assembled in the drawing room to discuss the day's tragic event which had such serious implications.

Deeply disturbed by the political assassination of the Austro-Hungarian archduke and his wife Vere felt, quite unreasonably, that from the moment Val had reappeared the idyllic life he had created at Knightshill had begun to disintegrate. Laurence had frequently spoken of his fears about a possible clash of arms in Europe, but Vere had not wanted to heed his warning because the consequences would be unthinkable. Yet, an hour ago, they had heard news which any man of intelligence must accept as the prelude to war, although even Laurence had been unprepared for such a development. Vere had fought the Dervishes in the Sudan, and had participated in the war against the Boers as an artist-observer. He knew what battle did to men, knew how it changed them. He also knew how quickly death came to some, and how agonizingly to others.

It was with a heavy heart that he surveyed the family he had only two days ago believed, with great happiness, would finally be complete. Young Tim was bouncy with excitement. He was sure to be taking up arms by the time the year was out. Simon was quietly elated because he saw an active role for his beloved flying machines. Margaret was understandably quiet. Her handsome, pleasure-loving son would be one of the first to face the enemy. Kitty was uneasy as she watched Simon expounding on the way in which aircraft would change the whole method of warfare. Vere understood his wife's dread. Aeroplanes needed pilots to fly them, and Simon had already mentioned that Sopwith encouraged their designers to take to the air in order to test their machines. They were such frail, temperamental things it did not necessarily take an enemy to send them crashing to earth. Vere was afraid for both young men.

His gaze then travelled to Val silently sitting beside John, with whom he appeared to have found slight rapport during a conversation about cattle ranching in America compared with Australia. Still wearing a set of his rough clothes because nothing else would fit him, Val had grudgingly agreed to add a tie for evening. It and he looked incongruous in the midst of dinner-suited men, and women in silk gowns, yet he would inherit this splendid house one day. Val's inflexible decision to spend the rest of his life defying his natural heritage had devastated Vere, leaving him with the single hope that his brother's son and heir, when and if he produced one, would love Knightshill enough to live here and preserve it. It was a faint hope, for Val's children would be products of the Outback, as tough as he had become. Small wonder Vere was beset by a premonition that life for the Ashleighs was about to change irrevocably while he watched all he valued slowly slip away from him.

Tim felt a different man from the one who had arrived in the shadow of a returning enigma. Val was living up to all his black-sheep qualities. He dressed and spoke like a backwoodsman, he drank nothing but ale, even at the dinner table, and had apparently come home merely to collect as much money as he could lay his hands on before going back to buy a place called Goonawarra. He would inevitably sink lower and lower into the morass of failure and die in some stinking place at the back of beyond, where the name Ashleigh would thankfully mean nothing. Surely Knightshill would then come to the son of the present owner's elder sister – and Tim had changed his name from Daulton in readiness.

The prospect of imminent war added to the swing of emphasis from the prodigal to the only soldier present. Aside from his elation at the grand opportunity for distinction in battle, Tim knew he was tonight the centre of attention and rose to the occasion. On his shoulders rested the honour of this proud family and they were all aware of it. He had no doubts about his ability to carry that responsibility – had he not won the accolade of excellence at Sandhurst? Although he had not yet had to lead his platoon against an enemy, they had engaged in mock battles often enough and obeyed his orders. Admittedly, he did not know each of his men individually but which officer did? They did not mix socially and Tim had no intention of becoming too chummy with rankers in order to court popularity. Some of his fellow officers had done that and lost the respect of men they had to command. No, he was confident that he had struck the right balance which would work well in action.

Laurence had made an unholy fuss about expending his youth and energy on women, but they were there to provide relief from the serious side of life and the man who ignored that basic need was more likely to fail his men in desperate situations than one who eased tension in pursuit of bodily gratification. All work and no play, after all! Yes, Tim Ashleigh would fully honour his obligations to his ancestors – which was more than the drunken drover had done.

Tim cast a glance at Val who was taking no part in the discussion on the dangerous powder keg in Europe. He was clearly prepared to turn his back on his country as well as his family. How typical! On the heels of the derogatory thought came a slight twinge of conscience. Whilst avoiding intimate conversations with other members of the family, Val had singled him out yesterday in a surprisingly friendly approach. Tim had initially questioned his own assessment of the man because, apart from the expletives he used so freely, Val had betrayed a sharp intelligence which defied his appearance and gave him an air of being in his most natural surroundings. The suggestion of true Ashleigh qualities had thrown Tim so that he had replied somewhat stiffly to penetrating questions about his early life and travels with an eminent diplomat. Why should Val pry so deeply into his affairs yet keep his own past such a close secret?

With the idea of working towards making a few probing inroads to Martin Havelock's mysterious career with the 57th Lancers, Tim had introduced the subject of the West Wiltshire Regiment speaking of his pride in being one of its officers and his intention of living up to those other Ashleighs who had served it with such distinction.

Val's attitude had changed dramatically. Fixing Tim with a curiously intense look he had said, 'Take my advice and forget about our bloody ancestors. Be your own man. Whatever *they* did was their flaming concern, not yours – or any other Ashleigh's. You owe them *nothing*.'

Immediately angered, Tim had whipped out, 'Is that your excuse for letting them all down?'

Val's eyes had slowly narrowed before he drawled in a swift reversion to type, 'You're really nothing but a jumped up little dingo's arse, aren't you?' Go ahead and worship at the shrine then, mate. It's the ideal place for you.'

The encounter had unsettled Tim until the news broke today, reviving his self confidence with overtones of patriotism. He would show the man which of them was the more worthy, and to hell with his insults. Tim was keen to end his leave tomorrow to get back to his friends and the regiment. Four days of his family were quite long enough at a stretch, and this get-together had been a total failure as far as cordiality was concerned. The only event which had saved it from disaster was the assassination news. The Elders were now being gloomy over the future instead of Val's decision to go back to his disreputable life in Australia, and the children had lost interest in their ruffianly uncle to focus instead on someone who would soon be defending them and England against the enemy. Tim could return to barracks tomorrow knowing his family were relying on him, and certain he would not be obliged to see Val again.

Kate was experiencing an echo of Vere's premonition that life for them was about to change dramatically. All the men save Val were discussing the political and military aspects of the war they were certain could not be avoided, and saying a great deal about the part Tim and Simon would play. Yet no one but she appeared to have considered the prospect of her own involvement. War brought wounding and maiming. She had read so many times the vivid accounts alongside Vere's magazine sketches of conflict in the Sudan and South Africa. Sister Bates had volunteered to work in an army hospital during the last year of the war against the Boers, and had spoken of her experiences in sombre vein. She always said illness was brought about by the hand of God, but battle wounds by the wickedness of man. Sister was inclined to be religious, but there was a great deal of wisdom in those words, Kate felt.

There were army nurses, of course, but were there enough without needing additional trained hands in a dire emergency? Would she volunteeer if the situation arose? Tending fever patients was one thing, but could she deal with broken men day after day? Kate thought again of that wonderful strong body she had seen as Val emerged from the pond in Leyden's Spinney. What if such a body were torn apart, deprived of a limb, reduced to skin and bone? Could she face that? More importantly, could she do what had to be done and remain calmly reassuring? She had told Val she wanted to do something useful with her life, but was she strong enough to carry out what would be demanded of her? What if Tim should be brought in without a leg or arm; or Simon? Would her urge to help them override all else? They were both so elated tonight. They saw war as their great opportunity to fulfil their dreams. She saw only a terrible threat to their youth and vitality, and was afraid. No, more than afraid: filled with inexplicable dread.

Glancing up she caught Val watching her. When he smiled across the room her eyes filled with tears. The announcement of his intended return to Australia, which had shattered her, now became a welcome event. Thank God he would not be caught up in whatever lay ahead. After tomorrow she would never see him again, but she could remember him as he was now and never be afraid that he had been blown apart or broken beyond recognition. He wanted no part in the war everyone else appeared to welcome, and she was liable to be so busy in her chosen work she would have no time to yearn for him.

Val lounged back in his chair listening to the conversation all around him. The great advantage of being a man who had lived in relative isolation for a very long time was that his mind was uncluttered, allowing him to see things with great clarity. Two days in his old home had blunted his initial sense of anger against the past, and tempers had mellowed. The assassination in Serbia had taken away all remaining family interest in him, for which he was grateful.

Val knew little of the power race which had been taking place in Europe, but years of studying in his youth the causes of armed conflict told him this murder was the match to a fuse and an explosion was inevitable. Those people who still believed in the things Val had seen debased, ridiculed and taken no deeper than face value by men of little understanding were right to be afraid. Before long, they would be as cynical and bitter as he.

Young Simon had dreams of flying machines changing the face of war. The British Army had believed their heavy artillery would be invincible against armed farmers in South Africa, until they had to drag them hundreds of miles across the *veld* in extremes of climate to find they were virtually useless against mounted men hiding in the hills. Yes, Simon would discover war made nonsense of theories and plans hatched over desktops in distant headquarters.

The red-haired young man was doomed to disappointment in another area. He clearly regarded Kate with more than brotherly love, but she was unaware of it. Val was sorry for the girl, although the little contact he had had with her suggested that she was self-possessed in following her desire to be a nurse. However, she appeared to belong to no one in particular, even when she was surrounded by a fond family. Val remembered her as a rather solemn little girl who had furiously defended those she loved if she felt they were being unfairly treated. Hence her urge to tend the sick? She might regret that inborn trait when she saw battlefield wounds.

Switching from such thoughts, Val concentrated on Tim sitting on the far side of the room. Kate's brother had troubled him most this weekend, because to look at him was to see himself ten to fifteen years ago. It was uncanny and acutely disturbing. Not only did Tim physically resemble Martin Havelock, he was as full of the same ideals and aspirations as that other young fool had been. Val had heard him airing them, and had argued heatedly with Vere over Tim's right to know the truth about the supposed hero of the regiment he had joined. Vere maintained that Tim's position in the West Wilts would be made intolerable if he had to serve with men who continually honoured a family member he knew to be a rogue and a coward. Val nevertheless thought his nephew should be prevented from mistakenly striving to live up to a myth, but Vere had remained firm.

'No, Val, if we tell him, we are obliged to share the shameful truth with *all* our children, and I can't condone that. Tim's capable of creating his own future regardless of anyone else's reputation. He did extremely well at Sandhurst.'

'Purely on merit, or because he changed his name to Ashleigh before entering?'

'That's rather a sour remark.'

'Not at all. I just wonder if a Daulton would have been named best bloody cadet.'

Val lost the argument but had not been able to resist trying to warn Tim of the folly of living in another's shadow. His friendly approach had been met with surprising coolness from someone who once had been a warm-hearted youngster full of eager admiration for the senior schoolboy determined to flout tradition and join the cavalry. Tim now wanted nothing to do with him, and had brushed off his advice with contempt.

Tonight Val watched him bathing in the limelight and realized there were differences between this young fool and the earlier one. While Tim was driven by the same longing to match the hero, he believed it would happen without much effort. Everything had come too easily to this golden boy. He was approaching the prospect of war with the same attitude, expecting heroism to descend on him by right. The schoolboy Tim had once admired had been totally single-minded in its pursuit, prepared to make any sacrifice. He now knew it was not worth the price. By the time Europe was echoing with the sound of gunfire he would be on the far side of the world in the peace of Goonawarra.

Throughout July governments strove to find a diplomatic alternative to war, but men of foresight like Laurence Nicolardi knew nothing would avert the culmination of too many separate aims just waiting for the opportunity to be settled with the use of force. Austria was threatening Serbia over the assassination of Archduke Franz Ferdinand by one of her political fanatics. Russia had mobilized her vast army which would support the Serbians if they were attacked by the Austro-Hungarian Empire. The Kaiser warned the Tsar that Germans would aid Austria in any power struggle. Italy swiftly declared herself neutral; the French openly supported oppressed Serbia. The British, struggling to avoid civil war in Ireland, desperately attempted to mediate as the giants girded themselves with swords. Those closely involved in the chaotic events of that sweltering July knew that each of these governments believed a show of force would be enough to gain its objective. They had been busily arming themselves to the hilt ready for a military walkover and had no intention of backing down until it was achieved. So, as the month drew to a close, the whole of Europe was waiting for someone to make the first move. On the twenty-eighth day Austria made it by declaring war on Serbia.

Within a week Europe was at war. On the fourth day of August Germany invaded Belgium, bringing Britain into the lists in support of an eighty-year-old treaty of alliance with France, Russia and Serbia. The army which only eleven years before had brought an ignominious end to the war against the Boers was disastrously under-manned, and called for volunteers. Young men flocked to the colours in droves, as they always had, fired with the spirit of adventure and mistaking it for patriotism. It would all be over by Christmas and no red-blooded, healthy male wanted to miss out on the ultimate experience.

In London war fever was rife. Men wearing any kind of uniform were flattered by wistful matrons, adored by romantic girls, slapped on the back by men too old to join them and given free cab rides to wherever duty was sending them. Recruiting centres were set up in all manner of venues; anywhere young candidates were likely to be garnered.

Val viewed it all with cynicism. He had no time or respect for the army. He had seen men die through hopeless leadership. He had watched battles being lost through indecision, ineptitude and poor channels of communication. His several years, first as a trooper then as a sergeant, had taught him to know men and handle them with understanding. As an officer he had earned the respect of those he commanded because he never thought himself a better man, merely a natural leader. Many of his commissioned colleagues were unsuccessful commanders because they had never had to follow. Martin Havelock had, and he had never asked of another man anything he would not do himself. Those qualities had been trampled in the dust of the *veld* at dawn one morning, because a cowardly weakling who was distantly related to minor royalty had been adjudged more likely to be truthful than a commissioned ranker with a doubtful background.

On his last day in England Val watched the busy scene from a window of Vere's London house, and felt bitterness well up strongly at the sight of a column of civilians being marched along the street by a sergeant and several corporals. They were heading for a nearby barracks, no doubt, and were being cheered by everyone they passed. Over-excited girls were throwing flowers. Some even ran up to perfect strangers in their fervour and kissed them. Val's mouth twisted. Girls had run after him from his schooldays, but he had been more intent on becoming a hero to follow in Vorne's footsteps. Julia Grieves had seduced him with a promise of that and he had never trusted a woman from then on. After his court martial on the *veld* he had never trusted another man.

He turned from the window and gazed around the room hung with dark velvet and furnished with expensive leather chairs. Vere had returned to Knightshill an hour ago. It had been a difficult farewell; he was still unable to accept that Val was about to leave the family, his inheritance and his country forever. Up to the very last minute Vere had used every form of persuasion to no avail. They had been in London for the past week finalizing the transfer of money to a bank in Perth. Val had been astounded at the amount to his credit, which had been gaining interest over a period of around fourteen years after his mother's bequest was accredited to his account. It had not been drawn on in all that time.

The Ashleighs' man of affairs had already completed the deed of purchase for Goonawarra when the brothers visited him to sign the last legal papers concerning Knightshill. Vere had added a codecil to his will which named as his heir Val's firstborn son or, in the event of his having no sons to inherit, the house and Wiltshire estate would go to Tim or *his* firstborn son. Val had known a brief moment of remorse when he saw how emotional Vere became at the point of removing his brother's natural succession to all that was his by right of birth. For a few minutes in a dusty legal office the old affection and loyalty had fought for recognition in a man whose faith had been cruelly broken, but the paper had been signed and the ties cut.

A passage was booked on a cargo ship leaving tomorrow

afternoon. The voyage might take a little longer, but Val refused to travel on a giant liner where passengers dressed for dinner, vied for seats at the captain's table and played bridge. Ash, the drover, would return the way he had come, even if he was now the owner of a vast cattle station with no small fortune to his name. He had planned to eat a substantial evening meal then walk in Hyde Park until it grew dark, but he was now thoroughly disturbed and restless. Vere had, probably unintentionally, done the worst thing he could just before he left, and Val was presently struggling to ward off memories he did not want to face.

With his bag packed and a cab waiting at the front steps, Vere had brought from a cupboard something which dealt his brother the biggest blow he had had for many years. 'I kept this until the very last minute in the hope that you would change your mind, Val. I know that nothing will do that, so I'll leave you to make your decision in my absence.'

As Val stared at the weapon his brother balanced on both his outstretched hands, Vere had added, 'I was very proud when I bought this sword in Kimberley to present to you on behalf of the Ashleigh family. You had well and truly earned your commission, whatever else you did before that.' Vere had swallowed emotionally before being able to continue. 'This arrived at Knightshill three days after Grandfather's funeral, together with a notification of the amount donated to the regimental widows' and orphans' fund from the auction of your horses and military equipment. Accompanying it was a letter from the daughter of your colonel, who very clearly had knowledge of your true identity.'

He had put the ornate sword on the table before saying, 'My pride in giving you this is no less now than it was then. It belongs to you Val, and always will.' At the door Vere had turned for a last word before the final break. 'Miss Beecham's letter is with it. I think it says everything for me. God go with you.'

For the past hour Val had been fighting the threat of reliving something he had spent half his lifetime expunging from his mind and soul. By producing the sword Vere had done more to bind Val to his past than anything else that had happened during these six weeks in England. He stared once more at the weapon he had last worn on that terrible dawn parade and felt sick with rage against the old man and the dead brother who had driven him to sacrifice his all. Vere was wrong. This ornate symbol of pride did not belong to him. It signified the destruction of an Ashleigh.

He crossed to the table intending to return the cause of his rage to the cupboard where it would remain until it rusted away, but he saw the letter lying with it and a perverse urge led him to pick it up. It was brief and in handwriting he recognized.

Dear Mr Ashleigh,

Sergeant Toby Robbins informed me that his friend once mentioned you as the person to whom his personal effects should be sent in the event of a tragedy. Everything else has been auctioned in the usual manner, but a sword is such a personal thing I thought you should have it. Please, I beg of you, do not believe ill of your brother. He is a splendid, courageous person who has been the victim of cruel injustice. I know him well enough to be sure he will overcome this to fight back and one day wear his sword with pride. Vivienne Beecham.

Val screwed the page into a ball in his tight fist. She had pestered him from his first days with the 57th determined to expose her 'mystery man'. Her interest had deepened into something he had seen as dangerously akin to that of her cousin, who had seduced him at Chartfield. He could see Vivienne's narrow freckled face beneath carrot-red hair, and recalled her delight in cornering him with a cross-examination designed to wrest a confession from him. She had guessed the truth with Toby's help, apparently, but Val was certain she would keep his secret. He threw the crumpled letter on the table. She *had* known him well enough, because he had eventually returned to Knightshill to fight back. What she was unaware of was the other Ashleigh secret – the one even he had not known until then.

With a sudden sweep of his arm Val sent the sword across the table to crash into a pedestal bearing a Chinese jar. The flimsy item wobbled; the jar fell to the floor and parted into two large irregular sections. Vere's heir had just lost a valuable asset! The room oppressed him; the house was too full of Ashleigh influence. He left it in great haste.

It had been another sweltering day and the streets were dusty, full of the smell of humanity. Val longed for the empty spaces of Goonawarra; the quietness, the anonymity. There was only one way he could get through tonight and he sought the nearest means of oblivion. The bar was full of voluble men in city suits who spared only a swift glance at someone whose rough clothes suggested he would be more at home among workmen and sawdust floors. After three quick drinks in succession Val left these *gentlemen* in search of more congenial surroundings where everyone became your mate and the language grew bluer by the minute. Then he would feel right.

He tried out two or three places but moved on in search of the noisiest, most basic atmosphere he could find. It was well into the evening before he wandered along an area of meaner streets, where houses were built close together with doors opening straight on to narrow cobbled lanes. It was not as airy there, and the unpleasant stench of rotting rubbish and bad sanitation was accentuated by the heat of the dying day. It was not remotely like the Outback where the air was clean and a man could see emptiness stretching for miles, but this place was eminently suitable for defiance of all the Ashleighs stood for. He wanted none of them tonight.

The bar was crowded; walls dark with the grime of years, windows so dirty it was impossible to see what lay beyond. Just as well, Val thought, because it was not worth seeing. There were women in here; females of uncertain age dressed in gaudy gladrags who were well away on cheap gin. There was a sing-song in progress. Even here war fever had got a hold. The words roared out by men in collarless shirts and flat caps were full of ridiculous patriotism – songs of the Boer War Val had heard in camps all over the *veld*. He began a systematic deadening of his senses so that he would be oblivious to them.

Before long Val discovered he was the lifelong friend of a black-haired man in a blue shirt and muddy trousers, who bought him a drink and began talking about the farm he had left behind. They got on very well, with two great interests in common – ale and cattle. As time wore on it became more apparent to Val that this man he called Toby had as many cattle as there were on Goonawarra, for the size of his herd had grown to thousands. That was when he knew they were going to be mates. Toby had always been a good mate. He had sent his sword back. No, it was the girl who had done that, except that he did not want it. She should have thrown it away. He told that to black-haired Toby, who heartily agreed and they drank to it. Everyone drank to it. They were *all* his mates.

Someone began to sing a new song. Toby joined in so Val did as well. It had something to do with marching, but he still felt the urge to bellow at the top of his voice and stamp his feet with the rest. They all sang it again, and several men hauled Val into their circle where they slapped him on the back and introduced him to everyone else. He stood them all a drink because he was going back to Australia tomorrow, then they all stood him one to remember them by. He lost all track of time. In fact, he lost track of everything, even Toby, but his mate soon found him and said he thought they should find a bed for the night because he felt sick.

They left together, holding each other up. Toby forgot his sickness enough to sing the marching song and stamp his feet when Val did. Stars were beginning to show in the blue-grey sky so it was definitely time to find the bunkhouse. They came upon it around the next corner; a long room, bigger than Val remembered, with beds down each side. Most of the boys were already there, stretched out and snoring, so Val made for his bunk realizing how tired he was. Someone stopped him and asked his name.

'Ash . . . you bloody fool,' he returned with an effort.

'We'll have to have more than that,' said the voice.

Val peered at the blur in front of him and gave a sly smile. 'Oh, *will* you. How about . . . how about Valentine Mar . . . tin Havelock Ashleigh. That flaming do?'

'Where are you from?'

'Goona . . . warra, you stupid . . . stupid . . .'

'All right. That's enough! Sign here or make a mark if you're incapable of writing.'

Val was fighting mad and grabbed at the blur. 'I could write before . . . before you could bloody walk, mate.'

'Do it now then, and get on one of those beds before I have you locked up for the night.'

Toby advised him to sign, because he already had and he wanted to lie down before he was sick. So Val scribbled his name as he had been doing on a number of occasions recently, except that he now had to be shown a blurred line to ensure that he wrote in the correct place. He reached his bunk just in time to pitch forward on to it. It had been a long time since he had been as drunk as this, but his mates did not think it was *disgraceful*. They were all as soused as he was.

In the morning Val discovered that he had spent the night in an army drill hall after enlisting as a volunteer, which was what the man he had called Toby had intended to do all along. There was no way out of the commitment. His name was on the form and he had signed it. Fate had added a further spiteful touch. Val had just become a private in a newly raised battalion of the West Wiltshire Regiment.

Tim was in his element. His battalion had been given orders to prepare for immediate active service. To say confusion had reigned for the past week was understating the truth. Everyone knew they were going to France, yet no one would actually say so. It was all a bit pointless, surely. To engage in active service they required an enemy, and the Huns were over there. Tim was to learn that Manners was a man who went by the rule book and never deviated from it, whatever the situation. As he walked beside John Marshall towards the parade ground for yet another inspection of the troops in full marching order, Tim was full of complaints.

'We've been running around like scalded cats for a week, John. The men are ready and all these parades are driving them crazy. What's Manners waiting for?'

'Orders.' John never appeared to grow flustered or worked up over anything.

'Who from?'

'*From whom*, dear boy. Mustn't let your grammar go to pot because of the Hun.'

Tim scowled. 'Does *nothing* excite you?'

His friend cast him a saucy glance. 'The waitress at the King's Head. You've no idea what she'll do for a few peaches or a bottle of cheap scent.'

For once Tim was not interested in hearing. He was eager for action and the chance to put into practice what he had learned at Sandhurst. 'Women are all the same. There are only so many things they can do and I've experienced them all.'

They parted at that juncture to take up positions at the head of their separate platoons of A Company, where they went through the usual ritual while Colonel Manners strolled along the ranks looking for the slightest fault in men growing more than usually disgruntled over this scrutiny. When they faced the enemy it would not be their polished buttons or shiny boots which would finish the Huns off, it would be their cold steel in the guts, they murmured to each other. Tim fumed inwardly. It was another scorcher and they were all standing here looking pretty while the German army was rampaging through Belgium and the French were reaping all the glory in battle. If Manners waited much longer the war would be over before the West Wilts got to it.

Finally, the inspection was over and the CO, instead of walking off with his entourage, took a position facing the four companies formed up with loaded packs on their backs. He then demonstrated that he had not lost the knack of making himself heard on the parade ground by announcing in stentorian tones that they would be marching out of barracks on the following morning to board trains to take them to the coast, where ships would be waiting to ferry them across the Channel.

No sooner had this stickler for correctness finished speaking than one irrepressible soldier raised a loud cheer. Within seconds he was joined by most of his comrades, who also shook hands or clapped each other on the back in their excitement. If there had been only a few there was no doubt Colonel Manners would have put them on a charge, but he could do little to teach six hundred men a lesson especially when they had marching orders for the following day. He decided to walk away from such indiscipline. The officers tried to bring their men to order without too much effort. They were all also grinning delightedly at each other. It would *not* be all over before they got there, but they would do their damnedest to finish it once they arrived.

Back in their quarters as they took off their thick jackets and poured a drink, Tim discussed with John what they should do on their last night in England. His friend had no doubts on his plans.

'I'm going to the Alhambra. There's a new revue on which only began its run last week. Garston and Raymond went on Saturday and said there were some ravishing girls in the chorus. Why don't you come with me?'

Tim liked the notion. 'And choose a couple of partners for afterwards? We could have supper at that little inn in Elderfield. I've used it before. If given a good tip mine host is very obliging and turns his back to the staircase leading to the bedrooms. What d'you say?'

John laughed. 'Why not? It's the night before we get our baptism by fire. Let's have wine, women and song.'

There were doomed to have none of those things. Apart from the married officers who did not live in the Mess, all others were refused permission to leave the barracks. Colonel Manners wished his officers to attend a meeting to discuss plans for the journey to France. The dinner hour was unusually subdued. Young men dying to let off steam who are told they cannot become resentful and rebellious, which was not the best way to embark on something which would demand of them complete loyalty and maximum effort when asked.

Tim was restless. He had set his heart on going to the theatre and having a chorus girl to make him happy for an hour or two. After thirty minutes of prowling around the sitting-room while John's pen nib scratched on paper, Tim had had enough.

'For God's sake stop being a good little boy and writing to Mama,' he demanded of John. 'The second house at the Alhambra will be starting soon and I'm going to it. Are you with me?'

John's response was immediate. 'Don't be a fool. We'd never get away with it. No one's allowed out except the married men. They know that at the main gate.'

'There are other ways to leave the barracks. I've used them before.'

'Tim, it's not worth it,' John reasoned. 'Read a book, have an early night. Better still, have a cold bath.'

As usual, opposition and unwanted advice made Tim all the more determined and, five minutes later, he slipped from barracks over a wall and through the grounds of a mental hospital to reach the street where he picked up a cab to the theatre. The third act had begun when he arrived, but he thoroughly enjoyed the show. He then had very little difficulty in persuading a pert brunette to drive out to the village inn with him for supper. When he told her he was off to France in the morning, she was up the stairs to a bedroom almost before the landlord could receive his tip and turn his back.

The battalion marched to the railway station through crowded streets. Shop girls came from the stores along the high street, typists leaned from office windows to wave, women pushing prams lined pavements, old ladies watched with tears in their eyes at the sight of youth passing by on the way to defend king and country. Cashiers stood in the doorways of banks gazing with envy, butchers, bakers and fishmongers waved their straw hats from the doorways of their premises, elderly men doffed their bowlers as a sign of respect.

Tim enjoyed every moment of that triumphant march. Riding his black gelding at the head of his thirty men he was a hero already. At the station the atmosphere changed dramatically. Confusion reigned as a thousand or more men milled around the long line of cattle trucks behind an engine whose funnel emitted a spiral of thin smoke. Aside from the men there were the officers' horses, the equipment of the Signals section, drugs and dressings from the medical room and a contingent of wagons, ambulances and fire engines plus the animals which drew them, all to be loaded on the flat wagons at the rear of the train.

After handing his horse to one of the grooms who were coaxing the beasts up ramps to the trucks, Tim went with John towards the khaki mêlée on the platform, saying, 'As soon as I get my platoon safely aboard I'm going to find a seat in the carriage reserved for us. I don't give a damn whether or not the rest squeeze into what seems to me to be nowhere near enough space for an entire battalion. It's ludicrous! What was the point of old Manners reading us a lecture on how best to get troops entrained in the shortest possible time, when the ratio of men to space makes the exercise damn nigh impossible?'

As they began pushing their way between soldiers already grumbling about the heat and how thirsty they were, John said above the din, 'I think the CO was referring to normal troop movements. This is war. All the trains are being commandeered at the same time.' After dodging the back-packs of men pushing and shoving to get to the front, he added, 'God help us when we get to Folkstone. Everyone'll have converged there and be fighting to get on the boats.'

'What boats?' shouted Tim, as he became temporarily separated from his friend. 'This is war, John, remember? There won't be enough to cope with us all.'

Tim's hope of soon finding a seat in the carriage was a vain one. Colonel Manners' rule book had to be ignored, for once. The trucks were slowly packed with far more men than regulations stated, and they were not happy. Tim sympathized, but had to remain brisk and official. He could do nothing about it and they probably had worse to come at the docks. Platoons and companies were split in the effort to get everything loaded. The chaos was not helped when a horse took exception to the wagon he was being led into and bolted along the platform, scattering men and setting officers vainly attempting to capture him.

The train departed two hours behind schedule. The sun beat down on those standing in open trucks, who quickly organized a rota so that a third of them at a time sat on their packs giving them some relief, although sitting amidst a sea of closely packed khaki legs was hotter than standing where the breeze could reach them. Progress was slow. The rolling stock was overladen and the engine had been brought out of retirement to cope with the demand. There were endless hold-ups, one lasting as long as forty-five minutes on a siding to allow normal services through. The officers walked the length of the train each time it stopped, checking that all was well and turning deaf ears to muttered complaints about the lack of a meal and nice strong tea. They were glad to stretch their legs away from the stuffy carriages, but they were also peckish and dying of thirst. The victualling officer rang through to Folkstone from one station to check that canteens had been set up to feed men on their arrival. He received a rather rude reply from someone trying to cope with a situation beyond one man's control. The officers passed along the word that everything would be ready for them when they reached the docks. There was no point in causing further disgruntlement. Men who had marched with such swagger through the town had reverted to normal.

Due to the overcrowding a number of the men fainted, so the Medical Officer was kept busy throughout the journey. There was also the problem of toilet facilities. Cattle trucks did not have such niceties so, although they had orders not to leave the train, large numbers of troops jumped to the ground during the frequent halts and used the railway embankments.

'So much for our gallant lads off to war!' commented Tim watching a line of men relieving themselves into some bushes.

'*We'll* be driven to that before long,' muttered a subaltern called Meyrick sitting opposite him. 'My brother was in South Africa and says one soon forgot all notion of good manners on the march.' He gave a short laugh. 'He said men easily sink to the lowest level when driven to it.'

Into Tim's mind came the memory of Val's arrival at Knightshill. An Ashleigh who had once been a Lancer Officer had certainly found it easy to sink there. Well, he was now on the high seas cruising back to that life. Tim's mouth twisted. It was the best place for a man like him.

'Who's for a quick cup of tea at the next station?' asked a tow-headed lieutenant from the corner seat. 'One of us pops out, smiles beguilingly at the girl behind the counter, and asks her ever so nicely to bring out a pot of tea and six cups.'

John looked doubtful. 'You'd have a mutiny on your hands when the men spotted her.'

'No, no,' the other said airily. 'We've worked damned hard to get where we are, so we're entitled to things they can't have. They know their place. Who's volunteering to be messenger-boy?'

'Ashleigh,' five voices said in unison.

'Why me?' he protested.

'You're the junior.'

'No, John was commissioned with me.'

John smiled at him. 'But your success with the fair sex is greater than mine.'

'If you don't go willingly we'll chuck you out,' promised Meyrick.

The threat did not have to be carried out. When they drew into Esher ladies in uniforms vaguely resembling those of nurses lined the platform. They had a number of urns on trestle tables covered with cups. In addition to tea there was an abundance of hearty sandwiches, currant buns and apples. Enquiries revealed the benefactress to be a titled lady who wanted to do her bit for the war by feeding hungry soldiers on their way to France. The presiders over the urns were eager volunteers who had formed themselves into a private organization operating without the blessing of the military authorities. They received the blessing of everyone aboard that train, however.

When it moved off with deep-throated puffs it was far too soon for the hungry passengers. The officers hastily jumped back into their carriages and settled in their seats much more contentedly.

'Got off lightly after all,' said Rob Meyrick to Tim. 'Didn't have to chuck you out.'

'You were getting on rather well with that brunette, Ashleigh,' said the subaltern in the corner seat. 'Never miss a trick do you?'

Tim grinned. 'Never. Pity we're off to war. She scribbled down her address to give me as we left. I could have done well if we'd been staying overnight.'

'Come on, read it out,' urged John. 'If one of us gets wounded and sent home before you, we can follow it up on your behalf. We'll tell her what a wonderful fellow *you* are, of course.'

'Oh no,' ruled Tim with a wag of his head, but the scrap of paper was tweaked from his hand by the man sitting next to him who opened it up and read what was written on it.

I hope you remember to close the carriage door, Mr Ashleigh. Good luck!

Tim ignored their demands to explain the meaning of the message. He was mentally back at Dunstan St Mary station with the girl who had made a bit of a fool of him. Moorkin's niece. What was her name? She owned a London café with her elderly husband. She had intrigued him a great deal on that occasion. Why had he not recognized her today, as she had him? He remembered her now, of course – dark hair, intelligent brown eyes, a well-shaped bosom and lace on her petticoat. What the devil was her name?

Tim had still not thought of it when they reached Folkstone, and the intriguing incident was forgotten at first sight of the total chaos around the port. Hundreds of thousands of troops had arrived to be transported across the Channel in any available seaworthy vessel, but these were unequal to the immediate task. The backlog was formidable and the men were camping out over a large area. As it was evening by then Tim knew they had no hope of getting to France until the next day. Tired out after settling their men for the long wait, he sat with John looking across at the faint blur that was the coast they longed to reach.

'With so many of us pouring across there the whole thing'll be over before we know it,' he said quietly. 'I want to go into battle, John. I want to know what it's like to face a *real* enemy instead of some of our men pretending to be them.'

'We all want that,' John said. 'Why else would we take up a career like this?'

'It's better than politics or the church.'

'But a chap doesn't get killed in either of them.'

'My father did.'

'Sorry. I forgot about that.'

They both continued to sit on blankets, leaning on their bent knees, and thinking their private thoughts until Tim broke the companianable silence. Gazing at the expanse of blue-grey where the sky appeared to have merged with the sea, he murmured, 'It's easier for you as the first man in your family to join the army. I have so much to live up to. My ancestors started the regiment, so one or other of them has been in almost every campaign since its formation. It's a hell of a record to support as it is, without Uncle Vorne's recent heroism in the minds of everyone these days.'

John turned to grin at him and attempted to lighten his mood. 'You *would* change your name to Ashleigh, man. Think how much easier life might have been for you as a Daulton.'

'I was a member of the Ashleigh family from birth, you idiot. The name makes no difference.'

'Then forget about it and just do your best over there. Be your own man, not a copy of a hero.'

The words so echoed Val's on the subject they effectively silenced Tim. Neither of them understood the obligations and pressures he would be under once he faced the enemy.

That moment was further delayed when a clerical error sent a contingent of Guards in their place the following day, and they were condemned to spending another twelve hours in Folkstone. Tim did not sleep well that night. A bad headache had developed, and he felt much too hot. When they eventually boarded an ancient cross-channel vessel at eleven a.m. his headache was worse and so was the heat of his body. During the calm crossing he was heartily sick, for which he was unmercifully ribbed by his fellows. Mortification was the least of his worries, because he was feeling so very unwell he feared he must be suffering from something more serious than seasickness.

At Boulogne they caught up with the backlog that had been at Folkstone. As far as the eye could see was spread a military patchwork of men, equipment, wagons, hastily erected huts, ambulances, artillery pieces of all calibres, ammunition in great stacks, motorcycles, small vans and thousands of horses. Facing enormous transportation problems at docks and railway station, harassed officials inexperienced with such demands were short-tempered and despairing. The officers of companies flowing in to the port very soon reached the same state, as they endeavoured to get their own men marshalled and under marching orders. No one appeared willing or able to state their destination. The general word going around the hot, exhausted men was that they would join up with the French, but there was some doubt as to where their present position was.

The men of the West Wilts spent another day of waiting beneath a very hot sun in cramped conditions, their only comfort being that they were at least on French soil now. Tim joined his fellow-officers in attempting to organize a meal and supplies of water for his men, and this took up the greater part of the afternoon. Throughout that duty he fought continuing sickness and a headache which made movement painful and magnified every sound into unbearable proportions. By early evening he was thankful to spread his bedroll on the ground and drop on it after being heartily sick again.

John was by now concerned over his friend's condition. 'Maybe something you ate has upset you. Food turns bad quickly in this heat.'

'Whatever it was has made me feel bally awful,' he moaned. 'If I came face to face with a Hun now, he'd just laugh and push me over as he went past.'

During that night Tim broke out in a cold sweat and began to shake uncontrollably. By morning he was so ill he could not even stand. The Medical Officer took one look at him and ordered him to the hospital recently installed within a nearby château.

'You're incubating measles,' he told the suffering Tim. 'There's an epidemic spreading over England. You must have caught it just before we left. Were you close to someone who had it, or whose children might have been suffering? Knowing you, it was a girl who passed on the infection. Good job she won't see her hero covered in spots.'

The West Wilts finally marched off to join the French making a stand at a place called Mons, leaving behind the young man who had vowed to be the pride of his regiment. He lay very seriously ill, suffering from a child's complaint instead of battle wounds like the first casualties coming back from the fighting areas. By the time Tim recovered enough to be rational he learned the unbelievable news of a total failure at Mons which had forced an Anglo–French retreat in some disarray. John Marshall was among the wounded, and the battalion had buried eighteen of its men who had been trapped in a wood during the retreat.

Deeply upset, and mortified by the cause of his own absence from the disastrous start to the battalion's baptism of fire, Tim could not be raised from the depths of despondency even by pretty, sympathetic nurses. He wanted to escape them and join the action. Incredibly, the German army had dug itself in and refused to be dislodged by some of the world's most formidable troops. What had gone wrong? Tim could almost weep at being forced to sit out the long period of convalescence, while his friends and the men he had expected to command were out there in the thick of it. His spirits rose dramatically when his company commander, Jack Moore, walked down the ward towards him one afternoon in mid-September.

Getting to his feet to demonstrate how fit he was, Tim asked eagerly, 'Have you persuaded them to sign me off, sir?'

'Didn't have to,' he replied. 'Orders came through for you today. Seems you're wanted urgently elsewhere. Been sitting on your backside surrounded by women far too long, lad. Time you did something useful.'

'It's what I've been wanting,' he said with a touch of resentment at the man's suggestion that he had planned his illness deliberately.

Jack Moore perched on the bed. 'Something of a linguist, aren't you?'

'I speak two or three languages, yes,' he agreed, wondering about the relevance of that information.

'Good. You're being sent on attachment to GHQ as from the end of the week. Prisoners need to be interrogated and there are all manner of nationalities there – French, Belgians, Dutch. They need someone who can translate and make sense of all the paperwork. I told them you were just the fellow, Ashleigh.'

Tim was shattered. 'I don't understand Flemish or Dutch.'

'Speak fluent French and German don't you?'

'Yes, but . . .'

'Then you're just the fellow for the job.'

'I want to stay with the regiment – my platoon. I'm a *fighting* man. Anyone can translate,' he cried.

'They *can't*. Sorry, Tim, but a man has to serve where he's of most use, and for you it's behind a desk at Headquarters.'

CHAPTER FIVE

The war was not over by Christmas. It would have been easy to believe it had not really begun, because the adversaries had established their 'fronts' and were pounding each other with shells from these positions without any significant advances in either direction. Each of the armies engaged in battle found warfare had changed so much it was impossible to conduct it as they had previously done. The nineteenth-century practice of advancing across a broad front to meet the enemy head on for hand-to-hand fighting was useless following the invention of the machine-gun. Heroic cavalry charges with cold steel could not combat heavy artillery hidden in forests. Modern rifles could fire rapidly, which was fatal to advancing troops who used to be able to take advantage of the time needed for reloading.

The old-time mounted gallopers, although still used in the heat of the battle, had been replaced by despatch riders on motorcycles so that valuable information reached battle commanders in time to make considered judgements. There was also wireless telegraphy to pass on even swifter messages. So, now that bold advances in huge numbers destined to put the fear of God into the enemy were no longer effective, the art of secrecy was the alternative. This was nullified by the ability to observe troop movements from balloons or observation aircraft, and to pass on the information very quickly. The opposing armies had therefore gone below ground level in enormous mazes of trenches to bombard each other with artillery while they tried to think of how best to make headway in these new, untried conditions. The generals had little idea. All their soldiering had been done in the old manner. In the meantime, thousands were killed or wounded as they stood in their holes in the ground while shells flew back and forth. Many others fell sick or died through causes previously unknown to medical authorities on the battlefield.

Kate was given three days off for Christmas. She initially declined it, but Sister Bates told her bluntly that she looked washed out and exhausted, which was no help to her or to the patients, then ordered her to go away and make herself fit for the work she would be required to do in the coming months.

'You have twice dropped a thermometer while shaking it, Nurse, and you almost fell asleep while feeding a patient yesterday. I want no would-be heroines in my ward, just efficient young women who have the sense to know when they have ceased to be so. There is far worse to come. Go home and *sleep*. Forget parties and merrymaking. Your duty is to come back ready to tackle the work of *three* women. Right now you seem unable to do the work of one.'

Mortified, Kate told Rosie she intended to stay in her room over Christmas. 'I haven't the energy to travel to Knightshill. The thought of climbing on and off trains is too much to face. I'd be sure to go to sleep *en route* and travel right down to Land's End without waking up.'

Rosie raised objections to that plan. 'Staying here won't help. You'd be disturbed by girls going on and off duty, and you don't think you'd get anything to eat, do you? Show your face in the dining hall and the Dragon would have you outside faster than she peels off soiled dressings. Go home, dearie! If I lived in a place like Knightshill wild horses wouldn't keep me from it.'

Kate glanced up from unlacing her shoes. 'I don't live there; I live here.'

'More fool you.'

She straightened up to confront the girl who had been her close friend during her spell at the hospital. 'Do you really think it foolish to want to do something useful instead of frittering time away with social calls and charity work?'

Rosie bent to pat her hand and smile fondly. 'Of course not, silly! But I wish you wouldn't take it so *seriously*. What we're doing is more than useful, especially right now, but we all need a break from pain and misery. Our boys are over there fighting for us, but they have fun whenever they get a chance. It doesn't make them lesser men to want a party occasionally, or a nice girl to kiss and cuddle before they get back to work. For goodness sake take yourself off to that lovely house in Wiltshire and have Christmas with your family.' She straightened up. 'And ignore the Dragon's order to forget merrymaking. A bit of that'll do you more good than a few hours' sleep.' After a moment, she asked, 'Will Simon be there?'

'I've no idea.' Kate continued to unlace her shoes.

'He sounds like such a lovely fellow.'

'So you've often said. He is.'

'Well . . . don't you feel the least bit attracted to him?'

Kate stood up and unpinned her crumpled starched apron. 'He's my brother.'

'No, he's not. He's the son of your uncle's widowed wife and a diamond prospector. No relation whatsoever to you.'

Kate unbuttoned her grey dress and shrugged out of it. 'I think of him as my brother; and he regards me as his sister.'

'Ah, so it's wicked Uncle Valentine, is it?'

Kate's head shot round as she began to roll down her thick black stockings. 'What do you mean?'

'My dear girl,' said Rosie, sinking on to the bed with a knowing smile, 'you haven't been the same since your last visit to Knightshill to welcome him home. I didn't get much out of you about your mysterious relative except a brief comment that he had come merely to lay his hands on the family fortune before going back to the other side of the world. You made far too much of your real brother's behaviour and how news of the assassination had upset everyone, but I saw through that, girl. If you didn't discover an unexpected passion for the red-headed Simon, it must have been your retrograde young uncle who caught your fancy.'

Kate bent over her stockings again to hide the giveaway colour in her cheeks. 'You read too many silly stories. I don't know how you find the time.'

'They're not silly, Kate, they're about love. We all need that to make the rest bearable.' Rosie's warm voice softened. 'I don't think this war is going to end quickly, and we're going to be caught up in it far more than we are now. If you imagine you can get through what's coming without something to remind you of what life's really about, you'll never survive it. We all have to have dreams to keep us going. They don't necessarily have to come true, so long as we have them to fall back on when everything gets too much for us.'

Rosie's words stayed in Kate's mind as she sat on a crowded train an hour later. She did not harbour dreams of Val because that would be pointless, but she lived with the certainty that she would love him all her days. The work she had chosen to do would certainly grow more demanding and difficult, but she would survive by doing it for him, by making it her expression of love. Val would never know but she would, and it would be her salvation from the surrounding pain and misery. Seeing him again had convinced her that he had suffered deeply. Why else would he be determined to reject all he had once loved, and return to eternal isolation?

In some curious way it would seem that his suffering must have been inflicted by the Ashleigh family itself, which made the situation even sadder and more inexplicable. The older generation refused to talk about it, yet they were all indisputably fond of Val, his decision to leave home for the last time plunging them all into depression. Tim's conclusion that Val had done something so totally dishonourable and shameful he had gone to the dogs might be seen as the only explanation, but she knew it could not be true. She had loved Val all her life, and the laughing, affectionate, proud Ashleigh boy could not have changed into a villain. Whatever had happened had been done *to* him, not *by* him. Kate would stake her life on it. She wanted to share his suffering but she could only do that by not sparing herself in devotion to her profession. Dropping thermometers and almost falling asleep on duty were signs that she was failing him, so she intended to obey Sister and sleep throughout Christmas.

Leaning against the side of the railway carriage, Kate gazed from the window at the winter version of landscapes which had looked so golden and glorious when she had travelled home in June. The few days' leave she had been granted since then had been spent elsewhere – a weekend with Rosie at her parents' cottage just beyond Oxford, and two overnight visits to Vere's London house which was used by all the family whenever they were in town. These three days constituted the longest break Kate had had since since the fatal visit to Knightshill.

As she had then suspected English hospitals had taken on a new role. Her own had been selected to expand its fever wards to take troops who had succumbed to a virulent strain of measles soon after the outbreak of war. Worried doctors had blamed the massive movements of men from every part of the country, which had caused isolated outbreaks to become a widespread epidemic of germs swiftly hatched in the unusual heat of that summer. An alarming number of young men who had rallied to the flag with hopes of glory died without even leaving England, victims of a disease normally associated with children. Kate had watched them slip away from life in their prime knowing they had given their all for their country as much as those who had managed to reach France. They had at least been spared the fate of being blown apart. Kate was still haunted by that, remembering Val's splendid body at Leyden's Spinney.

A month ago she had been forced to face that which she most dreaded. The epidemic over, her hospital had been told to prepare to take casulties. Overnight, extra beds had been pushed into the wards and the staff had awaited the first contingent of wounded soldiers. When they arrived it had been impossible to communicate with them because they were all Belgian. Several doctors spoke good French, and one or two nurses, including Kate, could manage the basics, but the patients had been simple men from rural districts who conversed in Flemish only. Luckily, they had all been so thankful to leave the war for safety in Oxfordshire all they wanted was to eat and sleep, and they had submitted to treatment without a fuss.

After the first day Kate had been sick. After the second she had cried and cried. After the third she had been unable to stop shaking when she climbed into bed. By the end of the week she was able to look at raw, bleeding stumps part-way down an arm or a leg and feel only the impulse to do what she must while smiling reassurance to the man who would never be whole again. The dread remained, but she was capable of keeping it subdued because these men were total strangers whom she had never known as robust creatures. How she would cope if confronted by a maimed friend or relative she dared not think. One advantage of being overworked was that she had no time to think.

Sitting on the train now she had too much of it, and her thoughts returned to that weekend in June when she had felt intuitively that life would never be the same again for the Ashleigh family. Tim was somewhere in France, she had no idea where. They had not corresponded for some years and he was remiss in keeping in touch with their mother, so Kate knew only that her brother was "at the front". He had been so jaunty when they parted at the end of June. Was he that way now, standing in a muddy trench being shot at? Suppose she walked down the ward to find Tim lying there minus his legs? She switched her thoughts from that very quickly as the train ran into Salisbury station, and she got off intending to buy a cup of tea before catching her connection to Dunstan St Mary.

As no one knew she was coming, Kate walked up to Knightshill from the station. The exercise warmed her, for it had turned into a raw day. This was a chilly area which frequently had snow when the coastal belt stayed free of it. She carried no luggage because she had all she needed in her room at home. Only when she was halfway up the hill did she realize that she had no presents for the family. Christmas had crept up on her this year. There had been greater priorities.

There was a tall tree in the entrance hall. It had been decorated with candles, garlands, sweets and tiny packages wrapped in silver paper. At the top was a great glittering star. Everything seemed as it always had been but, unusually, Kate did not become someone other than the woman she had been for the past six months. Knightshill would probably never have that effect on her again.

Thornton was pleased to see her, although he much preferred advance notice of anyone's arrival. 'I'll have fires lit in your rooms, Miss Daulton, and send Bridget to make every preparation for you. You'll find Mrs Ashleigh and Mrs Morgan in the morning-room with Misses Holly and Victoria, and Masters James and Charles. Would you care for tea?'

'Yes please, Thornton.' She handed him her blue fur-trimmed coat. 'It's turned so cold I need something to thaw me out. It's warmer in Oxford.' She gave a smile. 'Or perhaps it seems warmer because I'm on the go so much at the hospital.'

'I'm sure you will enjoy a few quiet days here. Mr Ashleigh is determined to celebrate Christmas in the usual manner. We have to keep to the old traditions in spite of the war, Miss.'

'I suppose so.' Kate thought of the wards decorated with holly and the carol singing she had participated in last evening. What a far cry from this lovely old house where a family would enjoy feasts and festivities with not a bandage or scalpel in sight.

Everyone was delighted to see her. The two aunts who had

reared her through her formative years hugged her and drew her nearer the fire.

'My dear, your hands are like ice,' said Kitty.

'And they look so rough and sore,' Charlotte added. 'You must soak them in glycerine and rosewater while you're here.'

The twins were full of curiosity. 'Why have they let you come away, Kate?' asked Holly. 'I thought there were *thousands* of wounded to see to.'

'There are, but we all have to take a rest occasionally or we could make disastrous mistakes.' Kate sat in a gold velvet chair, revelling in the depths of its comfort. 'I'd better not stay here too long or I'll go right off to sleep.'

'Is it *very* dreadful?' asked Victoria. 'Are they all most terribly hurt?'

'I'm afraid so, Vicky.'

'Kate won't want to talk about her work while she's here, girls,' Kitty said in reprimand. 'She's just told you she's been sent home for a rest.'

'You do look exhausted, dear,' Charlotte put in with her usual concern. 'Are you doing too much?'

'We all are, Aunt Lottie. No one was really prepared for what's happened, and medical staff are rushed off their feet. It was supposed to be all over by now.'

'Laurence said all along that was nonsense. He's very astute. Your mother and he are staying in the London house, but Margaret will be here this afternoon with the boys for a few days. She'll be glad to find you at Knightshill so unexpectedly.'

'Will she?'

Charlotte was constantly trying to create a stronger bond between mother and daughter, although Kate knew she was unlikely to succeed. Thornton brought a small tray for Kate and set it on a low table beside her chair. Then he turned to the mistress of the house.

'May I acquaint Cook with the number for luncheon, madam?'

Kitty smiled up at him. 'There will be nine now Miss Daulton has arrived. Mrs Nicolardi and her sons are not arriving until the three forty-five train. See that Parsons goes down to meet them.'

'He has already been instructed to do so by *Mr* Ashleigh, madam.'

'Thank you, Thornton.' When he left the room Kitty made a face. 'That man is immovable. Nothing will persuade him that women can be concerned with anything but the meals and flower arrangements in this house. Everything else is the province of the menfolk, in his experience.'

'Unlike dear old Winters who had no one but me to turn to during these years I was here alone with Grandfather,' said Charlotte. 'It will only be a light luncheon, Kate, because we have a party arranged for this evening and dinner will therefore be an hour and a half earlier than usual.'

'Mama, *please* let us come down for the party,' said Victoria from beside Kate's chair.

Kitty seemed exasperated. 'I vow if you say that once more I shall banish you to your rooms. You may both be fifteen years old by tomorrow morning, but you are still three years away from coming out. Your friends are invited on Boxing Day for a birthday party, and that will have to suffice. Your papa has agreed that you may stay downstairs for as long as you wish tomorrow night, which is a great concession, so let me hear no more of this nonsensical plea to attend the party.'

Kate smiled sympathetically at the twins who had been born each side of midnight on Christmas Eve. They already possessed signs of future beauty, and were physically mature for their age. They had been given a great deal of leeway due to their parents' liberal views and Vere's determination that Ashleighs should be free to follow their chosen stars – a revolt against Sir Gilliard's repressive rule. Kate had no doubt that these two would join the growing band of women fighting for recognition as soon as they officially became adults in three years' time.

'Who has been invited to the party, Aunt Lottie?' she asked, hoping for a clue to why the twins were so eager to be part of it. Did they have a secret fancy for a local stalwart who looked far too romantic in uniform? They were at an impressionable age.

Charlotte pulled up her shawl around her shoulders from where it had slipped across the arms of her chair, and Kate suddenly noticed that her aunt did not look well. Perhaps she should find out what ailed her before she went back to the hospital.

'It's not the usual kind of party, dear,' Charlotte said. 'We thought that would be inappropriate this year, so Vere came up with a splendid idea.'

Kitty smiled. 'He's so full of splendid ideas it's not easy to absorb them all. We're dealing with them one at a time, and this one has come up first.'

'Papa is the best and cleverest father in the world,' chorused the twins.

'You may already be aware that a great number of people have offered their homes as convalescent hospitals,' Charlotte continued. 'The Thurlows and Doubledays have done so, and the widow of Admiral Halsie has gone so far as to move out of Blakestone Hall with all her valuables and given it over to the Royal Navy for as long as they need it.'

'How generous,' said Kate with warmth, realizing how out of touch with local news she was. 'But what has that to do with your party?'

Holly could keep quiet no longer. 'We would have offered Knightshill, but Papa says it's too difficult to reach. Ambulances wouldn't get up here very easily, and it's often cut off by snow in winter.'

'So he's giving the London house instead,' continued Victoria. 'Isn't it exciting? As soon as Christmas is over he's going to arrange for our furniture to be stored so that hospital beds can be moved in.'

'If you two will be quiet for more than five minutes we can answer Kate's question. The poor girl is bewildered by all this conflicting information,' ruled Kitty. 'She looks half asleep already.'

Kate was, in fact, much wider awake now. What was being said interested her no end. 'It's very good of Uncle Vere. The London house will be perfect and so much more accessible than Knightshill. I had no idea this was being arranged.'

'You surely didn't imagine we would not play our part, dear,' said Charlotte.

'The delay was caused by trying to decide how best we could contribute,' continued Kitty.

'Then Papa came up with the most wonderful solution,' said Holly, who immediately covered her mouth with her hand and made eyes at her mother.

'As well as lending the London house to the military, we decided to use our theatre connections other benefactors don't have,' said Kitty, frowning at her irrepressible daughters. 'Vere and I are organizing concerts in London purely for troops on leave, and have put into action a plan to send performers around the country to various hospitals and convalescent homes. Unlike you, dear, we're unable to tend their physical wounds, but it's within our power to ease their mental ones.'

'Oh, that's so important, too,' cried Kate, thrilled by what she was being told. 'How very clever of you to think of it!'

'That's why we are having the party tonight,' put in Charlotte. 'Vere has arranged for some singers, dancers and a comedian to entertain the more serious cases at Foxington Grange. To do that they need space, so we have invited here for a party all those fit enough to travel by charabanc which will enable the medical staff to move away their beds to provide a stage.'

'We've also invited all the young girls in the district to come and talk to them and play party games,' cried Victoria defiantly. 'But *we're* not allowed to help. It's not like a proper party . . .'

'It's helping the wounded,' concluded Holly equally defiantly. 'We could do that, surely.'

'More likely make them feel worse,' put in Charlotte's son, Charles, who had been playing chess with his brother by the window. Apart from greeting Kate both boys had been intent on their game until now.

'Shut up, you beast,' cried Victoria.

'He's right,' mumbled James. 'You never stop talking. You'd give them all headaches instead of cheering them up.'

'That's enough,' said Charlotte crossly.

'From *all* of you,' Kitty added. 'If you can't make intelligent contributions to a conversation, make none. That's the rule in this house.'

Charlotte turned back to Kate. 'How fortunate that you managed to get away for Christmas. You'll know exactly how to treat these unfortunate young men.'

'I'd say they're just the reverse,' Kate pointed out. 'I had no idea you had all been so busy on behalf of our troops.'

Kitty smiled. 'With only one soldier presently in the family people tend to forget that the Ashleighs have a military tradition going back over thirteen generations.'

'We have *two* soldiers in the family,' Victoria announced firmly.

Kate looked from one aunt to the other. 'Not Simon! He hasn't been foolish enough to enlist?'

'It's Uncle Val,' stated Holly, swiftly adding, 'That's an intelligent contribution, isn't it?'

Turning cold, Kate fixed her gaze on Charlotte. 'He's in Australia. On the cattle ranch he bought.'

'No, dear.' She sighed. 'Bentley received a letter from him two months ago telling him to inform the people at that place Goonawarra that a manager would have to be put in. It seems,' she cast a black look at the twins who were now all ears, 'it seems Val enlisted on the night before he was due to sail for Australia. That's all we know. I imagine it was an impulsive decision, because he'd said nothing of his intentions to Vere earlier that day.'

From the chess game by the window came the faintly audible whisper between the two brothers. 'He'd been at the ale again and didn't know what he was doing. That's perfectly obvious!'

Kate decided to skip lunch and went to bed. Three hours later she gave up the vain attempt to sleep and went downstairs in the hope of stilling her unquiet mind in company. The first person she encountered was Simon coming from the stables area with grease-stained hands and smears of oil on his face.

He smiled broadly at the sight of her. 'I missed you at the luncheon table.'

'I didn't know you were home,' she replied, very glad to see him. 'Why didn't anyone tell me?'

'Did you ask?'

She ran down the last few stairs to reach him. 'I had no chance. The twins prattled on, as usual, and the aunts were full of their plans to help the troops. Oh Simon, your being here makes all the difference – even though you resemble a chimney boy at the moment.'

'I've been giving Jessie a bit of an overhaul. Don't have so much time to devote to her now.' He pretended to threaten her with his grimy hands, laughing at her grimace of horror. 'Give me five minutes or so while I wash, then we'll catch up on all the news.'

'I'll come back with you,' she declared immediately, slipping her arm through his as he started up the stairs. 'I've been trying to sleep, but it's impossible. Isn't it silly? At the hospital I feel I could nod off standing up. Then, when I've all the time in the world to spend in bed, I lie there staring at the ceiling.'

He grinned at her. 'You'll have no trouble sleeping tonight after I've danced you off your feet.'

They reached the landing where the staircase branched, and turned left to climb to the corridor off which Simon's room lay. 'I don't think I could cope with a party, especially one given to war casualties,' Kate said. 'I'm supposed to be getting away from all that for a prolonged rest. Sister saw me drop two thermometers and spill broth down a patient's pyjamas. I was so *mortified*.'

'Why, silly? It's not as if you'd cut off the wrong leg or something disastrous like that.' He stood aside while Kate opened the door for him with her clean hands. 'The Dragon might be mercy personified towards the patients, but she sounds downright sadistic in her attitude to her poor nurses. I'd like to tell her a few truths to her face.'

'I'm heartily thankful you're never likely to see her face, my dear,' Kate said, as he headed for his adjoining bedroom and bathroom.

He halted in the doorway to cast her a look she found puzzling. 'No wounded hero, me.' He disappeared from view and the sound of running water prevented further conversation for a while.

Kate wandered around the sitting-room she knew so well. Simon's personality was reflected in the contents – a writing desk so crammed with diagrams and specifications it could not be cleared, models of dirigibles and flying machines, pictures of aerial pioneers, a tall bookcase with an overflow of volumes piled at its foot, several pairs of powerful field glasses, one or two butterfly nets, a collection of birds' feathers. Simon was fascinated by anything that could fly, and steadfastly refused to take part in local grouse or pigeon shoots. Vere shared his distaste for killing creatures, which was fortunate for Simon. A step-father in the mould of Sir Gilliard could have made his life a misery.

Kate sat in a brown-ribbed chair by the fire, thinking of a room along the other wing of this house – a room containing a mass of sports trophies, photographs of thoroughbred horses, silver-backed hairbrushes, a stud box with the initials VMHA; possessions which no longer reflected the essence of the person whose boyhood had been spent at Knightshill. She recalled stealing in to look at him on that midsummer's evening, and her heart ached anew.

Simon appeared in the doorway wiping his hands on a thick towel. 'We're working on a new design. It's quite revolutionary, really, because it'll be possible to manoeuvre it in tighter turns at greater speeds. The problem is getting an engine powerful enough to allow this without adding too much weight. The greater the propulsion, the more fuel is consumed. There's little point in creating a fast machine that can only stay airborne for half an hour.' He grinned. 'I'm putting it in basic terms so that you'll see the problem.'

'I understand *that*, my dear, but not exactly why you should want tighter and faster turns.'

He came a few steps into the room and perched on the arm of a chair, the towel hanging loosely from one hand. 'At the moment aeroplanes are being used merely for reconnaissance – to find out what the enemy is doing and spy out the terrain ahead for advancing troops. Pilots are being shot at by artillery but have no means of defence. We need aeroplanes which are weapons in their own right. When the pilots see columns of enemy soldiers on the move they should do something to stop them, not simply fly back to send a communiqué on the subject. Valuable time is being lost.' His face was alight with a dream. 'Our flying machines should be mounted with guns and armed with grenades. Not only could they then attack any force on the ground, they could shoot down enemy machines to prevent them from reporting our own troop movements and gun positions.'

Kate protested. 'You'd then have a second war going on in the sky. Isn't one enough?'

'It'd be the *same* war. There's one going on at sea, isn't there? Naval participation in wars has always been essential and acceptable. Why not in the sky?'

'It's different,' she protested. 'Ships can bring invasion forces. That has to be prevented. What you're suggesting is, in fact, the *creation* of aggression where it's not necessary.'

He gave her a look of resigned patience. 'You're missing the most vital point. *Men have discovered they can fly*. They'll never stop in their search for a bigger and better machine. The world will be completely changed by this ability to take to the air, Kate. The future is certain to be dominated by the aeroplane. Before long someone will design a machine capable of carrying entire companies of soldiers to and from battlefields; ordinary people will be able to go from country to country in the air. Passenger liners will become obsolete.'

He was off on his hobbyhorse. Kate had heard all these wild dreams many times, but she was nevertheless concerned over the design he was presently working on. Flying was a precarious enough occupation without adding guns to enable aviators to shoot each other from the sky. There was enough killing going on on the ground.

'How far advanced is this new design?' she asked abruptly, bringing him from his visions of the future.

'Not as far as we'd like,' he replied with a frown. 'I think we've solved the problem of siting the larger fuel tank. We're waiting for amendments to the engine specifications. We need this machine urgently. The Huns are working on a fighter – we already know that – so it's essential that we get ours in the sky first.'

'Oh dear,' she reflected, 'then they'll make an even bigger one, and we'll have to do the same.'

Simon got to his feet. 'Isn't that what I've just been saying? That's what makes this whole aerial concept so exciting.' He smiled at her glum expression. 'There's nothing like flying, Kate. I'll take you up one day then you'll find out.'

'Take me up?'

'I'm having flying lessons – have been for two months.'

'*Simon!*'

'I've kept it quiet for mother's sake. I don't think she'd be too happy about it.'

Kate was not happy about it either. 'Why do it then? You're not in the RFC. You're a designer, not an aerial daredevil.'

Again that puzzling expression on his freckled face. 'How do any of us know what we really are until we try? If I expect other men to risk their lives in something I've designed, I must be prepared to demonstrate my confidence in it by flying it myself. Your RFC heroes have to do it in the presence of the enemy. The least I can do is test the machines safely over England, don't you think?'

She was still not happy. 'I shall worry about you now.'

'I've *always* worried about you.'

He disappeared into the connecting room leaving Kate feeling deeply disturbed for the second time that day. She had believed her beloved Simon to be free from the threat of what lay ahead for many young men; free from the fate of those she had tended since the war began. Was no one to be safe from danger? Her heart grew even heavier.

'Val has enlisted,' she called out, caught up in her thoughts.

Simon reappeared in the doorway. 'I know. Mother wrote the news in one of her letters. Said they were all relieved to learn of it from old Bentley.

'*Relieved*!' she cried in protest.

'Of course.' He studied her for a moment or two. 'Didn't they tell the whole story? When Father went to the London house a week after saying goodbye to Val, he was taken aback to find his clothes and that awful old bag still there, along with other evidence that suggested things had not gone according to plan. He contacted the freight line and was told passenger V. Ashleigh had failed to board the ship at Tilbury. Father was extremely worried, of course, but had no notion what to do next. Enquiries at the bank revealed that no money had been withdrawn from Val's account, which worried Father even more. Then Bentley received a letter instructing him to contact the legal man in Australia who must appoint a manager for the ranch until the end of the war because the new owner had enlisted in the army. Bentley wrote to Father right away. Of course, no one knows which regiment Val's in, or where he is, but it's better than knowing nothing.' He slung the towel over his shoulder as he pulled down his shirt cuffs. 'Val should have written to Father direct. Going through Bentley's an insult. Father was very decent to him while he was here – we all were. The very least Val should have done was to put everyone straight on his latest cavalier escapade. He's still heir to all this, after all.'

As he turned back to his bedroom, Kate cried, 'Why didn't you tell me about it when we met in London last month? You could even have put it in a letter. Why *didn't* you?'

Simon's face appeared around the door frame. 'I knew you'd be upset. He's one of your wounded soldiers, isn't he?'

Kate was left staring at the place where he had stood, his last sentence voicing the very situation she now dreaded.

Because dinner would be served at six-thirty, afternoon tea consisted of no more than biscuits and madeira cake. Parsons and the two parlourmaids brought it to the sitting-room in the sheltered west wing of the house at four o'clock, in readiness for the arrival of Margaret and her schoolboy sons. Vere joined the rest of the family in relaxed mood, having finalized his plans for the party, yet Kate sensed undercurrents of tension beneath the family togetherness. The twins were still in a huff over being denied attendance at a party they saw as deeply romantic, and their disgruntlement was accentuated by the prospect of the arrival of their Nicolardi cousins who always teamed up with the other two boys as overwhelming male opposition to them.

Kate had learnt that Charlotte's less than normal air of wellbeing was occasioned by worry over her husband's health. John Morgan was now in his mid-sixties and troubled by shortness of breath, which was not improved by winter weather. As Thornton poured tea for Rosie and Ginny to hand around, Charlotte was watching John with a frown of anxiety as he panted from the effort of moving a chair into the family circle.

For the first time Kate could remember, there was constraint between herself and Simon. Although they had this afternoon given each other accounts of what they had been doing since their meeting in London last month, the earlier exchange concerning Val had come between them in a surprising fashion. Simon kept glancing unhappily at her across the width of the room, and took no part in the conversation around him. He had made his views very clear, and Kate could not argue with them. The evidence against Val was damning. It suggested yet another desertion of his family without explanation or apology, but Kate clung to the belief that Val was yet again the victim of unrelenting fate.

A sweep of lights in the darkness outside told them all the carriage had arrived from the village with the travellers. Vere got to his feet, teacup in hand. 'Here they are!' He was always so pleased when the whole family gathered at Knightshill. He waved his free hand at the younger members. 'Hey, leave some of that cake for Jon and Dick. They'll be hungry after the journey from London.' He turned to smile at Kate. 'What a lovely surprise you'll be for your mother! We'll just see how long it is before she spots you there in your corner.'

There was a general shifting of chairs and positions to make space for the Nicolardis, by which time their voices could be heard approaching. Margaret swept in looking like a Christmas fairy in a pale pink coat trimmed with fluffy white fur, and with a Russian-style fur hat on her golden hair. She was positively aglow, and the reason for it and why she had not waited to take off her outer clothes became clear as she announced, 'Look who got off the train at Dunstan. Can you believe we had travelled all the way from London unaware of each other until we arrived at the station?'

Tim walked in to stand beside her. He cut a heroic figure in his khaki tunic and breeches with polished Sam Brown and high boots. The twins squealed his name and rushed at him in excitement. The Nicolardi brothers sidled in almost unnoticed and made for their cousins James and Charles, who were still eating cake.

'He's come straight from Paris on seven days' leave,' Margaret announced, caught up in the euphoria of the most wonderful Christmas present she could be given. 'Isn't that marvellous!' She now began unbuttoning her coat to reveal beneath it a tailored costume of deeper pink angora wool, with buttons and a brooch of carved ivory. 'Tim dear, come and sit beside me near the fire.' She patted the chairs vacated by Holly and Victoria, who were presently hanging on her son's arms. 'I have been so looking forward to tea in this lovely old house, and now I'm here I'm too excited to have any.'

'Have you killed any Germans?' asked Holly in awed tones. 'Is it terrible to have to fight?'

A shadow crossed Tim's face as he settled beside the mother who had eyes only for him, and he replied with a hint of self-consiousness, 'As it happens, I've been singled out for something rather important. I'm on attachment to Intelligence at Headquarters, to interrogate prisoners and translate vital documents. It's all very secret. We're not supposed to mention it to anyone . . . except our families, of course.'

'We won't say a *word*,' breathed Victoria, her eyes round with admiration.

'It's a splendid move, certain to advance his career,' Margaret enthused. 'He's in the perfect place to be noticed by high-ranking men of international repute, men who will be aware that his talents would be wasted in the mud of the trenches.'

During the general outbreak of conversation that followed, Kate watched her brother receiving the attention he always craved and knew their mother thought only of her own wish to keep Tim safely at Headquarters. Love for him should tell her that her son yearned to be in the muddy trenches, longed for a chance to be a true hero. He could not equal Uncle Vorne by translating documents. Poor Tim!

After a while Kate sensed that she was being watched, and turned to look at the other person in the room who was isolated in a corner. Simon smiled across at her with great warmth. She smiled back with a surge of thankfulness that everything was all right again between them. Then her smile faded as she recalled the risks he was starting to take in untried machines. Her gaze returned to Tim in warrior's garb. What of the family's *other* soldier. Where was Val? Had he named Vere as his next of kin, or would he one day die in a foreign land in the same lonely manner in which he had lived for so long? Might he lie fatally wounded for days in a field hospital with no one to comfort him, and would she learn about his slow death through some accidental source years later? The prospect was unbearable.

Kate was immediately sucked into the furious routine when she returned to the hospital from Knightshill. Those who had not taken a rest at Christmas went away to sleep over New Year, which drastically cut staff members at a time when patients were flooding in like an unstoppable tide. Conditions in the trenches had worsened. They were now getting a few British soldiers in the emergency wards who told a stark tale of the great adventure that had turned into a feat of dogged endurance instead. Winter had brought frost and snow. Although the mud had hardened enough to make trenches negotiable with greater ease, icy temperatures brought frostbite, bronchitis and an influenza epidemic. Both armies faced each other, sometimes with no more than a hundred yards between their front lines, suffering more from illness and the weather than from exchanges of fire.

Kate listened avidly to all this, even to the curious tale of opposing troops climbing from their holes in the ground on Christmas Day to exchange cigarettes or chocolate and sing carols together. The longing within her grew to almost uncontainable proportions as she carried out her duties, waiting for a response to her request for an interview with Matron. Five days had passed since she told Sister about it, and she tried to curb her impatience because she knew Matron had greater priorities than the personal problems of her nurses. Two days after New Year's Eve Kate received a summons to the office of the woman every nurse feared. It meant missing her tea, but the vital moment had finally come.

Miss Cavendish was unusually tall for a woman and her features were strong to the point of being mannish, yet she was indisputably a lady in speech and manner. She gave Kate grave scrutiny but there was a gentle note in her voice when she bade her nurse good afternoon.

'Good afternoon, ma'am,' Kate replied, in awe but fully determined.

'I'm sorry you have had to wait so long to see me, but our work must come before anything else, as I'm sure you agree.' Shrewd eyes behind spectacles fixed on Kate's face. 'I sincerely hope you have not come to tell me you have impulsively agreed to marry a young man on embarkation leave. I have lost three nurses since the start of December. As I told *them*, you will be of greater use to your loved ones doing this essential work than by sitting at home wearing a wedding ring and studying the casualty lists each day.' When Kate said nothing, the older woman prompted her. 'Well?'

Swallowing hard, Kate embarked on her rehearsed speech. 'I have given this a great deal of thought, ma'am. It's not a sudden decision. I know what it will entail, but it's what I feel I must do. I wish to transfer to the Imperial Military Nursing Service. They are desperate for trained nurses.'

'This hospital is desperate for trained nurses, Miss Daulton.'

'I'm sorry, ma'am.'

The weary woman behind a desk piled high with the paperwork now made necessary by the influx of military casualties gave a sigh. 'People are in need of our skilled help whether or not they are in uniform. A life is still a life even if it belongs to an elderly seamstress rather than a wounded soldier. That should be your creed, Nurse.'

'It is, ma'am.'

Another heavy sigh. 'I see. Are you able to give me a reason why you feel you *must* do this? Have you relatives at the Front?'

'No, ma'am. My brother is safely behind the lines engaged in Intelligence work. My other brother is an aircraft designer with Sopwith.'

'There is a young man you care for?'

'No, ma'am,' Kate lied. 'Something my aunt said during my Christmas leave is responsible for my decision.'

'May I know what that was?'

'Certainly. My family is converting our London house into a a convalescent home, and they are organizing concerts for troops on leave in London and in various hospitals around the country. When I applauded their actions my aunt said, "With only one soldier presently in the family, people tend to forget that the Ashleighs have a distinguished military tradition going back over thirteen generations". I'm the daughter of an Ashleigh, ma'am, and this is the first time a female member of the family has had the opportunity to follow that tradition.'

Kate had chosen her words well. It was an argument with tremendous appeal to a pioneering woman. Miss Cavendish absorbed it for a moment or two then gave a nod. 'A family of great military renown, of course, but only on the male side.' She pursed her lips. 'You are a good nurse – I read through your file before you came in – and the hospital can ill afford to lose you, but I shall not stand in the way of your application to transfer to the Army. Tradition is what makes this country great.'

Kate breathed out in relief. 'Thank you very much, ma'am.'

As it was clear the interview was over, Kate turned and made for the door. As she left, Matron said, 'Good luck, Nurse Daulton. You'll need every drop of the courage your ancestors possessed in the months to come.'

CHAPTER SIX

Tim faced Laurence angrily across the room in which Vere had handed the sword to Val before saying goodbye. 'I've been kicking my heels at Headquarters for *three months* while my men have been fighting this war. I'm not asking the impossible, sir. You could do it.'

Laurence looked tired and strained. Some of the fire was missing from his manner. 'Yes, I probably could, Tim,' he agreed quietly, 'but we are *all* fighting this war. I am holding exhaustive talks to persuade the Italians to become our ally. It's not essential to rush around with a rifle, although you very clearly believe it is.'

'Of course I do!' he cried. 'Diplomats talk. Soldiers rush around with rifles, and *I'm* a soldier. I know everyone is doing his bit in his own way – I'm forever being told that by Sir Reginald – but *my* way should be with my men, not sitting behind a desk translating documents.'

'Vital work.'

Tim scowled. 'A filched report on how many pairs of boots have been ordered for the Huns at Ypres?'

'Intelligence work often appears of little importance but when all the facts are assimilated they form an impressive picture.'

'But I'm not *in* Intelligence,' Tim stormed. 'I'm an infantry officer who happens to be fluent in French, German, Italian and Spanish – accomplishments *you* insisted upon.'

Margaret spoke up from the leather chair she occupied beside the fire. 'Please don't speak of Laurence's deep consideration for your future as if it were blameworthy, Tim. You have been given every advantage and, until now, you have used and appreciated them to the full. Any man can stand in a trench to be shot at. You have far more to give to your country.'

Tim turned on her. 'The men in the trenches are giving their *lives*. No one can give more than that.'

'Is that what you really want?' she cried. 'Do you want to die at twenty-five in a hole in the ground? Will that satisfy all you have worked for during those years?' She got to her feet in agitation and approached him. 'You say the men at the Front are giving their lives for their country. You're wrong, Tim. They're giving their *deaths* for it. Only by staying alive can you really serve England. Sir Reginald knows where you are of most use, darling.'

Tim stepped back as his mother tried to take his hands, a terrible suspicion dawning on him. 'My God, *you're* behind it, aren't you?' He swung round to confront Laurence. 'I've always known you'd do anything for her . . . but *this!* How long did it take you to talk Sir Reginald into appointing me to his staff . . . or did he owe you a favour for services rendered on his behalf?' Breathing hard he stepped further back. 'Have you any idea what you've done to me? For as long as I can remember I've wanted to join the West Wilts and follow Ashleigh tradition. All those men whose portraits hang at Knightshill went to war with the desire to prove themselves and match the courage of those who had gone before them. That's what I've wanted to do since I was a small boy. *You both know that.*'

Laurence was now losing some of his control. His dark eyes flashed with anger. 'This war will last a very long time – unless every impetuous young fool who craves heroism rushes to be mown down in the front lines, leaving no one to stand back and control the needless slaughter by using the talents they have been blessed with. You'll get your chance to prove yourself, boy.'

'Not if my mother has her way,' Tim snapped. 'She'll use her considerable influence to wrap me around with cottonwool and . . . and *crush* me to death.'

'*Tim*!' cried Margaret.

'Correct me if I'm wrong,' inserted Laurence with some heat, 'but isn't that what you've been seeking since maturity? "A cuckoo in the nest" is what I understand you have called yourself . . . and your resentment of your mother's fondness for your brothers has been quite open.'

Out of his depth against such argument, and filled with conflicting emotions which threatened his own control, Tim wanted only to leave and sort himself out. 'I'll go somewhere where my resentment won't be obvious to anyone. If I'm a cuckoo in any nest it's at Sir Reginald's safe haven. One infantry subaltern slyly inserted amongst Intelligence staff officers. Happily for you both, the mother hen hasn't yet spotted the interloper.' Reaching the door, he turned to face them again. 'I won't forgive you for this. *He's* out there fighting. In this family it seems a man has to be an out-and-out rotter who does as he pleases before he can make his mark. I've done everything right, but you're never satisfied with me, are you? *I'm* the Ashleigh who should be continuing the heroic tradition. All he'll do is make a mockery of it.'

He slammed the door as he left. Taking the stairs two at a time he reached his room, snatched up his cap, greatcoat and gloves, then descended to the hall in the same forceful manner expecting Laurence to come from the room at any moment. The door remained shut, and Tim let himself out into the street with the air of a prisoner escaping the confines of his cell. Too worked up to sit in a cab, he strode along the street seeing nothing of the passing scene. Why had he not guessed the truth at the start? Laurence had a number of influential friends, and his beautiful wife could persuade him to do as she wished. Tim knew how men felt about his mother. He had seen the admiration in their eyes, watched them flirt with her. It had made him uneasy when he first recognized the sexual overtones of those encounters. Then he had plunged into the game of seduction himself and taken it to its limits to banish adolescent resentment of Margaret Nicolardi's slavish admirers.

Why had she done this to him? Was her love so possessive that she would resort to such tactics to hold on to him? Or was she afraid that he would not live up to her expectations? Laurence had reminded him in June about his duty as an officer, and suggested cutting down his enjoyable *amours*. That had hinted at a lack of confidence in his ability, despite winning honours at Sandhurst. Tim strode on, collar turned up against the bitter wind racing along the street. Yes, it was not that she was afraid of losing him – she had two other sons by the man she adored – it was that she, and Laurence, did not believe he was up to the job of leading men in battle. They were afraid he would let them down. And yet that bastard . . .

Consumed by fury, Tim was oblivious of the interest he was

creating in women he passed. The twins had told him Val was not in Australia but in the army. He could not believe the man had enlisted out of patriotism. James Morgan's theory that it had happened when he was too drunk to be aware of what he was doing was almost certainly correct. The news had come as an unexpected blow when Tim was burning to get back with his battalion in the thick of the action. Admittedly, it was static action in that it mostly took place in a network of trenches, but Tim had not yet been in the vicinity of a shell or a bullet. He could hear the gunfire from his office – it could be heard from the coast of England – and he had sat day after day eating his heart out to be with his platoon. Another subaltern would have taken his place, of course, but the casualty rate was so high the need for trained infantry officers could not be satisfied.

Seven days' leave had offered him his chance, and he had headed for Knightshill believing Laurence would be there with the family for Christmas. His disappointment had had to be curbed until he and his mother returned to London today, but those three days at Knightshill had become almost intolerable after the twins had gushed on and on about their mysterious uncle. The thought of that drunken failure being in the place where he had a greater right to be accentuated Tim's determination to persuade his step-father to use his influence in getting him away from Headquarters. He had believed it would be relatively easy to accomplish, but Laurence's stubborn resistance had led to the dawning of truth. Perhaps he would eventually be able to excuse his mother's part in the move, because she was a woman and would not understand his need to fight alongside his men, but Laurence had now lost all the affection and respect earned from the day of Tim's escape from a tyrannical bigot of a father.

Tim marched on through London's West End saying silently over and over again, 'How *could* they have done this to me?' He was so lost in his misery he did not initially hear someone speak his name. Only when it was repeated in more emphatic tones did he glance up to find an officer he knew standing before him. Michael Calshore had been at Sandhurst with Tim, where they had several times been partners in wilder escapades John Marshall had refused to condone. Mike had joined the fuselier regiment his brother served so Tim had not seen him since that last riotous night at the Military

Academy. The dark-haired man with a smooth tongue and a talent for getting into tricky situations was presently grinning broadly. He had a girl on each arm.

'You couldn't have come along at a better moment, old son,' Mike declared. 'I rashly promised to find someone for Poppy within ten minutes flat, and you walked around the corner as soon as the words were out of my mouth.' He urged forward the blonde on his left. 'May I introduce Miss Poppy . . . er . . .'

'Gilpin.' She paused, giving Tim a comprehensive study with her round blue eyes. 'How d'you do, Mr Ashleigh . . . or shall I call you Tim?'

'We're on our way to paint the town. You haven't anything planned, have you? No, I thought not,' he added with a deliberate wink. 'You look as if you need cheering up. This is Eve, by the way. She's Poppy's friend. They work in the same shop. That's where we met. They gave me extra toast and the pick of the cakes, so the least I could do was take them for a nice evening out as a reward. Bit of luck you coming along.'

Tim assessed the girls, guessing the were the kind who were frequently rewarded for giving male customers extras. Poppy was gazing back at him as if he were a delayed Christmas present, and he knew she was just what he needed tonight. He smiled and offered his arm. 'Call me Bobby. All my friends do.' That name was all she would remember by morning.

'I bet you have a lot of friends,' she enthused, taking his arm.

'Hundreds! What's the plan Mike? A few little drinks, a show, then late supper?'

'Right first time, *Bobby*. And *my* friends call me darling.'

Both girls giggled, and Eve told him he was an awful flirt, which set the mood of the evening. Tim was in no hurry to get to the satisfying conclusion of this fortunate encounter. He needed a great deal of Poppy's awed admiration to restore his self-esteem before he embarked on something which would be a defiance of Laurence's warning about women. Poppy would not know what had hit her once he got going.

They found a large hotel full of Christmastide revellers, and officers on leave who were hellbent on pleasure. After two drinks the girls were laughing rather too loudly, so Mike signalled to Tim that it was time to put on the brakes. When the steward came in response to his wave Tim ordered four "special" cocktails and instructed the man in an aside to leave the gin out of two of them. The steward was experienced in these matters and did not turn a hair when asked to book two rooms, if they were available. He returned with the drinks carefully placed in pairs, but regretted he could not help the gentlemen further, it being between Christmas and New Year. It was a setback, but Tim was sure a room would be available somewhere, in a less plush place where he and Mike were unlikely to be recognized. From the way everyone around them was celebrating no one would be in a state to recognize much as time passed, anyway.

Mike recalled that he knew someone on the staff of a nearby theatre who would find them seats for the second house of a saucy review, so they drank up and left. To their surprise it was white underfoot and snow was tumbling down from the night sky in spirals driven by the wind. The girls snuggled close to their escorts for warmth, which suited them all. After an absence of several minutes when they reached the theatre, Mike appeared to conduct them to a box almost directly above the stage. Tim bought a large casket of chocolates for Poppy and Eve. After settling them in red velvet seats, the men took off their overcoats to hang on the hooks behind the door.

'How did you manage it?' Tim asked in a low voice. 'Do you really know someone on the staff?'

Mike grinned. 'We had a very good time on my embarkation leave. I had to promise to see her after the show.'

Tim was alarmed. 'I can't take on Eve as well as Poppy. I mean, I *could* but it's unlikely they'd be that willing.'

'Don't worry,' Mike whispered beneath the sound of the overture. 'The advantage of this war is that duty calls at the most convenient times.' He winked again. 'And they spend the night alone dreaming about what heroes we are.'

That last what not what Tim wanted to hear in his present mood, so he took his seat with a slight return to the anger of the afternoon. The revue was enjoyably saucy, which forced reluctant laughs from him as he held Poppy's hand and contrived to move his left thigh so that it rested against hers. When she made no attempt to shift her leg away, he began to make whispered comments on the show with his lips against her ear. She smelt of violets as did many girls of her class; it was a popular scent for those who could not afford the subtler perfumes from France. He did not particularly like the aroma of violets, but the glowing looks he was getting from her whenever he caressed her lobes with his mouth told him she was his for the taking whenever he was ready. Anger slipped away on the thought that he would have a woman whenever he damn well felt like it, and Laurence could go to hell.

They emerged into a veritable snow storm, but nothing daunted Mike. 'Come with me, children,' he invited with the smile which revealed his even, white teeth. 'Forget those overcrowded hotels. I've heard about a place which is getting very popular, but it's a short way out from here and unlikely to be crammed with the *hoi polloi* tonight.

Eve giggled. 'You say the funniest things! Doesn't he, Poppy?'

'Mmm,' agreed her friend brushing snowflakes from Tim's eyebrows with her gloved hand and managing to stroke his cheek at the same time.

They found a cab with some difficulty, then settled in its dim comfort with mutual desire for rather closer acquaintance. Poppy's lips tasted of chocolate – she and Eve had devoured them all during the show – and she was gratifyingly willing to let Tim's mouth travel down her throat as far as the collar of her blouse while his hand travelled upwards from her waist. Tim was reaching the stage where he felt that supper could wait when the cab came to a halt, and Mike called out, 'All ashore!'

From the outside the Regency Restaurant looked disappointingly sober and respectable. Tim flashed Mike an accusing look. 'Not exactly the hub of seasonal activity. Where in God's name did you hear of this place?'

'Chaps returning from leave raved about it. Said it's *the* place to go to now.'

'Yes, well I suppose *any* place seems good after trench-life.'

'Doesn't it just,' agreed Mike who had actually experienced the trenches.

Tim had lied about where he had spent the last months, leaving the other man to assume he had been with his battalion from the start. In any case, Poppy would be more impressed by that than by an account of his fluency in European languages. Girls of that sort preferred brawn to brain.

'Aren't we going in?' Eve asked in complaining tones. 'I'm getting frozen out here.'

'Me too,' said Poppy, tugging Tim's arm. 'Come on!'

The restaurant was not particularly large, but there was an air of spaciousness about the high-ceilinged room which suggested that two had been converted into one by the removal of a wall halfway across it. There now remained only a three-foot drop above the centre from which hung a row of elegantly painted glass lanterns. The walls sported paintings of Regency bucks driving racing phaetons across the grounds of their estates, with glimpses of majestic houses visible through the trees. Gold brocade curtains hung at the windows and at the back of a small dais bearing a piano and three chairs. Tables were covered with starched linen. In the centre of each stood a tiny glass lantern painted in the style of the overhead ones. The place looked full, but the diners were a surprise. Instead of middle-aged respectability to match the décor, the tables were mostly taken by young men in uniform whose partners were the sort who *could* afford French perfume. Tim looked at Mike across the heads of their girls for the night and rolled his eyes to express what he was unable to say. Mike merely shrugged and inclined his head to the snowy street outside, as if to say, 'It's this or the pavement.'

'Good evening. Do you require a table for four?' asked a female voice from behind them, causing the men to turn. 'If you're prepared to wait just five minutes one will be free. The gentlemen are dealing with the bill and fetching the ladies' coats. It will take only a few moments to reset the table for you.'

The woman was around twenty-three with an air of assurance normally found in more mature ladies. She wore a simple cream blouse with self-coloured embroidery on its long pointed collar, and a well-cut black skirt that hung to her ankles. There was an arresting quality about her candid brown eyes and her smile was neither cool nor over friendly. Tim had a curious feeling he had seen her before.

'Yes, we'll wait,' said Mike, with one of his hangdog looks. 'We are orphans of the storm and extremely hungry.'

The woman responded to his approach with a light laugh. 'I can satisfy your hunger with no trouble. All I can do about the storm, I'm afraid, is to invite you to take off your coats and warm yourselves by one of the fires. Would you care for mulled wine while you're waiting, sir?'

'Rather!'

'For the lady, also?'

'Yes, of course.'

She turned to Tim. 'And for you, Mr Ashleigh?'

'Er . . . yes,' he murmured, struggling to sort out sudden recollections of Moorkin's niece who ran a teashop with her elderly husband somewhere in the provinces, and linking them with here and now. This was far grander than a teashop, and where was the old man? Yet she knew his name, and he had definitely seen her before. He watched her walk away to speak to one of the waitresses and suddenly remembered a brief incident *en route* to Folkestone. She had served him with tea and sandwiches on the platform. And there had been a note wishing him good luck. What the devil was her name?

'Is she one of your friends, Bobby?' Someone tugged on his sleeve. '*Bobby*!'

He turned to see a face that was vastly different. Pale-blue doll's eyes, a turned-up nose rather cold from the chill outside, full lips and brassy hair which was now untidy after his attentions in the cab. Poppy's blue blouse was cheap and shiny, her navy skirt was too tight and fastened with overlarge, oval buttons that all faced in different directions. The scent of violets seemed overpowering in the warmth of this room. All at once Tim felt uncomfortable to be with her in a place like this, an entirely foreign experience for him. He wished he had not bumped into Mike. He knew nothing about this girl, and he usually aimed higher than café waitresses. There was no doubt in his mind that he had caught the measles germ from that actress he had slept with in impetuous defiance of his colonel's ban on leaving barracks. He could have died from the illness – men had gone under in large numbers during the epidemic, he knew – and he was now loath to risk intimacy with Poppy. It was a tricky situation to be in.

The mulled wine was very warming. It put gaiety into the other three, but Tim grew more and more unresponsive. When the two women went off to the cloakroom, Mike tackled him. 'Is our hostess an old flame you'd rather not have encountered?'

'Good lord, no. I don't know her.'

Mike's eyes narrowed in calculation. 'She knew your name.'

Tim shrugged. 'She overheard Poppy say it.'

'Oh no, old chap. That won't wash. She's calling you *Bobby*. Why're you so keen to hide your identity, anyway? You're not married.' His face fell. 'My God, you haven't gone and tied yourself down because of the war – obligations to the bloodline, and so on?'

'Don't talk rot,' Tim snapped, tossing back the last of his wine. 'If I was set on siring an heir before I fell in the call of duty, wouldn't I be at home getting on with the job?'

'Since setting eyes on that woman you've gone all broody, so there's *something* filling you with guilt. You *do* know her, don't you?'

Tim got to his feet and kicked a log on to the fire with the toe of his boot before turning back to Mike. 'I'm not particularly keen on seeing this through. After supper I'd like to get Poppy home, then make myself scarce.'

His companion whistled through his teeth. 'She *is* an old flame, isn't she?'

'*No*!' Realizing he had shouted the word, Tim pushed his hands in his pockets and stared at the floor. 'When I bumped into you I'd just had a fearful row with the parents. I thought this kind of spree was what I needed. Now I've changed my mind. Poppy's not my type, anyway.'

Mike stood up, too. 'They're coming back. All right, we'll take separate cabs when we leave here. You can do whatever you like, but I'm not going to spend the last night of my leave in bed by myself. In fact, I might drop Eve off then double back here. She's very easy on the eye.'

Tim looked up sharply. 'She's married.'

Mike's knowing grin said it all as he murmured, 'You old fox.'

They were shown to the table by Moorkins' niece – what *was* her name? – and they all ordered from a menu which was limited but surprisingly sophisticated. Tim felt increasingly awkward as Poppy giggled and consulted with Eve over her choice, while their hostess stood waiting with pad and pencil. He wished he could sink through the floor when Poppy turned to him and asked, 'What's solly mooneer, Bobby?'

'A very light fish dish, madam,' said the woman standing beside

Tim, with perfect poise. 'If you would prefer something more filling for a night like this, I recommend the beef ragôut.'

Poppy leaned over to gaze up into Tim's eyes as if moonstruck. 'You choose for me.'

After clearing his throat Tim gazed steadfastly at the menu whilst ordering soup followed by Châteaubriand for himself, and lamb cutlet with petit pois for "the lady". Mike followed suit, adding a bottle of wine to the order before Poppy asked in very audible tones whether or not she would like *purtypwa*.

'They're peas,' Tim murmured when he felt able to speak.

She fell into giggles again, turning to nudge Eve with her elbow. 'They're *peas*. I'll tell Mum I'd like faggots and *purtypwa* pudden for my dinner tomorrow. See her face!'

They were served by demure waitresses who had been well trained. Mike commented on the all-female staff. 'I suppose all the men are at the Front. Bit of a responsibility for our charming lady, but she copes with it very well.'

Tim glanced up from his soup. 'Is it the female dominance which has made this place popular when on leave?'

'Partly – but the best is yet to come, I believe.'

'Ooh, what?' asked Eve, dabbing at her dress where she had splashed it with soup.

'Wait and see,' Mike replied with a wink. 'The night is still young.'

Although he did his best to appear lively, Tim was all the time conscious of another presence in that room. He was recollecting more of that incident at Dunstan station as he watched her; how she had teased him over her destination, what shapely ankles she possessed, her dignity. Parsons had revealed quite a bit about her during the drive to Knightshill, but he had spoken of a teashop rather than a restaurant. She had been at Esher station when their train passed through. Tim grew hot as he recalled how he had flirted with her to the extent of asking for her name and address. She had instead written him a good luck message reminding him of who she was when it was too late.

They had just been served with their main course, and Poppy had said to Eve why had they not put on the menu chops and veg instead of all that about *purtypwa*, when there was activity at the far end of the dining-room which heralded three women in black dresses, each carrying a musical instrument. All eyes were drawn to the dais, and conversation quietened as the women settled themselves on the chairs.

'*This* is the real attraction,' Mike whispered. 'Just wait.'

As she walked on to the dais Tim remembered her name. *Amy*. Amy Sturt. She smiled and looked around the room. 'Ladies and gentlemen. We are about to give our second performance of the evening but, sadly, our pianist is indisposed.' To Tim's mystification this was met by a roar of laughter and stamping feet, but she continued quite calmly. 'We shall therefore have to manage without her, unless . . .'

More laughter broke out as some kind of scuffle occurred at a table near one of the windows. Cheers rose from various other groups, and male diners gave rhythmic encouragement by banging their hands on the tables. A young sandy-haired subaltern was being pushed forward by his merciless friends, and Amy stepped down with a smile to take his hand.

When they were both on the dais, he looking rather pink cheeked, she held up her free hand for silence. 'I'm delighted to tell you that we have a volunteer. I think we should allow him a minute or two to get to know the ladies he will be accompanying (howls from all the men in the room) then the musical entertainment will begin. Please enjoy your evening.'

Mike was looking very pleased with himself. 'Told you,' he said. 'She does that every time, and some poor chap gets "volunteered" by his pals if he doesn't go of his own accord. I wish to God I could play the piano. I'd have been up there like a shot. I heard that one night several fellows in the know took along a chum with a good tenor voice and made sure he aired it. Another time one of the women diners played Chopin with such fire she had to give three encores.'

Tim had forgotten the girls with him as he watched Amy introducing the khaki-clad volunteer to her two violinists and a red-haired girl with a cello. 'What happens if no one takes up her challenge?'

'She plays the piano herself, I suppose. But the word has got around now and there's always someone.'

Tim expected sedate 'spa' entertainment, but he was wrong. After selecting a dozen pieces from a huge pile of sheet music the tiny orchestra produced favorite melodies, ballads and popular songs, the latter prompting diners to join in and sing. The pianist swiftly lost his shyness and put all he had into his performance. The whole atmosphere in that place came alive. Tim had not experienced anything like it anywhere, and out of the blue Laurence's words returned to make a great deal of sense. *We are all fighting this war. It is not essential to rush around with a rifle to do so.* Amy Sturt was doing it by trying to banish the horrors for a short while. For some unaccountable reason that fact increased Tim's yearning to experience them. In the midst of this hearty crowd of men on leave from the Front he felt a terrible fraud.

It was very soon midnight and the evening was over. The restaurant was about to close so there was a general mêlée of people seeking cloakrooms and coats. The moment Tim saw his opportunity he crossed the room to where Amy was instructing a waitress on the clearance of tables. She did not see his approach.

'Mrs Sturt, may I have a word with you?' he began.

She turned. There was no smile for him, and her eyes contained more than a hint of coolness. 'Did you enjoy your evening, Mr Ashleigh?'

'Yes . . . with some reservations.'

'Oh dear, we try to please. Perhaps you would tell me what was wrong.'

'I believe I was rather rude to you when we arrived. I apologize for failing to remember your name.' For once in his life he felt awkward with a woman. 'It was six months ago and . . . well, a lot has happened since then.

'Yes, it has.'

She made no attempt to go, so he said, 'I appreciated your good-luck message at the station that day. I'm afraid I didn't recognize you then until I read it.'

'I was aware of that.'

It was not easy to have a conversation in the middle of a crowd of people anxious to leave and find cabs for the journey home, but Tim stuck to his guns. 'You must have thought me very presumptuous.'

'No more than you were at Dunstan Station.' It was said lightly but there was a caustic note in her voice.

Uncertain how to continue after that Tim was afraid his

momentary silence might end the encounter, so he said, 'Parsons told me a great deal about you as we drove up to Knightshill.'

'Oh?' It was not very encouraging.

'He said you and your husband owned a *teashop*.'

'We extended the premises last year and engaged an experienced chef. The change has been very successful.'

'More than that, I'd say. You're doing something quite exceptional here.'

'Thank you.'

Once more aware that she had effectively ended the conversation, Tim pressed on with determination. 'What part does your husband play in the business?'

'He died four months ago.'

'I'm terribly sorry,' he lied.

'It was a business arrangement only, Mr Ashleigh.'

'I see.' He was ridiculously glad about that. 'You manage extremely well.'

'I've always been in charge of this side of it, even when my father was alive. I enjoy it.'

Passing couples knocked into Tim again and again. He stepped nearer to her, smiling. 'It's like a cattle stampede, isn't it?'

'I've never seen one, I'm afraid. They just want to get home. It's snowing hard outside. Shouldn't you be joining your friends? All the cabs will be taken if you wait too long.'

'They're Mike's friends, not mine,' he said swiftly.

Her silence made him feel more uncomfortable than any words, and it was made worse by Poppy shouting across at him, 'Bobby, come on! We'll never get home.'

'I have two more days of my leave left,' he said before Amy could turn away. 'I'd like to come again.'

After a significant glance across the room, she said, 'It's the run up to New Year's Eve. I'm afraid we're fully booked for the next week.'

Everyone had gone except for Mike and the girls waiting impatiently by the door. Tim knew he must leave, but felt amazingly reluctant to do so. He tried one last shot. 'Would you allow me to write to you when I return to France?'

She shook her head in gentle exasperation. 'I'm asked that so very often by men whose judgement is distorted by these abnormal times. I always say no. In your case, Mr Ashleigh, I'll pretend you didn't even ask.' She nodded towards the door. 'Your friends are waiting. Goodnight . . . and good luck.'

Two hours later Tim let himself into a silent house and trod heavily up the stairs to his room. Poppy had played up so much when he tried to take her back to her own house, he had had no alternative but to get out and instruct the cab driver to head for her address. He had walked back through the snow-covered streets unable to forget the atmosphere in that restaurant, and sensing even more strongly that he had had no place amongst men letting off steam before going into battle once more. Amy Sturt had not known that or she would have been even more disparaging to a man she saw as no more than a wealthy philanderer.

Val walked back to his hut after peeling what he estimated must have been six million potatoes because he had been at the task for four hours. A chill wind was blowing across the downs and the distant sea looked cold and grey beneath lowering skies. The continuous rumble of thunder was the sound of guns across the Channel. It began at dawn and continued until dusk. All those shells, so many lost lives, and all for the sake of a few hundred yards which were surrendered again a few days later. It was not war as he had experienced it nor as any other soldier had.

He paused for a while to gaze in the direction from which the ominous rumble came, shivering in that exposed site along England's east coast and remembering the warmth and blue skies of South Africa. The part he had played in the war against the Boers had been an active one. He thought of the splendid horses and the sight of his troop trotting across the veld as the sun went down behind the hills, lance pennants fluttering proudly. He thought of the patrols far into areas believed to be held by the enemy, and the vain chase across endless grassland after men who merged into the foothills and appeared to vanish in an instant. He thought of the spread of tents beneath the stars, with camp fires gilding the faces of men yarning around them, and of the sense of pride and camaraderie within that cavalry encampment.

A gust of cold wind brought that long-ago eager horseman back to the present. Three years of wandering in that land had done little to banish the pain of being drummed out of a regiment he had served with all his heart and energy. Twelve years in another wild, wild country assaulted by the sun had slowly dimmed recollections of that tempestuous period and enabled him to exist without all those things which had once been his life force. He was now having to face it all again. After fifteen years he was back in a military routine which held a man captive to rules and regulations, and to laws for which, if he contravened them, he could be shot or so cruelly punished he would rather have died. Val found it difficult to obey the rules; impossible to accept any form of camaraderie. Most of all he missed the horses. He had always found immense affinity with them. For fifteen years they had been his loyal companions. He trusted them where he no longer trusted men. To be a soldier without a horse was unthinkable. Yet here he was.

Lady Luck had had her way to the last. She had taken from him his last refuge, his final attempt to be at peace with himself. If he had drunk to excess with any but that one particular man on the fatal night, he would have boarded the freighter and now be running his own property with a calm spirit. The mortality rate in France suggested that he was unlikely ever to return to Goonawarra, so he had left it in his will to young Kate. She seemed very much a lone member of the family; a woman who might have the courage to go out there one day and understand why he had stayed so long. He should never have left . . . yet *something* had driven him home. Lady Luck had been spiteful to send him into the clutches of the West Wiltshire Regiment. Still, she could have been totally vindictive and chosen the 57th Lancers.

During basic training Val had kept still when the sergeant major asked for men with military experience to step forward. Four weeks later he had been offered a stripe to sew on his sleeve. He had given it back. An interview with a pink-cheeked subaltern had resulted in Private Ashleigh being put on a charge for telling the boy officer where he should put the lance stripe. He had faced his company commander, Captain Wharton, twice since then for insubordination – which was why he had been peeling potatoes this morning.

There was no way that Val could hide the fact that he understood rifles and was an excellent shot, or that he was no stranger to things military, but he had the right to remain a private if he so chose. Using his natural skills was one thing – he had no inclination to pretend to be a bumbling idiot – but he would only do what he had to. The army had once taken all he could give then flung it back in his face. They would not do it a second time because he would give as little as possible. When they eventually crossed the Channel he would fire at the enemy if they fired at him and go over the top when the rest went, but he would very definitely not be out in front. Let some other fools do that. Meanwhile he continued to drink heavily to drive away thoughts of Goonawarra.

The members of Val's platoon were a mixed bunch. Two were a year or so older than him, but most were eager youngsters seeking the great adventure. Val had sized them up very swiftly. There were three or four who would go to pieces when the first shell whistled overhead; an equal number would swiftly get themselves shot through their bravado. The rest were sound enough except for a former blacksmith with sadistic tendencies. He would kill for the sheer pleasure of killing, and that would be his downfall because he would forget others would be out to kill him. Val was the only man large enough to be safe from Reg Snaith, who had no stomach for an even fight. Several of the smaller or more timid members of C Platoon went in fear of him. Val did nothing about it, remaining aloof from his fellows. After the first week or so they had given up trying to find common ground with him. There was none.

The coldness of midday drove Val to seek the relative warmth of his quarters. It would be time for tucker soon. He had to clean up before going to the cookhouse. No one was going to slap him on a charge for being slovenly – only for telling them what to do with their flaming rules and regulations.

He walked in on a potential drama. It was dim inside the hut which had been hastily erected as part of a transit camp for troops on leaving training. The gloominess of the day did nothing to improve the basic drabness of iron beds covered in brown blankets and two rows of dark metal lockers, in a room full of men wearing khaki. Once Val's eyes grew accustomed to the light he saw something he had been expecting to happen before long. At the far end of the hut, Snaith had cornered a mild-tempered youth who had formerly worked with his fishmonger father in a small market town. Unsophisticated, with a girlish giggle, Peter Barnes was a born victim for men with a sadistic bent. He was wearing only his woollen underwear and looked scared to death as he cowered against the wall. Snaith was enjoying every moment of power while the rest stood clear of the pair, looking on.

'Unless you want to go for dinner dressed like that you'd best do as I tell you,' Snaith said. 'I'm getting impatient, boy.'

'I c . . . can't.'

'*Can't,*' roared Snaith. 'And why's that?'

'You . . . you know why.'

The strapping blacksmith moved a step nearer in threatening manner. 'Maybe you'd prefer to go to dinner as God made you. I've made you take the other off. Maybe you should step out of the rest before I march you over to the cookhouse and push you through the door in your miserable skin.'

'No!'

'Then all you have to do is obey me and you'll get your coat and trousers back.'

The lad made an effort at defiance. 'I've cleaned your buttons and polished your boots like you said. I've done what you asked.'

'Yes, boy, but not well enough to please me,' Snaith sneered. 'Now all you've got to do is eat the rest of the boot blacking and wash it down with the brass polish, then we can all go for our dinner.'

The young private recognized defeat and began to plead, which was what bullies always enjoyed. 'Please, Snaith, I'll be ill. Might even be poisoned. Don't make me. *Please.*'

Someone in the cluster of onlookers said half-heartedly, 'Oh, leave him alone. You've had your bit of fun.'

Snaith ignored the voice and stepped right up to the victim with the boot blacking in his hand. Wiping his fingers around the tin he proceeded to spread black polish over the terrified boy's face.

Val walked down the room remembering a giant named Deadman who had tormented young trooper Havelock by repeatedly forcing his face into a bucket of horse piss and holding it there until he practically drowned. That same victim now pushed his way through the uneasy watchers, saying, 'You heard what was said. Leave the little bastard alone.'

Snaith turned his head, gave a superior smile, then deliberately forced a lump of blacking into the boy's mouth. Val saw red. Three strides, a right hook and Snaith was staggering backwards on to the nearest bed. When he struggled up and rushed at

Val, he was sent to the floor by another hefty punch in the stomach.

'I said leave the little bastard alone,' he told the gasping man. 'Unless you still haven't got the message. It's up to you, mate.'

Once more Snaith launched himself, but he had not the broad experience of a man from the Outback and this time he crashed into the onlookers who obligingly parted to let him through. He landed at the feet of Sergeant Lee, who had arrived unnoticed. He made no attempt to intervene. In fact, it was as if he was not even aware of anything amiss as he demanded in stentorian tones, 'Why aren't you lot at the cookhouse? Get over there smartish.'

Val crossed to his own bed to tidy up, saying as he passed the NCO, 'Why don't you do your bloody job properly instead of leaving it to me?'

Sergeant Lee followed to say under his breath, 'I can't punch any of you lot, as you know very well. Why don't *you* accept promotion and save yourself the bother of doing it for me, you bloody fool?'

Three days passed before Val was told to report to Captain Wharton. The summons surprised him. Sergeant Lee might be a man who saw everything in black and white, but he was surely too sharp to report the incident with Snaith. Having once been a sergeant Val knew regimental bullies had to get their comeuppance one way or another, so making an issue of it when he did was negative. Val deeply regretted his own intervention. Experience had taught him that to humiliate a bully in front of his victim only worsened the situation. Snaith could not take revenge on Val without several others to help him, and that was unlikely, so he would step up his persecution of the helpless Barnes. Yet the lad could not have been left to do as Snaith demanded – to swallow a lethal mixture. Only marching orders would save the lad now. Meanwhile, what was behind the interview with Henry Wharton?

Three feet inside company office Val guessed the answer. Sitting in a chair beside Wharton's desk was a short, stocky major with greying hair and moustache whose eyes were so pale they were almost colourless. Oscar Martin had been a very senior lieutenant the last time Val had seen him at Knightshill. That had been in

1898 at the Khartoum Dinner Sir Gilliard had held every January 21st to honour the family 'hero'. That fact, if no other, induced defiance in Val as he saluted his company commander.

Wharton spoke briskly. 'Ashleigh, this is Major Martin from the regiment's first battalion who has joined us as our Operations Liaison Officer. We have together been reviewing company strength and potential when we go into action. Your name cropped up, and Major Martin felt he would like a few words with you.'

I bet he would, thought Val as he noticed the triumphant gleam in the man's eyes. *He'll wish he had left well alone.* He opened the skirmish to take advantage, saying in his broadest Australian accent, 'Welcome to the battalion, sir. Me mates and me are flamin' keen ter go into action. You here ter give us our orders?'

The man appeared nonplussed and frowned at the other officer before looking back at Val. 'Eventually, yes. Um, Captain Wharton informed me that you are Australian, Ashleigh.'

'And bloody proud of it, sir.'

'Yes, quite so. You're a long way from home.'

'Too right I am.'

The Major's right hand began to fiddle abstractedly with some papers on the desk. 'Are you aware that you have the same family name as several of this regiment's heroes?'

'Well, that's me up for certain glory when we finally get at the bastards,' Val said cheerily.

With eyes narrowing in speculation, the officer said, 'The most recent of them was posthumously awarded a DSO for his gallant bid to save the life of General Gordon and the fall of Khartoum. It so happens he had a younger brother called Valentine.'

Val broadened his grin. 'Christ, that's also the same as mine. Can't fail ter be a hero now, can I?'

'You are not in any way connected with the late Lieutenant Vorne Ashleigh?'

He did not tell an outright lie. 'Never heard that Gran came across one of 'em in the Outback when Granpa weren't around.'

Oscar Martin's annoyance was scarcely disguised as he snapped, 'You enlisted in London. What were you doing there?'

'Going from bar to bar.'

The man got to his feet, bristling. 'Look here, Ashleigh, don't play a fool's game with me. You gave your address as a place called Goonawarra in the Northern Territories, so why were you in London last September?'

The grin vanished from Val's face. 'What I did before I joined the army is my own affair . . . sir.'

As he was far shorter than Val the antagonist lost advantage by having to look up at his subordinate. 'You deny any connection with the Ashleighs of Knightshill?'

'I'm a cattle drover from Goonawarra, as I swore on enlistment. We don't lie where I come from.'

Henry Wharton decided to intervene at that point. 'Ashleigh, it has been patently obvious to Sergeant Lee, Lieutenant Duncan and myself that you are well versed in military tactics and have great leadership potential. We both know, to your cost, that I have several times persuaded you to use that potential for the good of this company, the battalion and, ultimately, your country in this time of war.' He held up a hand. 'Yes, I'm well aware of your views on the subject. Don't be fool enough to invite further punishment by airing them in your normal frank manner. I just want to say this without interruption from you. Major Martin and I will do our very best for the men under our command when we get our embarkation orders. To do that we need total support from our NCOs. We have been reviewing the available candidates for on-the-spot promotion, and your name is on the list.'

He came around the desk to stand beside Oscar Martin. 'You have been a soldier in your time, it's pointless for you to deny it. Therefore you will surely know that during any advance officers and NCOs tend to be the first casualties by dint of being out in front. It's then necessary to replace them before the troops run amok for want of direction. You have made it clear that you refuse to take on responsibility of any kind. We can't force you to accept rank, but can we count on you to step in should there be a situation where men are left without a leader in the heat of battle?'

'No, sir.'

Major Martin was furious. 'Now, look here . . .'

'Ashleigh,' said Wharton at the end of his patience. 'You're a man of thirty-five with considerable experience behind you. Most of our troops are boys still wet behind the ears. Don't you feel a sense of duty towards them, an obligation to give them the benefit of your skill and knowledge?'

'Why should I? What have they ever done for me?'

'They might do a great deal in the coming months. One may even save your life. War makes heroes of some unlikely candidates.'

'I know what war does,' Val told him, all his bitterness welling up to make him forget who he was supposed to be. 'It makes heroes only to grind them into the dust. It gives weaklings a gloss of glory, and it allows cowards to fool everyone into believing they died with honour. I want no part of it.'

'Then why did you enlist?' snapped Major Martin.

Val turned on him. 'Because I was so piss-drunk I didn't know what I was doing.'

Two days later Val was again peeling potatoes as a punishment for insubordination, but Oscar Martin convinced Captain Wharton that he had discovered the missing Ashleigh brother. He had last seen Valentine sixteen years ago as a senior schoolboy who was as keen as mustard for a military career. The man presently in C Platoon was hostile, rough mannered and devious, but nothing could disguise the Ashleigh physique and the vivid blue eyes for which many of them were renowned. The truth had been obvious the moment he had walked in. Vere Ashleigh had declined a transfer to the West Wilts and had instead covered the war against the Boers as an artist, but the family had been very evasive when asked about the youngest brother who had vanished from the scene soon after that dinner Oscar had attended.

As Henry Wharton had said, Private Ashleigh was no stranger to military life and was the right age to be the youngest of Sir Gilliard's three grandsons. He had very obviously gone to the dogs, which had accounted for the Ashleigh family evasion on the subject. Major Martin was privately full of glee about his discovery. The regiment boasted so many of their number, one tended to feel resentful and a shade inferior. Why else had the latest member of the family regiment felt compelled to change his name from Daulton? It was time the Ashleighs had a failure, a black sheep. He, Oscar Martin, was in the delightful situation of being able to remind that pseudo-Australian of that fact every time he put a foot wrong in the coming days. The knowledge that one of the proud Ashleighs was doing cookhouse fatigues was enough to bring a smile to the face of a man who was small in stature, with unremarkable features and eyes that had almost lost even the faint blueness they had contained during childhood. The smile faded as an inner voice told him every Ashleigh was a born fighter and, with the attitude Valentine presently held, he would emerge unscathed and undaunted at the end of the war. Rotters usually did. It was the heroes who died.

A week passed before, at the start of April, the battalion received embarkation orders. Later that same day Private Peter Barnes was admitted to hospital suffering from the severe effects of poisoning which was accepted as self-inflicted. Captain Wharton took no steps to draw up a charge of cowardice for attempting to avoid active service because Barnes was also in a state of total mental collapse which made him unfit for further military duty if he survived his suicide attempt. Private Snaith suddenly requested a transfer to another platoon, but Sergeant Lee had an unusual lapse of memory. He forgot to pass it to Second-Lieutenant Duncan, and awaited with grim satisfaction the destruction of a bully by the ostracization by members of C Platoon.

Only when they were packed beneath the decks of a troopship were the men of the West Wilts, along with the battalions of other regiments, told the astonishing news that they were going to Alexandria, not France. They all cheered. Sunshine, blue skies, native girls – what more could they want? They felt sorry for the poor, lice-ridden devils still living in trenches deafened by the constant boom of artillery. It was as well they did not then know that far worse lay ahead for themselves.

CHAPTER SEVEN

Early in 1915 the British Government realized the war was going to be protracted and bloody unless some kind of decisive action was taken. There was stalemate on the Western Front; the Russians were facing extensive losses in attacks by the Germans, Austrians and Turks all along their borders. Millions were dying in frenzied bombardments followed by suicidal bayonet charges that gained no appreciable advantage. It was imperative for the Allies to find some means of changing the emphasis of the war.

The notion of forcing the Dardenelles Straits, capturing the Gallipoli Peninsula, then driving through to Constantinople appeared not to have been submitted by any one person in particular, yet it circulated so widely it became impossible to ignore. Like many campaigns throughout history, men of wisdom, with battle experience and proven courage, gave their reasons why the plan was not feasible, then leaders went ahead with it. As they saw it, taking the Dardenelles and racing through to Constantinople would demoralize the Turks into ineffectiveness, if not total surrender, and the Germans would be forced to take men from France to reinforce their eastern border. That would not only make a breakthrough on the Western Front possible, it would ease pressure on the Russians. British morale would also be boosted by a spectacular victory at Gallipoli.

In theory the plan could not fail, but theory never took account of human frailty. Riding on a wave of enthusiasm government, military and naval leaders drew up details of surprise landings on the peninsula followed by a sweep through to the Black Sea port of Constantinople. Along the way various astute men pointed out that little was known about the terrain the troops were to cross, and the absence of Intelligence reports left them in ignorance of Turkish gun emplacements and the strength of their forces all along the Dardenelles. However, what had started out as a tentative suggestion had become a burning passion for a glorious victory to offset the misery in France, and the cautions were ignored. As if that were not folly enough, the military leaders appointed to command the operation were either too old for it, too inexperienced in modern warfare, or at loggerheads with each other to the point of downright enmity.

Last-minute awareness of the problems of servicing and supplying land forces by sea through narrow straits with no existing jetties at the assault beaches, and with no certain supply of fresh water nearby, made them consider a naval assault instead. Warships were sent in the reigning air of administrative panache, only to encounter unsuspected defences. The entrance to the Dardenelles was heavily mined, so the ships could not safely enter until these had been cleared. Unfortunately, minesweepers could not do the job until the warships had gone in and blasted the heavily armed forts along the heights. Total impasse! The best that could be done by way of a naval attack was heavy shelling of the barren coastline where Turkish guns had started a bombardment of the minesweepers, thus betraying their presence.

Failure was unacceptable, so a second attempt was launched. Trawlers acting as temporary minesweepers penetrated the mouth of the Straits ahead of larger ships, and valiantly began hooking up the mines beneath the devastating fire of guns at close range. During daytime they made perfect targets in the brilliant sunlight; by night they were pinpointed by Turkish searchlights. Progress was slow and dangerous. When one vessel blew up after hitting a mine, the damaged trawlers with their crews of shattered and wounded men were withdrawn.

Yet another attack was launched. A veritable fleet was sent in through the mouth of the Straits with orders to pound the enemy gun positions until they were completely inoperative. The mines were considered to be worth braving in order to remove all land defences. Once that was done the mines could be dealt with at leisure, in safety. It sounded so sensible to those who planned the operation but would not be participating in it. A disaster ensued. Three ships sank with their crews, three more were severely holed. Although considerable damage was done to the shore batteries, it was impossible to achieve the objective and the fleet withdrew in disorder.

The original concept of military landings remained the only solution, so preparations for these went ahead with deaf ears turned to anyone who predicted further disaster. Disregarding the fact that all hope of secrecy had been banished by the naval attacks, military leaders drew up last-minute details of their "surprise" assault on six separate beaches around the tip of the peninsula by British and Anzac forces. Soon after midnight on April 25th ships laden with troops dropped anchor and were immediately surrounded by smaller boats of every description which were to effect the landings.

Val stood in a state of mental confusion with the rest of C Platoon on the upper deck of the ship that had brought them from Alexandria. The West Wilts battalion was to land with some men from other regiments, climb the hills leading from the beach and capture the Turkish guns at the top. Once that was done they were to hold their positions and await further orders. Oscar Martin had briefed them last night, and Val had been worried from that moment on about the lack of information given. How many guns had they to capture? How high were the hills? Were they scrub covered or bare; easy to scale or precipitous? How far back from these guns were the forward Turkish troop formations? Were the guns merely entrenched or were they fortified? Could they be overrun with a bayonet charge or must they be blown up with grenades?

Sleep had been impossible with these problems bothering him. He was a cavalryman; a horse soldier. He had never done anything like this before. He understood mounted tactics and his weapon was the nine-foot lance. His experience of war had taken place in areas of hills and vast plains hundreds of miles from the sea. His kit and equipment had been carried on his horse, leaving him free to use his lance if taken by a surprise attack. He had shot men with his pistol, but had never run one through with a bayonet, face to face. He was an unhappy infantryman. Even so, his inborn military flair told him there was something dangerous about this entire operation. They had been told to carry out an assault in the face of the enemy without knowing the first thing about what they were up against. Either their Operations Liaison Officer was inefficient or he did not know, either. If *nobody* knew what lay ahead, it could turn into as big a disaster as the naval attacks they had heard about, and few of them would live to record it.

Looking about him Val found nothing to ease his fears. Captain Wharton had fought the Boxers at Peking, and so had Sergeant Lee, but the three subalterns were all boys commissioned from the officer corps of their public schools, with no battle experience, and the majority of the men were volunteers from all walks of life. There were some good ones amongst them, but this operation suggested to Val that it needed professionals seasoned in action to carry it off. They were more likely to cope successfully with the unexpected than lads who believed it would be a great adventure. Reg Snaith, standing several inches above most of those closely packed on the deck, looked almost demoniacal in the faint green glow from the navigation lights. He probably could not wait to get going.

Val shifted the pack on his back. It weighed eighty pounds or more, so the small men must be almost bowed down by it. How they would climb these unidentified hills, he dreaded to think. Oh, for a horse, and an open plain to gallop across in pursuit of the foe! At that moment Val knew all too well why he had sacrificed his name and his right to a commission in order to join the cavalry, rather than his family's regiment. He had no enthusiasm for this.

The word was suddenly passed from man to man, then they began to clamber awkwardly over the rails to make their way down rope ladders to the waiting boats. The early hours were suddenly full of curses and grunts as soldiers grappled with the difficulty of descending swaying lightweight ladders with a load on their shoulders which tended to tip them backwards. Val swung himself over and looked down. The sea was black and choppy, causing the boat to dance in lively fashion, so he was not surprised when he was halfway down to hear a splash followed by a cry of "man overboard". He would go down like a stone, poor devil, unless he managed to shrug off his pack.

'All right, *steady* lads,' came Sergeant Lee's voice from the boat. 'No one else is going in tonight. Just take a rung at a time.'

He's a good sergeant, Val thought, *although he doesn't know his men the way I knew mine. It can't make his job today any easier.* Once in the boat it seemed to Val an age before a sailor gave the order to cast off, and they began to draw away from the large vessel which had been their home for some days. He felt curiously vulnerable so close to the water and drifting away from the tall side of the troopship.

They were in one of four open boats on tow from a motor-driven pinnace which could take them close in to the shore. It was cold out there on the dark water, yet Val was sweating. They were packed in so tightly those who suffered from seasickness spewed up over their neighbours, and tempers flared. In the faint light Val could see Henry Wharton and young Duncan standing together talking quietly in the prow. He guessed the Captain was doing his best to steady the nerves of his fresh-faced subaltern during the pre-battle period. Oh, to be in the saddle and moving through the pre-dawn across open grassland ready to spur your horse to a gallop!

Progress was slow – far too slow. Everyone had fallen silent, except those who were vomiting from the boat's motion and from pure fright. Val was taut as he stared ahead waiting for his first sight of the hills they must climb. All he saw now was the faint outline of the pinnace towing them; all he heard was the put-put of its engine seeming much too loud for the occasion. Surely the Turks on those hills would hear their approach. All around them in the darkness was a flotilla carrying a veritable army primed to invade this mysterious peninsula and slaughter those whose land it was. *Surely* they would be heard . . . and before they saw what awaited them, surely the gunners on the hills would pick out shapes moving on the sea.

Val shivered. The breeze had come up. It was chilling the sweat on his body beneath the khaki uniform that proclaimed him an enemy of those men awaiting them. Then, suddenly, he saw a darker darkness ahead and his heartbeat quickened as the pinnace slowed its engines. That darker darkness rose higher above them – dauntingly high. He knew about hills sheltering hidden marksmen. Thousands of British lives had been lost *en route* to relieve Ladysmith and Kimberley during assaults on South African *kopjes*.

Everyone around him now noticed the looming shape ahead and a burst of conversation began. It was swiftly silenced by Captain Wharton and the other officers. Then a new sound became audible. Waves breaking on a shore. They must be very near the beach now. The sailors with them took up their oars and began to row as the small towing vessels released them and turned to head out to sea again. There was no going back for the troops bearing on their backs supplies and ammunition enough to do the job they had been given. They must go forward whatever the cost.

Dawn began as a glimmer on their right then very swiftly spread to throw pale, eerie light over the scene to show boats on each side of them, all heading for the shore where waves broke in an uneven white line. With his head tilted back, Val studied the hills, which he would more properly have described as cliffs. They rose sharply from a mere strip of beach as a barrier of barren rock sparsely scattered with low scrub. Any gunners on the top would have total control of both shore and heights. *They had been asked to do the impossible.*

Next instant Val jumped nervously as the morning came alive with the thunder of heavy guns from the warships standing out at sea. Shells began to land on the hills ahead as the boat drew to within twenty yards of the shore and the word was given to stand by for landing. All eyes were on the hills, so the hazard in the water itself was upon them before they knew it. The boat ran on to barbed wire stretched along the shore, halfway under water, and was held fast. Captain Wharton gave the order to disembark and those at the front began jumping into the sea to wade ashore. At that same moment a fusillade of enemy machine-gun fire began, and men fell wholesale.

Once the forward movement had begun it continued as an unstoppable human flow into the sea. To stay in the boat firmly held by the wire was certain death; to leave it gave one chance in a thousand. Gone was any sense of discipline. The drive to reach the shore was such that men fought to jump over the sides for the partial protection of the surf. For many it was no protection at all. The Turkish gunners raked the edge of the beach with a relentless hail of bullets until the water grew red with blood, and the wire entanglement was hung with bodies, some still, others squirming with agony as fresh wounds were inflicted on them. The situation was worsened by additional boats arriving to become stuck fast in the human dyke. Those not already dead aboard them flung themselves into the sea to join the desperate, threshing mass seeking safety at the very foot of the cliffs.

Val saw and heard everything as if he were no part of it, as he jumped overboard to meet the cold wash of the sea. His mind told him it was madness to go on; his limbs took him along on the heels of others. They were all going forward when they should be going away. They could not do what they had been told to do. Why were they commiting suicide to prove it?

As before in battle Val was taken over by some other person, some force greater than himself. He felt no fear as he held his rifle clear of the buffeting waves, and pushed forward against them seeing everything in great clarity. The water was jumping with the rain of bullets; men were jerking off-balance with the impact of metal penetrating flesh before vanishing beneath the surface. Others clung grimly to a comrade, pouring their blood over someone they barely knew. Dawn was a chorus of screams and moans; artillery thunder and machine-gun rattle. The foot of the cliffs was an eternity away.

Val reached the wire. Sergeant Lee hung on it with half his chest gone and blood running from his mouth. The dark eyes which had missed very little now saw nothing. Men were trying to climb over the entanglement in their frenzy to reach safety, and being held fast to become perfect targets for the gunners in the hills. A small section had been opened by those with wire-cutters but such was the desire for escape to the beach most were unaware of it. Val made for the spot, pushing against a wall of khaki floating through the water like flotsom brought in by the tide. He was vaguely aware of boats coming in with fresh waves of troops, but half had already been killed. A greater proportion of those left alive were wounded. Why had they come? They could do nothing save add to the blockade of bodies along the shoreline.

In the act of pushing through to where a dead boy hung with a pair of wire-cutters in his hand, Val saw Henry Wharton standing a few yards away at the edge of the beach urging and encouraging his men forward. Then he gave a cry and fell to lie at the tideline for a brief moment before struggling into a sitting position holding a hand to the crimson stain on his chest. Still he called encouragement. Val saw his mouth opening and shutting although his voice could no longer be heard in the general tumult.

During any advance officers and NCOs tend to be the first casualties by dint of being in front. This man had gone ahead and was still risking death by staying as an inspiration for others to follow.

Val pushed through the hole in the wire and reached him in several strides. Stooping to pull the officer over his shoulder he ran across the sand through a scattering of men to where pitifully few were sitting with their heads in their hands, unaware of anything other than their own miraculous survival. Shouting to attract their attention Val put Wharton down with hasty care, causing the wounded man to groan with pain. Their eyes met momentarily in the kind of recognition Val had known before in his life. Next minute he dropped his pack and rifle before starting back across the beach.

Time became arrested; visions changed. Sergeant Martin Havelock was making a headlong dash across an open yard dominated by Boer rifles. Val Ashleigh was making a bid to score a try for Chartfield School in a vital game. He ran fast, pounding the ground with his boots as he swerved and weaved to evade his opponents. No, he was evading *bullets*. He entered the sea still running, and plucked the wire-cutters from a soldier who had failed to escape through the gap he had made. Soon, he was attacking the wire with strength born of rage. Against whom he was unsure. They stood no chance. Who had sent them here?

As he cut the thick strands he heard himself swearing and shouting at the khaki figures spilling from boats ahead of him. He moved along, leaping through the water, and began to cut another break for them to pour through. There was no more than a trickle. Most fell, then staggered up to fall again. Val was faintly aware of the wind rushing past him in the form of bullets, and of his own voice, full of authority, directing and encouraging as he widened the break in the wire. On and on came the boats; still men surged forward to add to the slaughter. Some sailors in one of the boats were dragging aboard the wounded, then action was suspended as the hilltop gunners targeted them. The wounded slid down into the sea and vanished. Vessels manned by corpses drifted on the tide, hampering others. The sun put blinding light on the water. Val half turned from it to concentrate on what he was doing and so did not see the great prow until it was rearing up beside him.

The boat knocked him aside so that he fell beneath the water, losing his grip on the wire-cutters. Gasping, he came up for air to find the boat firmly stuck in the hole he had cut. He felt giddy and there was an acute pain in his shoulder where he had been struck. Pulling himself up by grasping a rope on the boat's side he saw a face full of agony. This boy must have lied about his age. He did not deserve this. The thunder of battle continued as Val pulled the lad on to his own back, strengthened by anger, and began to trot towards the alien cliffs out of range of the guns above.

Henry Wharton was unconscious when Val reached the spot where he had left his rifle and pack beside the wounded captain. As he did what he could for the dying boy, Val's anger grew almost uncontainable. Wharton had fought the Boxers and been decorated for bravery. He did not deserve this. Gazing out to sea with aching eyes where the slaughter continued as the doomed landings went ahead, he told himself *none* of these poor devils deserved this.

Midday. The sun beat down on the handful of men lying against the wall of the cliffs. Following orders, an assault on the enemy positions was under way, manned by any who had survived the landings unscathed. Of the force of two thousand no more than fifteen per cent had clambered laboriously up the steep hillside in three waves in a desperate attempt to silence the guns. The first wave had been killed to a man, including the three officers. The second wave had gallantly risen up and been instantly mown down, leaving a dozen badly wounded who had fallen backwards and tumbled headlong amongst the last wave waiting in appalled silence knowing their final moments had come. Crouching along a ridge dotted with low, spiky scrub they were now waiting while the two officers commanding their wave conferred with another wounded in the second failed assault. The subalterns, one of whom was C Platoon's Andrew Duncan, were loath to commit more lives to an impossible objective. The wounded captain was of the school of officers who blindly obeyed orders, and he had seniority over the others.

Val lay with his cheek against the hot scree, his heartbeat thudding as he willed the two young second-lieutenants to override their senior. If they had the talent to command they should exercise it now and prevent further useless loss of life. In their place he would refuse to send his men up to face those guns. In fact, he would have detailed two to carry the captain back to the beach, for treatment, long ago, leaving the way clear to make his own decisions. Failing that, he would have knocked the man out and ordered a retreat. His word would have been supported by every person clinging to that inhospitable cliff if questions were asked. They waited immobile beneath the roasting sun. By twisting his head Val could look down on the blue waters where the mass of wounded was now slowly being collected by an assortment of boats shuttling to and from the hospital ships standing well off shore. This operation came under fire regardless of the mercy duty they were performing. Equipment and supplies destined for the beach remained on board vessels wisely moored out of range. To come close to the beach was to invite a swift end to life. There, out of reach, were food, fresh water, ammunition and tents. No one dared bring it in; no one dared go out for it. If there was a hell, Gallipoli was it.

On the heels of that thought, Val believed he must be doomed there for eternity when a fresh naval bombardment began. Shells started exploding all around them as they fell short of the summit. It became a cruel blessing. As some of the waiting troops were blown apart, an order to descend to the beach under their own steam was passed along the ranks. The stoical captain had had same sense blasted into him, it seemed. Only later did they all discover that the man had been finished off by a shell splinter, and the two subalterns had acted quickly.

Four p.m. They had long since drunk the water from their bottles and were suffering badly from thirst as they sweltered in the full glare of the sun. Their supplies were still out at sea. One boat had started to come in and been sunk. No other crew had since tried. Way out to sea small boats full of troops could be seen heading for beaches on the other side of the peninsula. Word was passed that other assaults had been more successful and reinforcements were now going in. Even against the heavy fire in their sector, Val could hear the sounds of battle coming from the beaches cut off from his sight by the jutting promontary. If only they could make their way around it to join up with the others. This assault had been a total failure through no fault of those participating in it. He still burned with anger against the men who had planned this campaign. They had suffered from incompetent command in South Africa, but this was unforgiveable.

Val lay face down on the beach, his cap covering his head to prevent sunstroke. His shoulder now ached abominably from the blow dealt by the boat, and he longed to sleep. The surviving officers had posted lookouts so that the majority could rest, but Val did not want to be overtaken before he could defend himself. If the Turks came down from the heights to attack it would surely be at dusk. They had not stood a chance up there on that cliff. He wanted a fighting one when they met face to face, so he battled against sleep.

The beach now gave off a stench to add to the trials of that long, long day. The terrible heat burnt the flesh of the dead along the tideline and roasted the open wounds of the injured who had been dragged or had crawled to relative safety out of range of the Turkish gunners. Everyone was forced to use the sands as a latrine, and flies had been attracted in swarms to crawl over their human prey. Worst of all was thirst; the terrible craving for a drink, for water to ease blistered lips. Those who had survived so far were beginning to feel they were not the lucky ones at all. Some gave up and staggered to the sea for relief from torment. The remainder watched through reddened, aching eyes as they died almost willingly.

Darkness. The Turks had not come down to finish them off. There was relief from the sun and flies. No fresh water or food was available. No one seemed to know what had happened to it. The boats had come in laden with tents, which were not so essential now the sun had gone, and entrenching tools. Some distant fool had thought bicycles would be of immense use to the campaign, and several dozen of these were off loaded by the pale light of the moon to the bewitchment of those watching with dry throats and empty stomachs. Cooking pots, tripods and several cases of shrouds were soon lined up on the beach, followed by rifles and ammunition. The most welcome thing to come ashore that night was a group of medical orderlies with stretchers to take off the wounded.

Val felt totally unclean. He went down to the water's edge to immerse himself fully dressed. His tunic was stiff with the blood of others and it stank. It was wonderful to feel the cold salt water on his skin, but he had to fight the desire to drink. He pushed his face in it and let some run around in his mouth before spitting it out. He washed the sand from his hair and from the thick stubble around his chin. When he emerged, his uniform weighed so heavily on him he squatted on the beach for a while panting with effort. Gazing with utter weariness at the dark shadow of the cliffs he knew he would remember this day and night forever, then realized forever was liable to be very short. By the law of averages he would be killed tomorrow.

The most senior officer left alive was a captain from another regiment, who reluctantly took command of the remnants of the original force. He and a handful of subalterns began to organize burial parties on a rota system. No man had the will or energy to dig for long, and it was a thankless business hollowing out communal graves. Val did his stint, then found a spot where he could lie propped against the cliff to recover. He closed his eyes and tried not to think about a glass of cold ale. Men condemned to death were always granted their last wish, so why was there not a boat coming in with a supply of it for him – for them all?

Drifting into half slumber Val wondered why he had not been one of those who had invited death earlier in the day. Fifteen years ago he had longed for it as he roamed the *veld*. Since that time he could not say that his life had been worth much. If Ash, the drover, had been trampled by a stampede or he had been bitten by a snake miles away from help the world would have been no worse off. He had planned on spending the rest of his days at Goonawarra, so even if he had lived his full three score and ten years his passing would have made very little difference to mankind. Why, then, had he not precipitated the inevitable during the purgatory of late afternoon? Surely suicide would have been the ultimate thumb of the nose to all the Ashleighs had stood for over the generations?

Tomorrow they would be told to make another assault on the Turkish guns. They would all die in the attempt. It would make them some kind of heroes; men who had given their lives for King and Country. He would be a member of the West Wiltshire Regiment killed in action. A true Ashleigh! Dear God, Sir Gilliard would get his way, after all. For a moment or two Val burned with the old anger, then it subsided. No, not *quite* the old man's way. He would be doing it because he had made a conscious choice today to stay alive and face tomorrow. He had made that choice for himself, not through a blind passion to emulate a family 'hero'.

When a hand fell on his shoulder Val became instantly alert. Andrew Duncan was squatting beside him. Moonlight accentuated the signs of strain on his face; his eyes were wide and staring, darkened by shock. He stank of blood and sweat, as they all did. His voice was little more than a scratchy whisper.

'We've just received word to withdraw. There's no hope of establishing ourselves here so the boats that have offloaded stores will start embarking men as from now. Our chaps on the other side of this promontary have managed to dig in and seem to be on top of the situation. We are to join them before dawn breaks.' He held something out. 'Fix these on your arm whichever way you can. Captain Wharton saw what you did yesterday, and before they took him off a short while ago he told me to give you acting rank until we get back to full strength.'

Val gazed at the three stripes on a scrap of cloth torn from a tunic the owner would not wear again. Martin Havelock had worn such rank with pride. Then his pride had been broken and ground into the dust of the *veld*.

The nineteen-year-old subaltern struggled to his feet. 'I'm new at this game, so I'm going to need you over the next few weeks, Sergeant Ashleigh. Don't let me down.'

Val looked up at Duncan's dim figure against the night sky. He had been as young when he had been kicked out of Chartfield School and joined the 57th Lancers. He was now thirty-five. The chances of this boy officer living to that great age were negligible, poor bugger.

'No, I won't let you down,' he croaked. What else could he have said? This was no time or place to tell the lad what he should do with his offer of promotion, as he had before.

They were all away from the beach before dawn, heading around the high promontary to join their comrades who had been more successful. No one looked back to where boxes of rifles and ammunition remained with the cooking pots, entrenching tools, shrouds and bicycles. The Turks would surely be as mystified over the latter as they had been.

* * *

September. It seemed incredible that any man could have stayed alive on the Gallipoli Peninsula for five months without going out of his mind. Sergeant Valentine Ashleigh had certainly become more than a little eccentric. He had also aged beyond all recognition. What he had seen and done since arriving on that rocky finger of land had turned him into a hollow-eyed, gaunt, nervous man with lines of strain on a face that had lost all remnants of youth. He lived, like thousands of others, on a cliff above a beach which was shelled daily by the enemy. Aside from two excursions across the top in futile bids to drive the Turks from their strong position, Val had spent his days in a warren of trenches hewn from the rock. Gallipoli was unique in that it was impossible for troops to have rest periods away from the din and danger of battle. There was no place to go, no quiet areas well behind the lines. The sea was at their backs. Unless a man was killed, or so badly wounded he had to be evacuated, he stayed in the front lines night and day. After five months of it, Val had become a stranger even to himself.

They had not broken through to Constantinople. Everyone but those in high command knew they never would. In five months they had not once advanced from the landing beaches without returning to them within a short time. Military reasoning in such stalemate situations dictated withdrawal to regroup and rethink. It was impossible in Gallipoli, so they clung to their cliff positions. All that could really be said with pride was that they had not been driven off by the enemy . . . or by the appalling conditions prevailing on that peninsula. Perhaps, like Val, all the rest trapped in that hopeless campaign had grown so bloody-minded they were determined to endure anything fate, in the form of their generals, cared to throw at them. It would take more than a parcel of stupid old buffers to finish them off. Tragically, thousands *were* finished off by the ineptitude of their own leaders.

Val still held acting rank because his unit had never been made up to full strength. There were only four of the original members left, and two of them were due to be taken off suffering from recurring dysentery. It would eventually kill them. It usually did when men were unable to recover for long enough to build up a little strength. Andrew Duncan was now an Acting Captain, showing tremendous potential as a leader. An unusual relationship had sprung up between Val and the young officer. Having much the same social background played only a small part in it. Each recognized in the other an instinctive military flair, which enabled them to see a situation objectively and decide on action that kept others and themselves alive. They shared an unspoken friendship that overrode rank without in any way endangering Duncan's officer status.

Val sat in the trench on a sweltering afternoon in mid-September taking an official rest. The early inhabitants of the cliff had excavated sleeping shelves in the sides of the trenches so that it was possible to withdraw into these tiny alcoves and lie full length away from the constant pedestrian traffic passing back and forth every hour of the day and night. They were known as sepulchres by some – an apt description when the occupants were victims of bombs tossed across by the Turks no more than yards from the highest of the tiers of trenches.

Val was thankful for his own shelf that afternoon. A naval bombardment had begun an hour ago, which always signalled an attempt to breast the cliff-top by some unfortunates who would never see dusk fall again. It was out of the question to dull the noise, but a little shade was welcome. He sat leaning back against a rolled blanket stuffed with his clean shirt and underwear in the relative seclusion of that hole in the rock, feeling sorry for the poor devils waiting to show themselves as perfect targets above the top of the front trenches. He knew what it was like. He had done it twice. That he had survived the first time was little short of a miracle; to have lived a second time could only be due to the hand of fate. Past experience with that inexplicable force gave him little confidence that he had been spared for any beneficial purpose. Something really malevolent was surely in store for him.

He gazed at the passing bodies for a while, then closed his eyes hoping for some sleep. Whatever fate had in mind he prayed Andrew Duncan was not destined to share it. His mind drifted to fantasy. He was almost old enough to be the other's father. If he had had a son he would want him to have been like young Duncan. Vere's will named his firstborn son as successor to Kinghtshill. There would now be no sons to inherit so everything would go to Tim, unless the silly young prig threw himself on to the nearest bayonet in a bid to die a 'hero' like Vorne Ashleigh. They should have told him the truth about his uncle.

Only at that point did Val think he ought to let Vere know where he was, especially if Tim had been killed on the Western Front. He owed his brother that much. Who would inherit if Tim could not? Charlotte's elder son, presumably. Not one of the Nicolardi boys. Pity he, himself, had none of his own. Although he had never wished to be master of Knightshill he should, perhaps, have done what he could to continue the bloodline, for Vere's sake. Too late now.

The bombardment stopped, and the sudden silence jerked him from his half-slumber with pulse racing as he mentally counted to six. Right on cue came the sound of yelling as men went over the top and, almost immediately, machine-gun and rifle fire interspersed with screams. It lasted no longer than ten minutes before a brief moment of silence followed by a whistle-blast signalling the second wave of assault troops. Val closed his mind to what was happening further along the cliff. It was the only way to remain sane. It would be his turn again soon and there would be no way of closing his mind to the horror then.

He scrambled from his resting place as a thought struck him. Before long there would be a procession through these walkways of those wounded who had fortunately fallen back into the trench, or had just gone down on the brink of it and had been pulled to safety by a comrade. Once that began he would have little chance of getting down to the beach. Making his way along the rocky corridors he passed men who were all strangers. Some of them were under his command. They were never there long enough for him to get to know them. That had advantages. He felt nothing at their inevitable demise. How far away from that war in South Africa this was! Over there he had cared for those he had led. Gallipoli had reduced a man to caring only about how soon he could escape as a stetcher case. Amazingly, there were very few instances of malingering. Gallipoli also bred a grittiness of character that kept men going against all odds. How else would they still be here in this burning, stinking hell?

On the beach there was the usual activity. Because of the attack presently taking place the Turks were not shelling the sands, so the constant to-ing and fro-ing of small boats, the offloading of stores and the embarking of the sick and suffering bound for the hospital ships standing out of range were going ahead unhindered. It would not last. In the short, peaceful interlude men were taking advantage of the chance to swim without the accompaniment of a hail of bullets. The sea was full of naked men frolicking and laughing as if on a summer outing. Val quickly joined them. It was marvellous to feel fresh and reasonably cool for a while. Beneath the waves he pretended he was in the pool in Leyden's Spinney, or in the tank at Goonawarra. Yet, when he surfaced, he could appreciate the barren beauty of that place. In time of peace it would surely be awe-inspiring.

As he floated on his back looking up to where the bloody crest of cliffs met the indigo sky, he grew conscious of the voices around him, and was back with the pretence of swimming in the tank with the other drovers. These men were Australians. A curious pang of homesickness touched him. Apart from a couple of changes, he had lived with the same group at Goonawarra for twelve years. They had been his substitute family. He had not known such companionship since then. If Andrew Duncan should be lost there would be nobody here for him.

Suddenly depressed, Val returned to the shore and began pulling on his underwear. Was he fortunate to have survived this long? Would it have been better to climb from the trench and die a moment later on those two assaults he had made? The pain of living would now be over.

'Well, damn my bloody eyes, it's *Ash*!' cried a loud voice from nearby.

Val looked up quickly to see a tall rangy man with a tangle of hair and a gap-toothed smile, who was coming towards him stark naked except for a slouch hat worn on the back of his head.

'Bugger me, you've walked straight out of my thoughts, Jed,' Val said with disbelief. 'I was in the tank at Goonawarra for a while out there, then you turn up like flamin' wallaby's uncle!' He strode forward to shake the man's hand. 'What are you doing here, for Christ's sake?'

'Same as you, I guess. How long you bin' here?'

'Since the first landing.'

'Jesus, you musta got a charmed bloody life! Chip's here too . . . and Bramber. Remember Jake? He got lost on the way over. Bloody

Turks shelled the boats. We all ended in the drink. Some Poms picked us up 'n brought us here. Talk about round pegs in square bloody holes! Some poncey officer took us on strength, but we want ter get with our mates in Anzac. That's where we was headed.'

'You're a long way from there and you can forget it,' Val told him. 'The only way you'll get off this beach is as a casualty, and then only if you're flamin' lucky.'

It did not seem strange to stand in his underpants on a beach criss-crossed by toiling troops talking to a man wearing nothing but his hat. It was the longest conversation they had ever had. Here was a face Val knew, a man he had shared twelve years of his life with. Jed was a friend in a sea of strangers.

'You flamin' let us down, you bastard,' the "friend" then said. 'We was told you'd bought Goonawarra and was on ya way back.'

'I did. I was.' Regret washed over him anew. The past five months had banished it. He had been too busy trying to stay alive. 'What's happened to the place?'

'Much you bloody care!'

'I flamin' *bought* it!' he shouted. 'That old windbag Johnson had instructions to pay you, as usual, until I got back.'

'Yeah, well you bloody never came, did you?' Jed countered aggressively. 'We carried on a while, but you gotta have a boss. None of us wanted ter take it on and . . . well, it just didn't work no more. House no more'n a pile of burnt timbers, and no one in charge. We kinda lost interest. They was recruitin' in town, so five of us went and signed up.'

Val sighed. 'I got drunk the night before I was to sail. Ended up in the army.'

'You'd been in before so you must be all right. Me and the boys, we don't fit in here.' He frowned. 'S'pose you couldn't put in a word for us.'

Val ignored that. 'What about the others – Mick, Spanner, Jugs – the rest? Did they stay on?'

Jed shrugged. 'Last I heard Mrs Collins sold out to a bloke from Adelaide who had his own team. I guess the lads moved on.'

'*Sold out! I* bought it,' Val cried. 'The whole thing was damn near settled by my lawyer in London. I signed the purchase document.'

'Yeah, but this bloke was on the spot. And *you* didn't bloody go back, did you? Mrs Collins needed it settled.'

Val sank on to his haunches having been transported to a memory place over the last few minutes. Goonawarra was *not* his. He had left to Kate in his will a place he did not own. It hit him hard, for some reason. There would be the money of course . . . but not to have anything of substance to leave behind him! No son, no property – no possessions whatever. He would pass out of life as if he had never entered it. Only if he was exceptionally lucky would there even be a biscuit-box cross bearing his name somewhere up on these stark cliffs.

'Don't take it to heart, mate. T'aint the end of the world.'

Coming from his thoughts at the sound of Jed's rough sympathy, Val glanced up. Then he was forced to grin. 'I've had to face some sights on this bloody peninsula, but nothing so gruesome as your balls at close range. For Christ's sake get some clothes on.'

Reunion with Chip and Bramber was too ecstatic in proportion to the closeness of their former relationship, but Gallipoli induced warmer reactions to others than in normal circumstances. When friends were being lost all around them, men tended to reach out to anyone as a replacement. The four former drovers talked as much in that happy hour as they had in a month or more at Goonawarra. Val finally learned their last names, given to him in the hope that he could arrange their transfer to an Australian unit despite his certain belief that it was impossible.

Shells landing on the beach told them the assault was over and normal routine had resumed. They did not hurry away, all the same. That Johnny Turk was sure to get you one way or another, was every soldier's belief, and they had grown blasé towards the weapons of death. The Australians showed Val the trench they had been allocated and they parted with an arrangement to meet on the beach in the morning, when the four were on offloading duty. As Val had feared, the stony hand-dug gullies were practically blocked by a downward flow of wounded on stretchers and mules. Val pitied the pack animals who were the nearest thing to his beloved horses on this narrow isthmus. The men at least knew why the noise and horror was being created. The poor beasts did not.

He found a temporary perch on an overhang while the procession passed his boots, yet he did not actually see the sad evidence of the failed assault because he was deep in thought. He may have lost Goonawarra, but there was no reason why he could not buy a stud farm for thoroughbreds with all that money. That would be something to leave for posterity – except that he was going to die in Gallipoli. He had left it too late.

Val eventually made his way up to his own section of the trenches oblivious to the sights and smells he passed. He was too lost in thought to see men writing letters on scraps of paper, reading from magazines, slavering over postcards of nude women, cutting a comrade's hair, carving a toy from a piece of wooden crate, playing cards with cigarettes as stakes, or merely staring with blank eyes at the rock wall a few feet away. He heard nothing of the sounds of a mouth organ played with some skill, of the curses and oaths of everyday conversation, of the groans of suffering from those afraid to move from the many holes which served as latrines, of the monotonous, nervous whistling of men on the edge of mental collapse. He was impervious to the smell of frying bacon, of overripe fruit, discarded tea leaves baking in the sun, of cigarette smoke, of dried blood, sweat and vomit, and even the strong eternal stench of the outpourings of dysentery. After five months it was possible to put all that to the back of the mind and concentrate on just one thing. All Val could think about was the possibility of ever getting to England to make himself a man of some property.

The next two nights were noisy. The Turks always retaliated after an attack. They were not content with slaughtering almost every man who dared to make it. Those occupying the front-line trenches were being bombed. When it happened in daylight it was often possible to catch them and throw them back. It had to be done quickly or they went off in the catcher's hands. In darkness it was not so easy to see them coming. Val's section was due to occupy the forward lines as relief. When they went up at dawn they would first have to clear away the bodies. It was not the most heartening task at the start of an unwelcome duty.

At three a.m. Val walked along to check on his men and found three unfit for duty because of fever. It was impossible to prevent germs from spreading through the ranks, and everyone went down with it at irregular intervals. Another two were absent in the latrines in the throes of dysentery. They had been marked for evacuation on the next hospital ship, so their loss was inevitable. They would be under strength when they took over from the depleted companies now looking forward to getting down to the beach for a rest. Val moved on to the corner dugout occupied by Captain Duncan and two subalterns who had just joined them from England. They resembled overlarge chubby babies with their full faces, pink cheeks and well-nourished bodies.

Val shook the boots that were cracked, dirty and thin soled. They would belong to the man who had been here as long as he had. Andrew's head appeared a few feet above the boots as he bent forward.

'You all right?' asked Val, his usual greeting.

'Yes. You?'

'Better than Stokes, Maple and Johns. Fever! That makes five short.'

'Only five?' came the placid reply. 'Are they ready to go?'

'If they're not they'll feel the toe of my boot up their . . .'

'They'll be ready. Time for a cup of tea?'

Val smiled his thanks in the darkness and squatted at the entrance. 'Dawn comes later every week. Wonder what winter will be like.'

'With luck we won't be here to find out.'

'Oh?'

'Don't jump to conclusions from that remark. All I've heard are *rumours* about pulling out.'

'They'll never do that,' Val reasoned. 'The folks at home wouldn't stand for it. All their boys killed for nothing.'

The young officer grunted as he twisted round in the confined space. 'This damn stove is bunged up with dust again. Can't light the bally thing.'

'Give it to me. I'm more used to them than you are. I can even get one to light after a cattle stampede.'

While Val cleaned the wick his companion asked, 'Will you go back to droving at the end of all this?'

Without changing his normal tone, Val said, 'That's a decision I shan't have to make, shall I?'

'Oh, I don't know. You and I are survivors.' After a pause, 'I wouldn't be here now if it hadn't been for you. You've taught me an awful lot.'

'And most of it is flamin' useless in a place like this.' Val lit the tiny stove and placed on it a pan of water Andrew handed to him. 'Quiet, isn't it! You can almost hear the stars twinkling.'

Andrew considered that for a moment. 'You're a paradox, you know. Most of the time you're heedlessly profane, then you suddenly become poetic.'

'Poetic? Not me. In the Outback you lie on your bedroll gazing up at the sky and it's so quiet you *can* hear the stars. You should go there some day. You can find the same phenomenon in South Africa. It's caused by the utter silence of a vast open area, I suppose.'

Andrew offered two tin mugs containing yesterday's tea leaves. They were invariably used more than once. Then he said quietly, 'You fought in the South African war, didn't you?'

Taking the pan of water from the stove Val began to pour it in the mugs. 'Having a cup of tea with you doesn't oblige me to tell you my bloody life story.'

'No, it doesn't . . . but I bet my boots it's worth hearing.'

'You're wrong,' Val said roughly. 'It isn't worth a tinker's piss.'

CHAPTER EIGHT

Three weeks later, the whole force gathered at that beach was warned to prepare for a major assault on the Turkish defences. The object was to overrun the enemy's front-line trenches and capture the hill beyond which would give them dominance over any troops amassed on the other side. The news gave everyone a renewed sense of being regarded as human garbage. They had twice before tried to gain that hill and failed to advance beyond the Turkish forward positions. Only by sending thousands upon thousands in relentless waves could they hope to succeed. In any case, dominance over the land beyond it would not get them to Constantinople. There must be millions of men with machine guns, heavy artillery and an arsenal of weapons between that rise and the Turkish port. All *they* had was a few thousand weakened, demoralized men with rifles, bayonets and a supply of bombs manufactured from empty jam tins. Their heavy guns had never left the beach. They knew they were being ordered to make another pointless sacrifice, and they prepared to make it because they had little choice. The alternative was to sit in their burrows on the cliffs until they all died of fever, or went mad and jumped into the sea with weights around their necks.

The men of the West Wilts were to form part of the first wave due to go over the top just before dawn. There was this time to be no naval bombardment for an hour beforehand to drive the Turks from their trench gun emplacements. Any men willing to think about the attack decided it was probably just as well. More often than not the timing between cessation of the ships' guns and the order to go was so ill-judged the enemy had time to get back to their positions. The element of surprise might work better, and the Turks would not be expecting another assault five days after the last so might still be slumbering.

Val waited alongside Andrew for the signal to come through on the field telephone. The three officers and four NCOs had synchronized their watches over an hour ago. The pair of untried subalterns had taken a wing each with a corporal as back-up. Val would go forward with Andrew and the main body of their force. A third corporal would bring up the rear to sort out any stragglers. The NCOs had been blooded before. It was the boy officers Val worried about. They had been sent to the Aegean straight from school. When he thought of them standing, lonely and afraid, in a dark trench fifty yards away ready to jump out revolver in hand at the head of thirty troops, he could not help comparing them with the arrogant Tim who thought he was a hero in the making because he had changed his name to Ashleigh. A month or two here would do him a world of good.

Andrew jumped nervously when the telephone rang. After a tense conversation he replaced the receiver and said, 'We go in seven minutes, on the hour. Tell Mr Bates and Mr Galloway, if you will. I'm not trusting the timing to a word passed along the line.'

Val went immediately, pushing his way past men standing tense and ready, speaking with soft reassurance to them as he headed for the first subaltern. He agreed with Andrew, it was imperative that they all moved as one, and a message passed from soldier to soldier could be distorted. When he reached Freddy Bates, the poor fellow seemed unable to speak. He merely nodded as Val insisted that they compared watches once more. Then he gripped the boy's shoulder. 'First time's the worst. After that you think nothing of it. Captain Duncan and I've done more of these than we care to remember. Didn't do us any harm, did they? Good luck.'

He shouldered his way back past Andrew and on to the other subaltern. This one was voluble and raring to go to ease his nervous excitement. Val issued a warning. 'Wait until dead on the hour. The success of this assault is going to depend on surprise and split-second timing. There are no bloody prizes for simply reaching the hill. We must have all our men with us, and we'll only do that by making a concerted attack. Good luck!'

He arrived at Andrew's side with a minute to spare. The officer said, 'I thought you were going to be left behind.'

Val grinned in the darkness. 'Not me. Who'd look after you? Watch what you're doing out there.'

'You, too. See you on the crest of the hill.' He was studying the dial of his watch. 'Ten seconds. Five. *Now*!'

They clambered up into the pre-dawn and began to move forward at a slow, stealthy trot. Somewhere in the darkness were several hundred men ranked on each side of him, yet Val felt vulnerable on that open stretch of land. He had grown used to the confinement of holes in the ground. The quietness was broken only by the occasional sound of a stone rattling away from the tread of a man's boot and by his own laboured breathing. For twenty-five years he had kept himself superbly fit. Five months on Gallipoli had reduced him to a weakling. The next thirty minutes might put an end to him altogether.

He had been a keen rugby player and now judged distance by recollections of racing across the pitch. The enemy trenches were two hundred yards away. Val knew he could not be far from them now. His breathing was growing more laboured and the equipment on his back seemed heavier with every stride. His nerves were stretched in expectation of the deafening fusillade they would surely face at any moment, yet the quietness remained. He trotted on certain he would tumble headlong into the Turkish trench before he knew it, but he had forgotten the element of surprise. There, just over ten yards away, he saw lamps glowing as the Turks relaxed unaware of their danger.

Val took just one more stride before the morning stillness was broken by shouts of alarm followed by the stutter of machine guns. The lookouts had grown aware of the attack and leapt into action far too late. To the sound of firing was added that of panic accentuated by the aggressive roars of the attackers. Val was also yelling in bloodthirsty fashion as he jumped into the narrow dugout and began stabbing in every direction with his bayonet. The yellow lamplight added a demoniac pallor to the faces around him already showing terror at being so defenceless. The trench was filled with threshing bodies as the men of the West Wilts had no mercy on an enemy who had shown none to them.

As before in battle, time and sound were suspended while Val acted instinctively as a man with the blood of generations of warriors in his veins. He thrust his bayonet again and again, or struck out with the stock of his rifle at those who threatened him at close range. His boots trampled on flesh, yet he felt no repulsion. His face was showered with blood as it spurted in that confined space. There was no anger in him; no hesitation or remorse. He laid about him with detached skill until there was no one left to prevent him from climbing out and moving towards the hill.

When he was once more on the flat his legs moved of their own volition and at their own speed. One of his arms felt wet. It was now light enough for him to see others clambering free of that blood-filled ditch. Not hundreds, but enough. He turned to yell encouragement at the stragglers; waved his sound arm to urge them to catch up. His blurred vision showed him someone he thought was Andrew Duncan on a level with him about twenty yards to the left. He was now without his pith helmet, as were many of them. Dangerous in this terrain.

Val was running slower than before. There was a red mist over one eye that hampered his view of the rise roughly half a mile ahead, so he was unsure of the shortest line of approach. His breath was now worse than laboured, it was wheezing in his chest where pain was growing with every ten yards he covered. The sun was fast rising to dazzle him, hampering vision further. Yet he was aware of a host all around him, moving forward to that hill across the scrub-dotted plateau. It was good to know he was not alone.

They reached the foot of the rise. It looked steeper at close quarters. Val's trot that had slowed to a jerky walk now became an arduous plod up the stony slope, his boots skidding on scree occasionally to set him back a yard or two. Gasping for breath through a parched throat, and light-headed with exhaustion, he sank to his knees and began clawing his way over the final stretch leading to clear blue sky at the summit. He had made it. *They* had made it. The hill was finally theirs!

Val collapsed full-length as he reached the crest and peered over, panting hard. It took some while for what lay ahead in the distance to stop shimmering and dancing before his eyes, and another delay before his dulled brain accepted it. He was not on the crest at all. Across a gully rose a higher ridge that cut off all view of the terrain beyond – another two or three mile march, then an arduous ascent. The prospect was so daunting Val bowed his head against the rough stones while he faced reality.

A flurry beside him heralded Andrew, his face coated with dust which little disguised his despair. 'Dear God, why weren't we told about this?'

'Because no one bloody knew – same as they don't bloody know *anything*,' Val grunted. 'You all right?'

'Yes, you?'

'Some bugger got my arm, I think. Nothing serious.'

The young officer sighed. 'This is a stinker. I'm not sure whether to go on or wait until the next wave gets here. I'm pretty certain the Turks will have defences up there.'

Val raised himself on one elbow. 'Too bloody true they have! The best we can do is to report back before the whole flaming force gets annihilated.'

'We've orders to push on and capture and hold the high ground.'

Val studied the person he had grown close to in a fashion he had never before experienced. Andrew had gone from boy to man without enjoying slow transition. At this moment the fate of more than a hundred men was in his hands, and he was not shirking the responsibility. He simply needed to discuss it before making the decision his rank demanded.

'Right, go ahead and obey orders, mate,' Val said with rough sympathy. 'They'll have heavy guns up there whose range will cover the gully from end to end, as well as this hill. They'll also have machine-gun posts that'll dominate the upward slope. And over the other side there'll be several thousand reserve troops waiting for any hero who escapes all the rest.'

Andrew's dark eyes, dulled by five months of fever, fatigue and fear flashed momentarily. 'I know all that. I'm not an idiot.'

'You will be if you push straight on and sacrifice all these blokes who trust us. It's not fair on them.'

'War's never fair,' the other snapped. 'In any case, I can't make decisions of this magnitude. I'm not a general.'

'You're a soldier on the spot who's therefore better able to assess the situation than any bloody general sitting out there on one of those ships in perfect safety.'

Andrew looked desperately worried and uncertain. He was a good officer with a great deal of intelligence, as had so many of the junior commanders. They should not be impelled to instigate needless slaughter. Val decided there was only one thing to be done. Forcing himself to his feet he addressed the troops presently lying or sitting along the crest in attitudes of dejection.

'Right men, on your feet. Let's show those blokes who murdered your pals what we're made of.'

As he guessed, as soon as the whole company was standing in full view of the further rise it became apparent to the defenders of it that the British had advanced thus far. Within minutes shells were raining down along the entire crest and others were falling beyond it to the flat where the second assault wave was advancing. Val and the others threw themselves to the ground again, but their presence had been betrayed and the bombardment continued. The tactic had revealed the intensity of the defences showing the potential cost of trying to advance. Andrew's uncertainty vanished. Ordering a withdrawal to halfway down the rise where it was comparatively safe, he conferred with the leaders of the other detachments of the first wave. They reported their situation and their belief that the true crest of the hill could not be taken by men with bayonets alone. They asked for artillery to be moved forward to support any assault. They also suggested large reinforcements for an action certain to bring very heavy losses. They were told to hold their present positions at all cost, and mount an assault on the heights in late afternoon when the angle of the sun would blind the enemy to troops advancing from the east. No mention was made of artillery being moved up, or of reinforcements. They could not believe what they were being ordered to do.

They lay all day in the blazing sunshine, tormented by thirst and relentless heat, while the enemy above pounded the area with shells in irregular bursts which took chunks from the crest of the slope they had believed to be the hill proper, and peppered the flat area they had already crossed at dawn. The second wave had lost men while crossing from the trench filled with dead Turks and some of their own number. The third wave remained at the trench, out of the guns' range, because the slope was now jam-packed with men waiting for the late-afternoon order to advance.

Val, Andrew, the surviving subaltern, Peter Galloway, and the two unwounded corporals regularly took turns to crawl to the crest looking for any sign of a counterattack by the troops they all felt certain were massed beyond the far summit. It was an unlikely move. The Turks presently held all the aces. All they had to do was wait for the British to commit suicide by either rushing the hill or remaining in their present position long enough to die of thirst.

The sun was as dangerous as the shells. Val shared his helmet with Andrew. Others did the same with comrades who had lost theirs in the trench. Even so, a few became delirious. Lack of water plagued them all. Stretcher bearers took advantage of the lulls between shelling to collect the wounded and dying. The dead were left in the demand of priorities and soon attracted swarms of huge flies grown bloated on the corpses of Gallipoli. Val had a small gash in his upper arm, but his sleeve had become glued to his flesh by dried blood sealing the wound. The whole arm throbbed but he endured it along with everything else. He was going to die by the end of the day, anyway, and nothing would cause him to desert Andrew at this point. They had been together from the day of landing here. It was fitting that they should stay together to the end.

At 3.30 p.m. the ships at anchor began a return barrage, raising hopes initially, but the summit was beyond their range so the shells fell into the barren gully and some among the British troops. Frantic messages took an age to reach the naval gunners, so the hapless soldiers were fired on by both enemy and friend for almost thirty minutes. When silence fell once more everyone nervously studied the angle of the sun. It was already possible to see an occasional flash as its lowering rays caught on metal objects up on the heights they must attack. The order to advance would come soon.

Andrew began organizing his available men. Second-Lieutenant Bates and two corporals had been bayonetted in the trench, according to their comrades, so on-the-spot leaders had to be chosen. As their sergeant Val was given command of Freddy Bates' platoon, and three of the steadier men were named as replacement NCOs until further notice. Andrew then crawled amongst those in his overall command, rousing them from their soporific state and attempting to instill in them a confidence he privately did not feel. Even the simplest mind could tell the operation was impossible.

At 4.30 p.m. the orders came through. Andrew passed them on to Peter Galloway and Val. 'We are to move off at seventeen hundred in waves, as before. When we capture the heights we are to hold our positions at any cost until dawn, when a second attack will be launched from the neighbouring beach as reinforcements to replace our losses. The message ends with a promise of artillery and rations in the wake of the dawn attack, and a helpful piece of Intelligence informing us that a stream runs through the gully to provide fresh water.' He looked at them both with the eyes of a man who believes he is in the land of nightmares. 'We're being led by bally maniacs. How the hell do they think we can all stop for a drink as we storm the heights, much less keep running down to the gully for one and hold our positions at the same time? They're raving mad – all of them.'

'The stream will have dried up, anyway,' said Val, 'and if bloody Intelligence knows about the stream how come they hadn't noticed this hill has a false summit?'

'It's all been done from the air,' put in the boy subaltern. 'I spoke to one of the pilots in Alexandria. It's bally difficult to make accurate observations when one's being shot at, of course. A ribbon of water shows up easily, but variations in terrain don't.'

'They will when we start climbing them – and *we'll* be shot at while doing so,' put in Val sourly. 'You'll be able to tell your mate all about it when you see him next.'

'It's imperative that we keep abreast during this advance,' Andrew told them. 'I don't want any small groups of men left isolated. We're in the first wave, of course, as we were this morning. But there aren't as many of us now.'

'That's all right,' said Val, his own voice as hoarse as the others. 'When you attack guns it's better to be widely spread out. If you're in a bunch they get you all with one shot.'

Andrew sighed. 'I didn't tell you the final phrase of that order. *England has every faith and confidence in her splendid fighting men.*'

'You shoulda told us that before,' drawled Val. 'Now we know why we're here.'

'But you're Australian,' pointed out the pedantic Galloway, missing the sarcasm in Val's comment. 'I hope you won't take it personally.'

'Not so long as I get a flamin' turn at coming down to the gully for a drink while you lot hold off the Turks,' he said, feeling sorry for this earnest lad about to offer his life in return for that professed faith and confidence. He was still young and idealistic enough to believe in it – as Martin Havelock had been.

For a moment or two, anger and disillusionment burned within Val again. He would be posted as "killed in action". Another Ashleigh hero: an ideal he had vowed to crush beneath his heel. Of course, he could run in the opposite direction at seventeen hundred and be shot for cowardice. What sweet revenge on that old man who had ruined his life! They really would execute him this time. There was no humiliating ritual as an alternative here. A man was already reduced to the lowest order by Gallipoli. Nothing could take him lower. So it would be the firing squad without a doubt.

'Synchronize watches, Sergeant.' The voice broke into his reverie and he came from it to see the face of someone he would be proud to call his son . . . or his brother. Someone who needed him. Val did as he was asked and the three prepared to split up to brief the men they would lead in to the valley of death. Funny how he had once thrilled to the words of Tennyson's poem; imagined himself one of the doomed Brigade galloping against the Russian guns. What a romantic fool he had been; a young hero-worshipper dazzled by the tales of an old general trying to regain glory through an eager disciple. Val glanced about him now, saw the emaciated, exhausted, filthy creatures lying beneath the late sunshine, lips parched and dry, eyes lustreless; saw the barren land stretching ahead as inhospitable as any he had seen in his thirty-five years and he knew there was nothing romantic about entering the valley of death. Perhaps that handsome, arrogant nephew of his had already discovered that, or perhaps Tim had died with his dreams intact.

'Where are you?'

Val concentrated once more on the young man beside him. 'Sorry.'

'That's twice you've drifted to some other place,' accused Andrew. 'Something wrong?'

He shook his head. 'I was thinking about someone who may never discover his own true worth. I'm glad it's you I have beside me right now.'

'Thanks. The same goes for me.'

Their glances said what they would not put into words. 'Watch what you're doing out there, lad,' said Val.

'You, too.'

'See you on top of the hill.'

'See you on top of the hill.'

They parted.

By the appointed time it was apparent that the sun would provide a glaring barrier to the Turks dominant view over the gully. It would help those coming from that direction, but it was their only advantage. Every soldier knew that courage and foolhardiness were close companions in some situations, and this was one of them, yet men who had suffered deprivation all day somehow found the resolution to get to their feet and go forward when told to.

The ground was stony and uneven, undulating quite drastically so that what had appeared to be a level gully was really a series of them. At the bottom of one was a dried out waterway. So much for their fresh water supply, thought Val. He walked steadily, glancing frequently at Andrew to his right. Way beyond him he could see Peter Galloway plodding along, revolver in hand. Pointless to have the weapon at the ready yet, but maybe it gave him confidence.

They had advanced more than a mile and all was quiet. Val glanced behind him. The second and third waves were two thin brown lines outlined against the sun. Could they be seen from the heights against the glare? His mouth was so dry he could not even summon up saliva to dampen his swollen tongue. His arm was still throbbing and he felt dangerously light-headed. Suppose he forgot what he was doing there and wandered off. Would they shoot him for cowardice?

He must have walked at least two miles. The steep rise was now very close. It looked deserted; as barren as the rest of this Godforsaken peninsula. After another half mile it occurred to his sun-baked brain that they were at too acute an angle now for the heavy artillery. That left machine guns. Once *they* started firing, their positions would be known and they could be put out of action. He and the two officers in front with him reached the foot of the hill simultaneously. They exchanged glances and Andrew signalled that they should continue as they were, straight up to the summit.

It was an easy climb for a trained mountain walker. With ammunition and equipment on his back each man found it a formidable undertaking. Val was soon breathing painfully. His boots slipped on patches of scree, causing him to slip downwards every so often. The sun was directly on his back with enough heat still to add to his plight. Worst of all, movement had reopened the bayonet wound in his arm so that blood began trickling down to his wrist. He glanced up. The summit was stained copper-red by the sun's dying fury. It looked formidable from where he stood; gaunt and hostile, the scrub standing out from it in dark spiky clumps.

In that moment, silence ended in an explosion of lethal sound. The hillside began to move beneath it. Stones flew in every direction as bullets raked the ground without pause; bushes flew apart as hand-thrown bombs exploded like a hailstorm of death. The air was suddenly filled with unearthly screaming. Something thudded against Val's helmet. Something hot brushed his ear. The bushes just ahead of him flew up into the air and disintegrated. He was temporarily blinded as dust rose in a great cloud.

Thought was suspended as Val's instinct took over the moment his sight cleared. The bushes blown away by the bomb blast revealed a low rock just ahead. He snaked up the incline to reach it, suffering a hit on his right shoulder as he moved through a sweep of machine-gun fire. He was a big man and the cover was barely sufficient, but he crouched there, heart pounding, stunned by the suddenness and ferocity of what had happened. All the way down the hill men lay dead. Those who were wounded perished beneath the next hail of bullets.

The slaughter continued as the sun sank so low Val could no longer see the hillside because of its glare. Yet he heard the continuing destruction of men who need not have died. It went on until the sun sank below the cliffs from where they had set off that morning, leaving a satantic plum-coloured dusk and unnerving silence. He crouched in a daze of pain and anger, unable to move for a length of time he was incapable of recording. Then he heard the rattle of a stone, loud in the sudden stillness. Fear led him to seize his rifle and peer round the rock. They were coming to finish him off!

Ten yards away the hand of a soldier was moving aimlessly against the loose stones. Val spoke to him through his parched throat, trying to make contact. There was no response. Several minutes later the hand fell open and lay still. Val gazed with shocked senses at the carnage all around him, praying for some other sign of movement to banish his sense of utter isolation, of being the last person on earth. Through aching eyes he thought he detected evidence that it was not so, but he continued to sit behind the rock unable to make a decision, keeping his eyes on a hump that appeared to show signs of life.

There was no moon that night, but the stars were abnormally bright. They cast enough light to allow confident movement. Val slowly unwound himself from the tight ball he had been in and estimated his chances. If the gunners were still at their posts he would be shot. If they behaved true to type and left the wounded – even their own – to their fate, no one should notice movement on the slope. If he stayed where he was all night he would die at their hands in the morning. He moved. It was a painful business. His shoulder caused him agony. His legs hurt as he began to stretch them out. The ground moved up and down in dizzying heaves. He decided it would be wisest to crawl. Somewhere on this shattered hillside there *must* be someone else left alive to keep him company. Once, he had craved solitude. Now he needed the comfort of another survivor for whom fate had further plans; needed it as much as life itself.

After a few minutes of laboured crawling Val heard laughing and singing. The summit was some distance from where he was, but the sound of the enemy's celebrations carried on the still air. He glanced at his watch. Three hours before midnight. They would be carousing for a while yet. He continued his macabre search amid corpses scattered thickly on a forbidding hillside far from home and loved ones. They would have no graves. The Gallipoli Peninsula would be scattered with human bones long after the living had abandoned the struggle and departed. He searched for sounds or signs of movement which would tell him he was not alone. Now and again he would croak a plea for someone to speak, driven on by the suspicion that fate had planned for him a lone and vindictive death here.

Two hours before midnight, and Val had found four others to join the search. They were all in pain, exhausted, shocked and dehydrated, yet the will to live was strong enough in them to seek escape. By one hour before midnight the group numbered fifteen. One of them was Andrew Duncan. He had a head wound and had lost a lot of blood, which caused him to slip in and out of consciousness. He had collapsed on trying to stand. Four others would have to be carried when they all moved off.

Seated in a group further down the slope Val put to them the difficulties ahead. 'Dawn will break at four-thirty. We must leave now so that we're beyond their artillery range when it grows light. Some of us might not make it but those of us who can, must.' He glanced around at their filthy faces just visible in the starlight. 'Fifteen of us, that's all. Fifteen out of a hundred and fifty-nine. If we stay here they'll bayonet us in the morning. We can't let them do that. *I'm* bloody not going to let them do that. And someone's got to get back to stop those poor sods ordered to come up here at dawn. When they see what's left of us maybe the bloody truth will sink in.'

'You're crazy. We'll never do it,' said one faintly.

'You stay here then, mate.' He faced them all almost savagely. 'Anyone else fancy a bayonet in the guts for breakfast?'

'I can barely walk, much less carry anyone, Sarge,' said another.

'Anyone who *can* walk must take his turn in carrying,' he ruled. 'Wouldn't you expect your mates to carry *you* if the position was reversed? I'll take Captain Burton all the way, but I can't carry the flamin' lot. Anyone who wants to get out, do so now. It's your choice, but time's passing and we've got to get moving as soon as we've done what we can for the serious cases.'

Twenty minutes later, after they had padded and bound with their uniforms the really bad wounds, they set out to descend a steep hill covered with the bodies of men who had been told England had every faith and confidence in them. So she should. They had given all they could. Once at the bottom, they then had to cross three miles of difficult uneven plateau to reach the false summit where they had lain all day. It was Val's fervent hope that the former Turkish trench they had overrun would be manned by their own troops, with help at hand. He knew that what they were attempting was almost certainly beyond their present physical capacity, but nothing would make him sit through a night on this hill so that some uncouth Turkish infantryman could stab him to death in the morning. Besides, he had to get Andrew to safety. And he had to prevent another massacre at dawn. It had nothing to do with being an Ashleigh. Anyone in his place would do it.

At 4 a.m. the group of Australians who had been shipwrecked and brought in to join the British force from which they longed to get away were on watch in the trench captured the previous morning. They had spent an uncomfortable night in the company of Pommy infantrymen and Turkish corpses. They were depressed, bad tempered and hungry. They were always hungry . . . or thirsty. There was to be an attack from another beach further up the coast. They had heard the force consisted of Anzac troops and each was wondering how he could slip away and join them. It was an impossible dream.

Jed Watkins was nevertheless dreaming it as he yawned and scratched his side. 'Bloody lice!' he muttered to himself. Then he turned to his mate from Goonawarra who was leaning listlessly on his rifle resting on the sandbagged firing step. 'What d'ya reckon we got for breakfast, Chip?'

'Biscuit'n bully, same's always.'

'You flamin' idiot,' Jed said explosively, comprehension hitting him. 'Who the hell d'you think's comin' in *that* way?'

'It's the firing step, mate.'

'For the *Turks*. They was going to shoot at *us*, you cock-eyed bastard. Come over here. If they come, it'll be from *this* way.'

'They won't come. Who'd want to take this flamin', stinkin', rat hole of a beach?'

Jed grinned in the starlit pre-dawn. 'Don't you like it here, mate?'

Chip's typical Antipodean reply was never spoken, because figures suddenly materialized on the flat area ahead. His mouth dropped open as he stared at a small group of lurching, slow-moving men in khaki with bundles on their shoulders. He put out a hand to shake Jed's arm. 'D'you see what I see?'

'They're bloody Poms,' his friend breathed. 'Where are they from?'

'Hell, by the look of 'em. Come on, let's give 'em a hand.'

They scrambled from the trench and approached the group of blood-stained men whose faces betrayed horror and the strain of endurance beyond words. The one who appeared to be leading was a big fellow carrying an inert figure across his back, and there was something about his filthy, hollow-eyed face that looked vaguely familiar. He refused to let them take his burden, just continued to push one foot before the other, saying in a voice barely audible, 'Stop the attack. Fetch an officer.'

'Christ, it's Ash!' said Chip.

'Well, do as he flamin' says. *Fetch an officer*!' Jed cried. 'These are the only buggers left from yesterday's assault.'

Small groups came in all through that dawn. Men from regiments which had attacked alongside those of the West Wilts. The second assault was called off. Of the four thousand who had gone the day before, three hundred and twenty two survived, most of them being wounded before reaching the heights. Only a handful escaped with no more than flesh wounds. They all suffered from shock, exhaustion and exposure to killing heat without water. Every one of them would never forget that day in September.

Val lay on the beach thinking that the only difference between today and yesterday was that he had been given water to drink. He was still in the same filthy clothes that stank of sweat and blood, and he was still lying in the full blast of the sun. The sound of waves breaking nearby was a vague comfort. With all the other wounded and sick he was tagged and waiting for a boat to take him out to a hospital ship. On the tag a doctor had written that the patient had a bullet lodged in his right shoulder, a festering wound in his upper arm and his temperature was dangerously high. This did not make him a priority case.

His eyes were closed but sleep would not come. Grotesque visions marched through his brain, ghostly sounds echoed in his ears. Something important hung tantalizingly outside his conscious thoughts. It bothered him more than the pain and kept him awake. He wanted to sleep. How good it would be never to wake from it. As his fancy courted that notion, an inner voice told him not to be a fool. To die an unsung hero would please the old man. He had to survive and get back to Goonawarra.

Out of the blue he remembered what was so important, and knew he must do something before it was too late. Gritting his teeth he rolled so that he was propped on his sound arm. The beach stood on end then dropped flat again. Through aching eyes he saw light dancing on beautiful clear water where small boats were plying back and forth around the makeshift jetty. He would surely be down there somewhere. It took more than a few minutes to attain a crouching stance when all around him undulated in sickening fashion. He remembered how to walk – he had done it for hours and hours last night. All he must do was put forward first one foot then the other. He tried it. It worked. The water's edge seemed a long way off but that was where he must get to.

Voices said things at him as he moved on. He ignored them, and everyone was too busy with other things to repeat warnings. The bodies by the waterline were those of the dying and most seriously wounded. Val did not recognize Andrew at first, until something about the set of his shoulders and the way his boots were laced identified him. He appeared to be asleep, but when Val spoke his name Andrew's eyes opened – two dark mirrors of experience beneath a swathe of gauze.

Val asked the familiar question as he sank beside him. 'You all right?'

'Yes. You?'

'I'll go when there's a spare space. Probably in the morning.' He lay back in the narrow strip of sand between his friend and a man moaning with pain. His gaze took in the large white ship bearing a red cross standing off shore. 'So, we're finally leaving.'

''Bout time!'

'Yeah.' He looked at the sea so incredibly blue and clear, then up to the stony cliffs harsh in the afternoon glare. 'I forget what the rest of the world is like, don't you?'

After a short pause, Andrew said, 'I expect we'll soon remember when we get there.'

Val rolled his head round to face him. 'See you in England.'

'See you in England.' Andrew moved his hand in a weary gesture. 'I haven't thanked you.'

'You're here. That's enough,' said Val roughly.

'Yes, I'm here.' Another pause. 'Look, if we never meet up again I'd like you to know there's one thing you taught me that I'll never forget.'

'What's that?'

'Stars *can* be so bright you can hear them twinkling. I heard them last night while you were bringing me back.'

'Christ, what a bloody useless thing to teach you!'

'It kept me sane.'

'No one who's been here as long as us can be sane.'

They lay quietly for some while, then Andrew said, 'In my report I made a recommendation for you to be awarded a DCM, and for your name to be put forward for a commission.' He glanced at Val with a ghost of a smile. 'Don't tell me what to do with the medal, it'd be too painful.'

Val began to laugh and there was a touch of hysteria in the sound. Martin Havelock had been given a DCM and officer rank, then had them taken away as a mark of his dishonour. Fate was indeed playing a wickedly devious game with him.

The Turks began shelling the beach again five minutes later.

CHAPTER NINE

The London house did not look very different from outside, but the moment Kate stepped through the door she was deeply impressed. Vere had spared no expense in making his home over to a private hospital for convalescent officers. The wide hall contained a number of wheelchairs, and young women in very attractive outfits suitable for no more than the administration of bromides or gentle soothing of brows flitted back and forth on each of the four floors. Kate could see them as she gazed upwards through the stairwell. The smell of antiseptic was barely noticeable. It was smothered by the scent of flowers in massed arrangements wherever she looked. The doors leading from the hall bore boards stating, MATRON, RECEPTION and STAFF ONLY, and the recessed cloakroom was filled with khaki greatcoats and black cloaks edged with scarlet, but it was a very far cry from the massive grey stone military hospital she had just left. The men who came to Ashleigh Court must believe they had entered some kind of paradise.

The door marked STAFF ONLY opened and out came a tall golden-haired woman in a dress of pale lavender silk finished at the neck and cuffs with white organdie. On her elaborate piled curls was a tiny organdie cap. In her hand was a sheaf of papers. She caught sight of Kate standing near the door and came forward with a smile, looking devastatingly lovely in her version of a uniform.

'May I help you? Good gracious, *Kate*! We were not expecting you, were we?'

'No, Mother.' She went forward into the light. 'I guessed you'd all be here. There wasn't time to go way out to Knightshill.'

'Oh, my dear, those *dreadful* clothes! They're even dowdier than the uniform you wore before. Does the army *really* imagine you'll cheer up your patients dressed like that?'

Kate gave a faint smile. 'They go as far as to forbid us to "cheer up patients" in the way you suggest. *We're not women, we're nurses. Our job is to tend their wounds, not raise their temperatures*! I must say *you* look good enough to heal anyone at first sight of you. It's what they need, you know. A reminder that there are still beautiful things in the world.' She picked up her bag. 'I hope there's enough space for me to stay here for two nights.'

'Of course.' Margaret waved her hand containing papers in the direction of the stairs. 'You can have Lottie's room. She's returned to Knightshill. John's not at all well. We're all worried.'

Kate was disappointed that she would not see the aunt who was closer to her than her glamorous mother. 'Uncle John should slow down at his age. His heart's not too strong.'

Margaret shook her head. 'He'll die behind the plough. The estate has been his life. Poor Lottie.'

Reaching the foot of the stairs, Kate asked, 'Is Aunt Kitty here?'

'Yes. Between us we've made this venture highly successful. Her experience of running a hotel in South Africa has been invaluable with the administrative side of things, and my acquaintance with so many influential people has enabled me to raise additional funds so that our patients lack for nothing. Vere's presently in London organizing a charity concert in aid of the Red Cross.' She smiled. 'I think no one can say the Ashleighs are not doing all they can for the war effort.'

'Is Tim safe?' she asked, knowing she must work up to what she really wanted to say.

'*Quite* safe, dear. He's still working with Intelligence well behind the lines. I see no reason why things shouldn't stay that way.'

'It'll break his heart if he never goes into battle.'

'Better that than his mind or body being broken, like so many we see here.'

Kate held back the urge to say that her mother had seen *nothing* yet. She instead asked, 'How's Simon?'

Margaret began turning away. 'He's upstairs talking to Kitty. In London overnight to attend a meeting concerning the RFC, I believe. I *must* consult with Matron about these lists of donations.'

Kate watched her mother go, then tackled the stairs with an eagerness her limbs did not share. How fortunate that her substitute mother, father and brother should be here. They were the people she really needed to say goodbye to, and she could ask Simon for news of Val. The girls in pale lavender dresses, white aprons and floating veils gave her pitying looks as she reached each landing. They were, without exception, young and pretty. The patients' temperatures must be dangerously high the whole time!

Catching sight of herself in a long mirror she saw the comparison. A pale young woman with dark circles beneath her eyes, wearing a close-fitting grey bonnet, an ankle-length grey dress, thick black stockings, sensible shoes and a long, drab travelling cloak. Small wonder her friend Millicent said they resembled angels of death rather than angels of mercy. Kate made a face at her image in the mirror then continued up the stairs.

However dismal her appearance, Kitty and Simon were delighted to see her arrive in the doorway of a former service room, now acting as an office. Kate dropped her bag to hug her aunt. Then she impetuously flung her arms around Simon. 'Finding *you* here is a lovely bonus,' she told him, thinking he looked as pale and tired as she. 'The RFC must have taken pity on me and arranged the meeting to coincide with my leave.'

Kitty cirled them with each arm. 'No work for the next hour, children. We deserve some tea. Let's go to my room where Clarice can bring us some while we catch up on all the news. Do you realize I haven't set eyes on you, Kate, since your Christmas visit to Knightshill. Nine months! So much has happened in that time.' They began walking along the broad corridor lined with gold-coloured carpet. 'Lottie went to Knightshill two days ago. John collapsed. Trouble with one of his lungs, Dr Arkwright said. He does too much.'

'Mother told me Aunt Lottie wasn't here. I'm disappointed.'

Kitty glanced at her. 'You've seen Margaret?'

'She met me in the entrance hall. She looked so beautiful I'm sure the patients, whatever their age, must worship her from afar.'

'Yes. She's done wonders for fund raising,' she said in vague manner. 'Is she coming up for tea with you?'

They reached the door of one of the large bedrooms and entered. 'I don't think so. She spoke about a consultation with Matron.'

The subject was dropped as Kitty rang the bell and turned back to Kate. 'My dear, those dreadful clothes,' she exclaimed with a slight giggle. 'But are you happy – really happy? Did you make the right decision to transfer to the army?'

'Clothes are not important. What Kate does is far more worthy and responsible than the cosseting given by the girls here,' said Simon, making Kate aware that it was the first time he had spoken since her arrival. 'If *I* was sick or badly wounded I'd think Kate was the most wonderful person in the world, as I'm sure her patients do.'

'*I'm* sure they do, Simon,' agreed Kitty quietly. Then she asked Kate, 'How long will you be with us?'

'Two days.'

'Shame on them! You've had no leave in nine months.'

Kate shed her cloak then sat in one of the tapestry chairs. 'There have been odd days off – never long enough to make the journey home. Although I'm fully qualified, the army demands that each of its members goes through their intensive training before being allowed to serve abroad. I'm on embarkation leave.'

'*No!*'

The word burst from Simon, startling them both. Kate was astonished by his vehemence and by his increased pallor. 'I *applied* for a transfer overseas,' she explained. 'My reason for joining the army was so that I could be of the greatest use. The casualty rate is dreadfully high – and so many might be saved if they are given treatment in field hospitals at the Front. I'm needed *there*, Simon.'

'I'm surprised you haven't changed your name to Ashleigh, like Tim. That *is* what it's all about, isn't it? The drive to follow family tradition.'

Deeply shaken by this attitude – she had believed him to be the only person who would always understand – Kate was silenced by the entrance of a maid or, more correctly, one of the new kitchen staff also dressed in mauve, who brought tea and fingers of buttered toast. Kitty calmly dispensed this while chatting about the show Vere was organizing with Gilbert Dessinger.

'Gil is surely past seventy, although he will never admit to it, but he has thrown himself into this project with the energy of a man half his age. His finest *coup* has been to persuade some of the cast of *Tonight's the Night* to perform an excerpt from the show as a finale.' She smiled at Kate. 'The twins are presently in love with the leading man and are pestering Vere for an introduction.' She glanced at her son. 'Have some toast, Simon. If you're going to be drinking for an hour before luncheon, as gentlemen tend to do, it will be as well to eat something first.'

'Is it to be a very important meeting?' Kate asked politely – ridiculous formality towards her closest ally.

He darted a glance at her then looked away swiftly. 'Yes.'

'About the new aircraft you're designing; the one you mentioned to me at Christmas?' Again terribly polite.

'That's right.'

'Is it too secret to tell about?'

'Yes.' He ignored the toast, tipped back his teacup, then stood up. 'I'd better collect my notes and set out. It's difficult to get a cab unless you're wearing a uniform. Quicker to go on foot.' He walked to the door. 'I'll be back in time for dinner, Mother.' Pausing with his hand on the handle, he added quietly, 'It's good to see you, Kate.'

There was a short period without conversation after Simon left, during which Kate studied her aunt. In a blouse of cream cambric and a long amber-coloured skirt, with her hair in a chignon, she looked attractive in a more businesslike fashion than Margaret. Kate guessed this woman was the main reason for the success of Ashleigh Court's new role.

'Simon doesn't look well,' she said, as Kitty refilled her cup.

'No. The poor lad is working all hours on this new aircraft. The RFC is crying out for a true fighting machine because they have information that the Germans have one in prototype.' Kitty leaned back with a frown. 'I don't consider myself unintelligent, but it does seem to me to smack of lunacy to start sending young men into the *air* to fight each other. Isn't it enough that they're already doing it on land and sea? Has the world gone completely mad? I dare not say what I think to Simon, of course, yet I see other mothers' sons suffering here and know a sense of responsibility to speak out.'

'To whom?' Kate asked over the top of her cup. 'Not the RFC, surely?'

'Not to any *masculine* body,' Kitty retorted smartly. 'They're all too steeped in a sense of superiority to listen to me. I just wonder if I could influence their wives – some of the indomitable, influential women Margaret knows on fairly intimate terms. Surely they would see the utter madness of taking war into the sky. There's no territory to be gained up there; no national frontiers to extend. It's merely a place where men could kill each other for no better reason than that their politicians have declared them to be enemies. Kate, it's . . . it's . . .' She threw up her arms in annoyance. 'A fine orator I'd make. Can't even think of the perfect word of protest with just you as an audience.'

Kate was impressed. 'Aunt Kitty, you're a Suffragette in the making.'

'No, not that, my dear,' she responded with a hint of sadness. 'I'm just a woman from a country which was torn by war at the start of this century – a war which need never have been fought but for the want of understanding and common sense. Vere arrived at my inn in a fearful condition after Colenso. I used to watch the Red Cross trains go past laden with young men whose youth had been lost in a matter of moments, and thanked God my son was too young to fight. My heart goes out to the mothers and wives who come here as visitors . . . and I still thank God my son is safe. Yet he's helping to develop the means of taking death *above* the battlefields, so that other mothers' sons can die or be broken up there. The Suffragettes demand rights for women; *I* feel a strong compulsion to demand rights for our young men. They're suffering so deeply in this war. They *cannot* be sent into the air to suffer there as well. It's too inhuman.'

'I think you're a *splendid* orator,' Kate said, so moved by her aunt's sentiments she went to kneel beside her chair and take her hand. 'All you say is sane and sensible, but there's very little you could do even if you won over the women you feel have some influence where it matters. The patients at Ashleigh Court need only rest, plenty of untroubled sleep, and a few weeks' reminder of normal life. If you should ever see the cases I've been nursing it would break your heart. Yet, if you said to any one of them what you've just expressed with true compassion, they would not support you. I'm constantly amazed by their courage – *immense* courage – and their unshakeable belief in what they're expected to endure. You and I see things through women's eyes. Not one of the men I have cared for would condemn aerial warfare. They'd go up and take part in it themselves, given a chance.'

Kitty sighed. 'How foolish men are.'

'Not foolish; different. The past nine months have taught me so much about them – things I'd never have learnt if I'd stayed at Knightshill as Ashleigh women have always done. My patients come from all walks of life, and from every part of this country. Some are cheeky, others quiet and rather shy. There are some who keep the whole world laughing, and others who calm their fears at dusk by reading poetry or singing softly despite their own pain. There are even a few big, strong fellows who deliberately make a fuss when their dressings are being changed just so the boys beside them with more serious wounds won't feel ashamed when they cry silently over their agony. No, Aunt Kitty, men aren't foolish. They simply need to be understood.'

To Kate's consternation her aunt had to dab with her handkerchief at eyes filling with tears. Intuition overtook her. 'There's more to it than your need to speak out about the war, isn't there?'

Kitty put out her hand to stroke Kate's light-brown hair. 'You always were a perceptive child, my dear. As an orator *you* are most persuasive. I'm sure Simon was right to say your patients must think you the most wonderful person in the world. I see now that any effort on my part to speak out against building fighting aircraft would be more of a betrayal of them than championship.'

'Go on,' Kate urged, guessing there must be more prompting those tears than her own description of suffering.

A smile touched Kitty's mouth briefly. 'I see there's no deceiving you.'

'No more than I can deceive you. We're like mother and daughter, aren't we?'

'I'm so glad you feel that. Yes, you're right, dear. There *is* more to my protest about war in the air. Simon is doing vital work at Sopwith. He's a talented young man and his heart is in the design of aircraft. He sees them only as wonderful pieces of engineering, not weapons of destruction. The men he has gone to meet today want a killing machine, and the team Simon has joined will do their utmost to provide it. Yet they will be solely occupied with its creation as a challenge to meet. What others do with it when it's built won't be their concern, because they'll then be enjoying a tussle with the next challenge. At work, Simon is perfectly happy. When he leaves he's made very conscious that he's not wearing a uniform, and I know he's getting edgy about it. He wouldn't say anything to me if there had been upsetting incidents, but I suspect he's not immune. Girls are known to shout insults at young men in civilian suits – even throw stones at them – and he's right about finding it difficult to get a cab. The British public has many ways of making life hard for anyone they feel is not pulling his weight.' She dabbed at her eyes again. 'I've been so afraid he'll do something impetuous one of these days. I'm as foolish as any mother. Margaret persuaded Laurence to get Tim a safe posting as a translater, and *I* want to keep *my* son safe. What you've told me about the men who've become casualties has now made me ashamed of myself.'

Kate leaned forward to embrace her aunt. 'That wasn't my intention. Of course you worry about Simon, and Mother tries to protect Tim. It's what all mothers are doing. I was simply putting *their* side of it. If Tim ever suspects what she's done, he'll never forgive her. I understand why . . . and Simon will have to be allowed to do what he feels he must, no matter what the British public thinks of him.' She smiled. 'If you and a host of worthy ladies succeeded in banning the flying machine, you'd rob your son of the love of his life and drive him into a khaki uniform. Have you thought of *that*?'

'You're so sensible, dear . . . and very, very sweet. If you were *my* natural daughter I'd be so proud of you.'

'You have two to be proud of.' She sat back on her heels. 'How are the twins?'

'Maturing too fast. They have Vere's flair and determination. Holly is still set on becoming a musical comedy actress – quite out of the question, of course – and Victoria is fascinated with the idea of stage design. She flatters Gil Dessinger into taking her behind the scenes to meet men she believes will help her when she embarks on what she's convinced will be a brilliant career. People are enchanted by her – she's growing disturbingly pretty; they both are – but she's hoping for the impossible.'

Kate chuckled. 'That's why she wants it. She and Holly are typical Ashleighs, always seeking the highest pinnacle.'

'They're terrors whenever they come here. Vere has had to ban them from the wards. They'd persuaded several young subalterns that they were actresses in a revue, and were all set to go to supper with them on the day the boys were discharged as fit.'

'The war has changed everything,' said Kate with a slight frown. 'I suppose it'll never again be like it was. When I was fourteen I spent all my days at Knightshill with straight-laced Miss Purley. The only boy I knew well was Simon. The twins are living in exciting times, and patriotism is a romantic ideal at their age. I suppose I had my private heroes, but Lord Byron, Mr Darcy and the Duke of Wellington aren't needed when there are so many flesh-and-blood ones all around the girls. And *wounded* heroes are even more compelling.'

Kitty gave Kate a searching look. 'You haven't mentioned your greatest hero – the one whose photograph gave you back the power of speech.'

She could not laugh it off, because her aunt had given her the perfect opening. 'Have you any news of him?'

'Do sit back in your chair, dear, and have another cup of tea.'

Kate remained on the floor, suddenly afraid. 'It's bad?'

'It's not good, I'm afraid.'

'He's not . . .'

'No, we would surely have been informed. Several months ago Vere received a letter from a man called Oscar Martin – a major in the West Wilts who had occasionally visited Knightshill in Sir Gilliard's day. He's the merest acquaintance. Vere's not met up with him for years. In fact, he was hard put to remember the man at all. It was the oddest letter, written as if they were accustomed to correspond. Towards the end of a brief reference to his *many* pleasant evenings at Knightshill, Major Martin wrote that he had "bumped into" Vere's young brother who, he understood, had been in Australia for some length of time. He added, in what we considered was a spitefully smug tone, that Private Ashleigh was finding difficulty bowing to discipline but acquitted himself well enough in other respects.' Kitty frowned. 'Although Vere says he's a singularly oafish person it was unlikely that the man would write a pack of lies, so he made enquiries of a friend at the War Office.'

'Yes?'

'A Valentine Ashleigh definitely enlisted in a new battalion of the West Wiltshire Regiment raised at the outbreak of war, then travelled with it to Gallipoli and took part in the initial landings. What's left of the battalion is still there.' She put a hand on Kate's shoulder. 'We would have received notification if Val had come to harm, so we must assume that he's all right, dear.'

'*All right*!' she cried, scrambling to her feet in deepest agitation. 'I've heard the most terrible stories. How can *anyone* be all right in that place?'

'We have to believe he is on the evidence of Vere's enquiries. For some reason of his own Val abandoned his plan to live in Australia – Bentley told Vere the sale of the property over there had to be forfeited on a legal technicality – and joined the very regiment he had suffered so much in order to shun. He must have a personal quest to fulfil. He's an Ashleigh, Kate. The highest pinnacle, didn't you just now say?'

Kate was no longer listening. She had worked hard to be eligible to apply for foreign service, so that she might possibly be near him in France. She was going there next week, but the man she loved was instead living in hell on a spit of land in the Aegean.

When he returned from his meeting, Simon was in a more relaxed mood, although Kate still sensed an underlying tenseness in his manner. She was hardly able to make reasoned judgements on others when her own spirits were so heavy. Normally able to put on a brave face in front of her family, she found the effort almost beyond her at dinner that evening. A bout of weeping before they all gathered prior to the meal had left her looking paler than ever, and so weary she longed to go to bed and miss the meal altogether. When Vere greeted her with evident fondness, and concern over her imminent departure to France, she made a greater effort to hide her misery. After all, there was hardly a woman in England who was not beset by fear and anxiety for someone dear.

Vere lightened the atmosphere by giving an account of the progress of the charity show he was arranging and partially financing. 'Gil has asked me to work with him on a décor for the item closing the first half,' he told them. 'It's to be a concerted number featuring a flirtation between a Russian countess and two hopeful suitors, with a full corps de ballet. The setting is a frozen lake where she has arranged to meet them both for a skating party.' His charming smile showed he realized that they were all distinctly bemused. 'I know it's romantic and possibly slightly näive for a show designed to raise funds for an association engaged in tending our battle wounded, but Gil and I feel strongly that the audience needs a little light in the darkness of this year.'

'They do,' said Kate. 'Everyone does.'

'Where's *your* lightness?' asked Simon immediately. 'All you see every day is pain and blood. Now you've asked to go to France where there's even more of it.'

She had a ready answer. 'I'm a nurse. Those things are part of our everyday work, even in peacetime. You've never made that point before, Simon.'

'You've never looked so pale and exhausted before.'

'None of us looks rested,' declared Margaret, radiant as ever, 'but the very least we can do is to devote ourselves to helping in any way we can.' She glanced around at them all. 'I suggest we think about Vere's näive, romantic Russian scene and forget the details of Kate's work while we finish our meal. It's so important to keep life as normal as possible whenever we can, don't you think?'

'I'm sure Kate would like to hear more about the show,' put in Kitty. 'You have a new recipient for your enthusiasm, Vere. Unlike the rest of us, she hasn't yet heard a scene-by-scene description.'

Vere gave his wife a glance of rueful challenge. 'Have I really driven you to the edge of boredom on the subject?'

'No, darling.' Kitty smiled her love at him. 'As Margaret said, we all need to escape into an unreal world for a while. You and Gil are providing it for us.'

'I'm the person driving Mother and Aunt Margaret to the edge of boredom,' put in Simon. 'If I'm not talking endlessly about flying machines, I'm introducing unsuitable subjects at the dinner table.'

Kitty said immediately, 'Introduce a suitable one instead.'

Her son was silent for a moment or two, then said, 'I met a fellow this afternoon who's also keen on butterflies. He asked if I'd be interested in helping him with the compilation of a book on the subject.'

'Simon, how exciting!' exclaimed Kate, who had accompanied him on a number of youthful excursions to net the many species around Knightshill. 'Did you agree?'

A deep flush covered his pale face. 'I suggested he talk with me again after we've won the war . . . or contact some old duffer presently able to indulge in things like that.'

'What did he say?'

'His words aren't suitable for the dinner table.'

Into the subsequent lull Vere asked casually, 'Who was this man?'

'A pilot brought over from France for the meeting. You'd think he'd be more interested in the machine we're developing than butterflies, at a time like this.'

'I still play the piano between my duties here,' his mother said. 'Everything pleasant doesn't have to stop because of the war.'

'And I still enjoy doing an occasional watercolour,' Vere added. 'Pity you said no to the book. I might have attempted some of the illustrations for it.'

'You did beautiful miniatures of butterflies in the old days,' mused Margaret. 'Lottie has always maintained they were better than your war pictures.'

Vere shook his head gently. 'Lottie's a countrywoman through and through. She doesn't appreciate my later work because she has no affinity with the subject matter. Nevertheless, I think I'd enjoy tackling a few rural pictures for a change. Those I did in the Sudan and South Africa were successful because they illustrated what was happening halfway across the world. This war is on our doorstep. The images are too immediate. They can be seen wherever one looks. I've no desire to paint a nation's ordeal when reality speaks more forcefully.'

Back to the subject they seemed unable to avoid they all fell silent, until Kate asked how her step-brothers were liking their new term at school. Margaret loved talking about her clever sons, so the meal ended before she had run out of things to say. After they drank coffee, Margaret pressed her daughter to make the rounds of the wards with her. Kate would far rather have stayed in her comfortable chair, but got to her feet and prepared to please her parent in one of the few ways she could.

'I go every evening after dinner,' Margaret explained as they left the room. 'I sometimes feel too tired, but they look for me, you know, and would be disappointed if I failed them.'

'I'm sure they would. Life on a hospital ward is often very dreary, so the patients welcome those things that brighten their day. I'm certain you do that, Mother.'

Margaret was sweeping ahead in her elaborate evening gown of bronze chiffon, and said over her shoulder, 'I wish you had chosen something more attractive than that old blue silk you have owned for several years. They like to see pretty things to offset their pain.'

'I've only three dresses here. The rest are at Knightshill,' Kate said with commendable patience, as she trailed behind her mother. 'I need evening gowns so rarely it's pointless going to the expense of buying new ones.'

'You've adopted Simon's attitude, which is very narrow. We have to accept the demands war makes on us all, but we certainly don't have to abandon all else because of it. I should have thought your training as a nurse would have included the truth that without the beautiful things of life we would all sink into the morass of depravity.'

'Perhaps it should be included,' Kate concurred, 'but our main concern is to heal the outcome of depravity, not fend it off with culture. Uncle Vere's doing that. Unfortunately, there's little hope of it in the trenches.'

'Yet you have volunteered to go there. I seldom understand you, Kate.'

There was an obvious response to that, but Kate remained silent as they entered the first of the 'wards' containing three beds, each with a screen for privacy. Lucky patients, thought Kate, as the impact of flowers, floral curtains and counterpanes, elegant bedside lamps and restful gilt-framed landscapes on the walls took her full attention. When she glanced at the men sitting in armchairs by the window she saw only smiling faces and sound bodies clad in silk dressing gowns. Yet they had come from the battlefield as bloody and stressed as others, no doubt . . . and they knew they had to go back. There was no resentment in her as she compared this scene with ones she saw every day at her hospital. Let them bathe in the light before they returned to darkness.

It was very evident that Margaret contributed to their present peacefulness. Kate saw why as her mother chatted and laughed with gracious ease, making each feel he was more a welcome guest than a man being prepared to be thrown back to the wolves. Margaret Nicolardi was a woman of beauty, wit and immense charm. She sparkled in that room fast darkening with the onset of night, and the young officers responded to her brilliance. All at once Kate saw the reason for her mother's great love for Laurence.

He had released her from the captivity of being Mrs Daulton. What a terrible waste of her talents if she had not run away with Laurence and instead sailed to Africa with a violent zealot. She would have been murdered with him – they all would have been – and her true purpose in life would never have been realized.

As they said goodnight and moved on to the next room, Kate's thoughts remained on the subject of fateful decisions. They touched on her own to volunteer for overseas service, Simon's in turning down the chance to collaborate on a book of butterflies which once he would have jumped at, Margaret and Laurence's conspiracy to keep Tim safely behind the lines and, finally, Val's inexplicable move to abandon his return to Australia. Was she destined never to meet up with him again? Would Simon regret a wasted opportunity? Would her mother lose the son she adored if he discovered what she had done to prevent his opportunity for battle honours? Was Val now regretting an impulse to revert to all he had discarded with apparent finality twelve years ago? She pondered yet again Kitty's curious choice of words: *joined the very regiment he suffered so much in order to shun.* Would she ever learn what he had suffered, and why?

The Elders retired earlier than they did at Knightshill, because they rose earlier. Kate and Simon remained beside the small fire lit to counteract the late September chill. She was surprised when he poured himself a brandy and asked if she wanted a drink.

'No, I'm half asleep already,' she murmured, still wondering what Val had suffered. 'I'm surprised to see you indulge. You never used to.'

'I've changed,' he said tensely. 'Everything's changed. So, you've done the rounds of Ashleigh Court and seen the cute little ministering angels. Rather different from what you're used to, I imagine.'

'Very different,' she agreed, disturbed by his bitter tone. 'But any kind of nursing is of great value. Mental wounds need as much help as physical ones, and all the men here know they have to return to danger soon.'

'Why haven't you answered my letters lately,' he challenged, in a deliberate change of subject.

She frowned. 'I meant to. I enjoy receiving them.'

'Do you?'

'Of course.' Watching his restless fingers playing with the tassel on the arm of his chair, she wondered if something had been said by Kitty and Vere to upset him while she had been absent from the room. 'Simon, is the new aircraft posing problems? You're nothing like your usual self today.'

He looked across at her swiftly. 'Mother believes she is running an inn once more, Father is carried away by visions of Russian princesses on frozen ponds, and Aunt Margaret presides over this place like Lady Bountiful.'

She sat forward in her chair. 'That's more the kind of thing Tim says in an effort to be amusing . . . and she's a Russian *countess*.'

'You're not exactly your usual self, either,' he continued forcefully. 'When I'd heard you'd transferred to the army I guessed why, but you've gone too far now. It's really not necessary to face the guns in order to fulfil your desire to do something useful with your life. You could do it just as well in England as a civilian nurse, couldn't you?'

Kate was dismayed by his manner. 'Don't let's quarrel. We may not meet again for some time, and we've always been such close friends. *Always*.' She got up and walked to his chair. 'Something's upset you. Please tell me what it is. We've never kept secrets from each other before.'

'We've never spent so much time apart before.' He looked up at her and she was further dismayed by the unhappiness in his eyes. 'Since you became an army nurse our meetings here have stopped.'

'They've turned the house into a hospital,' she pointed out, 'and it's no longer a convenient halfway point.'

'You used to come to my digs sometimes on your days off.'

'I'm too far away for that now. Even coming here for two days is something of an expedition, but I had to see the family before I sailed.'

He stood up. 'If I hadn't come to London for the meeting today you'd have gone without seeing *me*, wouldn't you?'

Putting a hand on his arm she said gently, 'I'm not free to do as I please, Simon, and unless you tell me what's wrong I shall go to France feeling very unhappy. I shall also finally feel like a cuckoo in the nest.'

'You'll never be that now,' he said swiftly. 'You've conformed.

I'm the odd one out. I suppose I could change my name from Munroe to Ashleigh but, unlike Tim, I've no Ashleigh blood in my veins. I'm the only member of the family who's a complete outsider. On Mother's side I believe I have Brinley blood, which is pure enough, but my father was a diamond prospector with few scruples who abandoned us in the heart of the *veld* by taking the horses and riding away during the night. My ancestors weren't noble officers who offered their lives for sovereign and country. We don't know the Munroe family history, but if my father was an example of the line it's probably better not to know.'

Greatly concerned, Kate said, 'You've always been aware of all that. Why are you upset about it now?'

He let out his breath in a heavy sigh. 'Everyone's doing something very obviously patriotic. Tim's upholding regimental tradition, even if it's not in as bloody a manner as he'd like. Val's being heroic at Gallipoli – I'm sure you've already discovered that – and you've seen what's happening here. Now you're off to France in uniform. The Ashleighs are doing what they always have done. No one sends *them* white feathers.'

As the import of his words dawned on Kate she gave an involuntary cry. 'Oh Simon, no!'

The pain of it was evident in his expression. 'I think I know who's responsible, and she's an empty-headed little thing, but she's only done what others would like to do. I've stopped going out unless it's to go to work. You'd never believe how insulting quite respectable women can be. I even had a basin of vegetable peelings emptied over my head from an upstairs window, one morning. Men can be as bad. Fathers with sons who've given their lives or limbs have to vent their rage on someone, and I'm fair game. I left Jessie at Knightshill in June. I was afraid someone would damage her. That would upset me very much. I don't care what they do to me, personally.'

'You do!' she contradicted fiercely. 'It's made you angry, irritable and ridiculously guilty. What you're doing is *vital* to our success in this war.'

'But it's perfectly *safe*,' he pointed out bleakly. 'I'm not risking anything to do it.' He kicked at a log falling from the fire and gazed at the heart of it for a moment or two. 'That fellow who asked me about the book on butterflies – several years younger than me – had crashed six times, walked away from three wrecked machines and ended in hospital on the other occasions. He had an air about him, a bravado rather like Tim's, and I found him immensely likeable. Curiously, it was his enthusiasm for what I was doing, his admiration for men who could *design* a machine that would allow him to take it into the air that bothered me the most. This afternoon I'd have given anything to change identities with him.'

'That would be a tremendous waste of the talent God gave you,' Kate said softly. 'If there weren't men like you there wouldn't be men like him. How far do you imagine the Ashleigh ancestors would have got if gifted civilians hadn't designed swords, guns and bigger, more lethal, missiles to hurl at the enemy? A horse and a fancy uniform isn't all it takes to be an obvious hero.' When he glanced back at her Kate could not resist adding, 'I overheard something Val said to Tim when they were both unaware that I was outside the window last summer. He told Tim to forget about his ancestors and be his own man. Perhaps you should heed that advice.'

Simon gave her a strangely intense look before saying, 'Val hasn't forgotten them, has he? Why else would he have thrown up his plans to spend the rest of his days in Australia, and joined the family regiment? You Ashleighs will always follow your heroic pattern.' He appeared unsure how to follow those words, then changed direction completely. 'I have to be up early to catch the milk train, so I won't see you before I leave. Take care of yourself over there.'

Before she was aware of his intention he pulled her against him and kissed her on the mouth with great passion before releasing her just as suddenly. 'I love you, Kate. I thought you should know that, and I shall worry about you every minute of every day you're over there.' At the door he turned to add, 'I just hope he appreciates what you're doing for his sake . . . if he ever finds out.'

She watched him go, held motionless with shock. The one person she loved and trusted implicitly had just alienated himself. They could no longer be friends, and he was badly in need of one right now.

Two days at Ashleigh Court left Kate drained, instead of refreshing her ready for even more demanding work. She arrived back at the hospital heavy-hearted and still shaken by Simon's declaration of love. It had spoiled everything. He had been her one true ally and confidant in the midst of aunts more like mothers, a parent who was a sophisticated stranger, an uncle who deputized as a father, a brother she barely knew and a welter of half and step-relatives. She now faced the facts of her substitute brother really being a suppressed suitor, and her own unrequited love for an uncle who was not presently in France, as she had thought. Far from being a cuckoo in the nest, she was unsure which nest she should rightly be in . . . and she no longer wanted to go on foreign service.

Millicent Hapgood, who shared Kate's room, was already back from leave and sorting out her spare items of uniform. Small and dark, with a ready sense of humour, Milly had become a firm friend during their nine months' intensive training following their transfer from civilian hospitals.

'You're in the wrong room, ducky,' Milly greeted, taking in the appearance of her friend. 'Patients should be occupying a ward.' In response to Kate's wan smile, she asked, 'Did you find it hard saying goodbye to your large, complicated family?'

Kate flopped on her bed, close to tears. 'I wish they were more conventional at times like these. They're all so terribly talented. Uncle Vere's a renowned artist turned impressario; Aunt Kitty is administrator of a convalescent home and budding peace campaigner. Mother combines being a distinguished diplomat's wife with fund raising and charming dispirited young officers into confident good health, and Laurence is making vital decisions on foreign policy. Tim is translating everything under the sun into as many languages as he can think of, Simon is creating an aeroplane to outsmart the one the Germans have built, the twins are impossibly captivating and destined to dazzle on West End stages in no time at all, and my Nicolardi half-brothers have such brilliant brains I don't know how the world will manage to cope with them once they leave school.'

Milly sat on the side of the bed looking down at Kate with understanding. 'You haven't mentioned Big Bad Uncle Valentine. It *is* his photograph you keep hidden in your drawer, isn't it?'

Kate would normally have fired up but she was too weary. 'If it's hidden how do you know it's there?' she murmured.

'That time you had influenza, I had to get clean nightgowns

for you. One look told me he's a born heartbreaker. Has he broken yours?'

It was a relief to speak about it to someone who was not a relation. 'Not knowingly. He's not the kind of person to do that.'

'Yet you told me he's the black sheep.'

She shook her head on the pillow. 'You deduced that. I only said there was a mystery connected with his decision to live in Australia for so long. Val wouldn't do anything wicked.'

'Pity,' Milly said lightly. 'That picture suggests he'd be a great deal of fun if he did.'

Her friend's nonsense brought a faint smile. 'He was barely twenty-one when that was taken. He's now thirty-six.'

'Mmm. Time he lived up to his erroneous reputation, in that case. Where's he now – did you find out?'

'Gallipoli.'

All Milly's lightness fled. 'Oh Lord, poor lamb!'

'See what I mean about the family?' she said. 'If he hadn't been an Ashleigh he'd have gone back to Australia and been quite safe.' Before she could stop them she was shedding the tears she had held back throughout her farewells and long train journey.

Milly offered a handkerchief smelling of violets and let Kate cry for a moment or two. Then she said, 'If they've received no notification it means he's alive, and if he can stay alive in a place like that *nothing's* going to finish him off. Now, blow your nose and sit up because I have several important things to tell you. I'll make a cup of tea while you're coming back to earth after two days with the fascinating Ashleighs.' As she left to make for the tiny kitchen shared by the nurses, Milly said, 'I suppose it didn't occur to any of them that *you* are quite as talented as the rest. Dressing wounds, giving injections and assisting with operations is too depressing to be flaunted publicly, but it takes courage and enormous hard work to get where you are, ducky. Don't ever forget that.'

During Milly's absence Kate took from her bag the photograph which had travelled with her. It always did. The young Lancer officer did look very much an Ashleigh. Handsome, smiling, proud – an almost exact copy of Tim. Kate knew her brother was an inveterate flirt. He even played up to the twins. Did he break hearts? Did Val? Had there been any women in *his* life? Was someone waiting in vain for him to return to that place Goonawarra? As she studied the face of someone she had known so well up to the time that picture had been taken, Kate knew that person no longer existed. All she knew of Val now was what she had seen of him during that weekend at Knightshill over a year ago. She was hopelessly in love with a stranger.

When Milly returned, the photograph was back in the drawer and Kate had taken off her coat and bonnet. Her friend set down on the locker two thick china cups and saucers filled with strong tea. 'Drink up while I tell you the news.'

Kate sipped the tea gratefully. 'They haven't changed our orders, have they? I couldn't face it now I've told everyone I'm going.'

'We're still off tomorrow afternoon, but you've time enough to write and tell whichever one of them is most important to you that you are now a *Staff* Nurse. The appointments came through while we were on leave. We're both on the list.'

Kate was thrilled. The promotion put them both up to the equivalent of officer status and one step away from becoming a sister. 'How exciting! We should be celebrating with something more bubbly than tea,' she declared, feeling warmth flooding back through her chilled senses.

'*Nurses will never be seen drinking alchohol,*' ruled Milly, quoting the severe regulations governing their lives.

'I'm so glad we've both got it. It would have been horrid if one hadn't.'

'I should have lorded it over you unmercifully,' Milly said with a broad smile. 'You'd have hated me.'

'And I'd have given *you* the bedpans and vomit dishes to clean.'

'I wager your mama and aunts have never done *that* in their hospital.'

Kate's smile began to fade. 'They would if they had to. That's what makes them so . . . so . . .'

'So much like you. You keep forgetting you are one of them. Staff Nurse Daulton! Sounds grand enough, doesn't it?'

Kate leaned across and embraced her friend. 'It sounds wonderful! Congratulations, Milly. We both deserve it, don't you think?'

'After the hours and hours of studying? I should say we do.' She broke free and took Kate's hands. 'I did something impetuous on leave. Now I'm back I find it difficult to believe I agreed to it.' She frowned and bit her lip. 'I became engaged to Pip. I'm wearing his ring on a ribbon around my neck.'

Kate was astounded. 'What about your work? They won't let you stay if you get married.'

She played nervously with Kate's fingers. 'I'm only engaged. Don't tell anyone.'

'You said he was just a friend.'

'He was until we met again last Sunday. He smiled at me as I walked into church and it struck me how much I'd missed him. It went on from there, really. His people invited me to lunch. Pip and I went for a long walk by the river and he asked me to marry him when the war was over. When I hesitated he begged me to become engaged, at least. He bought a ring the next day and we told both sets of parents. Everyone was delighted, especially Pip. He was dreading going back to France next week. Now he has something to keep him going.'

'Is that why you did it?' Kate asked quietly.

'I . . . I suppose so. Now I feel terribly responsible for his life. Isn't it foolish?'

'You're responsible for a great many men's lives, every day. Once you get to France you'll be able to see him and get more used to the idea of marrying and leaving all this.'

'No, I won't. That was the other thing I had to tell you. We're not going to France. Because the big August offensive in Gallipoli failed, there's an overwhelming demand for qualified nurses to help with the sick and wounded out there. You and I are joining a group going to Alexandria tomorrow.'

CHAPTER TEN

Staff Nurse Daulton discovered that she had a strong stomach when the ship hit a heavy storm in the Bay of Biscay. As one of the small number of passengers remaining on their feet, she was called into service by the ship's doctor trying to cope with several broken limbs and an emergency appendicectomy along with several hundred seasick passengers. Kate little knew the next few months would follow a similar pattern and she would be glad of her immunity from *mal de mer*.

Cruising through the Mediterranean was pure joy. The sea was calm, the sun shone, the world was opening up before her eyes in a dazzling vista of blue skies, white buildings and rich green foliage bearing exotic fruits. Kate very soon realized why she had so little in common with her mother, Tim and the Nicolardis. They had all travelled extensively while she was passing her formative years at Knightshill. Twenty-five year old army nurse Kate Daulton was open to enchantment with everything she saw, and blossomed more with every day of the voyage.

Fresh sea air, long hours of undisturbed sleep and sunshine turned the pale, drawn, overworked young woman into someone in whom the Ashleigh good looks once more became apparent. Kate herself could scarcely believe the difference in her image in her cabin mirror. She looked five years younger. How much of the change was due to the fact that she was drawing nearer Gallipoli with each knot was hard to assess, but she stood at the rail during every sunset gazing in the direction of that doomed peninsula, willing Val to survive the coming night and day while praying they would somehow meet. The prayer was conditional on the meeting not being a professional one. She longed to see him just once more.

The rules aboard the troopship were strict, so made to be broken. Romance was part of the Mediterranean lure, and the officers on board were all too ready to persuade the only women there to succumb to it. Some did and were caught by Matron, whose wrath and subsequent punishment suggested they had danced naked in front of the entire ship's complement when all they had done was to spend an hour chatting to one of the officers on a secluded part of the deck. The nurses were not irresponsible enough to indulge in compromizing situations – they were going to a war zone to do an important job – but they were human, and as they were forbidden to stand alone with a man in public view they went where they could not be seen. Some nurses managed to escape Matron's eagle eye and enjoyed pleasant interludes with young officers destined for Gallipoli, who staved off their dread with harmless flirtation.

Kate and Milly enjoyed the general sociability but each was too involved with thoughts of someone special to be tempted into a particular friendship. Even so, Kate found herself for the first time in overwhelming male company which was healthy, vigorous and amusing. It brought home to her the fact that she was a novice at dealing with men, unless they were helpless in bed and she was immune behind a starched apron. Her hesitant manner made the men try harder to draw her out, which only complicated her problem making her wonder what she would do if her prayer was answered and she came face to face with Val in a street in Alexandria. What she would give for a little of her mother's charm and self-assurance!

At Alexandria the last vestiges of romance were banished by the return of reality. The streets were swarming with troops and military vehicles, many of them bearing a red cross. The harbour was busy with boats plying to and from the Dardenelles, the outgoing ones filled with men and supplies, the others bringing back sick and wounded. The sight of the flood of casualties and the constant traffic of ambulances from docks to hospitals must have chilled those officers who had laughed and teased in light-hearted fashion through the Mediterranean. Sad goodbyes were said and the nurses were driven off in bone-shaking trucks to their quarters in small hotels commandeered for their use.

Kate and Milly opted to share a room with blinds drawn against the sun, furnished with two beds, with a small chest between, a narrow wardrobe, two upright wooden chairs and a dresser bearing a jug and bowl. On the stone floor was a rush mat with one corner badly frayed, as if some creature had made a meal of it. The atmosphere smelt fusty and in need of some antiseptic scrubbing.

They looked at each other with noses wrinkled. Kate said, 'It's a far cry from our room in Yorkshire.'

'It's better than a trench at Gallipoli. Sheer luxury, in comparison. We'll smuggle some antispetic up here and soon have it smelling better.'

Within a week they no longer cared about the curious aroma in their room. A large number of men in the hospital they served were dysentery cases brought from the beach-bound forces on the peninsula, where disease was now as fatal as bullets. For the first seven days of their overseas duty, Kate and Milly helped out on one of the wards set aside for men in the throes of the terrible debilitating affliction brought on by the insanitary conditions prevailing in defences which had been occupied constantly for six months without the necessary facilities. It was a relief to them when a change around of staff resulted in re-allocation of duties. Milly was given a surgical ward and Kate's earlier experience with fever patients would be put to good use again.

The hospital was clean and airy with plentiful equipment and good subsidiary staff. Two additional wards had been opened after the landings in the Dardenelles. There was an atmosphere of order and competence which helped staff and patients alike. The challenge of her profession returned strongly in Kate as she presented herself at Ward 9 immediately after breakfast. Sister Howell arrived thirty seconds later, which was excellent timing by Kate, and revealed herself to be a friendly, pleasantly human woman in marked contrast to some Kate had worked with. Tall, dark haired, around thirty, she exuded energy.

'Have you grown accustomed to the heat yet?' she asked after Kate introduced herself. 'It's very trying for the first few days, but one soon forgets discomfort on seeing these poor lads who have suffered so. We'll go round the ward together and I'll tell you about each one as we get to him.' She smiled. 'No time to stand around chatting.'

They started down the ward past two nurses who were clearing away what passed for breakfast in a fever ward. Two more were preparing bowls of water to wash the patients before the doctor arrived. They all seemed to be cheery, efficient girls, Kate noted with relief. She was not keen to chastise, as her new rank demanded she must. Some patients were awake but their eyes were dull and they had little expression on their faces. Others were asleep, too exhausted to wake up. Those with screens around them were in a world of their own, muttering wildly and turning their heads from side to side in the height of their fever. Kate and Sister stayed longer beside these beds while they discussed details of the cases and the severity of their condition. One kept calling with desperation for *Katie* as he went through the throes of fire and ice unaware of where he was.

'Poor lad,' said Sister. 'He's been asking for her non-stop for two days. I wish we could persuade him she's here. It's driving the others mad.'

'My name's Kate,' she said. 'I could try to reassure him.'

Sister's expression changed. 'We are here to do what we can for their physical ills. There must be no *personal* involvement with any patient. On no account must a patient be given a first name or any other piece of information which is not concerned with his condition. We dispense compassion and medicines, that is all. We are not women, we are creatures of mercy.'

Kate bridled. She had been reprimanded as a probationer and as a nurse. She did not expect it now she was more exalted. 'I'm well aware of the wisdom of the rules, Sister, especially in wartime when men have undergone unnatural, extremely stressful experiences and tend to seek emotional consolation. But when one is dying, as this man almost certainly is, I believe he should be given whatever comfort he needs to make it easier.'

'You do?'

Telling herself she was making an enemy for life here, Kate nevertheless added, 'If I were a mother I'd hope a nurse would make my son's passing a little less lonely in any way she could.'

Sister Howell looked her straight in the eye. 'Don't air those views to anyone else . . . and make sure my back is turned before you act on them. Now, shall we move on to the next patient?'

It was fully half a minute before Kate realized this woman was unofficially on her side, and that working with her promised to be extremely fulfilling. She had struck lucky indeed to find someone prepared to bend the rules for the good of the patients. So many senior nurses were totally inflexible.

Two beds from the end of the ward another set of screens surrounded a patient, but this one was quiet, almost deathly still.

'This case is somewhat unusual,' Sister told her, taking up the temperature chart from the end of the bed. 'He was well on the way to recovery when he succumbed to fever. He was transferred to us two days ago on the point of being sent home. He came in from Gallipoli with a bullet embedded in his shoulder and a festering laceration in his upper arm. Like all of them he was also suffering from exhaustion and malnutrition. What they endure during the voyage is infamous. It worsens their condition in so many instances. He responded well enough to the operation on his shoulder, and he was fortunate that the onset of gangrene of his arm was stopped before it really took hold. He could well have lost the limb. Having fought his way through that, he had a sudden relapse and was sent across here. We're watching him carefully. The fever broke last evening, but he seems unable to emerge from it.' She hung the chart back on the bed. 'According to his record he was among the first to land in April. There's not many of them left. He's lucky to be still alive.'

Kate began to grow cold as she noticed the name on the chart. She stepped nearer the bed, forgetting all else but the pain of finding him in such circumstances. It was what she had dreaded. Val's face was burnt brown, very thin and covered with an infant beard. His throat and shoulders, also darkened by the intense sunshine, were hollowed by malnutrition. He looked a shadow of the man from Goonawarra. She recalled pushing back his thick blond hair as he mumbled, 'Not me, lady. It's another dose of that bloody fever.'

A voice beside her asked, 'Is he someone you know?'

Kate nodded, unable to speak.

'I'm so sorry. The sum total of young manhood seems to be passing through the wards of hospitals, so it's inevitable that we find ourselves treating friends, relations – sometimes a person who means a great deal to us. That's when we have to remind ourselves that we're merely creatures of mercy.'

Kate did remind herself of that maxim during the next two days, scrupulously avoiding showing more interest in Ashleigh V.M.H.

than any other man on the ward, conscious that Beth Howell was watching her. When she went off duty she said a silent prayer, and when she arrived the following morning she looked straightaway at the charts dreading that his name might have been scored through by the night staff. His condition remained the same. Artificial feeding continued but he did not respond to treatment. He was not in a coma, yet he remained unaware of anything but the subconscious thoughts which made him mutter unintelligibly, sometimes for long periods. If a nurse spoke to him during those times, asked him what was wrong, he gave no sign of hearing her.

The doctor who was responsible for the ward was overworked and perpetually angry. Kate suspected James McIntosh of having a secret fondness for Sister, to whom he expressed his opinion of 'elderly buffoons' who allowed the Dardenelles horrors to continue. His professional heart bled over losing so many strong men unnecessarily through illness which drained their lives away. He treated the rest of the ward's staff with complete offhandedness, including Kate. His principal concern was the patients. Kate admired his devotion to duty and emulated it despite the presence of the man she loved. She did not even tell Milly the situation in case the news reached McIntosh's ears.

During her third morning on Ward 9, when she was in sole charge in Sister's absence, Kate glanced up to see someone standing just inside the entrance. She left the table where she had been listing Captain McIntosh's comments on his rounds.

'Can I help you?' she asked.

He was no more than nineteen yet he wore the rank of captain. There was a disfiguring scar running from his right ear to his shoulder. Lucky man, Kate thought. Another inch either way and he would not be standing there with all his senses intact. He had a shy smile which was rather moving in someone who had clearly been forced to deal with more than he should at his age. It was a common story, however.

'I was told Sergeant Ashleigh was here, Sister,' he said diffidently. 'I know there's a rule about visiting only between certain times, but I'd hate to miss seeing him before I sail this afternoon.'

'Not back to Gallipoli?' she asked with concern.

'Oh no, they've decided to give me some leave.' He fidgeted with the cap he held. 'We were together from the first landings. He saved my life. Would it be possible . . . ?'

Kate did a rapid mental calculation. The meeting Sister was attending would not end for at least fifteen minutes. This boy knew Val and details of what had put him in his present condition. There was a chance he could get through that barrier preventing recovery.

'I'll put screens around the bed so no one will see you,' she said, leading the way down the ward. 'He's unwilling to return to us yet. Talk to him. It might help.'

Once they were behind the screens the young officer revealed a story that drove Kate to the edge of forbidden tears. At the end of it he added, 'He's something of a mystery man. Australian. Bit on the rough side.' Again his shy smile. 'You'll have to close your ears to his language once he starts getting better. Yet he's clearly been well educated. He refuses to speak about his past, but I've never known anyone more loyal or determined. I've put his name forward for a medal.' He glanced back at the man in bed. 'He'll probably refuse to wear it, but he can't stop it being gazetted for all time. If he ever has a son the boy will be proud to read about it.'

'I'll leave you with him,' Kate said, knowing that she must find a solitary place for a few moments. 'Speak to him in reassuring tones. Perhaps he'll hear. Five minutes, that's all.'

When the visitor walked back up the ward Kate had not only composed herself she was ready to face Sister if she should return unexpectedly.

'Thank you for letting me see him, but I'm afraid he's still out for the count.' Troubled dark eyes appealed to her. 'He's going to be all right, isn't he?'

'Oh yes, his constitution is quite strong,' Kate told him with confidence. 'He's simply too weary to face the world. When he's ready, he will. I'm sorry you have to leave without making contact. Is there a message you'd like to leave with me?'

'Just tell him I'll be listening for the stars to twinkle. He'll understand.'

Two men on the ward died that afternoon, and a ship docked with a fresh batch of casualties. Extra beds were added to every ward to deal with them, and day staff worked alongside those who came on duty at sunset until every man had been undressed, washed and seen by a doctor. Kate reached her room just before midnight. Milly came in just afterwards. They were both too tired to say much, but Kate lay thinking of all she had been told about Val, feeling ridiculously jealous of that mature boy who had been so close to him for five months.

Captain McIntosh was late making his rounds due to the influx of patients, so not until afternoon the next day were the men in Ward 9 seen by the man who could have them sent home for convalescence or back to active service. They all wanted to get to 'Blighty' and waited with apprehension if they knew they were about to be discharged. Kate accompanied the doctor because Sister was temporarily standing in for another who had fallen and broken her leg. The news did not please James McIntosh, who grunted and muttered that the medical staff were not expected to become patients. His mood led him to make decisions Kate thought unfairly harsh on three men she considered unfit to return to duty without recuperation in England, and she vowed to tackle him at the end of his round.

They reached Val's bed and the doctor made a cursory examination while Kate stood watching and remembering that same body at Leyden's Spinny. It was wasting away all the time he refused to come out of his long period of unconsciousness.

'Hmm, it's time this man was up and about,' ruled McIntosh morosely. 'Can't let him carry on like this much longer. Are you making *every* effort to implement my recomendations?'

Kate was angry at this slur on their efficiency. 'We *always* carry out your instructions, sir. I learned yesterday from Sergeant Ashleigh's officer that he was not only wounded in an assault, he led a group of survivors in a four-hour trek to safety, carrying his commander all the way. I'm not in the least surprised that he's taking all this time to recover.'

Bushy eyebrows rose. 'Are you not? How long have you been in Egypt, miss?'

Kate felt her colour start to rise at his sarcastic approach. 'Almost three weeks, sir.'

'And you have already become an authority on fevers and their recovery time!'

'I worked for two and a half years on a fever ward at St Martin's before I transferred to the army,' she said, unwilling to be downtrodden by this arrogant man, 'and knowing a little of this patient's history, I . . .'

'Christ, it's little Kate,' said a quiet voice from the bed. 'What are *you* doing here?'

She turned with only one sensation – relief that he was back in the land of the fully aware. In that hollow face his eyes were still amazingly blue despite the haze of illness. She smiled, but remembered just in time to be impersonal. 'Welcome back, Sergeant Ashleigh. The other patients have been referring to you as Rip Van Winkle.'

'I could go a jug of beer,' he murmured. 'I've got a bloody thirst.'

'Plenty of time for that,' said McIntosh brusquely. 'Get yourself up, man! You've been occupying this bed for too long.' He wrote on his pad, then moved on to the next patient.

When they returned to Sister's office Kate made her representations on behalf of the three she wanted to help, depite the doctor's obvious aggression towards her. She gave sound reasons for her request that they should have home convalescence. To her surprise McIntosh altered his decision in writing, without argument.

'The ships are overflowing, of course, but I daresay they won't care about that,' he muttered as he scribbled. 'We'll have no men left out here by Christmas if you have your way.' Without looking up, he added, 'Don't expect special treatment for Sergeant Ashleigh.'

'I never have, sir,' she replied.

'You didn't mention that you knew him.'

'He's a patient like everyone else in the ward.'

'Hmm.' He shot a piercing glance at her. 'Your young man?'

'My uncle, sir.' She cursed the flood of colour that crossed her cheeks.

'Very *young* to be your uncle.'

'I always thought of him as an older brother.'

'I see. Difficult for you having him here.'

She made no further comment and he spoke on medical matters for a few minutes longer, then prepared to leave. 'This war has men – and women – doing the impossible. A four-hour walk carrying his officer was a considerable feat in his condition.' He gave a dry smile. 'Determination runs in the family, it seems.'

Kate knew she had miraculously made a friend of this irascible Scot and her day was brightened further. As soon as she had informed her nurses of any change of treatments and checked the tea list so that distribution could begin, Kate went to speak to Val. He was staring at the ceiling but quickly turned his attention to her.

'It *is* little Kate, isn't it?'

'I'm not so little now.'

'Look, where is this place? It stinks of the Middle East.'

She smiled. 'You're still in Alexandria, I'm afraid. You were laid low with fever before you could be sent home, and they transferred you to this ward. I've only been out here three weeks. It was a shock to walk in and see you in one of the beds, although I knew you were in Gallipoli.'

'How about a beer?'

'I'll help you with a drink of water, or just a little weak tea.' His expression spoke volumes, and she said, 'You've been quite ill, Val. We can't rush your recovery. It'll have to take it's own time.'

'How did you know?' he asked then.

'Know what?'

'That I was in this part of the world?'

'Aunt Kitty told me when I went on embarkation leave. A Major called Oscar something wrote saying he had met up with you, and so on. He used to visit Knightshill and remembered you, he said.' She sighed. 'They'd all been so worried. Why didn't you let them know where you were?'

He did not answer that. 'When are you going to help me with a drink of water?'

She raised him with an arm beneath his shoulders and allowed him to take short sips before lowering him back to his pillow. 'I'll tell the nurses to see that you're given a drink at regular intervals. You'll have to be rationed until you're able to accept greater quantities of fluids.'

When he smiled it warmed her right through. 'You always were a caring little thing. When I woke and saw you at the end of the bed I thought I'd passed out at Knightshill again. Then I recognized the uniform. All Ashleighs get into one sooner or later . . . but you've done it for a far worthier reason, little Kate.'

'You'll have to stop calling me that,' she warned, conscious that two nurses were now very near with the tea wagon. 'And I'll have to call you Sergeant Ashleigh. It's the rules.'

He was still smiling. 'I never heed bloody rules.'

'I guessed that some time ago. Val, it's *so* good to see you again and to know you're on the mend. They'll send you home when you're well enough.'

'Have they evacuated Gallipoli yet?'

'We hear rumours, but they're still bringing wounded over.' She smoothed the sheet over his chest, saying quietly, 'I'll come and talk to you when I can. Please do all you're asked. You'll build up your strength more quickly. I'll check that you're all right before I go off duty. Be prepared to lie awake most of the night. You have been asleep so long your mind will want to compensate. Do your utmost to relax. Thinking about Gallipoli won't help.' As she straightened up she remembered the young officer. 'Someone came to see you yesterday before he embarked for home. He told me to tell you he would be listening for the stars to twinkle.'

Val's sharp response surprised her. 'He was being sent home? Was he all right?'

'Oh yes, but sad that he couldn't speak to you.'

'Yeah, well I only teach him flaming useless things when I do.'

'I imagine you taught him rather more than that, Sergeant Ashleigh,' she told him as the nurses arrived at his bedside. 'Rest now. You'll be surprised at how much stronger you'll feel tomorrow.'

By the end of a week Val was eating well and gaining some of his lost weight. Kate could not spend much time with him because they were rushed off their feet, but it was enough for her to know he was there, and whole. She thanked God the gangrene in his arm had been treated in time or the mutilation she dreaded would have been inevitable. She still hated treating amputees and had to struggle against being too sympathetic towards them. Captain McIntosh continued to be brusque on his rounds, but he made the occasional dry comment when they were alone which showed he no longer thought of Kate of an automaton in a starched white apron.

When Sister Howell returned to take charge of Ward 9 she brought news that discouraged Kate. 'There is an emergency situation at Gallipoli, I fear. When has there not been? Winter arrived with such violence it has brought fresh problems. Torrential rain first flooded the trenches making them uninhabitable, which caused excessive casualties because the men lost their only protection from the enemy. Now everything has frozen, leaving them exposed to heavy snowfall and icy temperatures with no shelter whatsoever. It's being said that winter clothing on its way to them was mistakenly diverted to the base at Lemnos, so those poor lads are now *freezing* to death.'

To Kate's consternation this energetic, capable, self-assured woman's voice suddenly broke as her clenched fist thumped several times in the palm of her other hand. 'It's *infamous*! War brings battles and I have pledged my skill to help those who suffer as a result, but the Dardenelles campaign is a horror beyond hell. When it finally ends those responsible should be put on that peninsula and left there. I would gladly row them to it single-handed and enjoy coming away with the only available boat.'

As Kate stood silently thankful that Val was safe from such unimaginable suffering, Beth Howell swallowed back her emotion by taking several deep breaths. Then she forced a faint smile. 'Even the most determined of us sometimes forget we're merely creatures of mercy. You must remember that in the coming weeks. To deal with these cases of frostbite, exposure and near starvation casualties are being taken in much greater numbers to Lemnos on every available vessel. Extra nursing staff is needed, and each hospital has been requested to supply twenty. I have put your name on the list, and Captain McIntosh has endorsed it. You are a very capable nurse well able to deal with unusual or unexpected demands. Your devotion to duty has been apparent while you have been on this ward. I'm sorry to lose you, but you'll be serving our troops better on a hospital ship than here.'

In the face of such praise Kate had to hide her distress. 'When am I to go, Sister?'

'Tomorrow afternoon. It takes two or three days to reach the peninsula, and the situation is urgent. You'll be issued with a winter uniform, and I'd advise you to get hold of extra underwear in the morning. You'll probably need to wear two of everything.' She glanced at the watch pinned to her apron. 'Gracious heavens, we must get to work!' Picking up the reports left by the night staff, she began scanning them. Then, as Kate walked from the tiny office, she said quietly, 'I can't allow it when you're on duty, but if you'd like to have a chat with your uncle when you finish this evening there is a secluded corner you could use on the terrace. I'll make certain Night Sister understands the situation.'

'Thank you. I'd like that,' said Kate, knowing Captain McIntosh had discussed Val with Sister Howell, because only he could have told her of their relationship. Kate had said nothing to anyone else. Surely she was not being sent away because of it. She had been so careful not to favour Val more than any other man in the ward, and had scrupulously timed her conversations with him to ensure they were no longer than usual with patients.

During the course of the hectic day Kate managed to pass to him the message about the proposed meeting. Val merely frowned and said, 'Righto.' It was difficult to keep her mind on her work as she wondered about the routine on a hospital ship. It would be an entirely new experience. How would patients be accommodated, where would dressings and medicines be stored, would she be allocated a sleeping cabin, how would the men be transferred from the beaches to the ship? Only when she finished duty, said goodbye to Sister Howell, the nurses and patients, and made her way to the terrace, did it occur to her that she could learn most of the answers from Val.

He was waiting in a cane chair with faded blue cushions. There was another beside him. Kate sat in it and smiled. 'How cosy. Did Sister put these here for us?'

'No, that little girl with yellow hair. She tried to stop me coming out here but I lifted her out of the way. Next minute she arrived with a chair and insisted that I use it. I found the other one around the corner.'

'It's probably Sister's.' She looked from the balcony at the scene spread before them. Lights were springing up in the dusk-tinted streets. The distant docks were already ablaze with them. The great liners' funnels were just visible where the heads of cranes and gantries reared into the mauve sky. The evening hour was filled with the sounds of traffic, voices calling and answering, the babble from the nearby market, the braying of asses; the humid air bore the pungent smells of cooking, incense, animal hides, rotting garbage and unwashed humanity. Yet there was romance there, Kate found, as she contemplated leaving it tomorrow. She had been in Alexandria five weeks and had just grown used to the heat, the noise, the stuffy room she shared with Milly, and her staff on the ward. This foreign city had brought her an insight to things her family knew well, and it had brought her the chance to be with Val. Sitting beside him on a terrace with no one else near, and with stars growing brighter as the sky darkened, was a time she would remember all her life.

She turned to him and briefly saw an echo of the young officer in the photograph she had in her bedside locker. He was recovering well in the peace of Alexandria. 'What did your young friend mean about listening for the stars to twinkle?'

He shrugged it off. 'Something I once said caught his imagination. It made a change from most of the stuff I told him.'

'He thinks a lot of you.'

'It's mutual. You get like that in Gallipoli.'

'I know. So many patients say the same thing.' She did not want to remind him of horror, so she said, 'Uncle Vere's turned the London house into a convalescent home called Ashleigh Court. You could go there for a while when you get home.'

He gave her a straight look. 'You know that's a flamin' cock-eyed suggestion, so why make it?'

'The aunts and Mother all spend time there, although Aunt Lottie was at Knightshill when I left. Uncle John's not too strong.'

'Pity. He's a nice bloke.'

'He was always kind to me – to us all – when I was small.' She pushed on in the determination to give him all the Ashleigh news. 'Uncle Vere's putting on a grand charity show on New Year's Day in company with Gilbert Dessinger, and the twins are planning careers in the theatre. My half-brothers are astounding teachers and family alike with their brilliance. Aunt Lottie's boys are hoping the war will last long enough for them to take part, and Simon's working on the design of a new fighter aircraft to better the one the Germans have.' Remembering his kiss and declaration of love, she hastily added, 'Poor thing was rather upset because he'd been sent a white feather. I hope he doesn't do something impetuous over it.'

'He'll be a silly bloody fool if he does. A man's entitled to do what he likes with his life no matter what anyone else thinks. Well, go on, girl. You've mentioned everyone but that brother of yours. Tell me what damn fool things he's been up to, then we can talk about something more interesting.'

Kate was seeing yet a different person, one who touched her even more than before. Gone was the anger, the aggression against everyone and everything that he had displayed at Knightshill eighteen months ago. Gone was the man of few words and most of them oaths; the reluctance to commit himself to a discussion. Here beside her was someone who appeared to have come to terms with the unnatural life he was trapped in, whose quietness was now within rather than jealously guarded from without. This man in a dressing gown beside her in the warm dusk charmed her anew with his soft, accented voice, with his physical impact and, mostly, with all the things he had done which hinted at a personality she might never uncover. Yearning for that made her bold.

'Val, why did you enlist instead of going back to Australia?'

For a moment she thought he would refuse to answer because he looked away towards the bright lights of the docks. Then he said, 'There are things in life you never forget – you'll find that. Vere reminded me of one of them and I went on a binge. When I woke up I was in the army.' He gave a short dry laugh. 'In the bloody West Wilts.' Glancing back at her, he added, 'Don't tell me they all thought I had done the decent thing for once.'

'They didn't know about it until Mr Bentley let on you'd written to him. They . . . they would have liked you to tell them yourself.'

'Yeah, we all like to be told things, little Kate. *All* of us.'

The slight hint of bitterness in his voice prompted her to venture further. 'Simon said your purchase of the place in Australia has been invalidated.'

'That's right. I bumped into one of the drovers on the beach. He'd been shipwrecked and forced to stay put. He told me the news.' His eyes gleamed in the gathering darkness as he studied her. 'I'd made a new will leaving Goonawarra to you. Now you won't have it.'

She was astonished. 'Why me?'

'Why not you? All the boys in the family will get plenty – the

Ashleighs are only interested in their males – and you're the one who'd have appreciated it the most. When I was at Knightshill I thought you were something of an outsider there. Now I know why. You're not doing this for glory or because it's expected of you. Good on you!'

'That young officer said you'd saved his life. Wasn't *that* expected of *you*?'

'As a soldier, not because my name's Ashleigh. I did it because he didn't deserve what they'd done to him, that's all.'

There was a short silence while they both thought their own thoughts and gazed into the night sky brilliant with stars.

'I'm leaving tomorrow,' Kate told him. 'I'm to be on a hospital ship taking off wounded.' She related what Sister had told her, and asked him about his evacuation from the peninsula. What he said was not in the least reassuring and she well understood why so many patients were more seriously ill than their initial diagnosis suggested, when they arrived at Alexandria. At that point she spotted Sister Biggins in the doorway of the ward looking along the terrace at them. She stood up knowing this parting would be unbearably difficult. Given more time she might have won his confidence to the extent of his confiding the secret she would give anything to know. She now had to leave and survive on the memory of these few minutes, never knowing if they would meet again.

'Our time's up, Val. They were very good to allow us to come out here for a private goodbye.'

'So that's what it was all about. I thought they'd softened up the rules for once.' He got to his feet. 'You still haven't mentioned Tim. He's all right, isn't he?'

'Mother and Laurence conspired to get him attached to Intelligence as an interpreter. He hasn't been into action yet.'

'Poor little bugger!' he said explosively. 'Ashleigh ghosts are demanding a hero and his doting parents are afraid to let him try to be one. He'll hate them for it. Any man would.'

She looked up at him puzzled. 'I thought you and Tim were daggers drawn.'

'His is drawn. I just feel he doesn't deserve what they're doing to him, because they'll end up destroying him . . . if he doesn't destroy himself first. I tried to talk some sense into him, but he told me to . . .'

'Sergeant Ashleigh, your supper is about to be served,' called Sister Biggins briskly. 'You *must* come inside.'

Val put out his hand. 'Goodbye, little Kate. I'll buy something else to leave you in my will.'

She gave a wobbly laugh thinking how inadequate it was to shake his hand when she longed for him to do what Simon had done. 'Just ensure you don't *need* a will.'

He gave her cheek a fleeting brush with his fingers, and it almost broke her composure. 'The Ashleigh ancestors won't know what to make of you. You're beating them at their own game. It's time somebody did.'

When he was halfway to the door she called his name, making him turn. '*Please* look after yourself.'

'It's out of my hands. Fate's doing that.'

He went inside leaving her to gaze at the ship which would take her away from him, knowing he would always think of her as the little girl of his youth.

The island of Lemnos stood some fifty or sixty miles from the Gallipoli peninsula. Greek-owned, it was being used as a supply base for combined forces fighting the Turks, and hospitals had been set up there because the harbour at Mudros was wide and deep enough to allow large ships to dock. Such was the confusion on the battle beaches, and the overwhelming flood of casualties, it was not possible to separate minor and serious cases when shells were falling all around. The priority was to get the wounded away as speedily as possible. So they were packed aboard the transports willy-nilly, and men whose lives or limbs could otherwise have been saved often were left for hours unattended and received treatment too late.

Kate and Milly, along with the others selected as reinforcements for the overworked medical staff in the area, arrived at Lemnos in the heart of a storm. The friends were glad of their 'sea legs' when some nurses succumbed to violent seasickness, but their first sights of the island filled them with awe. Kate gazed at the barren hills being bombarded by sleet and hailstones, at the mass of tents many of which had collapsed in the gale sweeping through, and the hundreds of ships of all sizes in the harbour, and experienced a surge of chill excitement. She had now arrived in a war zone.

This was where Val had survived for five months, where he had fought and had been wounded. This was where he had led men to safety and thus saved their lives. This was a part of his secret life she longed to share. That she *was* about to share in it thrilled her and leavened the dark aspect of what lay ahead.

The transport ship docked, and the passengers were let ashore before unloading commenced. Kate was glad of the uniform her mother had thought so ugly, and she wrapped the thick cloak close around her body as she fought her way across a stretch of mud to where the senior medical officer was waiting to check them all ashore. There were six doctors and sixty nurses, with two dozen male medical orderlies. When they had all assembled, buffeted by wind, drenched by the sleet and up to their ankles in mud, it was to learn that there was no transport on hand and they must walk two miles to the hospital complex where they would be given their orders.

Milly gave Kate a furious look, saying under her breath, 'They knew we were arriving. How do they expect us to walk there in weather like this?'

Picking up her suitcase Kate replied calmly, 'They expect men to *fight* in these conditions. Surely we can walk in them.'

As she tramped through the mud Kate's gaze was fixed on the stormy heights, imagining a sergeant, a young officer, and a company of men climbing up a similar hell knowing what awaited them at the top, and she knew in that moment that love for Val would sustain and inspire her in this place. Whatever she was confronted with here she would not falter or fail. Every man she treated would be him, everything she was expected to do would be done for him, every day she spent here would keep close the memory of that haunting farewell. Gallipoli held the essence of the man she had almost reached.

Crowded into a hut, the new arrivals were given mugs of tea while sitting on their luggage. The doctors had gone to the Officers' Mess. The nurses and orderlies waited for Matron or the Senior Medical Officer to arrive with their orders. They all warmed their hands around their tin mugs as they sat soaked through and frozen after the warmth of Alexandria. Milly remained silent beside Kate, who wanted to compensate for her earlier comment. Knowing Pip was somewhere in France she should have thought before she spoke, but her own feelings were so overwhelming at present they overrode every other consideration.

'I hope we get a room together,' she ventured. 'I'd hate to split up during a stormy night.'

'Room? A tent, more likely,' Milly pointed out. 'That's all I saw during our walk.'

In the event Kate spent the night once again at sea. Milly was to stay at the base hospital with a dozen others. The remainder were allocated to ships. When Kate was told she would be serving on one of the small boats plying from the Gallipoli beaches to the large hospital ships, her pulse quickened. Maybe she would see the very place where Val had lived through and endured five unimaginable months. She bore his fortitude in mind when told she would now have to walk all the way back to the jetty.

The friends parted regretfully. Milly said, 'If Big Bad Uncle Valentine comes into my ward I'll keep him there until you can visit.'

'I've already seen him,' Kate confessed. 'He was one of my patients in Alex.'

'And you said nothing to me! Now I *know* you're sweet on him, ducky. Is he going to be all right?'

Kate nodded. 'He's going home . . . and he'll then be sent to France, won't he?'

''Fraid so. They send all the best fellows there.'

They seized hands and each forced a smile. 'I'll pop in and see you when I can,' Kate promised.

'Bring me a Christmas present from Turkey, but nothing too exotic. I'm no Sultan's favourite.' Milly walked with her to the door. 'How does he regard you, Kate?'

She paused before stepping out into the storm once more. 'As his little niece. Take care, Milly.'

The ship sailed in the early hours to arrive at dawn. Kate was taken aback by what she found aboard. Intended only as a transport to move serious cases to the fully equipped hospital ships, the *Romaine* had only basic facilities. A handful of beds, a large number of dirty, blood-stained stretchers, an inadequate supply of dressings and medicines, but plenty of bowls, sponges and soap. She soon discovered why these were so plentiful. There were no cabins, as such, merely bunks curtained off from a general companionway. The nurses who had been on the ship for several weeks told her she would have no time to sleep, just rest a while on the outward journeys. They all looked pale. One bemoaned the fact that she had been unable to wash her hair for two weeks. Kate knew such things mattered when everything else was grim. She was certain the soldiers grumbled about small deprivations in the midst of their endurance and courage.

Too excited to sleep, Kate waited for her first sight of Gallipoli. Although the storm had abated, freezing rain and a bitter wind made the decks treacherous. As day dawned she stood apart from Sister Johns, a plump silent woman nearing thirty, and the other nurses, watching for land to loom from the greyness ahead. This was a milestone in her life. This was something the much-travelled members of her family had never done. This was a battlefield. Even Tim had not been this near to one.

The Gallipoli Peninsula identified itself by sound before sight. It was said by people along the English Channel coast that the guns in France could be heard when the wind carried the sound across the water. Kate had never been near enough to hear them, but she heard guns now and swallowed nervously. This was real; this was war. This was something Val had known in South Africa and here on this finger of land. She could now share it with him. As the rocky cliffs bordered by a narrow beach materialized from the obscurity ahead, she turned cold. He had said there were some things one never forgot. This moment was one of them for her.

The *Romaine* cast anchor a short way out, unable to sail further without going aground. Small barges were already on their way from the makeshift jetties, causing sudden alertness on board. Sister Johns moved forward and stood beside Kate, staring with dulled eyes at the activity.

'One's first sight of this place is extremely moving,' she murmured. 'After a week you'll feel nothing. Don't try to do the impossible. It can't be done. Just do what can. It's little enough.'

The meaning of those words was soon made clear. The casualties were swung aboard by cranes, lying in pairs in shallow wooden crates where they had been for most of the night. From the moment the first arrived there was no time for anything but them. Their uniforms were bloodstained, caked with mud and stiff as boards. Some were frozen to the wearer's skin, others had become part of open wounds. The men were gaunt, bearded, unaware or uncaring of where they were. Kate set to work with scissors and pails of hot water, like the rest. Cutting off their clothes was difficult and time consuming, but as many as possible had to be washed clean before treatment could be started, even if they had to wait until they reached Lemnos. Doctors examined the labels attached to each man and made notes. The label was tied to the patient's toe after he had been stripped and washed, so there would be no errors.

Kate had tended men with terrible wounds during her time in an English military hospital, but they had arrived from France in pyjamas having received preliminary treatment in field hospitals. She had never seen anything like this before and her heart bled. As a Staff Nurse she was told to leave the washing and start on dressings and injections. With Sister and two others of her own rank she followed the doctors and carried out their instructions, while more and more stretchers were swung aboard. She lost track of time as the ship slowly filled. She regretted being unable to soothe those who cried out in pain, as she had always done. The brief minutes she spent with each patient as she tended him were all the time she had in which to comfort him with words and a smile. Then she must move on. The ship soon smelt of Gallipoli; a stench those who had been there would forever remember.

When as many as possible had been packed inside, the decks were lined with casualties. These could not be stripped of uniforms they had worn for weeks on end – that would have to be done at Lemnos – nor could they be examined in the biting cold and rain. These unfortunates were covered with heavy blankets and tarpaulins, their only comfort being that they were getting away from the beach being shelled almost constantly. While working on the deck Kate once more became aware of the bombardment and realized shells were falling into the sea not too far off. She paused for a moment, on her knees beside a stretcher, to gaze in astonishment at a great spurt of water rising up as shells exploded between the laden barges.

'They're firing at the wounded,' she cried in open protest.

'They're rotten shots, though,' said a male voice nearby and she turned to see a good-looking doctor making notes of the labels on each man. He smiled across at her. 'They haven't hit us yet. This is your first time, isn't it?'

'Yes, sir.' She continued what she was doing. There was no time for conversation. They sailed when not another body could be fitted on the decks. Everyone was given a drink. Thin broth was offered to those who could take it. Those who could not had nothing. Despite rolling seas a large number of serious cases on the decks were exchanged with an equal number of minor ones below, who then had to suffer the cold and the rain.

'It's infamous,' Kate muttered to a nurse beside her.

'It's what they're used to, and it's only for a couple of hours,' came the reply. 'At least the end of it is in sight for them. Those left on the beach have to carry on until they get hit and are brought off by us . . . or put in a grave. These lads are the lucky ones.'

They did what they could for the extreme cases during the return voyage, then helped to get them all ashore when they tied up in Mudros harbour. The rain had stopped and a watery sun was out, but it provided no warmth from the winter temperature and biting wind as the *Romaine* set off once more for the Dardenelles. The brief voyage provided time for the nurses to wash themselves and their filthy aprons, then take a short rest. Kate understood why these women had no chance to wash their hair, yet was certain the *Romaine* was full of lice from the soldiers. Whatever would she do if they got in her head or clothes? Hot on the heels of that thought she reminded herself of her rebuke to Milly. If the men could fight with lice crawling over them, she could sail in this ship with them.

She had an hour's sleep before being woken by the thunder of guns to find they were back at the battlefield, where barges were again setting out across that stretch of water within range of Turkish guns. The medical team steeled themselves for the next batch of cases with scissors, bowls of water, antiseptic, dressings, medicines, morphia and hypodermic needles. Kate forgot weariness and the prospect of lice in her hair as the first poor wretches arrived aboard. She was now aware of the routine and set to work with more confidence. She could cope with anything in the face of this extent of suffering.

It was as well she could, because the *Romaine* ploughed back and forth day after day and the medical staff never set foot on land in all that time.

* * *

Two weeks before Christmas *Romaine* made her normal dawn visit to the doomed beaches. Kate was by now too exhausted to watch their approach. The ship's crew alerted them when they dropped anchor, and she woke with the others to prepare for the exacting routine. She still felt moved by the sight of the cliffs and the sound of battle, contrary to Sister's claim. In good visibility she could see the soldiers moving about their precarious stronghold and her heart went out to them. Each time they weighed anchor she imagined that those left behind must all watch with longing as the ship grew further and further distant. Christmas. All their thoughts must be of their homes and families. Kate could not imagine a bleaker place in which to spend the Christmas festival. They must believe God had forsaken them all. She knew from what men had told her on these trips that they already believed their country had done so. After three weeks on this mercy run, Kate had to agree with them. They were taking off so many she had begun to fear that anyone in Alexandria considered fit enough for duty would be sent back to Gallipoli, rather than to France via England. There must be so few left on the peninsula they would be wiped out to a man if the Turks decided to take the beaches. The casualties said that would never happen because the enemies had more sense than to want them. Only madmen inhabited such stinking, pestilential graveyards.

The first men were lowered by crane and taken from their box-like containers by orderlies. The nurses moved forward, scissors in hand and smiles on their faces. There was a new condition known as trench foot, which was afflicting progressively more on each trip. The percentage of wounded was growing smaller as the severe conditions prevented any serious assaults being made. Most of those who came aboard now had dysentery, frostbite, fever, pleurisy or pneumonia. They all wore what Kate called the Gallipoli Glaze – a haunted expression and eyes that appeared to see something other than their surroundings.

One or two managed to be chirpy; nearly all asked for tea or a cigarette. They were offered the usual water or thin broth according to their condition. There were fewer than there had been three weeks ago, so no more than a dozen lay on the deck covered with tarpaulins. The washing began. Some of the older men were embarrassed over this, but it had to be done and doctors were moving between the stretchers the whole time to prevent any problems over it.

Romaine got underway and Kate went with Sister, alongside doctors on the emergency cases. The good-looking captain who had said the Turks were rotten shots on her first day had made several overtures to Kate during rare opportunities for personal conversation, but she had not encouraged him. In a tight military régime such as theirs it was best to avoid friendships. Sister frowned on any contact between her nurses and the doctors which was not on a professional level, but Kate seemed to be the only nurse aboard who was impervious to his considerable attraction.

Halfway through the return voyage Kate happened to be near him when an emergency occurred. A corporal with pneumonia suddenly began gasping with painfully indrawn breaths which rattled in his throat, and he thrashed his arms in panic.

'Nurse, raise his head,' said the doctor with urgency.

Kate stepped around the stretcher to help lift the distressed patient choking on the rising fluid in his chest. They had scarcely begun the task when there was a deafening bang and Kate was thrown off her feet by violent movement of the ship. The lights went out; someone shouted, 'We've been hit!' The emergency alarm began and the staccato order to report to boat stations was repeated several times over the loudspeakers. The thrum of engines faded and stopped. Feet began thumping on the decks above. The boats were being run out.

Kate scrambled up, her eyes growing accustomed to the dimness. They all knew the emergency drill and began to implement it with quiet efficiency. The captain would not be preparing to abandon ship unless it was certain to sink. *Romaine* had been fatally holed, but by what Kate could not think. Surely not another ship. It was daylight and weather conditions were better than some she had experienced. She felt no fear as she made her way to the boat deck and the station she had been allocated to. The priorities were clear – nurses and patients would occupy the boats; the crew, doctors and orderlies would remain until the last minute.

It was bitterly cold as Kate and the other nurses at Station 9 donned lifejackets and climbed down into the boat hanging out over the sea to wait for the casualties. Her only concern was that there were no lifejackets for the men from Gallipoli. *Romaine* was a small transport performing a duty for which she was not designed. Aware that they had begun to list, and that black smoke was pouring from the starboard side, Kate prayed there would be enough time for everyone to escape before the ship went down.

According to the drill, a double chain of men had been formed to bring up the sick and the wounded, but it was slow work as blanket-wrapped men minus their stretchers were handed into the boats and laid in rows by the nurses. It was a perilous task because the boat swayed with every movement, but Kate and her companions worked with a will knowing speed was essential. There was no time to reassure the men who had escaped one hell to enter another. Her hands were so cold she found it difficult to grasp anything and was terrified that she would lose her grip and cause someone further injury. They all suffered equally as they struggled to maintain their hold on the inert bodies of men often weighing twelve stone or more.

All at once the evacuation was halted because the list to starboard had increased so much the boats on the port side would have to be lowered before it became impossible to do so. Kate was dismayed. There was space for more. What would happen to those still aboard? The boat's crew jumped in and the boats were lowered with such speed they hit the water with a great smack, then rocked so violently the men lying on the bottom were thrown into a heap. Sailors manned the oars and began to row away from the stricken vessel. Kate was so busy helping her colleagues with the pile of suffering soldiers she was dismayed when she eventually sat back and saw how far they were from the *Romaine*, which was now almost completely on her side.

In numb horror the occupants of the boat watched casualties being dropped into the sea where they might stand a very slight chance of survival, swiftly followed by the able-bodied men. Almost at once *Romaine* capsized, signifying the end of anyone who was still aboard. The circle of boats standing some distance away began to converge on the heads bobbing in the water, visible only as they crested the waves. There was something particularly awesome about the sight of that rusty hull turned up to the lowering sky, and those exposed to peril in the waves.

Kate was icy cold. It was as if her body was hollow; empty of all sensation and emotion as the other boats arrived amid the survivors. Some were pulled aboard; others clung to the ropes on the sides, too weak for further effort. Bodies undulated between those men trying to keep above the surface long enough to be helped. After a while Kate noticed other boats there, empty save for sailors pulling to safety all remaining bodies, alive or dead. On these lifeboats was the name *Bastille*.

Kate's crew began pulling towards a vessel standing a short way off. 'It's a Frenchie,' said a white-faced sailor wielding his oar near Kate. 'Lucky they was near when we hit that mine.' He wiped his sleeve across his nose, and she realized he was crying. She wondered why she was not. 'Thought the sweepers 'ad picked 'em all up,' he continued. 'This 'un must 'ave drifted up in the storms. Poor old *Romaine*.'

Tears were now streaming down his cheeks, so Kate looked away to where the ship that had been her home for three weeks was no more than an obscene shape fast disappearing below the surface. Pushing her tumbled hair from her eyes she stared at that shape across a heaving, leaden sea and found it difficult to believe what was happening. How could they have been victims of the enemy? They were protected by immunity from acts of aggression on humanitarian grounds. The wounded, and those who tended them, were counted as non-combatants and allowed to go about their work. How could this have happened?

Kate was still staring at the last section of the upturned hull where men had died after surviving all Gallipoli had done to them, when they reached the French troop carrier. They were offered hot coffee and blankets. These were declined as the nurses worked alongside the doctors in saturated uniforms who had jumped from the sinking ship, to do what they could for those casualties still able to be helped. Then they covered the dead. Among them was the corporal who had been choking just before the disaster.

'He wouldn't have survived, anyway,' said a quiet voice, and Kate glanced up to find the friendly doctor beside her. There was a trickle of blood oozing from a bad laceration to his temple.

'You're hurt,' she said dully. 'Let me attend to it.'

'It's nothing. I hit my head when I slipped on the deck. I'll slap something on it later. We've enough casualties without you turning me into one.' As they laid out more unfortunates, he asked quietly, 'You weren't afraid out there?'

'There was too much to do. Didn't you find that?'

He shook his head. 'You women are marvellous! You've quite as much courage as any of these men.'

Kate glanced at the row of blanket-covered bodies. 'They always deny having courage and say they were just doing their job. That's what we've been doing.'

Three hours after reaching Mudras harbour, when the land-based hospital staff had taken over and Kate had had a bath, washed her hair and crawled beneath the blankets of a spare bed in someone's tent, she began to sob and could not stop. Her precious photograph of Val was in the sea beneath the wreck of *Romaine*.

On December 10th the evacuation of the Gallipoli Peninsula began, stealthily by night. During daylight hours stores and small numbers of troops continued to be landed at various beaches; life in the trenches appeared to be continuing as normal. Small boats slipped in under cover of darkness to take off men with cloth wrapped around their boots to muffle the sound of concentrated movement. Supplies of alcohol were withdrawn to ensure that the soldiers would not celebrate and give themselves away whilst retreating. Smoking was banned in case matches flared to reveal men on the move. Graves were dug on the island of Lemnos ready for the many certain to be fatally injured during the exercise. However, night after night thousands were taken off unharmed and the Turks appeared to suspect nothing.

As numbers decreased those remaining worked hard to maintain the deception, moving from gun post to gun post to keep up a steady fire and making very obvious displays of sorting out stores on the beaches. During the last two days, the skeleton force outnumbered by at least ten to one set up self-firing mechanisms at front lines, with explosive material whose detonators were timed to activate while they were climbing into the boats.

From way out to sea the last troops to leave stood with tears on their cheeks as they heard the stutter of rifle fire and saw the flash of explosions from positions occupied only by the ghosts of the legion of dead haunting the cliffs.

CHAPTER ELEVEN

Tim arrived at Victoria Station on the afternoon leave train from France at the end of April 1916. He had not been home during the fifteen months since discovering that his parents had engineered his safe posting to GHQ. He spent his periods of leave in charming villages well away from his fellows, where the girls were happy to compensate an English officer for all he had suffered in the trenches. Tim lied without compunction because he *would* have suffered if he had been allowed to. It was no fault of his that his uniform was immaculate and his revolver had never been fired. Girls showed little interest in guns, and he was more usually *out* of his uniform when he was with them, so his role as the valiant warrior was never questioned.

More recently Tim had spent some delightful weekends at the country home of one of his French colleagues whose sister's flirtatious eye had roamed in the direction of the blond, handsome friend on a visit last Christmas. Yvette was happily uninhibited by the conventions of her class and had given herself freely to the insatiable Tim on his first visit. From then on he had concentrated on the shapely brunette with aristocratic features but the morals of a whore. Erotic sessions with Yvette eased Tim's professional frustration, resentment and impotency.

Sexual lust partially bolstered his masculine pride but he could not banish his yearning for the chance to prove himself in battle. He had come home for this seven-day leave because it was apparent Yvette's roving eye had finally come to rest, and her family was expecting him to make an honest woman of her before long. The overriding reason for his arrival in London was of greater moment than the evasion of matrimony, however.

He walked from the platform feeling unexpected envy of soldiers being hugged and kissed by ecstatic wives, sweethearts or mothers. Even if he had written of his arrival there would be no one to greet him in that fashion. As he pushed his way between the reunited couples he knew a sudden longing for a girl to be there searching the faces for *his*, which was so dear to her. A girl who truly loved him; someone who held his happiness in her hands. It was not an image he had before considered, yet it was one he could not shake off as he broke free of the excited press of people and hailed a cab.

London looked unusually appealing to Tim as he gazed from the windows at St James's Park where blossom trees provided umbrellas of colour and scattered petals like bridal confetti on the paths beside the lake. Flowers rioted in the beds and wildfowl preened and splashed in the spring sunshine. The promenaders were all pairs arm in arm, he noticed with a fresh pang. A day for lovers. No, a day for people *in love*. He had been the lover of countless women, yet had never walked with any one of them beneath a canopy of fragrant blossoms. All at once he wanted to do just that.

The cab pulled up outside the family's London house now rather grandly named Ashleigh Court, but Tim was reluctant to get out. The familiar rooms were full of wounded heroes. Some of them would be nineteen year olds with a higher rank than his. Promotion was swift in the trenches. Although he was now a full lieutenant Tim knew he might well be an acting major by now if he had stayed with his battalion. He had just had his twenty-seventh birthday and must be one of the oldest subalterns in uniform.

'This is it, sir,' said the cabbie pointedly.

'Right . . . thank you.' Tim stepped out to the pavement and put his hand in his pocket. 'What's the reckoning?'

'That's all right, sir. Come in on the leave train, didn't yer? I never charges fer the first trip back in Blighty.' He gave a cheerful grin. 'When you go out on the town wiv a young lady that'll be different . . . and I never looks at what's goin' on in the back. I was young meself. 'Ave a good time, sir, and God bless yer.'

When Tim entered to find the smell of antiseptic and the sight of a number of wheelchairs in the hall, his mouth was set and his eyes were bleak. The cabbie had asked God to bless someone who had been sitting behind a desk translating documents, while thousands had died in their efforts to prevent the Germans from overrunning the area where he worked in comfort and safety. The sight of those wheelchairs exacerbated his bitterness. His mother was playing ministering angel to other women's broken sons while ensuring that her own remained whole. She was a bigger fraud than he.

He asked a passing redhead dressed in a sugared-almond outfit where he would find Mrs Nicolardi. Her lustrous green eyes signalled that she would like nothing better than to get him on a bed and give him a blanket bath, but she merely said that Lady Nicolardi was with Mrs Ashleigh in the third floor office.

'*Lady* Nicolardi?' he repeated hollowly.

'Yes, sir. Sir Laurence was knighted last month. We were all so proud. The patients gave them a lovely party.' Her face glowed. 'It was kept secret. We brought the bubbly in beneath our cloaks, and one of the boys telephoned Fortnum's to make up hampers of food which we smuggled in with the laundry baskets. They were both touched, although Lady Nicolardi scolded the boys for spending their money so extravagantly. She's marvellous with them and they all adore her.' When Tim walked off without comment, the nurse called out, 'Do you have an appointment?'

'I don't need one, I'm her son,' he mumbled feeling even more bitter. Someone could surely have told him. He had not answered his mother's letters, admittedly, but *someone* should have let him know she had been elevated to the peerage through Laurence so that he was not given the news by a little pseudo-nurse he could have for breakfast every day of the week and still feel hungry. Why had they not known at GHQ? Sir Reginald was in cahoots with Laurence over his appointment there, so he would surely be aware of the honour. *Of course* he would be! Was it general knowledge among the staff? Did they all believe he was being modest in not speaking of it? Was *that* why Yvette's family were hinting at a betrothal? His mother and Laurence had once more made a fool of him.

He walked without knocking into the room marked as an office. Margaret and Kitty were holding a discussion with a grey-haired woman in a severe dark-blue uniform. They all looked startled to see him. Then Margaret got to her feet with an expression of joy.

'*Tim*! Why didn't you let us know you were coming, you wicked boy?' She came forward with a flurry of mauve silk and floating chiffon to take his hands. 'Darling, it's lovely to see you. Words can't express how I feel,' she added, tears shimmering her eyes.

He kissed her cheek in no more than dutiful fashion. 'Hello, Mother. Aunt Kitty.'

Margaret dragged him forward. 'Matron, this is the son you've heard me mention almost daily.'

Matron's smile warmed her features miraculously as she greeted him, then she suggested the meeting be continued later. As the woman left the room Kitty expressed her delight at seeing Tim and declared that she would have tea brought to the sitting-room for them all. At the door she said, 'Come along when you're ready. I'll leave the toast until then.'

Tim said, 'We'll come now. I'm hungry.'

'Just a moment.' Margaret put her hand on his arm. 'I think we have a few things to say before tea, my dear.'

The door closed behind Kitty leaving Tim alone with the mother he had parted from in a mood of hostility. He continued in that vein. 'Do I now address you as m'lady?'

She regarded him with regained poise. 'I'm surprised you are here to address me as anything. You've been very cruel, Tim. Don't you realize everyone is aware that you would have been granted long leave at some time during the past fifteen months?'

'That bothers you – what other people think?' He moved further from her. 'You don't mention your own cruelty in denying me what I dearly want.'

'You *want* to die, throw away your future in a senseless attempt to become a posthumous hero?'

'You said all that before, trying to justify your actions. It didn't.'

'Is that why you refused to reply to my letters?'

'I suppose so.'

'Did you read them?'

He declined to answer. He had scanned each one in search of atonement, some hint that she and his step-father acknowledged their fault. There had been none. He returned to the prime issue.

'I admit I had colourful ideas of heroism when war was first declared, following in Uncle Vorne's footsteps. Of course I don't *want* to die – no single man out there at the Front does – and I certainly would never do anything crass in order to be dubbed a hero. Just getting through the hell of winter in the trenches creates them, anyway. All I needed was to be allowed to follow my profession as an infantry officer. If I had had ambitions to be a linguist, translator and interrogator I wouldn't have joined the West Wilts. You've robbed me of the chance to show that I'm a real man.'

Margaret's eyebrows rose slightly. 'I always understood you to do that in a direction other than soldiering.'

Tim's cheeks grew hot to hear such words from his mother, a woman of great refinement and taste. From another male they would have been something of a compliment. She made his sexual activity sound like a tawdry substitute for military action. He hit out. 'As you so clearly disapprove of your first husband's son I'll find a hotel for the rest of my leave. I really only came here to tell you you've lost the game. With the advent of Spring several new offensives will be launched, so the regiment needs every officer it can get. I've finally worn down Sir Reginald's resistance. He's released me. At the end of my leave I'm to join the survivors of my old battalion who have spent the winter near Ypres.'

Turning pale, Margaret sat very abruptly on a nearby chair, gazing at him in stricken manner. 'Please stay with us until you have to go back. I've only borne your treatment of me because I knew you were safe and that, one day, we would forgive and forget. Once your leave is over I'll no longer have that comfort. Do you really have no notion how much I love you; why I have been obliged to hide it from you? Please don't walk out on me.'

Tim perched on the arm of a chair, saying awkwardly, 'I thought there were no spare rooms here, that's all.'

'Laurence has been given an apartment in Chelsea. We live there.' She swept on, needing to say what she had bottled up for a long time. 'You've always resented being Philip's child, seeing your brothers as the children of love. *So were you.* Before your father turned to missionary work he and I were deeply happy. Both you and Kate resulted from that happiness. I have watched you grow sturdy and handsome with nothing in you of Philip Daulton. You are all Ashleigh. I have seen you excel in everything you do, and I've been filled with pride when others speak of your charming manners and delightful personality.' She reached for his hand. 'Darling, there is something very special between mothers and their firstborn. I *pray* you'll be spared so that one day your wife will experience it and you'll understand, at last. Please give me these seven days, I beg you.'

No son would be proof against such a declaration, certainly not one in the mood Tim was in. He put his arms around his mother and promised her the week she asked for.

It was a charity function: an auction to raise funds for the new experimental technique for reconstructing badly damaged faces. So many of those wounded in this way condemned themselves to solitude because of hideous scars, but the surgeons were working miracles in their efforts to reconstruct jaws and other vital facial bones. It all cost a great deal of money which the British Government did not have. Before the main business of the day, lunch was served to the VIP guests. The Ashleigh party was large. Vere had come up from Knightshill, where he was spending a great deal of time since Charlotte and John had departed for America on their annual visit to the family property in Texas. Although he was in doubtful health John had insisted on making the journey, claiming the change of climate and scene would do him good. Laurence was one of a number of diplomats and parliamentarians whose presence added distinction to the event, and the family were joined by Gilbert Dessinger, a soprano named Madeleine Metcalfe, the one-armed Colonel Dunwoody, late of the West Wiltshire Regiment, Major Edward Pickering – a friend of Vere's from the South African war – and his wife who was a renowned equestrienne, and the owner of an exclusive art gallery accompanied by the woman known to be his patroness, who had two unconventional daughters each fathered by a different young aspiring artist. Mrs Cullinan was exceedingly wealthy and influential so London society chose to ignore her bohemian private life. Her daughters, one blonde and one redhead, fell in on each side of Tim on his arrival and kept him under feminine close arrest from then on.

For once Tim did not respond to their challenge. The mood induced at Victoria Station was still on him. Maybe the knowledge that, within five more days, he would finally be risking his life emphasized the feeling of having missed out on those things he had subconsciously set aside for when he had finished with the wildness of youth. All at once he was aware that he might never reach that time; that it might be too late. Betsy and Maria Cullinan were the kind of ripe plums he had always encouraged to fall in his lap, but today he found them too artificial and too voluble. Madeleine Metcalfe cast regular dramatic, burning glances across the table at him, but even her generous bosom and pouting lips failed to excite his interest.

He had been in London less than forty-eight hours. In that time he had been conducted around the wards of Ashleigh Court by his mother who, despite her hints at the secret work her son had been engaged in, had failed to banish Tim's certainty that the patients all knew he had never seen a trench, much less lived in one. Tim had also learned that his sister Kate had been rescued when the ship she was serving on had been sunk off the Gallipoli Peninsula, and that she was now on the staff of a military hospital in Salonika. Worst of all was the news that Val had taken part in the Gallipoli landings and had appeared wounded, five months later, in Kate's ward in an Alexandria hospital. She had written of their meeting and of the officer who said Val had been nominated for a medal.

There could be no greater salt in Tim's wound than details of *that* man's battle exploits. How could a coarse drunkard distinguish himself to the extent of earning a medal? No one knew where he was now. Tim prayed Val would not be in Ypres when he got there next week. Surely fate would not be *that* unkind to him.

The lunch went on too long for Tim. He tried to be his usual self, but his heart was not in it. It was a relief when they all went through to the great salon where the auction would be conducted. All the items had been donated by benefactors – Vere had given a set of his sketches from the South African *veld*, and a pair of candelabra from Knightshill – and these donors were also expected to buy it all back by the end of the afternoon.

Still flanked by his female guardians, Tim entered the room to find himself looking into a face he knew. He had returned to GHQ at the beginning of January last year with that face clear in his mind, yet he had forgotten it in the ensuing months. There had been so many others smiling with invitation, so many pairs of bright eyes, so many lips he could bruise. Seeing again the intelligent brown eyes, the serenity of her features, the neat coil of dark hair and the tiny sapphire earrings she had worn on that other occasion, Tim recalled an out-of-town restaurant on a snowy evening and two teashop waitresses who had made him feel ashamed in front of her.

Amy Sturt looked at him and at the girls clutching his arms, her lips twitched with disparagement. 'Mr Ashleigh, I trust you are not to be one of the items on offer here.'

The crowd came between them and Tim was dragged forward by the giggling sisters to where the other members of their group were being ushered to reserved seats. Anger rushed through him. How *dared* she say that? The day had been bad enough before their encounter. How *dared* she suggest he could be bid for like a male slave?

The auction began. It followed the usual pattern of large amounts being offered for items worth only half the sum by people who could afford to be generous. One or two genuinely valuable antiques were the objects of calculated battles between collectors, which spiced up the proceedings, but Tim only grew interested when bidding began for an ornate lamp and the aristocrat acting as an auctioneer took bids he attributed to The Regency Restaurant. Twisting in his seat, Tim spotted Amy Sturt four rows back on the other side of the room. She was with a middle-aged man of heavy build who was signalling the bids, but she was instructing him. Tim resented the fact that she did not look or act in the least out of place among the famous and wealthy. The lamp became hers within a very short time, to her obvious delight.

When a further glance in that direction during the next period of bidding encountered an empty seat where she had been, Tim was overtaken by impulse and went in search of her before he understood why. She was nowhere in view, so he strode across to the uniformed doorman.

'Have you seen a young woman in a black and white costume, and a dark-green hat with a feathery thing on it?'

The man smiled. 'That would be Mrs Sturt, sir. She left a few minutes ago.'

Tim thrust open the heavy door to reach the top of the steps. He spotted her across the street, walking briskly towards St James's Park, so he ran down to the pavement before darting between traffic to gain the opposite side of The Mall. Impulse still ruled him as he vaulted the low railing and caught up with his quarry after a swift dash across grass.

Amy was astonished by his sudden breathless appearance. She stopped, gazing at him as if he had sprung from beneath the ground like a khaki-clad genie. He took advantage of her silence. 'You were extremely rude to me back there.'

She had the grace to blush. 'It was . . . I spoke before I thought. I apologize.'

'Thank you. And now you've said you're sorry, you can atone by having tea with me,' he said.

The blush faded quickly. 'Don't be absurd! I've admitted I was a little harsh on you, but my comment wouldn't have sprung to mind if you didn't behave this way. The Cullinan sisters clearly regard you as theirs for the day. Shouldn't you fulfil their expectations?'

'Damn *their* expectations. I'm more interested in my own, and I want you to have tea with me.'

She turned away. 'I think you should rejoin your family and friends.'

Tim fell in beside her. 'They're Mother's friends, not mine.'

'When you came to the Regency you told me you were with your *friend's* friends. Haven't you any of your own?'

'It's difficult to make them when people treat me as you're doing. It's quite a change in tactics. You were extremely nice to me at Epsom Station – even wrote me a good luck note.'

'You were going to war. We all gave out good luck notes.' She halted and faced him frankly. 'Please go away. People are starting to stare.'

'I'm not surprised. You're worth staring at. That's why your restaurant's full every night.' A look of disdain crossed her face as she walked on again, but Tim never gave up easily and accompanied her. 'Do you still pull that trick of asking a pianist to step in at short notice?'

People *were* very interested in an attractive young couple apparently at odds with each other, so she answered his question in conversational tones. 'You'd know if you had ever come back.'

'I couldn't. Unhappy circumstances prevented me from doing what I most wanted.'

She glanced up swiftly and there was a softer note in her voice. 'You've been in hospital. A long time?'

''Fraid so,' he said with sufficient pathos to melt the coldest of hearts. 'That's why I so badly want you to have tea with me.'

Her steps faltered until she stopped beneath a flowering tree beside the lake. 'I'm sorry, I have to arrange a special celebration for twenty-six tonight. That's why I left my floor manager to pick up the lamp I bought.'

'Tomorrow, then? The Savoy at four.' He was at his most persuasive. 'Please don't turn me down a second time.'

After visible hesitation she nodded. 'I know somewhere less ostentatious than the Savoy. Collect me from the restaurant at three, and I'll take you there. It'll be quiet and peaceful, and I don't think the journey will tire you too much. You've been convalescing at Ashleigh Court, I suppose.'

Perhaps it was the yearning mood he had been in, or maybe it was the prospect of what awaited him when he returned, but as he looked at this girl with a scattering of pink petals on her hat and across the shoulders of her jacket he wanted something other than the usual shallow flirtations.

'I lied,' he confessed quietly. 'I was never in hospital. The reason I haven't been back to The Regency is because my parents used their connections to trap me in a posting well behind the lines. I couldn't forgive them, so I stayed in France.' As Amy seemed uncertain how to deal with this piece of unexpected frankness, Tim continued. 'On that night we dined at your place I'd just discovered what they'd done. I walked out on them and met an old acquaintance quite by chance. He was looking for someone to help him out with the girls, that's all.'

After a moment she said, 'So you willingly "helped out" with the girls. That's your forte, isn't it?'

He drew in his breath slowly. 'I suppose so.'

'Your reputation is well known in Dunstan St Mary.'

'Is it?'

'You lived up to it that day at the station . . . and at Epsom.'

It was undeniable. He had seen her as easy prey. He looked beyond her to the glassy water overhung by trailing willow fronds, where drakes were courting ducks with every trick they knew. It was spring and life was there to be enjoyed before youth ran out. He met her eyes once more. 'I didn't *ask* the Cullinan girls to hang on to me like that.'

'You wouldn't have to. I'm sure they're also well aware of your reputation.'

'They have reputations of their own, believe me.' He sighed with resignation. 'I'm really not *wicked*, you know.'

'I didn't say you were.'

'What *did* you say?'

She was nonplussed by his demand. 'I . . . I'm not sure. I must go.'

Tim closed in to cut off her retreat. 'We're still having tea together tomorrow, aren't we? In spite of my reputation.'

A faint suggestion of a smile touched her lips. 'It won't be enhanced by a very proper tea with a widow, beside the river.'

'Let me worry about that.'

'Goodbye until tomorrow, Mr Ashleigh.'

She offered her hand which he thought far too formal now they were getting on so well. He wrapped his palm around it in a manner more intimate than shaking hands, and murmured, 'Please call me Tim.'

Amy broke contact. 'Shouldn't it be *Bobby*?'

As she walked off briskly, Tim's smile faded. She was still refusing to take him seriously.

Amy was waiting for him dressed in a navy-blue costume with spotted silk on the collar and on the deep swathed waistband. She looked classically striking, in direct contrast to the vivid creatures he normally favoured. For a brief moment he thought of them as bidders at the auction of his virility, then pushed aside the ridiculous metaphor and concentrated on his companion. Her hat sported a feather so long it kept brushing Tim's face until he said they must change places before he was tickled to death. They laughed about it, and Amy spoke about changes in fashion introduced by the more active roles women were now undertaking.

'I think we shall never return to the frills, flounces and restrictions of Edwardian fashion. Women who have always had servants to do everything for them are now discovering they can quite easily manage the heaviest of work, and need clothes they can *move* in. It's amazing how even the most aristocratic creatures are turning their hands to anything asked of them. It's a splendid development.'

'You've worked all your life?' Tim asked.

'Only in the most genteel way.' She wrinkled her brow. 'I

wish I had the courage to emulate your sister. So many girls have volunteered to be Nursing Aids. I admire them so much.'

'But you have the restaurant to run.'

'I could put it in the hands of an elderly manager. Instead, I do what little I can to provide the brighter side of life in the midst of so much pain and sadness.'

Tim put his hand on hers lying on her knee. 'That's what *I* try to do.'

Amy immediately brushed his hand aside. 'There's a subtle difference. You were doing it long before the war began.'

With their fragile rapport temporarily suspended they arrived at the Waterfowl. The tea pavilion was a far cry from the Savoy, but the riverside setting was scenic and more intimate than the hotel frequented by the upper set. It appeared to be a favourite rendezvous of military officers, most of whom appeared to know Amy. As they were shown to a table by a window alcove, the men called greetings and their girlfriends waved. Amy Sturt was a minor celebrity, it seemed.

No sooner were they seated than a middle-aged man bustled up with a broad smile, and embarked on an effusive conversation during which Tim gathered that he was a former employee of Amy's father when the Regency had been a teashop, and that Amy had been invited to be his guest whenever she could get away.

'I'm delighted that you agreed to come at last, Mrs Sturt. I reserved this table for you after your message last night. As you can see, business is booming and I have you to thank for it.'

Amy smiled. 'All I've done is to mention the Waterfowl as a delightful place to take tea. I'm pleased my recommendation has been taken up by so many, Robert.'

Tim was introduced, but the proprieter was intent on proving to Amy his culinary skill by boasting of a new cake he had created, the recipe for which he claimed the pastry chef at the Dorchester would steal or kill. It was all too histrionic for Tim who began to grow bored. He was not taking Amy to tea, *she* was taking *him* and it was an outing she had been waiting for an excuse to make. So much for the intimate tête-à-tête he had wanted and thought he had won from her by his honesty.

Tim was not asked for their order. Tea, sandwiches, scones and a pot of honey were brought to the table by a waitress who gazed at him with the brand of admiration he had expected Amy would now be showing. Even with the tea before them they were not left in peace to enjoy it. As other customers finished and prepared to depart they approached to chat with the popular hostess of the fashionable Regency Restaurant. Amy identified them all without being prompted, but addressed each as *Captain* This or *Mr* That – no first names. It made her determined formality towards Tim more acceptable, although the progress he had hoped to make with her seemed less likely as time passed.

When Robert brought to the table a covered plate and lifted the lid with an excited flourish, Tim played second fiddle to a cake for the first time in his life. While Amy and her companion enthused over a circular confection topped with thin slices of lemon, Tim gazed out of the window. Unsure what he had really expected of this meeting, he only knew he was not getting it. Out on the river, ducks and drakes were doing what their counterparts had done in St James's Park. The drakes were having more success than he. Couples were strolling arm in arm along the towpath, absorbed in each other. *He* could not even outshine a gâteau today.

A hand fell on his arm. 'You're very quiet.'

He looked round to find Robert had gone and Amy was smiling at him. 'I'm overawed by that cake,' he said acidly.

'Have a slice. Perhaps when you sink your teeth into it you'll feel better.'

'I doubt it.'

She put down the cake slice and studied him shrewdly. 'I'm not sure why you came after me yesterday when you appeared to be perfectly happy in a large, cultured group, but I agreed to do this because I thought you were still upset with your parents.'

'Not because Mr Waterfowl has been pestering you to visit, and I was a convenient escort?'

'I thought you'd enjoy it here.'

'I would if we could be left alone for longer than five minutes.' He moved his hand along the tablecloth until his fingertips were touching hers. 'I'm going into action when I go back. They're building up numbers for a big new offensive. I wanted a nice memory to take back with me.'

It was a moment or two before she asked. 'Are you lying to get my sympathy?'

'Good God, no!'

'You lied about being in hospital. You admitted it.'

'So that's what becomes of being truthful about lying,' he said in disgust. 'You now don't believe *anything* I say.'

'It's better than lying about being truthful.'

'I've done that before now.'

'That's an unwise admission.'

'Give a dog a bad name,' he countered morosely.

'The dog needn't necessarily live up to it.'

'He might as well, if it's more fun.'

There was silence between them for a while, then Amy said, 'I have to eat a slice of this before we leave, I'm afraid. Robert's anxious for my verdict. Can you bear to wait or would you prefer to go on home?'

'I'll wait. I'm not a complete outsider.'

'Perhaps you'd like a short walk beside the river. I don't have to be at the Regency until six and the sun's still out.'

'It'll have gone in if you don't soon start on that cake,' he pointed out.

She smiled at that. '*Do* have some yourself.'

'No, thanks. Robert wouldn't like my verdict.'

'It's very good,' she said with her mouth full.

'It would be!' He watched a drake happily copulating with any willing duck and told himself he could now be doing much the same with both Cullinan sisters if they had had their way. Why had he not taken up their invitation? His gaze wandered to a captain of a rifle regiment standing with a girl in a pale-blue coat and hat. They were unaware of anything but each other as they exchanged shy secrets. Neither was older than nineteen – mere children caught up in the urgency of life before they parted at Victoria Station in a day or two. They had found something he had never experienced. Was it too late for him?

Amy raved about the cake as Robert handed Tim his cap, gloves and cane, refusing to let him pay for their tea, then they stepped outside into a springtime atmosphere only found beside a river. The air was full of the sounds of quacking, chirping, splashing, children's laughter and dogs' barks. The world and his wife appeared to be enjoying the early evening sunshine along the towpath.

'Oh lord, if we go that way we'll run into a few hundred more of your admirers,' Tim said in dismay.

'There weren't *hundreds*, Mr Ashleigh,' she chided lightly, 'and it's my dinners they admire.'

'Don't you believe it. If I had to choose between you and a dinner, it wouldn't be the dinner.'

She set off along the crowded towpath as if he had not spoken. A spark of anger flared as Tim followed her in half-hearted fashion. She was not allowing him to control any part of this meeting. He was not one of her restaurant employees to jump to her command and the sooner he proved it the sooner she would realize who she was dealing with. How dared she ask if he was lying about going into action? How dared she ignore him in order to fuss over a *cake*? She was making a fool of him, as she had at Dunstan Station. He would put an end to her game.

Catching up with her in three strides, he grabbed her elbow and began to march her up the gentle grassy slope leading to some trees. 'I said I didn't want to go along the path,' he told her firmly. 'I invited you to have tea with me so it's time you paid me some attention. The only place where there's any hope of getting you all alone is up here.'

Amy tugged her arm free and faced him, tight lipped. 'I was prepared to walk with you, but only along the footpath where there were people around. I should have guessed what you had in mind.'

She was away down the slope, but fury sent Tim after her to bring her to a halt with a fierce grip around her wrist. 'What do you take me for? No matter what you've heard about my reputation at your uncle's inn, I can recognize icy purity when I see it. I had no intention of luring you to fate worse than death, believe me,' he said. 'I've no idea why you're so afraid of me – I'm not the blackest sheep in my family, let me tell you – but I'll leave you to find someone you trust to escort you home. There are any number of men along that path who'd jump at the chance to show you what sporting fellows they are.' He touched the peak of his cap with his cane and strode away without a backward glance.

It was almost nine when Tim walked into the Regency Restaurant that evening after fighting a battle with himself, and lying to his mother and Laurence who wanted him to accompany them for dinner with diplomats and their wives. Every table was occupied. There was much laughter and conversation between girls in silk or lace, and men who drove fear and exhaustion away with determined high spirits. Tim was surprised to find changes. The décor which had been interesting before was now sumptuous, in keeping with Regency fashion. The ornaments and lamps in niches were genuine antiques rather than copies, and the curtains of rich green and cream stripes were embellished with heavy tassels. The dining-chairs were now upholstered with green velvet and the dais was edged with heavy velvet drapes looped and tasselled like theatre curtains. Amy Sturt must be doing very well if she could afford these improvements.

Tim spotted her speaking to a foursome in a far corner and willed her to look his way. A waitress drew Amy's attention to a single man waiting in the reception area, and she gazed in disbelief for a moment or two before speaking to the girl in an aside. Tim was treated to a pink-cheeked smile as the waitress told him with visible regret that they were unable to offer him a table tonight. 'It's best to make a reservation in advance, sir,' she told him. 'I could ask Mrs Sturt to do that if you like.'

'Ask Mrs Sturt to find me a table for tonight,' he said persuasively. 'I'm on my own, very hungry and my leave runs out in a day or two. She'll surely not be cruel enough to turn me away.'

It worked like magic, restoring his faith in himself. Amy crossed between the tables, resisting invitations to stop and chat with the uniformed diners. She looked pale and determined, but Tim was set on controlling this situation. She had run circles around him at the Waterfowl and would not be allowed to repeat her performance tonight.

'There's no room,' she said immediately. 'You can see I have no spare table.'

'Put up an extra one. I'm alone.'

'Don't be difficult, Mr Ashleigh.'

'There's a space over in that corner by the dais, and I can't believe you haven't a very small table somewhere on the premises.'

'I'm extremely busy.'

'I'll wait until you have time to organize it.'

'It's out of the question.'

'Perhaps you'll send over some mulled wine while I wait.'

'Please leave.' It was not a command, more a desperate request.

He stood his ground. 'I gave up a dinner invitation with a well known ambassador so that I could come here. You wouldn't want me to go hungry, would you? *I* didn't have a slice of Mr Waterfowl's cake to sustain me.'

Holding on to her poise she said, 'If you've come to apologize, I'll take it as said. Goodnight, Mr Ashleigh.'

'I was expecting *you* to apologize. You treated me very badly this afternoon. I'll accept dinner instead of humble pie from you.'

She turned with every intention of walking away, so he called softly, 'I mean to spend the evening here.' When she spun round to confront him, he added, 'Unless you ask some of those sporting fellows you appear to regard very highly to throw me out, it won't do your reputation any good to have a fracas on the premises. And it'll get known that you ejected a British officer who was causing no trouble whatever, on the eve of his return to France. Is that less of a risk than letting me stay?'

The waitress returned with mulled wine while a table was put up then set with white linen and cutlery. The same girl conducted him to it and took his order. Amy paid no further attention to him, but Tim knew she was aware of his presence as she moved about her restaurant. Her colour was higher than usual. She looked particularly attractive in a dark-green silk dress whose skirt was panelled with subtle jet beading. She had come a long way from her humble origins, much the way Kitty had done.

Dining alone was an unique experience for Tim. He was invited to join them by couples at tables around him, but he declined saying that he was Mrs Sturt's special guest and she would soon be free to sit with him. When the female trio appeared on the dais a ripple of expectation ran through the room and several men made a play at hiding beneath the tables. Laughter broke out as a dark-haired subaltern rose, put one foot on his chair and began to warble in falsetto tones *Oh, you beautiful doll* before one of his colleagues pulled away the chair and he fell. Another produced a comb and paper which was snatched away after a few bars of an unidentifiable tune. A captain stood up and blew a hunting horn which caused further merriment, and Tim then understood why every army officer on leave appeared to know Amy Sturt. She was certainly providing the brighter side of life in the midst of pain and sadness.

When she stepped on to the dais and held up her hands for silence, her audience complied immediately. Her face was glowing with life as she began to speak. 'Ladies and Gentlemen, I have to announce the sad news that our pianist is indisposed so . . .' The remainder of her words were drowned by a great roar of laughter and thunderous applause augmented by stamping feet. This was the highlight of the evening, the reason why the Regency was the first choice for officers on leave. Tonight, even Amy was visibly thrilled when two blond lieutenants, identical twins, mounted the little platform. There was rapt silence as they played several piano pieces for four hands.

They were followed by a portly major who sang two ballads accompanied by the string trio. Then a young woman left her table to play a Chopin étude. Finally, an RFC captain took over the piano stool and joined the three women to entertain with all the popular songs of the day, which everyone sang. Everyone save Tim. He was busily watching Amy sitting in the chair vacated by the volunteer pianist. She was a rather extraordinary woman, he realized. Small wonder she had little time for him. He had done nothing to suggest he was other than the practised womanizer she believed him to be. He remained the only silent person in that room as he cast around for a case for his defence and found there was none.

Tim lingered while everyone else departed. Amy had adopted the practice of standing at the door to bid her customers goodnight. She added a good luck message to all those on their last night of leave, and Tim was struck by her dignity as well as the near-reverent manner of the men. Had she found his own behaviour this afternoon petulant and more suited to the type of women he normally escorted? He should not have come tonight. He still did not understand why he had; did not understand why he had run after her at the auction. Was he possessed by the desire to make her capitulate and accept that she was as susceptible as other women? If so, that desire was certain to be thwarted. Was he merely tired of lust which briefly satisfied but had no lasting value? Was he still piqued by her comment about his being an item for auction?

Gazing moodily at the last diners beside their hostess, Tim

experienced once more that curious ache brought on by the loving embraces at Victoria. In three more days those same women would be in tears as the train pulled out taking their menfolk back, perhaps never to return. Who would cry for Tim Ashleigh? He would find a seat in a carriage and read a newspaper while all around him others were expressing the kind of devotion he had never known – had never needed. As he got to his feet at that small table set for one he experienced a terrible sensation of loneliness.

They met halfway to the door and then only because Tim weaved between tables to ensure that they did. 'You were leaving your post before all your guests had gone,' he said quietly.

'I have a great deal to do.' She made to pass, but he sidestepped to prevent her.

'I have two more days in England. I'd like to make a reservation for tomorrow evening and the one after that.'

'We're fully booked.'

'I'll have the same table. That can't be booked because you set it up just for me.'

She studied him with exasperation. 'Why are you determined to pester me? Sitting here alone on the last two evenings of your leave, refusing to join in with the others, will do you no good at all. If you truly *are* going into action . . .'

'I am,' he confirmed swiftly. 'You still think I was lying about that?'

'I don't know what to think where you're concerned,' she said, half her attention on her waitress hovering near the door to the kitchens. 'There are any number of girls in London who would be happy to entertain you until you return to France.'

'I know that,' he agreed, 'but I want to come here instead. Please reserve that table for me. I promise to behave myself.'

'Very well, I'll leave it where it is. If you turn up you may use it.'

'You don't believe I'll come, do you?'

She looked up at him frankly. 'You're a man of impulse. Tomorrow, it will be a fresh one. I have to attend to my employees now.'

He sidestepped once more to keep her there a moment longer. 'I was wrong about the apologies for this afternoon. I *was* the one at fault. It was unforgiveable to leave you as I did. I hope you found a more worthy escort.'

She moved a chair to get past him. 'I'm a widow and a businesswoman, Mr Ashleigh, perfectly capable of getting from A to B without an escort. Goodnight.'

Tim left the Regency the only man that night who was not sent off with a friendly smile from his hostess. He did not get one the next evening, either. Amy looked suprised when he arrived but merely conducted him to the single table then sent the waitress to take his order and serve him. The tremendous atmosphere of camaraderie and laughter was created once more, increasing Tim's alien sense of loneliness. The thought of banishing it in the bed of a nameless blonde or brunette who called him Bobby was repugnant to him. In fact, he had no idea how to shake it off. He was denied the opportunity of speaking to Amy because the man who had been with her at the auction commandeered her as the final group of diners departed, and all Tim got was an impersonal 'goodnight' when the pair crossed the far side of the room as he collected his cap from the vestibule.

On the following day, the last of Tim's short leave, Ashleigh Court was invaded by the youngest generation of the family on their spring vacation. His half-brothers, Jonathan and Richard, arrived in the early afternoon along with Charlotte's two sons. All four could speak of nothing but the war and how they hoped it would last long enough for them to participate. It seemed unlikely. Jonathan, the eldest at fifteen, still had three years to go before he could enlist. Most of their schoolfellows had older brothers, or even fathers, at the Front, and sisters who were contributing to the war effort even if it was simply rolling bandages or knitting comforters for the troops. They were naturally caught up in a notion of glory that bore little resemblence to what was apparently happening in all areas of the conflict.

As Tim listened to the boys' enthusiasm, he remembered himself saying much the same things at Knightshill on the day of Franz Ferdinand's assassination. Had he then sounded as immature as these lads did now? He grew hot under the collar as he thought of his words spoken in the presence of Vere, who had known war in the Sudan and South Africa, and the cattle drover who had once been a Lancer officer decorated for bravery on the *veld*. That same man had apparently been decorated again for valour on Gallipoli. Tim grew even hotter with secret embarrassment and was subsequently quiet in response to the questions shot at him by these schoolboys concerning his posting to the Ypres salient. Luckily, Margaret put a stop to all the talk of war by entering the room at that point accompanied by the twins, who had been lunching with Gilbert Dessinger and his protégée, the soprano Madeleine Metcalfe.

Tim was taken aback by his female cousins. Holly and Victoria were considerably more developed than when he had last seen them. He could not prevent instinctive appreciation of their full breasts, tiny waists and neat ankles visible beneath hems they must have shortened whilst at school because Kitty would never have approved such daring in fifteen year olds. They were going to be beauties – were already more alluring than schoolgirls had a right to be – and their parents clearly had a duo of mischief on their hands. For once, the twins did not fuss over Tim; they were more concerned with the patients at Ashleigh Court. Wounded heroes, no matter what they looked like, were of greater interest to females than a multi-lingual subaltern who had been translating top secret orders.

Before the girls had been home thirty minutes, Tim sensed they would be packed off to Knightshill with Vere and the boys on the morrow, before they could create havoc amongst the pyjamaed warriors occupying the bedrooms of this home. Tim knew what his reaction would be if one of the girls sat on the edge of his bed to offer sympathy when he was feeling sorry for himself. The poor devils here would stand no chance. His cousins were fully aware of the power they wielded and clearly loved to use. He was concerned. They were safe under this roof, or with young inexperienced lads awed by feminine emancipation, but if they encountered men like himself they might very soon be in serious trouble. Males could play the field with impunity; it was very different the other way around.

Tim's concern soon changed direction when he realized he was expected to be present at a family dinner planned for his last night of leave. The unwelcome news was broken to him by Margaret, who was unaware she was doing just that. She clearly believed he had expected the arrangements, and gazed at him in disbelief when he said he had a prior engagement for the evening.

'You can't have, Tim. It's your *last night*.'

Guilt made him snap, 'You make it sound as if it's my

last night on earth. I'm going to France tomorrow, not to eternity.'

Laurence who had come home early from the Foreign Office said sharply, 'That's a particularly cruel thing to say to your mother.'

From the depths of his armchair Tim retaliated. 'I'm sorry, but no chap wants a sort of "last supper" when he's going back off leave.'

'That's a ridiculous notion,' his step-father reasoned. 'You haven't been home for fifteen months and it so happens that the evening before you go back the whole family save Charlotte, John and Simon are here. It's a rare occurrence which should be welcomed.'

'What about Val? Hasn't someone contacted *him* with an invitation.' It was said from the extent of Tim's conflict between a sense of duty and his personal desire to go to the Regency. 'Why is it no one expects *him* to fulfil family obligations? He's the heir, after all.'

'Val has his reasons for staying away,' said Laurence enigmatically. 'Is this prior engagement of yours of vital military importance?'

Tim got to his feet, stomach churning. 'I'm sure you know it isn't. The "vital military importance" won't apply until I get to Ypres. But the engagement is important to *me*.'

Laurence's dark eyes held a hint of hostility. 'I suppose it concerns a young woman.'

Although he was a shade taller than his step-father, Laurence's slender figure in the trappings of a diplomat, and the dignity which suited his elevation to knighthood, now made Tim feel like a tenant caught out by the lord of the manor. 'What it concerns is my own affair, sir,' he said stiffly.

'You have made it ours, by giving it as an excuse for shunning your family tonight.'

'I'm not *shunning* you,' cried Tim, knowing it was a fool who attempted to best an expert in presenting a case.

'Then can you tell us what you *are* doing?'

'You're hurting *me* unbearably,' said Margaret from the chaise-longue. 'You made me a promise on the day you arrived, Tim. I have accepted your absences from functions when I hoped you would be beside me, but any mother would expect her son to spend his la . . .' She broke off just in time, and amended her protest. 'I deserve to have you to myself tonight.'

'You wouldn't; you'd be sharing me with the whole family.'

Laurence resumed his strategy. 'You speak as if the question is settled. Until you offer us a sound reason for your unavoidable absence tonight, the issue is still open.'

Tim had his back to the wall, he knew. 'I made a promise to be elsewhere.'

'A promise which supercedes the one you made to your mother?'

'As it happens, yes.'

'Then it must have been made to someone who means a very great deal indeed to you. A young woman, as I thought?'

Tim declined to comment. Laurence was quite wrong. It was just that he *had* to occupy that table tonight after insisting on reserving it. He could imagine Amy's smug derision if he failed to turn up. She would think he was behaving true to character.

'Tim . . . *is* there a special young woman you want to see?' probed Margaret, rising and approaching him in the manner she used towards Ashleigh Court patients who needed extra sympathy. When he remained tight lipped she put her hand on his arm. 'Darling, ask her to join us. If she's fond of you, she'll understand that you want to share your last night with us all.'

Tim moved away from her. 'Mother, it's *not* my last night. I intend to live a lot longer yet.'

Laurence put his arm around his wife's shoulders in protective fashion. 'My dear, why don't you leave us to sort this out man to man?'

'Oh, for heaven's sake, this isn't a matter of international diplomacy,' cried Tim. 'All right, you win. I'll dine with the family.'

The breach in his relationship with his parents widened once more. Margaret put on a brave show in front of the others, particularly her two sons by Laurence, but it was plain she was distressed by the incident and by Tim's imminent departure. Laurence's attentiveness to her seemed like further censure of the son who put his licentious pleasure before his mother's feelings. Vere was as genuinely interested in Tim as always and Kitty did her utmost to lighten the atmosphere. The younger ones were so lively and noisy Tim wished them back at school. They had no conception of adult situations; no sensitivity to atmosphere. He could cheerfully have strangled them all that evening.

Throughout the meal he watched the clock wondering how soon Amy would notice that he had not come. Although he was physically in the chair next to his mother's, his mind was at the Regency throughout the evening seeing the happy faces, hearing the laughter, picturing Amy as she wandered between the tables chatting to men and women who were helped through a difficult time by her original method of providing brightness in the midst of pain and sadness. He imagined the moment when the trio appeared on the dais and jokers anticipated what would come next; that roar when Amy announced that her pianist was indisposed; the volunteers who were pushed forward by their friends or who went willingly in the spirit of comradeship evoked by the atmosphere in that restaurant. He yearned to be there, to be part of that unique experience, to see her smile and make that announcement which must surely now be known to officers of every corps and regiment serving in France.

All at once the yearning grew too great and he got to his feet. The meal was over and they were drinking coffee in the general sitting-room used by the owners for their private use. He looked down at Margaret. 'You will have to excuse me now, Mother. Goodnight everyone. I'll see you all in the morning unless you're still asleep at seven forty-five, in which case I'll see you on my next leave.'

Casting Laurence a look that dared him to say anything, Tim hastened to Chelsea and scrambled into his uniform cursing the rule that demanded he wear it in public. It took up precious time. Fifteen minutes passed before he captured a cab from which a rowdy group had just tumbled, and the journey appeared to take far longer than it had before. On arrival at the Regency he found everyone leaving in high spirits. He paid the driver and pushed forward against the tide.

'Left something behind,' he murmured several times to ease his way through. He could not define Amy's expression when she saw him, but she continued with her warm farewells until the last of her customers had gone and waitresses began clearing the glasses and coffee cups from the tables. The small one by the dais had been set for him. When he and Amy were face to face Tim's natural assurance deserted him. What on earth was he to do now?

'Hallo,' he said to fill the silence.

Amy was slow in responding and there was no smile from her. 'I'm afraid you're too late. We're closing.'

'I knew you would be when I set out.'

Again a momentary pause. 'Then why come?'

'So that you'd believe I meant what I said about dining here. Unfortunately, my entire family converged on Ashleigh Court today and my parents cut up rough when I said I had a prior engagement. They insisted that I join them for my last night. Oh hell, *I'm* saying it now!' He was ridiculously nervous, afraid he would say and do all the wrong things. 'I really couldn't get out of it. Do you understand that?'

'Of course. I told you sitting here alone wasn't a good idea. It doesn't matter that you were unable to take up your reservation.'

'It matters to me. I *wanted* to be here tonight.' Conscious that his voice carried across the empty room to the girls clearing the tables, he asked, 'Isn't there somewhere more private where we could talk?'

'I have a great deal to do, Mr Ashleigh.'

'I've come all the way out here to see you before I go back in the morning.' As she seemed about to dismiss him, he added, 'Just a few minutes. I'm sure you'd spare them for any of those other fellows you're so friendly with.'

Casting him an inscrutable look Amy led the way to a door in the vestible, flung it open and stood back for him to enter. The room was merely a tiny office, not at all what he had in mind. Its only advantage was that they would not be seen or overheard by the staff, even though Amy left the door standing open and remained between it and Tim. He did not miss the inference.

'I'm really not as black as I'm painted,' he said pointedly.

Amy was visibly disconcerted by the comment, but soon got to the heart of the matter. 'What did you wish to say?'

'I suppose there's no chance of a glass of mulled wine while we talk?'

'I'm afraid not.'

For the first time in his life Tim was alone with a very attractive woman and unsure what to do. Amy wore dark red tonight. The colour enhanced her dark, glossy hair swept back into a simple arrangement of curls, and it emphasized the soft blush in her cheeks. He realized she was also nervous beneath her outward calm and wondered why. She was always perfectly relaxed and natural with other men.

'I wanted to tell you that what you're doing is every bit as important as Kate's work,' he said for want of something more effective as an overture.

'That's rather dismissive of your sister, isn't it?'

He sighed. 'Look, I see what's being done at Ashleigh Court. It's very praiseworthy, but not as tricky and skilled as the work of a fully trained nurse. All the same, the women at our family house are doing what is within their power for convalescents. Kate does the same for patients who need much, much more help. The men who are still physically fit also need something; something to keep them going until they become a candidate for places like Ashleigh Court or clever women like my sister. I've watched what happens here each evening, and you're creating a kind of magic which somehow holds at bay the spectre of those other possibilities. I would much rather have been here tonight than with a family trying too hard not to mention what I'll be doing tomorrow.'

'It must be difficult for them, especially with your sister also on active service.'

'You know a lot about my family.'

'My uncle at the Stag's Head keeps me up to date, although why he thinks I'll be interested I can't imagine.'

Tim seized on that. 'You shouldn't believe below-stairs gossip and judge a person on it.'

'I don't, I go by the evidence of my own eyes.'

An impasse appeared to have been reached. Amy was certainly showing him no encouragement to stay, and he had no idea how to prolong the encounter now she had as good as reminded him of her mistrust. His impulsive gesture had reaped nothing but her further disparagement of his character. Hot on the heels of that thought came another impulse, and he acted on it before he could stop himself.

'Well, give a dog a bad name,' he murmured, and proceeded to live up to it. Amy's reaction was totally unexpected. Instead of struggling to free herself she was at first rigid in his arms, then slowly melted as his expert kiss softened her mouth until it parted beneath his. The warmth of her back came through the silk beneath his palms, and the perfume of her hair and skin spread through his senses to soothe him with exciting subtlety as he held her body close against his.

When he released her he was totally nonplussed to see that she was wide eyed and trembling, gazing at him as if in shock, making no attempt to retaliate with a smack around his face or a tirade of contempt. Suddenly, his years of experience told him an astonishing truth.

'By God,' he breathed, 'no one has ever done that to you before!' His brain was racing. She had lived with her father until his death, then had married an old man – a marriage of convenience. No one had ever made love to her; she was a stranger to sexual passion. Marriage had at first protected her from others' attentions, then demure widowhood. Amy Sturt was an untouched virgin who remained so by making every man a respectful friend and none her lover.

'So *that's* why you're so afraid of me!' Tim declared softly, drawing her back into his arms with a tenderness foreign to him. His lips touched her forehead, her eyelids, her cheeks, her throat, and finally her mouth in a far gentler kiss than the first. She still seemed mesmerized by what he was doing, and her body continued to tremble beneath his caressing hands as he came to terms with his discovery. When he reached the point where he knew he must leave, he held her away from him, absorbing the signs of awakening awareness in her dark eyes so that he would remember that moment until he came back to her.

'Keep that table for me, Mrs Amy Sturt. I'll be here again before you know it.' Edging away, holding her hands until the last moment, he added softly. 'I'm going to write lovely letters to you every week, whether you answer them or not. That's a promise.'

She was still gazing at him as if in shock when he turned the corner and left.

CHAPTER TWELVE

Tim's experience of trench life was delayed. On reaching Poperinghe, the rail centre for the entire Ypres complex, he was told by a transport officer that the West Wilts had been relieved from the front line two days ago and were presently resting in a hamlet named Roget's Wood. It was one of the rest centres used by the thousands of Allied troops who had occupied this large sector of Flanders since the beginning of the war, neither advancing nor retreating more than a mile or so in that time. Ypres itself was a ruin of no use to anyone, yet the Germans continued to shell it daily and made periodic attempts to take it from the British living in the ground beneath the charred remains of buildings. After eighteen months they had not succeeded.

As Tim waited for a vehicle going in his direction he experienced a revival of the old yearning for glory which had been slowly deadened at GHQ. All around him was first-hand evidence of war. Fleets of mud-covered ambulances moving to and from the railyard; staff cars and motorcycles, some with sidecars carrying senior officers and others driven by dispatch riders used to slithering over mud, ploughing through floods, dodging shell craters and bullets in order to deliver their vital communiqué; long columns of weary soldiers coming in from the horror to go on home leave, others marching away from the trains which had brought them back to face more. Over all these stirring images Tim heard the rumble of heavy guns like an approaching storm, and his pulse quickened. He was the great-grandson of General Sir Gilliard Ashleigh and the nephew of Vorne, the Hero of Khartoum. He had an obligation to these men, and those who had gone before them, and he would meet it in full. He could finally justify his right to assume the family name and be counted amongst their number. His mother did not understand his need to do that.

The journey to Roget's Wood was enough to make any new arrival's hair stand on end. Driven by a slap-happy lance-corporal named Minns, and accompanied by two cavalry officers who were as drunk as lords and who encouraged Minns to "take the fences like a man" or to "clear the sticks with a tally ho", Tim clung to the sides of the bone-shaking vehicle as it raced and bounced through potholed lanes, occasionally taking a short cut over streams or across the corner of a derelict field. The two cavalrymen tumbled from the back seat at the entrance to a large remount camp, where horses tried to graze on new grass struggling through the mud and rough-riders attempted to break in a fresh consignment of animals.

'*Cheerio*!' chorused the pair as they staggered off, supporting each other to remain upright.

'Very nice gentlemen, sir,' commented the pixie-faced driver. 'Real sports.'

'Yes,' agreed the bemused Tim, wondering what they were like in the saddle.

'New to Wipers, is you, sir?' he asked, using the troops' name for Ypres.

'That's right. I've been with GHQ.'

'Ah.'

Tim wished he had not mentioned that. Minns' expression suggested that he thought little of the men behind desks. It was a warning to keep quiet on the subject. He had only let slip the information because he was overwhelmed by this new experience after the sedateness and discipline at Montreuil, but the chirpy lance-corporal fell silent and remained that way until they entered Roget's Wood.

'This is it, sir. The wood's no more'n a few charred trunks now, but it's a friendly place for all that. I'll drop you at Tilde's Bar – that's where the officers congregate. You're bound to find someone there to help you.'

Minns swerved across the cobbles with scant regard for his vehicle or passenger, and pulled up with a flourish outside a small *estaminet*, narrowly missing an old man on a bicycle and two riflemen chatting to a local girl. They started to shout a protest, then saw Tim and broke off to salute. He returned it as he climbed out very conscious of the pristine state of his uniform compared with those of the men filling the street. Standing with his kit beside him as Minns drove away, Tim took in his surroundings. The *estaminet* stood in the midst of a row of Flemish cottages facing a similar row opposite them. At the end of the street he could make out the broken spire of a church. That appeared to be all the village comprised, but the army had augmented it with a series of tents forming a casualty clearing station, offices and stores. What had once been a peaceful, sleepy hamlet was now a miniature military camp shaken by the continuous thunder of guns from the front line to the south. The sound of it excited Tim further. He was going into action at last.

The street was filled with troops, a few nurses and local peasants. As Tim took it all in he was accosted by someone who had approached him from the rear.

'Hallo, you look lost. Must be a new boy. You look too clean and scrubbed to be one of the Wipers Brigade.'

Tim turned to see a captain with a live duck under his arm and a patch over one eye. The man nodded at the *estaminet*. 'That's the best place to find someone who'll tell you what to do about bagging yourself a bed for the night. I'm Jarvis, by the way. Take no notice of the eye. I'm not another Nelson – it's a bally infection that won't clear. Been to see the Doc – rather a pretty nurse handling my case, you see – and picked up Jemima along the way.' He held up the duck. 'Promised Madame de Brouchard something for her birthday tomorrow. Caught some oaf trying to wring her neck – the duck's of course – and liberated her. Well, come on. Sure to be some West Wilts boys in here. Hard drinkers, the whole pack of 'em.'

Tim picked up his baggage and followed this breezy character into a small bar so filled with cigarette smoke he could only make out hazy figures. As he waited for his eyes to grow accustomed to the dimness, a voice called out, 'Are you Ashleigh? We've been told to expect you.'

Tim turned in the direction of the voice. 'I'm looking for Major Reeve.'

'You won't find him here. He doesn't approve of Demon Drink!'

Stepping forward Tim found a group of four subalterns of his regiment sitting around a table bearing glasses of red wine. He did not know any of them. They all looked very young.

'I've just got in from Poperinghe. I was expecting you to be in the forward lines.'

'Lucky you. We left two days ago,' said a beefy second-lieutenant who would have looked more appropriate in his school's rugby kit than a battle-stained uniform. 'Have a drink. We've got nothing else to spend our money on so we'll buy you one. *All* of us'll buy you one, chum.'

Tim realized the boy was well under the influence and decided to decline. 'Thanks. Later, perhaps. I'd like to find my quarters. I've been travelling since yesterday morning. You know how it is. Where *will* I find Major Reeve?'

'At his devotions,' said another of the intoxicated quartet in ultra-solemn tones.

'He's quartered in the church annexe,' said a third, who appeared more in command of himself than his companions. 'I say, is it true that Vorne Ashleigh was your uncle?'

'And you're the great-grandson of General Sir Gilliard?' asked the fourth thickly.

'That's right. Look, I'll see you later.' Tim did not want his ancestry discussed in public by commissioned schoolboys who were not regular members of his family's regiment. He preferred to find his battalion commander so that he could settle in and have a wash. The journey with Lance-Corporal Minns had induced a pressing need to relieve himself before he sought the church annexe, and he guessed there must be a urinal to the rear of this bar, so he picked up his baggage and went in search of it. Above the general chatter he was able to hear a voice say, 'Now *he's* joined us the war's pretty well bally won. Hurrah!'

Tim gritted his teeth. Major 'Rocky' Reeve had been a frequent guest at Knightshill although he, himself, had only met the man twice. Vere liked him because the Major had spent his childhood in China with a missionary doctor and nurse for parents, and not only spoke several Chinese dialects but knew a great deal about the history of the Orient. Vere's fascination with the subject had fostered friendship with this colourful character, named Rocky because he was an amateur geologist and collected chunks of stone wherever he went. He had enhanced his reputation during the Boxer Rebellion by dressing as a coolie and mingling with Chinese to pick up information. Tim had initially been pleased to be posted to this man's command. He had not expected him to be idiotic enough to infect everyone with the notion that another Ashleigh hero would be joining them. He had had no opportunity to be one yet. Well, he would soon show them the stuff he was made of to counter their sneers – especially those of mere boys who had enlisted for the chance of a jolly lark and joined the regiment Tim had pledged his life to serve.

Tim did not recognize Major Reeve. He remembered him as having thick dark hair and a moustache, and mischievous blue eyes. The man he encountered in the chilly stone hut beside the church was almost bald, clean shaven and so thin his shabby uniform hung on his frame. Expressionless eyes gazed at him for so long after he announced his identity, Tim suspected the man to doubt the truth of his claim.

'I'm pleased to be with your battalion, sir,' he added to breach the silence. 'I've come straight from London. My uncle gave me a letter for you.' He unbuttoned his pocket and took out an envelope. 'It's rather crumpled, I'm afraid. You know how it is, travelling.' When Reeve made no attempt to take the letter, Tim put it on the corner of a rough table serving his CO as a desk as well as a place to eat. The room, divided into sleeping quarters by a couple of army blankets hung over a rope, smelt vile. Tim could not define the aroma but it was not that much different from that in the crude urinal behind the *estaminet*. He was considerably shaken by the change in this man and by the conditions he lived in.

Reeve finally spoke. 'By God, you've upset me, lad. Coming in here all spruce and full of life. You're the spitting image of that portrait of Vorne Ashleigh hanging in Headquarters' Mess. Haven't seen you for some while – never in uniform. A young sprig at Oxford, if I recall. You shouldn't have come. Not the place for the likes of you. Should have stayed at Montreuil with Intelligence.' He got to his feet with difficulty and went to stare at a window so filthy it was opaque. 'They all come, these children with rosy cheeks and no notion of what it's all about, and they go before you even remember their names. If they don't go with the first wave they sit and cry for those who did.' He turned his head to look at Tim. 'They sit in the mud and *cry*. They don't know what it's all about, you see.' He turned back to the window. 'You're a *real* soldier, like me. Something you wanted to do from the moment you saw a red coat. Given your life to soldiering. Proud of the regiment and all it stands for. Fought the Mahdi in the Sudan, put down the Boxers outside Peking. Proper soldiering. Marched by night; bivouacked during the heat of day. Chased the devils every yard of the way. They saw our red coats and knew what they were up against. And we stood shoulder to shoulder as they came at us, never wavering. When you fell another stepped into the gap, unafraid.'

Tim watched this man who commanded a battalion and was filled with deep dismay. Reeve was sick. How could he lead others?

'This is no place for us, young Ashleigh,' he said then, turning to walk right up to Tim. 'All they need here are boys who can climb out of a trench to start to advance. *Skittles*, that's all they need. Stand 'em up to be knocked down. Simple as that. Anyone can do it. If they refuse to be a skittle, we shoot 'em ourselves. Ever done that, eh? Shoot your own men? Turns your stomach, but it's got to be done or none of 'em would go. Is that what we pledged our lives to? *Is* it? Is that what the West Wilts stands for? They've all gone stark raving mad.'

A long silence followed as Reeve's blank eyes bored right through him. Keen to get away, Tim asked, 'What do I do about quarters, sir?'

'See the Adjutant. Find him at Tilde's. They all go there.'

Tim saluted, picked up his kit and went back to the *estaminet* feeling extremely uneasy and inclined to agree that everyone at Roget's Wood was mad. So far, he had met no one who seemed the least bit normal. His reappearance was greeted by a cheer from the four subalterns, one of whom asked if Major Reeve had handed over command of the battalion to the man whose ancestors had created the West Wiltshire Regiment.

Tim ignored that. 'Is the Adjutant here? I was told he would be.'

'Through that door.' The beefy rugby player pointed. 'You can always find him in there.'

Tim dumped his baggage and walked through to what he supposed would be a separate bar where more senior officers gathered. The room contained a bed upon which a naked man was indulging in a pastime much enjoyed by Tim. A contorted face twisted to see who had entered. 'Get out, you bally stupid bastard. Go on, *clear off*!'

Tim backed out fast to be met by howls of laughter from a host of officers occupying the tables in the bar, who must have heard and seen that encounter with his adjutant. Furious, and feeling totally out of his depth, Tim snatched up his things and left the *estaminet* for the cobbled street once more. Were *these* the so-called heroes of the Western Front lionized at home?

He sensed movement beside him and turned to find another boy officer there. Not one of the four he had already encountered. This one held a rank above his own although he could only be twenty.

'You must be the new chap,' he said in friendly tones despite the lack of a smile. 'I saw you pop in earlier, but you left again rather quickly. I suppose you'd like to find a billet somewhere.'

'That's what I was endeavouring to do.' Tim spoke brusquely. He did not want this captain seven years his junior adding to his anger.

'There's room at the Roquefort's. The MO and the Padre are officially quartered there, but they very rarely leave the hospital so you could have one of the beds. Actually, there isn't anywhere else. I'll take you there, if you like.'

'I . . . what about the Adjutant?'

'He'll be busy for a while yet. Come on, it's just up here at the end of the street.' Picking up Tim's bag he began walking. 'Good lord, whatever have you got in this?'

Tim fell in beside him carrying his military kit. 'I can take that.'

'It's all right. It's so heavy I thought you might have books.' He glanced at Tim. 'My weakness. I was going to take Modern Lit. Thought I'd be England's next great novelist.' A very faint smile appeared. 'I've left the field open for some other conceited blighter.'

Tim began to relax. This fellow was saner than the rest. He also seemed older than his years – certainly more mature than the quartet in the *estaminet*. 'There's still time. You're not exactly Methuselah.'

'You're fulfilling *your* ambitions,' the other said as they tramped up the street, their boots ringing on the cobbles. 'It must be difficult for men like you, who've been through Sandhurst and emerged trained to the hilt to find yourselves with subalterns created almost overnight because they have brains, or come from the right background. Don't you resent us?'

Nonplussed by this from someone who was one of the people he described, Tim hedged. 'Since the war started I've been at GHQ. Amongst the huge shoal of staff officers I felt a very small fish, believe me.

'A very brainy one, I guess.' He skirted a motorcycle on its stand outside a slightly larger cottage. 'This is where the Paymaster's billeted. We all got three months' money yesterday. That's why Tilde's is so popular today. Clothilde was the woman beneath Freddy Thomas, by the way. Did you see anything of her?'

That brought a smile from Tim. 'She has very plump knees.'

The other man grinned back. 'Wait until you see the rest of her. But she's the only woman poor old Teddy can get. The village girls are well chaperoned, although one or two have been known to oblige, so I've been told. The nurses are out of bounds, even to officers, which is a pity. Most of them are quite pretty, and it must be awfully lonely for them here.'

'Don't you believe it,' said Tim, wondering which of the cottages just ahead was to be his temporary home. 'My sister's an army nurse surrounded by men who think she and the others are angels personified. Unfortunately, Kate's so totally dedicated to her work all the admiration's lost on her.'

'I hope not,' said his companion thoughtfully. 'They deserve every bit of it. I was in hospital in Alexandria and those women were just wonderful.'

Tim stopped. 'My sister was out there for a while. What were you doing in Alexandria?'

'Recovering from a head wound. I might have met your sister, but I don't recall a Nurse Ashleigh.'

On the point of saying that her name was Daulton, Tim held back. He had no wish to tell this chance acquaintance about his family tree and leave himself open to further silliness from his fellow officers. Instead he asked, 'So you haven't been here long?'

'Since the beginning of March. I had a month's convalescent leave at home then joined Two Battalion.' He walked a few yards to a cottage with clean lace curtains and knocked on the door. 'This is the Rocquefort house. Madame looks a crone but I gather she's only forty-five. Her husband ran off with a gypsy, so the story goes, and her son is fighting with the French. She never smiles, but likes British officers because they're such gentlemen.' He made a comical face. 'That's what I've been told.'

'You've learnt an awful lot about this place in a few weeks,' said Tim, thinking the woman must be out and he would be back where he started again.

'There's nothing much else to talk about when you live in a hole in the ground. It was worse in Gallipoli. There were just the Turks and us. No village rest centres to provide a bit of gossip.'

The door opened before Tim could react to the news that his companion had experienced action in a place which had already become legendary. Madame Roquefort wore a long frock of black homespun covered by a calico apron. Her greying hair was severely drawn back from a face that was lined and sallow. A woman around Margaret Nicolardi's age, who looked old enough to be her mother. Tim felt like an intruder as the situation was explained in halting schoolboy French by the man who had assumed responsibility for taking him there. The woman was bewildered by references to Captain Bosworth and the Reverend Pierce, who never came but were there in her house on paper. Eventually Tim thought he should take over.

'Look, let me talk to her a moment,' he said, and began an explanation in excellent Flemish he had learnt at GHQ. Within moments they were invited in and offered coffee.

'That was pretty impressive,' said the envious captain, as they were shown into a small room containing two truckle beds already made up with coarse sheets and grey knitted blankets.

'It's what I was doing at GHQ – interpreting.' Tim dumped his heavy kit beside one of the beds which he then sat on to test its depth of comfort. 'My step-father's a diplomat. I travelled around a lot when I was young and picked up other languages. That's the easy way of learning them.' He got to his feet again; the bed was board hard. 'Actually, she's not a bad sort once you communicate. It can't be easy for the civilians here.'

'It's not exactly easy for us.'

Madame Rocquefort brought strong coffee then left them to drink it after telling Tim she would cook a nice dinner for him that evening because she had been given food for the two Englishmen who never came.

'I hope to God they don't turn up, for once,' commented Tim, pulling a face over the coffee. 'No wonder they're not keen. This is terrible.'

The other man's brown eyes met his over the rim of his upturned cup. 'Wait until you taste trench coffee. You'll think dishwater's marvellous in comparison.'

Tim changed the subject. 'I knew Major Reeve some time ago. He's changed quite drastically.'

'It's shell shock. Everyone stays clear of him on stand down. During an attack he's first rate. You wouldn't think he was the same man. Professionalism tells. That's why he was pleased to learn you were joining us. We've only one other regular officer in the battalion – James Player. Know him?'

'Heard of him. Crack shot at Sandhurst. His name was on the list of cup winners.'

'And yours!'

'Mine came later,' Tim said, feeling awkward. Surely 'Rocky' Reeve had not mentioned *everything* about him to these instant officers. 'Look, I don't know what the CO has said, but . . .'

'He told us we were privileged to have joining us a fellow who was the great-grandson of a famous general and the nephew of our regimental hero. It wasn't hard to guess you'd be pretty hot on anything connected with soldiering.'

It was hard not to like this frank, friendly young man who was much older than him in experience yet treated him with a measure of respect. Tim spoke on impulse. 'The thing I'm *not* hot on is going into action. I haven't got around to that yet.'

'You will.' He put down his empty cup. 'I'll leave you to settle in.'

Tim asked. 'What's the drill?'

'The drill?'

'The duty roster, inspections – I mean, I'll have to meet my men.'

He laughed. 'They won't want to meet you. We all turn a blind eye during rest periods. That's why Freddy Thomas told you to clear off. You joined us at a bad time. No one will show the slightest interest in you for now.'

'You did, and I appreciate it. You haven't told me your name, by the way.'

'Duncan. Andrew Duncan.'

Tim smiled. 'Well, thanks for taking pity on a new boy.'

'It wasn't only that, to tell you the truth,' Andrew said with a surprising hint of diffidence. 'You remind me very strongly of someone I knew in Gallipoli. An Australian sergeant. It's an amazing coincidence that his name was also Ashleigh.' He smiled at his reminiscences. 'A big, bronzed chap who could blaspheme like nobody else I know. Said he'd enlisted when he was too drunk to know what he was doing, yet he was never under the influence there. A born soldier and a born leader. A mystery man, I thought him. He'd never speak about home or his youth, like everyone else did.' The smile faded as he focused on Tim again. 'We struck up a friendship which kept us alive for five months. He taught me all I know about battle tactics. I was sorry when we split up at Alexandria.' He made for the door, then turned back. 'If you feel like company after you've had dinner there's Tilde's or a canteen run by a women's charity organization just beyond the church. The men go there mostly, but there's a separate room for officers. If you don't fancy either, I'm billeted three doors along on the other side of the street. I rarely go on the razzle in the evenings. You're welcome to join me for a quiet drink and a chat.' He hesitated, then said, 'When you walked into Tilde's I had a bit of a shock. There's an amazing resemblance between you and that Australian. Under different circumstances I'd have said you could be his younger brother. Strange, isn't it?' In the open doorway, he added, 'He saved my life. I'll never forget him.'

Tim stayed at Madame Rocquefort's that evening.

It proved impossible to avoid Andrew Duncan because he was Tim's company commander – a situation neither was happy with. It seemed ludicrous for a volunteer of twenty to give orders to a regular, fully trained officer seven years his senior, and yet Andrew was battle hardened. Tim acknowledged this, nevertheless resenting a situation which he felt exposed him to secret derision from the other subalterns, all as young as Andrew. After the ridiculous advance introduction Major Reeve had given Tim, it was unavoidably embarrassing for him and, surprisingly, for Andrew, who was a quiet, sensitive young man keen to establish genuine friendship with the new arrival. Tim also found this aspect hard to deal with.

There was something extremely likeable about Andrew who, it emerged, had attended Chartfield School and remembered Charlotte's sons as juniors, although the Nicolardi boys had been there too short a while for his recollection. Naturally, though, he knew about Tim's Uncle Vorne, a former pupil whose heroic exploit in the Sudan was celebrated in School House with a plaque outlining his valour. He was also aware of the long line of Ashleighs who had been taught at Chartfield since its inception, including Sir Gilliard. Tim was thankful Laurence's professional commitments had prevented him from following family tradition, because he would have had to own up as being registered as T. Daulton.

Andrew made no reference to a Valentine Ashleigh, yet Tim's young uncle had won endless sporting laurels during his years at Chartfield. The omission seemed rather odd, but Tim kept off the subject of the family's black sheep. As yet, Andrew appeared not to connect his Australian sergeant with them, and Tim determined he would not. Even so, he was certain the youthful captain was drawn to him only because he so resembled Val. Andrew spoke about that unusual friendship at Gallipoli many times. Through these recollections Tim was given an impression of a far finer man than the one who had staggered into Knightshill.

Those days at Roget's Wood dragged. There was so little to do, and Tim was in no need of the rest so much enjoyed by a battalion straight from the trenches. He borrowed a horse and rode through the open countryside. This was not Montreuil with its pretty villages and untouched landscape, so the sight of devastation only further lowered his spirits. He avoided Tilde's and the canteen because he did not feel at ease with fellow oficers who constantly chaffed him about his antecendents or his distinction at Sandhurst until he wished himself back at GHQ where the élite were happy together.

Twice he awoke to find someone in the other bed. The Padre had taken time off to catch up on some sleep. He was a pleasant man numbed by what he was experiencing and grateful to chat with someone who, as yet, had not also been numbed by it. The Reverend Pierce was a volunteer for the duration of the war so was unfamiliar with the regular officers Tim knew. But he had once visited Dunstan St Mary and climbed up to view

Knightshill's famous Great Window during a bicycling holiday to see architectural landmarks. Tim extended an invitation to visit the house on his next leave, saying that his Uncle Vere would be delighted to host someone so knowledgeable on the subject. Tim spent his evenings drinking alone in his billet unless he found it impossible to refuse Andrew's overtures for a get-together.

During that rest period Tim wrote twice to Amy giving his divisional mailing address in the hope that she would reply. He thought about her constantly and, each evening at around ten o'clock, he would imagine the gaiety and horseplay when she announced that her pianist was indisposed. He caught himself longing for her as he never had for any other woman, and the longing was not necessarily physical. He wanted to talk to her, walk with her arm in arm. He would even go back to the Waterfowl and enthuse over a cake if he could just be with her – and he could not forget the shock of dawning awareness on her face after he had kissed her. Because of it he filled letters with lies about what he was doing, then tore them up and wrote the unexciting truth. The most dramatic thing he could tell her was that the ground shook from the continuous gunfire and that it would not be long before he was in the thick of it. He signed off saying she was in his thoughts and he could not wait to go to the Regency on his next leave.

The rest period ended abruptly when the battalion received orders to march south across the border into France. Tim was taut with excitement as he inspected his platoon, fully accoutred and ready to set off. It was the first time he had really faced them in regimental fashion, and he was gratified to find that, unlike his fellow officers, these men were visibly glad to be commanded by a more mature regular officer from a family so closely connected with their regiment. It gave them confidence, a sense of being in good hands. They had had enough of eighteen year olds who gave orders in high-pitched, nervous voices and were often discovered vomiting after a severe bombardment, or even crying. The troops were mostly inexperienced boys themselves and needed an assured leader. Tim was all of that as he walked along the ranks speaking encouraging words to those who looked listless, and exchanging a little banter with the more cheerful ones. He knew none of their names, but was blessed with a sergeant named Phipps who was thirty and also a regular soldier. Tim was prompted with names by this tough, wiry NCO so that he appeared to recognize men individually. It was a promising start to his first engagement with the enemy, Tim felt. They were on the march four days; four gruelling periods over roads pitted with shell holes, past woods now no more than a collection of bare, splintered trunks, through villages whose residents had deserted before their ruined cottages collapsed on them. All along the way they passed clusters of rough wooden crosses with names and regiments scrawled on them. Here and there they encountered emaciated dogs scavenging on the corpses of army horses, left where they had fallen. Everywhere there hung in the air a terrible stench. And the guns never stopped firing.

They halted late on the fourth evening at what had once been a farm. While the men got out their rations and began to eat their bully beef and biscuit supper, Major Reeve spoke to his officers. He was, indeed, a different man now. They gathered around him in the shell of the farmhouse, hot, tired, hungry and in need of a wash, but what he said brought little hope of a rest.

'Well, gentlemen, our job is to capture this wood to the east of our present position. From available Intelligence we know that it is held by Germans who, despite several frontal attacks by our forces eight miles to the south, refuse to surrender it. It's to be hoped that they are unaware of our arrival – all their attention will have been directed further south, as are their guns.' He tapped with his cane the rough map spread on the ground. 'We shall dig in *here*. At nightfall we shall cross three meadows as far as Point A,' his cane moved to a larger cross, 'and create a trench complex to the north and south of it. Then we shall lie low and await orders to go. An hour before our assault, the infantry who have been unsuccessful in gaining the wood will begin a feint attack, which will keep the Huns busy while we surprise them with bayonets up their arses.'

It sounded an excellent piece of strategy, so they all laughed and nodded their approval before dispersing to tell their men the unwelcome news that they would have little sleep that night. Then they washed the grime from their hands and faces before gathering in the ruin to eat their own unappetizing supper. Andrew contrived to sit next to Tim on the ground.

'See what I mean about the change that comes over him?' He

nodded at their CO. 'Wait until we really get going. He's a walking dynamo.'

'I hope he'll be a *running* one or he'll be mown down before he gets to the trees.'

'Walking or running, it makes no difference when shells burst. And that's what they'll send against us. I've seen it happen before. They save the bullets until you're almost there. More chance of hitting the target.'

Tim studied his companion wiping bread around his plate to capture the last crumbs of meat. 'Are you scared?'

Dark eyes looked up into his. 'Aren't you?'

'Not really. Just anxious to get going.'

'That's good,' said Andrew. 'If I go down you'll take over the company as senior subaltern. You should be in command, anyway. They need someone like you to put their faith in, and you won't let them down because soldiering is in your blood. Like your namesake, Sergeant Ashleigh. I'm pretty damn certain he'd fought before, in South Africa. Made a comment about the silence of the *veld*. When I picked him up on it he more or less told me to mind my own bloody business.' He smiled in reminiscence. 'He was like that. Swore like a trooper.'

'Did you let him get away with it?' Tim asked acidly.

Andrew cast him a curious look. 'Gallipoli brought men down to the same level. War makes no discrimination between generals and privates. Their bodies fly apart equally easily. So long as orders are obeyed and loyalty is strong the niceties of rank don't matter a damn. Please don't take offence, but when we advance on that wood you'll be glad the men do what they must even if they don't call you sir.'

Tim did take offence, but it was because of this boy's overt admiration for Val Ashleigh rather than his gentle admonition.

With darkness came rain. It fell relentlessly all night while 2 Battalion dug itself in. By first light they had no greater shelter than shallow trenches in which they were compelled to crouch to avoid being visible above ground, but they did not expect to occupy them for more than a day. They remained there for a week, awaiting the arrival of another infantry battalion as a back-up force for the attack on the wood. During that week it rained on and off most of the time, and it turned unseasonably cold. The shallow dugouts were soon ankle deep in liquid mud. Tim's smart uniform finally grew dirty and sodden, his highly polished boots were constantly caked with mud, and he never felt dry. He wished Amy could see him. She would *have* to take him seriously.

On the seventh day he crouched in pouring rain to look through field glasses over the now-familiar fields leading to the wood. RFC information was scant because aircraft had been unable to take off in the worst of the rain and, when they could, the pilots found it next to impossible to see anything from the air. One had reported an enemy column on the move, but no one else had spotted it so the information was considered doubtful. Tim scanned the trees looking for signs of anything different. He and the two second-lieutenants had been maintaining a constant watch from their sector of the line, but it was a boring business. The trees remained undisturbed and one's eyes ached from staring through lenses in search of things that were never there. Sleep was spasmodic and extremely uncomfortable. Tim began to understand why the others had welcomed the doubtful comfort of Roget's Wood. They appeared able to drop off in sitting positions in pouring rain, whereas he found it impossible. In consequence, he was tired and irritable.

Glancing at his watch Tim saw that his relief, a diamond merchant's son with a flop of brown hair and large green eyes, should be sloshing through the trench at any moment. Thank God! He could soon crawl into the tiny earthen cave that served as a sleeping quarters for C Company subalterns and try to doze off for a while. Raising the field glasses once more he gazed listlessly at the far-off wood. His pulse accelerated painfully as he noticed movement – indistinct but certain. He adjusted the focus and wiped the lenses, then raised the glasses to his eyes again. What he saw set his pulse racing even faster.

Pushing back from his prone position on the slippery bank of the trench he set off in a crouching trot towards the centre of the line, where Major Reeve could be found in another earthen cave. Progress was not fast or easy. His boots skidded on the spongy floor of the trench putting him in danger of falling headlong backwards several times, and he sent up showers of muddy water over the troops lining his route.

'Sorry, lads. Can't be helped,' he said as he passed them.

'What's up, sir?'

'They're not coming at us, are they?'

'You see somefink, sir? Somefink 'orrible?'

'Yes, *you* Murphy,' muttered the man's neighbour.

'Is the Huns after us, Mr Ashleigh?'

All these questions remained unanswered as Tim reached his own sleeping hole and grabbed his relief by the sleeve. 'Get up there, Piers. I've got to see Major Reeve. And move!'

'But it's not eighteen hundred yet,' the boy complained, jerking his arm free. 'There are five more bally minutes before my watch begins.'

'Do as you're told and keep your eyes peeled!' Tim snapped, then continued on his way hardly able to contain his excitement. His vigilance had paid off. No other officer had seen it. At least, he hoped not. He wanted this feather for his own cap alone.

Major Reeve was reading a book of Greek poetry and Teddy Thomas, the Adjutant, was asleep with his mouth agape and his boots upturned over a small folding stool. Water still dripped from inside them.

'Sir, the situation's changed,' Tim panted as he ducked his head and squatted on his haunches in order to speak to his CO. The seat of his breeches was now in the mud, but he hardly noticed the new discomfort as he waited impatiently for Reeve to place a bookmark in the page before closing the worn volume with care amounting to reverence.

'Which situation, Mr Ashleigh?' he enquired in unhurried tones.

'In the wood, sir. They've moved the guns – *are* moving them. Unless they've brought in others, that is. I detected movement, saw men amongst the trees directly facing our position. Then I could make out the shape of heavy artillery. It's not easy to see them because they're camouflaged by overhanging branches, but they're there all right.'

Reeve put the book in his pack, still unhurried. 'Are you certain of this?'

'Yes, sir, *quite* certain.'

The CO's eyes which had lacked expression back at Roget's Wood, were now sharp with intelligence as he shook the Adjutant's foot very hard. 'Wake up, Teddy, and put your boots on.' He turned his attention to Tim. 'No one else has reported this.'

'They're there, sir,' he repeated with utter confidence. 'We can't possibly mount a frontal assault now.'

'Correction, Mr Ashleigh. It would be *madness* to mount a frontal assault now. It's still quite possible.'

'But it would amount to suicide,' he cried.

'You're a mere platoon-commander, sir, not OIC operations,' Reeve cut in harshly. 'And we have yet to establish the truth of your sighting. Return to your men. Your company-commander will be informed of any fresh orders as they become available.'

Tim was furious, yet he had no choice but to do as he was told. He resented being put in his place in front of Thomas, who had never forgiven him for interrupting his sexual interlude with Clothilde, but he resented even more being told his vital information had to be corroborated before it was believed and, even then, might be disregarded in the overall plan.

'Tim,' called Reeve, as he raised himself into a crouch once more ready to go. 'You have sharp eyes. Well done.'

'Thank you, sir,' Tim replied stiffly. The praise had come too soon after the reprimand to please him and he squelched his way back to the sleeping hole still furious. His anger very soon faded beneath tardy conjecture on his CO's comment about a frontal assault. No one in their right mind would order one, surely, and yet he had hinted that such a piece of lunacy might occur.

The rain developed into a cloudburst just then and Andrew Duncan's voice reached him. 'Shelter here for a moment. There's no one in but me.'

Tim ducked instinctively from the sheets of rain, and entered the comparative protection of the little cave. 'Christ, if this is Spring what the hell's Winter like?'

'You'll find out when it comes – if you live that long.'

'I shan't if our CO has his way.'

Andrew offered cigarettes. 'That's an enigmatic statement. I thought you were Major Reeve's blue-eyed boy.'

Words burst from Tim as he related what had happened, ending with a declaration that the battalion would be all but wiped out if they attempted to overrun the wood now. 'The Germans know we're here. Why else would they turn their artillery? The essence of surprise was our ace. If we had attacked the day after we arrived the wood would be in our hands now.'

'We didn't have reinforcements,' Andrew pointed out.

'They took too long to get here.'

'They were bogged down in a village and had to capture a bridge before they could reach the road. They lost half their number.'

'They're a fat lot of good to us as reinforcements, in that case,' Tim said in disgust. He smoked in silence for a moment, reflecting on how calmly his companion was taking his words. 'Have you got a girl waiting for you?' he asked out of the blue, thinking of Amy.

Andrew shook his head. 'I fancied a chap's sister once, but she made it clear she thought school prefects were mere children so it never came to anything. I haven't had time since then.' He smiled. 'I suppose it's just as well. They have an awfully difficult time worrying about us, don't they?'

Tim made no reply. Was Amy worrying about him? Probably not. She had fifty admirers every evening. Why should she be concerned with someone she had no faith in? Now he had woken her to the joys of passion she was probably sharing them with anyone she fancied.

'Have you?'

Andrew's question brought him from his thoughts. 'Have I what?'

'A girl waiting for you?'

'No, I've always played the field. Love 'em and leave 'em. It's the best policy.'

'I'll bear that in mind when I next go on home leave.'

Tim exhaled smoke slowly. 'The dear creatures won't think you a mere child now. Smart uniform, jaunty air, a few tales of dashing exploits and they'll be eating out of your hand. Make the most of it. We're only young once.'

An eerie whistling filled his ears making them hurt. Next minute he was thrown off his feet as the cave disintegrated into a shower of earth and mud which rained down on him with a roar that drowned the whistling. He knew what was happening. Any man who had fought even mock battles could recognize the noise of an exploding shell. For an instant he feared maiming, but when he started to struggle free of the weight of mud and felt no agony, he knew he had been fortunate.

'*Christ*, those guns have our range!' he panted. Andrew Duncan could not respond. He lay spreadeagled with a shard of metal through his chest, staring at Tim with sightless eyes in a face streaked with dirt. He must have died instantly. Tim sat motionless in a pool of mud, plastered with ooze from head to foot, going through every soldier's sense of shock on first seeing a comrade killed at his side. Exaggerated friendship flooded through him. Andrew Duncan seemed the dearest person on earth in that moment; his loss unbearable. Why had Val saved his life for this?

Another whistle; another great roar. More earth flying up, this time a few yards further along the trench. Men shouting. Screams. Tim began to make his way towards that area, those sounds. His mind was adjusting to shock. *If I go down you'll take over the company as senior subaltern.* Training surmounted emotion. He had to bring order from chaos. The men must have a leader. All hell had broken loose and it was impossible to traverse the trench. Great mounds of earth blocked the shallow channels so that he had to claw his way over the top, then was faced with deep craters where bodies sprawled and water cascaded down on them. Whistles were being blown, voices cried for help, officers yelled for stretcher bearers. Above it all was the infernal thunder of exploding shells and the shrieks as more followed them through the air.

It took no time for Tim to accept that mock battles were nothing like this. It was impossible to rally his men. He had no notion where they were; he could recognize none he saw. It was a case of each man desperately fighting to stay alive beneath a storm of death. Retaliation was out of the question. Regrouping and planning fresh tactics did not apply here. This was real. This could bring any man's last moment on earth.

Blast from another explosion threw Tim backwards into a crater. There he saw what his duty should be. Forget exercises at Sandhurst, and manuals on tactics under fire. War had never been fought this way before. Solutions to this had to be invented on the spot. Struggling up he now saw several soldiers almost totally buried by mud, and he began digging to free them. It was too slow manually. He snatched up a tin helmet of no further use to the head it was on and excavated with that. He shovelled like a maniac, all the time assuring the entombed men in a steady voice that they would be free at any moment.

He had grown amazingly calm. The clamour of the bombardment

continued as though he were no part of it, so intent was he on what he was doing. He freed two from burial alive and dragged them high enough up the side of the crater to leave them clear of the water rising in the bottom. He then pulled the wounded clear of it, too, promising to direct stretcher bearers to them right away.

Emerging from the hole he knew they were empty promises. Medics were certainly in evidence, but the makeshift trenches had been so battered there was no clear access. Even as Tim watched through eyes assaulted by heavy rain, he saw two stretcher bearers blown apart as they lifted a casualty. There was total confusion; wholesale slaughter. If only he had spotted those guns earlier. What would be left of 2 Battalion West Wiltshire Regiment when darkness fell?

During the next hour Tim did his utmost to ensure that as many as possible stood a chance of survival, but wounded men were helped by their fellows only to be killed by a subsequent shell. He eventually found his own platoon – his own *company* now Andrew was dead – but the German bombardment was so intensive Tim could do little but help the men who fell and pray he, himself, would survive until the order to fall back was given. He could not understand why Reeve had not issued it long ago. As far as he could tell he was the only officer in sight along C Company's stretch of what was now little more than an area of craters and heaps of earth. The temporary trenches had vanished.

Picking himself from the ground once more Tim felt a surge of anger possess him to the point of acting on it. The only thing to be done in this situation was to retreat to the farm where the reserve battalion was encamped, and make a stand there when the Germans attacked under cover of darkness. No one would move until an order was issued. Reeve could be dead. The messenger bringing the order was probably buried beneath earth or bodies. They would stay here until no one remained alive unless someone told them to go. He was an officer, expected to lead. He would bloody well lead these poor devils away from this needless sacrifice.

Blowing continuous blasts on his whistle he waved his arms to signal to those around him that they should fall back. Against the din of the bombardment a whistle could be heard only by those in the close vicinity, but they acted on his signals with speed. Setting off as fast as they could go, some limping, some carrying wounded over their shoulders, the first few were spotted by others who abandoned their posts thankfully and also began to retreat. Before long, men all along that broken line were crossing the rainswept countryside heading for the farm. There were pitifully few of them.

Tim reached the rear lines just as dusk was falling. Because the sky was so full of rain it came early that evening. The farm was not harbouring a battalion of reserve troops. There could be no more than two companies, in Tim's estimation. They were now augmented by less than their own number, half of them wounded. He made his way to the ruined farmhouse weary, sodden and filthy, recalling what Andrew had told him about their reinforcements meeting stiff opposition at a bridge. This meagre force would never repulse a German assault tonight. What had happened to the troops to the south who were to mount a feint attack? Had they been wiped out?

As he entered the ruin Tim was joined by Captain James Player, crack shot at Sandhurst and the only other regular officer in the battalion aside from Major Reeve. Trailing dejectedly behind him were two junior subalterns, one holding a bloody handkerchief to his nose.

'Reeve's dead,' said Player tersely. 'Teddy Thomas lost a leg. Won't last out the night. Hopkins disintegrated. Judge and Campion caught it. No one's seen Billings or Duncan.'

'Andrew was killed by the first shell. My two subalterns are also out of it,' Tim told him. 'Wentworth was carried off with a stomach wound. No idea whether they got away safely.' He sighed. 'So we four are the battalion's only officers.'

Taylor nodded. 'God knows who gave the order to retire.'

'I did.'

The other man goggled at him. '*You*! Who gave you the right? I'm the senior here.'

'Oh, for God's sake! Someone had to. There'd have been no battalion left,' Tim cried. 'Why didn't *you* give the order? It was the only thing to do.'

'We were told to hold that position,' Taylor yelled.

'Ready to advance on an enemy force whose guns were trained in another direction,' Tim shouted back. 'They *moved* them, didn't they! How the hell could we hold that position, much less mount an assault on the wood? We should have fallen back at the outset.

When I estimated that all the senior officers must be gone, I took command.'

'*Christ*! Because your name's Ashleigh? It doesn't cut any ice with me, and *I hold senior rank*. As from now *I'm* in command of this battalion!'

'*Then bloody well command it*,' Tim roared. 'You have me to thank for having any men left to lord it over.'

'Why, you little . . .' Taylor's aggressive move towards Tim was halted by sudden silence; a silence so intense it hurt the eardrums. The uncontrolled outburst between two shocked and exhausted men was forgotten as the implication of that silence got through to them.

Within minutes, the four West Wilts officers, the youngest of whom was suffering from no more than a heavy nosebleed to which he was prone, had rallied what remained of the battalion to combine with the infantrymen already positioned around the farm out of range of the German heavy guns. Star shells began to burst above the area just beyond the scene of the recent massacre as the defenders waited for the first sight of the enemy advance. The bright green lights showed only a few stragglers making their way to the farm with agonizingly slow progress. The watching men could do nothing for their comrades who would surely be overtaken by the enemy coming out of the darkness behind them. They longed to tell those wounded to lie and pretend to be dead, otherwise they soon would be.

Tim crouched behind a low broken wall with the survivors of C Company – eleven in all – and watched those desperate men struggling to reach the farm; to reach the living. They had escaped from the dead, but they were reaching out for something doomed to destruction. There was nowhere to fall back to this time. Fear was an abstract thing when there was no way of evading it, Tim discovered. Death was advancing on him somewhere out there. He prayed it would be a bullet, not a bayonet in the guts. He prayed it would be quick.

His heartbeat leapt so dramatically it was if he had stopped breathing momentarily when he saw a long line of dark shapes materialize from the rain-filled night. At that same moment a shattering salvo of machine-gun fire had him jumping nervously as their own defence of the farm began.

'Wait until they're close enough, lads,' he called to his men, in a voice grown husky. 'Don't waste bullets. You're all *excellent* shots, remember. As soon as they're near enough, make every one count. Wounded men can kill you. Dead ones can't. Keep that in mind. If they get as far as here, you know what to do. They're the *enemy*. They've just slaughtered your pals out there. Make 'em pay for it.'

The first line came on in spite of the machine guns. The star shells revealed another line not far behind them. It was a concerted attack by overwhelming numbers. The night became a scene from hell as the brightness overhead faded and the enemy blended with darkness until another shell exploded showing them there, much nearer. First they were in sight, then gone, then there again. It was unnerving. It was awesome. A long moving wall of aggression bearing vicious cold steel coming out of the rainswept night; on and on no matter how the guns spat bullets at them, how many fell.

Tim cocked his revolver. His heartbeat was thundering through his body. His throat was so dry he had to keep swallowing in an effort to ease the pain in it.

'Nearer, just a few yards nearer,' he breathed, his eyes aching as he stared into the darkness.

Then they were there, clearly visible without the aid of lights. A deafening fusillade began all around Tim. The Germans rushed the farm, yelling savagely to instill fear in their victims, and it was then each man for himself in hand-to-hand fighting. Tim fired and killed his first human being. He kept firing, swinging round in every direction as the German troops overran his position. The night became a cacophony of shots, screams, yells, grunts and blasphemy as the grey horde mixed with the khaki. All around Tim were vicious faces, steel helmets, crashing rifle butts, thrusting bayonets and heavy boots kicking and stamping. There was no time to think. It was kill or be killed. His protective helmet was knocked askew and fell to the ground. He twisted around to see a raised rifle butt above his head. He ducked. The blow fell on his left shoulder causing immense pain, knocking him off balance. He dropped to the ground and rolled over instinctively in time to see a muddy boot descending on his face. He turned to protect his eyes. Darkness overtook him.

* * *

When consciousness returned there was the thickness of blood in his throat, almost choking him. He rolled his head sideways to spit, and groaned with pain. When he tried to open his eyes only one obeyed. The other appeared to be sealed. He saw part of a broken stone wall in the faint light from a lantern. He tried to speak, to beg for some water. His lips felt like two balloons that refused to form words. He merely grunted. With enormous effort he attempted to raise himself. His left shoulder was racked with acute pain, causing him to cry out. Yet he somehow managed to prop himself against the stonework in a semi-lying position. The movement brought overwhelming nausea and he vomited violently over the boots of a man lying near.

A dark shadow loomed from the dimness. Tim peered up at it with his single eye. It was impossible to make out features or detail, merely that it was a man in uniform.

'There is no need to be afraid. I give you my word you will be well looked after.'

Instinct told him to give no sign of understanding, but the words brought inner pain far greater than his physical agony. He closed his eye before giveaway moisture could form. He would sooner have died than be the only Ashleigh ever to be taken prisoner by the enemy. His wounds were not even 'honourable' ones. He had merely been stamped on by a German soldier.

CHAPTER THIRTEEN

Vere sat in the train heading along a branch line to the small village on the western boundary of Wiltshire. After two years of silence Val had written to ask for a meeting during the following week. Vere's anger over the letter which gave no reason for the request was muted by strong family loyalty. Hence his journey from Knightshill this morning.

He was heavy hearted these days. His fear that the war would irrevocably change all he held dear was being justified. John Morgan had died last month leaving Charlotte widowed at forty-five. His loss meant that Vere had to be more often at Knightshill. Ordinarily he would like nothing better, but Kitty was so involved in Ashleigh Court it meant they spent a great deal of time apart. Neither of them was happy about that. In addition, Vere had pledged his assistance to Gilbert Dessinger's various projects to the extent that both his wife and the estate suffered from his preoccupation with theatrical matters. Then there was the American ranch. He and John had made alternate annual visits to check on the stock and finances. He would now have to go over each year. He had discussed with his sisters the advisability of selling it, but Val's agreement would have to be sought. In any case, profits were booming because, ironically, the beef was being bought by the British Government to feed the troops. Vere did not regret his offer of the London house as a convalescent home, but he did sometimes wish it was again the sophisticated haven he used to enjoy so much.

He thought of his family. Simon was patently unhappy. It was not only due to overwork, although the new aircraft was posing many problems. The news of Kate's shipwreck had upset him greatly. He had suddenly, and quite unreasonably, begun to resent being the only member of the family group with no Ashleigh blood in his veins. It was a good thing he would never know he was the child of an adulterous love affair between Kitty and a widowed diamond prospector, not William Munroe's son. Vere knew it must be difficult for his step-son, and the twins tended to tease him about his lack of family traits. Those girls were becoming unruly. There was a streak of wildness running through the bloodline which threatened to develop in them, and they were also real beauties well aware of the fact. Vere was certain the war, with its greater emancipation for women, was basically responsible for their waywardness. Each time they returned from school they worried him more, yet Kitty remained philosophical.

With John's death came the obligation to take a measure of responsibility for James and Charles. Boys needed a father figure when they reached puberty. If only they were his own sons! He would have no fears then for the succession. Margaret and Laurence were devoted to each other and going to the top in diplomatic circles. The Nicolardi boys were clever and talented. The only cloud on that particular horizon was the fate of young Tim, although he now seemed certain to survive the war. As for Kate, she was spending her youth amidst suffering and death when she should be enjoying flirtations and carefree days at Knightshill. The end of the war was nowhere in sight. The summer offensive on the Somme had failed with a loss of thousands, and the Germans were now bombing London with greater frequency. Yes, the peace and contentment of pre-war years had gone. Nothing would return to how it had been when hostilities ceased, and an entire generation of young men would have been lost.

When Vere alighted at Blecton Mere station it was with a sense of foreboding. Val was certain to add to his problems today. The ageing station master waiting to take his ticket was full of bonhomie.

'It be a lovely day, sir, but bein' August so it should. I see you've a gennelman meeting you, so you won't be needing Ned Hawkins' trap. Good day to you.'

Vere nodded absently, his attention taken by his brother waiting in the yard beside a smart dog cart. In well-cut breeches and a tailored jacket Val looked every inch an Ashleigh. His thick hair shone gold in the sunlight enhancing his strong resemblance to Tim and, even more so, to the profligate Vorne. Handsome devils, all three. What had brought this change? Surely not five months in the Dardanelles.

'Thanks for coming,' said Val, offering his hand.

Vere shook it. 'I almost didn't.'

'I wouldn't have blamed you. Get in.'

As soon as Vere climbed up they were away, smoothly and swiftly, setting a spanking pace. He had forgotten Val's skill with horses. The lanes were bordered with hedges thick with both wild roses and blackberry. Summer had produced a mixture of unseasonable weather, causing havoc to nature's timetable. The beauty of rural Wiltshire was lost on Vere, for once, as he puzzled over this unexpected encounter. He challenged his brother.

'Why aren't you in uniform? You *are* still in the army, I take it.'

Val glanced briefly over his shoulder. 'I haven't deserted, if that's what you think. I'm just breaking the rules.'

'Not for the first time, I'll wager.'

'Too right.'

Anger triumphed over loyalty. 'What's this all about? You've treated your family pretty shabbily, you know.'

Another brief glance. 'No bloody word about how the family treated me.'

'Grandfather has been dead fifteen years . . . and Vorne didn't *ask* to be held up as a heroic image to emulate.'

'He would have, if he'd survived his act of treachery.'

Vere sighed. 'You haven't yet forgiven me for not telling you the truth earlier than I did.'

'No, I haven't . . . but men do worse things to each other, even to their brothers.'

Silence fell for a while, birdsong and the beat of the piebald's hooves filling the gap until Vere tried again. 'Why didn't you let us know you hadn't gone back to Australia? We heard from Benson that you'd enlisted, and that pipsqueak Oscar Martin wrote to me in sickeningly gloating terms to reveal that he'd met up with my elusive young brother. That's how we knew you were with the West Wilts in Gallipoli. After that we received a letter from Kate telling us you were a patient in her ward. Why the *hell* did we have to hear all that from others?'

All Val said was, 'I guessed that little dingo's arse didn't accept my act. I did my best to put him off the scent and denied even hearing of the Knightshill Ashleighs. Don't worry. He won't have told many others. Our Operations Liaison Officer died of cholera soon after we landed. *He* stayed safely aboard the command ship, of course. Just proves death'll bloody get you wherever you are.'

Val's language had certainly not improved, yet Vere detected a slight softening of the tough manner of two years ago. 'Kate wrote that you'd been recommended for a medal.'

'Ironic, isn't it? Give one, take it away, then offer it back.'

'The first one was awarded to someone called Martin Havelock,' Vere pointed out.

His brother gave a short, mirthless laugh. 'I'd like to see their flaming expressions if I told them I was the same bloke.'

'But you never will, surely?'

'He died on the *veld*.'

It was harsh and final, so Vere thought it time to broach the main subject. 'Why did you ask for a meeting after ignoring the family for so long?'

'We're almost there. Someone's preparing lunch for us.'

Against the continuing use of blasphemy came further evidence of change. All meals had been *tucker* two years ago. The Antipodean drawl in Val's voice was also less apparent. Vere grew even more intrigued. The village had been left behind a while ago, and a lake lay sparkling at the foot of some gentle hills to their left. A true beauty spot in a region popular with landowners. Who was preparing lunch for them, and where? All at once he leapt to a staggering conclusion. His brother had married in secret. How typical! Annoyance was nevertheless tempered by the prospect of Val having a son to inherit Knightshill. He just hoped to God the wife was acceptable, but doubts flew as Vere told himself Val's smart appearance and improved attitude could only be due to a woman of taste and gentility.

The dog cart took a sharp turn to the left through a curved entrance giving on to a long driveway winding across meadows where horses grazed. Thoroughbreds of no small merit, Vere noted. Of course Val would marry a horsewoman! A wealthy one if this was her family estate. Happier anticipation ran through him. Had his brother finally done something right?

A tall grey stone arch straddled the drive. Beyond it Vere could see a mansion covered with ivy, and a spread of stables. As they ran beneath an arch a swinging sign announced the place to be Woodlands Stud Farm. Vere was delighted for Val, and for the family. Maybe the past could now be set aside and a new, closer bond with the runaway Ashleigh could be forged. It was good to find a spark of hope amidst the gloom and worry of wartime.

Val brought the vehicle to a halt outside the stables and jumped from the driving seat. A man of around forty came from the nearest building and took charge of the horse, smiling at Val. 'You made excellent time, sir. I take back all I said about driving yourself.'

Val returned his smile. 'You'll learn to think it, not say it where I'm concerned.' He turned to Vere. 'I'd like you to meet Philip Bostock, the manager here. There's nothing about horses he doesn't know.'

The man in breeches and a shirt with sleeves rolled to the elbow wiped his palm on his hip before shaking Vere's hand. 'You brother's exaggerating, Mr Ashleigh, but what I don't know *he* does so Woodlands is very lucky in its new owner.'

'Come up to the house,' Val said to Vere. 'I'm sure you'd like a drink before we eat. No good offering you beer, I suppose. It'll have to be a more gentlemanly sherry.' He looked back at the stud manager as they walked away. 'You'll give us the tour after lunch, Phil?'

'Yes, sir. I'll be here.'

Vere was all at sea as he stepped out beside his brother. 'I think you should explain what the devil's going on before we go inside. Bostock suggested something quite astonishing.'

'What's astonishing about owning this place? I lost Goonawarra, so I've bought Woodlands instead. It's a bloody good investment.'

'You've bought it for *yourself*? There's . . . no one else?' Vere asked with a sense of disappointment.

'I've bought it for little Kate,' was Val's disconcerting reply which silenced Vere until they reached the house.

Mary Vernon, the housekeeper, greeted them warmly and said lunch would be served in half an hour. Then Val led Vere into a long, attractively furnished room, which commanded a comprehensive view leading to the lake. Vere stood gazing from the windows as he took the sherry Val poured. A moment later Mrs Vernon entered with a glass of cold ale on a tray. After she left, Val took several pulls at his preferred drink before saying, 'You're quiet.'

Taking his gaze from the tranquil beauty of the scene, Vere faced his brother. 'After your return from Australia I thought you could do nothing more to rob me of words. I was wrong. What's this all about?'

Val perched on the arm of a chair and spoke frankly. 'It's about dying and having nothing to leave for the next generation. This war's not like the one we knew in South Africa. Gallipoli was hell on earth. Everytime I woke up I expected to be killed that day. After a couple of months I bumped into some blokes on the beach; drovers from Goonawarra. They told me someone else had bought it. After that I started caring about staying alive because I was bothered about the fact that I owned nothing – absolutely nothing. I had money, a great deal of it, but nothing of substance.'

'There are things of yours still at Knightshill,' Vere said quietly.

'Things that belonged to a boy lost on the *veld*.' His mouth tightened and Vere realized, with a pang, the depth of bitterness still within his brother. It was in his eyes as he added, 'When you brought out that sword and offered it to me, it reopened the wounds with a vengeance. I went on the town with the full intention of getting drunk, and ended up selling myself to the King for a shilling once more. I tried to desert, but they were ready for volunteers who changed their minds in the cold light of day. After that I stopped fighting it. It seemed to me Grandfather had won, after all. I was in the West Wilts as an Ashleigh, and I'd be killed in action wearing the right uniform. The only way I could continue to thwart him was to remain a private and declare myself an Australian with no connection to the family.

'I made a will before leaving England. I wanted Kate to have Goonawarra – my only possession – because I felt her worth and dedication were unrecognized by all the talented, exotic people I found at Knightshill.' His brow furrowed slightly. 'Perhaps I thought she might one day go to Goonawarra and find – I don't know – an echo of someone she once knew. Something not possible with a financial legacy.' The frown deepened. 'When I discovered that I *didn't* own the station, I felt I'd let her down.'

'That was foolish,' said Vere, knowing all too well the pressures men faced during war. He had had those feelings of inadequacy, and had fought his own battle with their grandfather. Because of that he was caught up in all his brother was saying.

'Foolish! What a bloody feeble way to describe the sense of loss when Jed Watkins told me about Goonawarra!' Val drained his glass and wiped his mouth with the back of his hand, lost in recollection of that tragic campaign. 'We became *nothing* out there, you know. We were filthy, covered with lice and sores, running with dysentery, black with flies; just skin and bones. When I heard that the only decent memorial I'd leave behind had been sold over my head, I knew I didn't want to go out that way – like a sewer rat. I wanted to survive long enough to . . .' He broke off abruptly to go off at a tangent. 'I vowed to buy some other place for Kate. Woodlands is it. I bought it as it stands from a war widow who couldn't bear to live here alone. The sale was completed last week.'

'Not by Benson, or he would have told me.'

'No, not by Benson. He made a bloody mess over Goonawarra. I wasn't going to risk losing this. He should be retired . . . or shot.'

Vere was aware of how much Gallipoli had changed the drover who had turned up at Knightshill. He had begun to fight back once more, not through a mistaken sense of atonement for his past but for his future, however short it might be. Was there an additional reason? Kitty maintained that Kate was in love with Val; perhaps an extension of childhood adoration but very positively an emotion which affected her strongly. Was it reciprocated? Did his brother nurture affection deeper than kinship for the girl? Was that why he was doing this?

'You haven't touched your sherry,' Val said.

Vere put the full glass on the windowsill. 'Does Kate know about your gesture?'

'When we met in Alexandria I hadn't even begun looking for a property.'

'Did you know the ship she was serving on hit a mine off the coast of Gallipoli? The medical staff were picked up safely, but a number of the wounded were drowned.'

Val reacted. 'The *Romaine*! I read about the disaster during the voyage home, but I had no idea Kate was involved. Poor little girl!'

His brother was disturbed, but not as much as a man in love would be. As much as Simon had been. Vere cast aside the unwelcome possibility with relief, and probed further. 'You'll leave the house shut up, and Bostock in charge of the stud? Isn't that a little risky?'

'Phil's been running it for years. I trust him as you trusted John Morgan when you went to war.'

'John had been *with* us for years, but you've only just met that man.'

'Good God, Vere, I'm trusting my *life* to strangers every day. Horses are Phil's world. He won't let me down. Mrs Vernon will remain as housekeeper. She lives in the village. I've instructed my new man of business to handle the finances. The army has first claim on our bloodstock, of course, but the poor beasts aren't suited to the purpose they have to fulfil. Hundreds perish in the mud and extreme temperatures. It's a bloody awful world.'

'It is at the moment,' Vere agreed, 'but I'm glad you've found what you were looking for.'

Val seemed oblivious to the wider implications of that comment, and kept on the subject of Woodlands. 'I'd be glad if you'd come over now and again just to check on the house. Mrs Vernon won't handle more than the cleaning.'

Vere was dismayed at the thought of additional responsibilities, but he merely said, 'Of course I'll come over. If you let me know your movements I'll send you regular reports.'

'Thanks.'

As his brother made no attempt to elaborate, Vere asked, 'Where are you stationed at the moment?'

'Henley. I've been with a training battalion since they shipped me home just before Christmas.'

'Why on earth haven't you been to see us?'

'I should have thought it was obvious.'

Back to that! Vere pressed on. 'Still *Private* Ashleigh?'

'They made me a sergeant at Gallipoli – on the first day. The other poor buggers had been machine gunned as they landed, so I had no choice. I turned down the commission they offered me at Henley. I couldn't stop them giving me a medal, but I can refuse

Grandfather the satisfaction of having me listed as an officer on the regimental roll of honour.'

So he had not entirely abandoned his hostility to Ashleigh tradition! 'It may never come to being listed on the roll of honour.'

His brother's vivid eyes met his. 'The summer offensive is continuing all along the Somme. More wholesale slaughter which gains little. Another winter will kill as many as the bullets do. Then we'll try again next spring. The chances of survival are slim.'

'They were in Gallipoli.'

'A bloke's luck runs out sooner or later. I'm on seven days' embarkation leave. That's why I called you here.'

Mrs Vernon announced that lunch was ready, and they walked through to another pleasant room overlooking the hills and lake. It was a simple lunch of the kind that would normally have been served to the last owners. There was no question of Val shovelling it into his mouth, despite his description of life on Gallipoli. He drank ale rather than wine with the meal, but he otherwise appeared to have slipped into his former style quite naturally. Vere sensed that the Australian drover had become the English landowner without looking back, and he was thankful despite the news that his brother would soon be in the front line. Val had something to live for now – if his luck did not run out.

They discussed the problems of owning property, and Vere spoke of John's death and the necessity of an annual visit to check on the Texas ranch. 'It's not only time consuming, it's getting risky to cross the Atlantic where German submarines prowl. Profits have doubled during the last two years, and Lottie's boys love the place enough for perhaps one of them to take it on later. Even so, we've considered selling it. We'd need your consent in writing, of course, because Mother made you the major shareholder.'

'I'll give it to you today,' Val said instantly. 'You've done all the work on the place, so you must do whatever suits you all the best. I'm sorry about John. He was a decent bloke.'

As he made no enquiries about Charlotte, Vere guessed Val had no love left for his sister. 'It's a good thing Lottie has her work at Ashleigh Court to occupy her. She's taken her loss very well. Kitty helps her as much as she can, but she's worried about Simon.'

'What's wrong with him?'

'She's afraid he'll volunteer in spite of being exempt.'

'He'll be a damn fool if he does.'

'I know.'

'What about that young gladiator, Tim?'

Vere sighed and pushed away his plate. 'We had notification two months ago that he was missing in action. You can imagine how that upset everyone. Then, yesterday, there was an official letter stating that he's a prisoner of war.'

'*Poor little bugger!*' It came out explosively. 'He'd be better off dead.'

'Val!'

'So he would.'

'For God's sake, the boy's safe for the duration. Margaret's overwhelmingly thankful. We all are.'

'Then you're all bloody fools,' Val cried with mounting anger. 'Ever since he's been old enough to understand, he's been fed honour and glory, as I was. Vorne was held up as the shining example to follow. *As he was to me*. After Margaret married Laurence it's evident Tim was pampered and spoiled by her and, later, by a legion of willing women until he can't take advice – especially from me. I tried to talk some sense into him, but the little prig hit out about honouring our ancestors. You should have told him the truth about Vorne. He deserves to know.'

'We decided against it,' Vere said stiffly, resenting the outburst of condemnation.

'As you decided against telling me until it was too late. Christ, I wonder if any of you has an inkling what you've done to him by your silence. He's had everything he wanted. Now, at the most vital time of his life, everyone has begun saying *no* to him. When he was all set to live up to the heavy burden of heroism on his shoulders, Margaret made sure he couldn't by arranging to have him kept at GHQ. I guess he finally broke out, and tried again to become another Vorne. Now the Germans have ensured that he can't. He can't be like any ordinary prisoner of war, you know that. *He's an Ashleigh of Knightshill with obligations to his ancestors*.' Val was so worked up he got to his feet. 'Being locked up for the rest of the war will break the poor bastard, and you know who'll be to blame? Not Grandfather, this time. As you said, he's been dead fifteen years. It'll be you, Margaret and Lottie – for allowing him to be weighed down by an obligation he doesn't owe. Take my word, none of you'll be "overwhelmingly thankful" when you see the man who comes home when it's all over.'

They marched in from the Front Line 'filthy, famished and fagged out' as a young church-going soldier put it. The majority found riper adjectives to describe their condition. Sergeant Ashleigh could come up with even bluer ones, but he kept them to himself and instead encouraged the men to sing as they plodded through muddy puddles in dazed state, cheering them with promises of square meals, baths and untroubled sleep.

'You can keep all them, Sarge,' chirped an irrepressible lecher, 'just give me a mamzelle for each of me arms.'

'You're in no fit state to handle one much less a couple, Bates,' Val retorted, making another check on his company for stragglers as they neared the small town where they would 'rest' until going forward again in time to spend Christmas as close to the enemy as they could get. 'You're running with lice, covered in sores and ugly enough to frighten the Huns more than a bloody tank heading straight for them. What's more, you haven't taken your clothes off for weeks. When you do and see what's underneath you'll settle for a game of cards instead. No man can stoke the fire with a flamin' rabbit's foot.'

This brought a ragged shout of laughter, but Bates' scowl was deliberately assumed. He knew and understood good-humoured ragging, and he would find himself a girl without much trouble. He always did.

'I don't know whether to first jump into the marble bath with gold-plated taps and relax in the steaming hot water with a good book, or saunter into the restaurant and eat a châteaubriand with fresh vegetables, washed down with an excellent red wine,' mused a lad who had formerly been on the staff of a baronet's household and enjoyed mimicking the gentry.

'Wash *yerself* down with red wine,' advised his neighbour in the column. 'It'll take somethin' like that ter get the muck off yer skin. Water won't be no good.'

'I'm going right to sleep,' vowed a former printer. 'Just come along every four hours and shove food in my mouth. I'll be fine.'

Val stepped out and reached the head of D Company once more, marvelling at the tenacity of these men who, like himself, had miraculously survived two desperate actions along the Somme in a last bid to secure total breakthrough of the German line before winter set in. Half the battalion had been lost, but that was a mere drop in the ocean against the total casualty toll of a campaign that had lasted five months and had achieved only limited success. For the past month Val had been in command of D Company, there being no officer available. The remnants of the battalion were led by a junior captain, but they numbered little more than a company, and the companies were merely the size of a platoon. During their time in reserve they would be reorganized and re-manned. Those who had been there since June would go on home leave, which had been resumed now the summer offensive was over. Val was among the number who had arrived halfway through as reinforcements and therefore had no hope of leaving this doomed landscape for an indeterminate time.

Life in French trenches was much like it had been in Gallipoli, except that it was cold and wet instead of dry and sweltering. There were compensations, however. It was possible to take a rest in reserve for a while. Supplies did not have to come in boats, and the wounded did not have to be ferried out by them. He had, himself, been treated for a minor flesh wound practically on the spot. The fear of gangrene leading to amputation had been with him since Alexandria. He had been lucky then, but a man's luck eventually ran out.

Another difference here was that his true identity was known. Fate had played yet another trick by sending Valentine Ashleigh to join a battalion served by a captain named John Marshall – the one presently in overall command. The new sergeant's name, in addition to his marked resemblance to Tim, made it impossible for Val to deny being the uncle from Australia Marshall's friend had gone to Knightshill to greet. Despite what Val was certain Tim had said on returning from that meeting, the officer had tackled him in pleasant manner and remained on friendly terms. It was not the kind of relationship Val had shared with Andrew – John Marshall was a fully trained regular soldier in his late-twenties with two years' war experience – but they had respect for each other, which was valuable when the going was tough.

It was inevitable that the news travelled. While many of the officers found it difficult to accept a sergeant who was a member of the regiment's founder family, the rank and file responded warmly to a man who could be as foul-mouthed as they, roughed it without complaint, and stood up for them against anyone, whatever his rank. When he then proved steady and sure in action, they were ready to follow him anywhere. Right now, however, Val could not wait to see them settled so that he could get his clothes off and scrub himself clean before finding what passed for a Sergeant's Mess to eat until food came from his ears. After a decent sleep he would search out the cavalry regiment he heard was in camp just outside the town, and make a mate of their sergeant roughrider. He could not wait to get among horses again.

As he limped along on feet grown spongy from standing in water day after day, his back ached, the shoulder they had dug a bullet from in Alexandria gave him sharp twinges of pain because of the constant wet weather, and his eyes were sore from lack of proper sleep. He chose to ignore the heavy mass of rice pudding that was once his brain. The only thought it could presently produce was an instruction to keep going until he reached a place where he could satisfy all his basic needs.

The little town was overflowing with troops, vehicles and horses. The streets were so full it was impossible to march in column through them. John Marshall halted them and spoke to his subordinates – a subaltern, two sergeants and three corporals. 'We've entered Bedlam. I'll go with Sergeant Ashleigh to get details of our billets, messes, etcetera. Pointless to wander around in this damned circus hoping to come across our patch. Give the men a rest, even if you have to kick a few of these fresh-faced new arrivals out of the way. We were here long before them.'

As Marshall and Val walked off, the weary West Wilts sat down on the wet cobbles regardless of pedestrians and military vehicles then caught in a bottleneck. They were not going to move for *anyone*. 'I'm amazed they hoofed it this far,' the officer commented. 'I've a feeling I'm about to have a blasted great row with someone, because our hopes of food, baths and decent billets look doomed. This place can't possibly sustain these numbers. Are you in a suitably aggressive mood?'

'The first neat and tidy bloke to deny us what we're entitled to will get a bloody punch on the nose,' Val promised.

'A few of your choice expressions will suffice,' came the response from a man nearing the end of his tether. 'You don't want to spend your break behind bars . . . and I don't want to lose one of the best sergeants I've ever had.' They pushed their way through a rowdy group tumbling from the door of an *estaminet*, with dangerous disregard for *their* merry state and their own present exhaustion. Then Marshall asked, 'Are you still adamant about taking commissioned rank?'

'I wish you'd stop bloody asking,' Val grunted, giving an inebriated Highlander a hefty shoulder charge reminiscent of his days on a rugby pitch, then regretting it because the old wound made an acute protest.

'You're doing an officer's job. Why not get paid like one, with all the additional advantages?'

Val flashed him a pointed glance. 'You've been standing in the same flaming trench as me, with water up over your boots. You've been shelled and bombed, like all of us, and you've got just as wet, muddy and terrified each time there's a gas attack. But *you* have to go over the top in front of the rest – out there on your own, a perfect bloody target. No, thanks!'

They fought their way through a contingent of French cavalry halted by a fleet of supply trucks heading in the opposite direction. Neither would give way and exchanged expletives in several languages while worsening the pandemonium in the narrow thoroughfares. When they emerged from the throng of mud-caked animals and riders, Marshall said, 'It's nothing to do with going out in front, is it? You've been doing that without turning a hair for the past three months.'

Relatively free of pedestrians now, they were suddenly drenched by a deluge of muddy water sent up by an ambulance racing past. '*Christ*!' swore Val, 'which bugger said a few weeks in reserve would set us up as new men ready to tackle the Boche single handed?'

'I did.'

They exchanged looks then began to laugh. If the laughter held a note of hysteria it was understandable. When they calmed down, Marshall said, 'Whatever your reasons for your attitude, I'm sorry. You're the epitome of all your family stands for; all Tim was sure he'd be. It's such a waste.'

Val remained silent. John Marshall had just added the finishing touch to his deep depression. The last thing on earth he wanted to be was the epitome of all the Ashleighs stood for. He had spent fourteen years trying to be the opposite.

While Marshall gave a balding billeting officer the unexpurgated version of his opinion, Val did the same in the office of an ageing sergeant attempting to feed an unknown number of troops who had come in from the front lines.

'Now, look here,' said this harassed individual, 'don't use that tone with me. You shouldn't never have been sent here. Gawd knows how many expects feeding already, and I ain't Jesus satisfying the multitude, you know.'

'And I'm not flaming Hercules wiping out the German army with one stroke, but I've put enough of them out of action to let you sleep safely in your dry, warm bed. I don't give a tinker's piss about who is in this dreary little hole, *we're* here and I want hot meals for the West Wilts before it gets dark. *Today*, mate!'

'How would you like to wait your turn?' he asked nastily.

Val grabbed the front of the man's tunic and pulled him to his feet. 'How would you like a knee in your balls?'

It worked. The poor man somehow produced a miracle and the men of the decimated battalion enjoyed a hot, satisfying meal before they bedded down on the ground beneath some overcrowded, sodden tents for the best and longest sleep they had enjoyed for weeks. The hot bath had to wait, but they did not grumble. They were too tired to wash, anyway.

Val and the other NCOs created their own accommodation in a small hut beside the railway station. It smelt unpleasant, but that was something they were used to, and it was big enough for them all to have a decent place to themselves once they had thrown outside some lengths of rusty rail and a pile of mouldy sacking harbouring a rat's nest. They had eaten with the men, but had been luckier in scrounging a bath from some Rifle Brigade NCOs who took pity on them. The bath consisted of a large oil drum filled with tepid water and carbolic, but it was wonderful to strip right off and wash with soap even if the water had been used by many others. Val exercised his seniority and went first, but was soon hauled out by his impatient fellows. Dressing again in khaki stiff with mud spoilt the fresh feeling, but they all slept as soon as they stretched out in the hut they had appropriated and not even the rattle of passing trains disturbed their slumber.

It was not until two days later that Val was able to make his way to the cavalry camp and win over the sergeant roughrider. Val claimed to be a horse breeder to explain his knowledge of the creatures he loved to be with, and made no mention of the 57th Lancers. The man enjoyed nothing more than to talk horses with someone who was a fellow enthusiast, so the morning flew past ending with an arrangement for Val to ride with his new pal on the morrow down the road to a nearby halt where fodder was normally offloaded.

Val said goodbye and began to walk back to town. The rain had stopped, although low cloud kept the midday atmosphere gloomy and cold. He tried to blot out the sight of a town whose typical French rural houses had become a collection of half ruins, alongside broken streets filled with a khaki horde that blended into the muddy devastation stretching for as far as the eye could see. Instead, he struggled to conjure up a visual memory of Woodlands. He did his best to shut off the sounds of clattering boots, shouts and coarse laughter, the repetitive clangour of klaxons endeavouring to scatter pedestrians to allow vehicles through, and the roar of motorbikes driven by shell-shocked dispatch riders, and remember instead the chorus of birdsong and whinnying of horses in the peaceful fields around the place he had bought for Kate.

Was it only three months ago? Would he ever see it again? There would be no more major battles until early next year. If his luck held to keep him safe from routine shelling throughout the winter, he might get some leave in before the onslaught of 1917 began. He would like to go to Woodlands once more. A week was no time in which to put his own mark on the place. If he was killed before he could go back it would scarcely stand as a memorial, and Kate would feel nothing of his presence there as she would have at Goonawarra. Time and war had hazed his memory of the vast brown Outback so that he no longer yearned for it. He now wanted the green, cool beauty of Blecton Mere, the joy of riding across meadows gleaming with summer dew, the sweet smell of hay and well-groomed horses, and a bed with crisp linen sheets in a room in a house so far from any other place it was quiet enough to hear the stars twinkling. All at once he wanted these things so much he felt tears stinging his eyes.

Shaken by a depth of emotion he could not handle, he turned from the road to sit on a chunk of wall ending and beginning in the middle of nowhere, letting the tears spill over. He had seen and done so many terrible things and remained controlled, yet thinking of a place which had been his for so short a time had broken his composure without warning. He prayed no one would see him. It was the horses, of course: being with them again had weakened him.

He sat for a long time, oblivious to the cold, sharing the cause of his tears with young Andrew Duncan who did not deserve what he had suffered at Gallipoli, with little Kate who had been shipwrecked when she should have been enjoying the idle pleasures of youth, with a legion of nameless men who had risen up on the blast of a whistle and advanced into the smoke of gunfire never to be seen again leaving a legion of mourners, with the horses he had just seen who should be running free in meadows instead of struggling through rivers of mud under shellfire, with a young man burning to prove himself who was imprisoned by the enemy and, lastly, with another young man who had tried too hard and destroyed himself.

Chilled and further exhausted, Val looked at his watch and saw that he might be too late for what the army called 'dinner' for other ranks and 'lunch' for officers. Although he no longer felt hungry he knew he must eat all he could before going back up the line, where it would be bully and biscuit again. Then he would sleep. It was his off-duty day so he could do whatever he liked. He got to his feet and forced himself to head back to the mêlée.

'*Havelock*!'

Val stopped abruptly and turned in a state of icy shock to see a woman in shapeless khaki standing beside an ambulance she appeared to be washing down with a mop on a long handle. He scarcely recognized her after seventeen years, but only one girl had ever called him by that name. As they stared at each other wordlessly, all the pain and humiliation young Martin Havelock had suffered afflicted him as strongly as it had during those lost years on the *veld*. Vivienne Beecham had sent his sword to Vere; the sword that had affected Ash, the drover, so strongly he had drunk himself silly and wound up back in the army. She looked to be in a state of shock, too, as she held the mop motionless and dripping above the bucket of dirty water, but as Val stared at her white face he was back on an open plain during a dawn punishment parade designed to break even the strongest of men.

He backed away from her, crying through his haze of continuing shock, 'Don't *ever* call me that again!' When he pushed his way onward through the usual khaki mob he was mentally still on that South African plain.

Val ate stew with potatoes and cabbage without tasting it. How *could* that girl be here? How could she have known *he* was here? He was a man of thirty-seven. How could she have recognized in him the arrogant youngster of twenty; recognized him as he happened to pass by? Why, oh why, had she to be here at this very time? It was obvious she had not changed. She had always delighted in addressing him as Havelock, even when he became first a sergeant then an officer; she had always delighted in riling him by trying to probe further into his background. She had claimed he was a mystery man, and every encounter with her had been a fencing match. That she had finally succeeded in discovering his true identity was proved by the fact of her sending his sword to Knightshill.

He had been looking forward to his rest; he badly needed it. She could ruin things for him. Of course, she was now a woman almost his own age, no longer the pert, eighteen-year-old daughter of his colonel, but if she tried to behave in the same headstrong way she would find herself upturned in her bucket of water. God knew in what capacity she was here – she had not been dressed as a nurse and they surely did not wash vehicles – but he was no longer ruled by the obligation to treat her with respect. If she thought she could carry on where she left off, he would soon disillusion her. All the same, her reappearance was a blow. She had been present at the destruction of Martin Havelock. Deep down inside him the humiliation and shame remained. Each time he looked at her it would rise a little further.

He left the large mess hut without having said a word to those around him. No one cared. It happened all the time. Men received letters from girlfriends and clammed up, or someone got killed and his chum grew morose and hostile. Every so often men sank into sudden depression, and all of them had times when they were sick to death of everyone around them. It was a fool who did not recognize these signs and respect them.

Outside the hut beside the railway Val found Vivienne sitting on an upturned tin drum he intended fashioning into a brazier after he had slept for a while. He was furious. 'How the *hell* did you know about this place?'

She seemed unperturbed by his anger. 'I asked a very good looking West Wilts subaltern where I could find Sergeant Ashleigh, and he directed me here.'

'Then I'll direct you straight back.'

'Please listen to what I have to say,' she said quietly. 'This is as much a shock to me as it clearly is to you, except that *I've* been hoping against hope that it would happen one day.'

'You'll bloody soon wish it hadn't,' he vowed.

She still looked very pale. Her unattractive khaki coat with a stained fleecy collar enhanced the impression of work-worn weariness. She had never been pretty, he recalled – too thin and with shockingly bright hair – but her freckled face had always been very expressive and her large green eyes had betrayed feelings that boded him no good. He saw the same message in them now. When she got to her feet he prepared to fend her off.

'It's very cold out here. Can we talk inside your hut? I know there's no one in. I knocked.'

'No.'

'Why not?'

'Because I just said so.'

A strained smile just touched her mouth. 'You haven't changed. You're still truculent.'

'And you're still a damned nuisance.'

She studied him for a moment or two, then said, 'I came to apologize.'

'Righto. Say sorry, then go.'

A train rattled past billowing smoke around them both. When it cleared she was nearer to him. He stepped back instinctively, but she did not come in pursuit. 'Seeing you suddenly after waiting so long, I spoke without realizing what I was saying. Although I've known all these years that you're Valentine Ashleigh, I can't think of you as anything but Havelock.'

'Don't think of me at all. That should solve the problem.'

Another train passed in the opposite direction. It was a busy time for bringing in enormous quantities of stores ready for the spring offensive. The smoke cleared and Val was shaken by the intensity of feeling her expression held. 'I can't *not* think of you. For seventeen years I've wanted the chance to put things right. I did my best to trace you, but all my enquiries resulted in no more than a vague suggestion that you were living abroad. I kept on trying in case I one day got lucky, but I didn't. When the war began I joined the First Aid Nursing Yeomanry because several detachments were going to Flanders. Of course I wanted to help in any way I could but I also believed that, somehow or other, you might be caught up in it – soldiering was once your life – and that, if fate was kind, we'd meet. I still can't believe it's happened.'

'You call this fate being *kind*?' he asked harshly.

She looked even more upset. 'Please, Havel . . . oh, I'm *sorry*! What . . . what do your friends call you?'

'We don't have friends in this game. They're never alive long enough.'

Suddenly and shockingly she began to sob, bending forward almost double as her shoulders heaved and the racking sounds of deep distress were forced from her. Val was appalled. He had never before seen a woman break down so totally. It was terrible to watch this hunched figure in shabby khaki standing on muddy cobbles beside a smoke-darkened hut, oblivious of those passing only a few yards away, and remember the unconventional, self-assured girl who had tried so hard to befriend him all those years ago. He had no idea what to do, until he could stand and watch no longer. Putting an arm behind her he coaxed her into his makeshift quarters and settled her on an upturned box which served as a table. Her sobbing sounded even worse in the confined space. There were no windows in the hut, so it was a case of burning candles or leaving the door open. He left the door open. It was not only a handy escape route, the fresh air dispelled the rather foul odours he had not really noticed before.

Vivienne continued to sob, so Val opened a bottle of beer, poured some into his tin mug and offered it to her. He had no notion what else to do. He was no hand with women. In his experience they were best avoided.

'Here you are, have a drink of this,' he said in desperation. When she appeared not to have heard, he drank the beer himself and continued drinking until the bottle was empty. He needed it.

Another train rattled past sending smoke in to dim the hut further. Val leaned back against the door staring at the lengths of track leading into the distance, and saw instead another track curving around tall aloe-dotted hills where a young man dying of thirst, exposure and a broken spirit struggled to dismantle sticks of dynamite tied there to blow up a train filled with British troops. The train passed safely, but Martin Havelock was unwittingly shot by those he had saved. For three years he had wished black men had not witnessed it and carried him to a nearby mission hospital. Clearly, he had not been meant to die then. He had not been meant to die at Gallipoli – not here on the Somme these past three months. It was unnerving to sense that his life was part of a deliberate plan.

'I'm sorry. *So sorry.*'

He turned at the sound of her voice roughened by the racking sobs. She was gazing up at him through strands of hair stuck to her cheeks by tears. Her eyes were red ringed and large with distress. She looked a pathetic sight. He sighed, remembering his own weakness just before their encounter. 'Would you like some beer?' When she nodded, he opened another bottle and filled his mug for her.

She drank and wrinkled her nose at the taste. 'You always preferred this to wine, didn't you? Some of the officers saw it as a sign of your unsuitability to be in the Mess. If *only* they had known you had a greater right to be there than most of them.'

Val could not tell her to go until she had recovered a little more, yet he had to cover the awkward moment even though she had introduced a subject he would rather avoid. 'How is your father?'

'Unhappy in retirement. A back injury makes riding difficult and painful. You'll understand the effects of such a penalty for a cavalry colonel. He and mother live in Kent. They've given over most of the land to the military for a training camp.'

'England's become one huge training camp.'

'I've never forgiven him for letting that be done to you,' she blurted out with great feeling. 'It's the first time he's ever given in under pressure from others. It was wartime and he had the perfect excuse to abolish the beastly ritual. I *burned* to tell him your real identity, but I kept your secret as I'd promised you.'

It was time to get rid of her. 'He knew who I was long before we went to South Africa.'

'He *knew*?' She was incredulous.

'It put him in a very difficult position. I appreciated that. He's a good man. If you had more sense you'd see it instead of condemning him unnecessarily.'

She put the mug aside. 'Is that all the thanks I get for defending you?'

'I never asked you to. I kept telling you to mind your own business.'

She got up wearing an expression he well remembered. 'You're still fighting me.'

'Too right, I am. I don't want all that raked up. It's now over and forgotten.'

'No, it isn't, or you wouldn't be so worked up about it. And you wouldn't care if I called you Havelock. It *is* one of your names, isn't it?'

'You seem well enough to go now,' he said pointedly.

'I will, if you'll accompany me.'

'You got here on your own.'

'No. The handsome subaltern brought me.'

'Then he can take you back,' he said remembering her determination to get her own way. 'We've only one subaltern, at present, handsome or otherwise. I know where you can find him.'

She came to where he stood in the doorway. 'So many, many times I've imagined our meeting. I knew exactly what I was going to say to you, how calm and understanding I'd be. So much for my advance planning.'

'You look terrible,' he said defensively, stepping aside.

'I can look quite nice when I'm neat and tidy. Come along this evening and you'll be surprised.' When he said nothing, she added, 'If I'm forbidden to call you Havelock, what name can I use?'

'Sergeant Ashleigh,' he said promptly.

Her smile changed her entire appearance. He recalled that it always had. 'I was dreadfully afraid that when we did meet up again, you'd be so full of Ashleigh aura I'd be well and truly disillusioned, but you're just the same. Your bark's worse than your bite. And I still want to be your friend. I've never met anyone as stimulating as you.' Her smile grew more persuasive. 'Please walk back with me, *dear* Sergeant Ashleigh.'

'I'm supposed to be sleeping. It's the only chance I'll have to catch up this week.'

'You can sleep when you get back and you'll be nice and fresh for this evening. Shall we go?'

He cast her an exasperated look. 'You really are the bloody limit.'

'I have to be where you're concerned. That's why our friendship is so special.'

Knowing the only way he could get rid of her was to do as she wanted, Val began walking at a brisk pace. Vivienne ran after him and fell in alongside, asking if they need go at breakneck speed.

'Yes. I need that sleep.'

'You won't get much in that awful hut with trains rattling past.'

'I've slept in worse places.'

Although they drew glances from the passing troops there were no jeers or catcalls. Vivienne was neither young nor pretty enough for ribald speculation, and he was marching her along in such purposeful fashion no one would mistake him for a hopeful swain.

'Are you married with a string of children?' she asked out of the blue.

He was tempted to say yes, but denied it.

'I'm glad you didn't lie. I checked with the handsome subaltern.' She met his fierce glance with another sunny smile. 'I'm not, either. I was engaged to a lieutenant in the Coldstream Guards when I was twenty-five, but I threw the poor man over after six months. When I reached thirty and everyone began hinting that I was destined to be an old maid, I accepted a proposal from the son of a motorcar manufacturer. He was drowned after driving his car into a river on returning home from a very wild party I wasn't free to attend. I was sorry his life ended so prematurely, but it got me out of a commitment I knew deep inside was a great mistake. Does that sound heartless?'

'It sounds flaming stupid to have done it in the first place,' he said as they reached the end of the street and turned towards the outskirts where the hutted hospital had been erected.

'You speak differently – rather like the Australian lads we often pick up in the ambulance. Is that where you lived for a while?'

'Yes.' That was all he was prepared to say on the subject. 'I didn't know nurses had to wash their vehicles.'

'They don't. I'm not a nurse. I've no medical qualifications.'

He glanced down at her. 'You nursed the wounded in Kimberley.'

'Of necessity. We were under siege. Everyone had to help as best they could so that we could hold out. I joined FANY to drive an ambulance. My second fiancé taught me a lot about vehicles.'

'You have a man along with you, of course.'

She stopped and faced him, her eyes lively with challenge. 'There's no "of course" about it. Our organization aims to free men to fight. We have another driver with us, in case she has to take over, and we both help to load the stretchers. A nurse travels inside to give emergency treatment and keep an eye on the patients.'

'What happens if the vehicle breaks down?' he asked with a frown.

'We hop out and put it right. If we can't, we have to ask the nearest unit to telephone for another ambulance. We sometimes get stuck in the mud and have to beg help to push ourselves free, but we're mostly self-sufficient.'

His frown deepened. 'Does your father approve of what you're doing?'

'I'm thirty-five and run my own life, but no, he doesn't. He's the old-fashioned type. Don't tell me you're the same.'

'Too right, I am.'

'You lived in Australia too long! Aren't the Ashleigh women emancipated?'

'Kate's a nurse. But that's different.'

'Why?'

He cast around for a reason. 'It's part of a woman's nature to care for people. Driving ambulances around battlefields isn't.'

She smiled. 'Isn't it? When you come this evening we can discuss that further.'

'Now, see hear . . .'

'It's the least you can do after I drank your horrible beer.'

'I didn't force it down your throat.'

She tried another tack 'We're both off duty and who knows when we'll get another chance to talk? We have a tiny room set aside for entertaining friends. It has comfortable chairs. Our tea is very drinkable, and there's homemade cake on offer.'

'I have to see to my men,' he said, determined to go down fighting.

Her eyes grew moist with a suddenness that alarmed him. '*Please* come. You said these days people are never alive long enough to make friends. Our friendship goes back a very long way, and we know we shall be alive until tomorrow morning, at least.' She began backing away. 'About eight? Knock on that brown door in the corner.'

CHAPTER FOURTEEN

Val could not sleep when he returned to his hut. He lay on the floor listening to rain thundering on the roof like a hail of bullets, thinking about women driving ambulances through mud and storms in order to release men to fight so that they could later pick them up from emergency aid posts and drive them to field hospitals behind the lines. The macabre absurdity of it all kept going round and around in his mind until he sat up, opened a bottle of beer and the door of the hut, and stared out at the rails running alongside piles of saturated wooden boxes. Vivienne Beecham had revived memories ruthlessly crushed while at Goonawarra.

Wrapped in blankets against the cold, yet appreciating the fresh air wafting through the door, Val allowed recollection full rein. He was a nineteen-year-old trooper on punishment duty inflicted by the foppish subaltern Audley Pickering, who had mounted a hate campaign against a new recruit who could ride superbly and knew more about cavalry drill than he – a newcomer with obvious breeding and intelligence, who must have committed some sort of offence against society and gone into hiding with the 57th. As Trooper Havelock rested from his labours in the stables, a young girl with carroty hair had passed on a lame mare which threw her at his feet. The girl looked him over with frank admiration which so reminded him of his recent humiliation at Chartfield, he put up all his defences. His attitude did not please her. She announced that she was the colonel's daughter and a mere trooper should do as she commanded. That red rag to the bull set a pattern which brought them into lively conflict each time she engineered a confrontation.

It addition to her sensual baiting, she told him she believed none of the supposed details of his background and was determined to get the truth from him. Worried by her prying, and increasingly wary of her growing admiration of his strong physique and professional ability, he found her as big a thorn in his side as Pickering – except that her motives were not vindictive but incomprehensibly feminine. Vivienne Beecham was sharply intelligent and caught him out on several occasions, which made him even more defensive in her company. She was irrepressible; he was limited to how rude he could be to his colonel's daughter. She longed to be his friend – they had much in common – but he feared it was more than friendship she wanted from him and took refuge in his lowly rank.

There was a fire in the stables. Martin Havelock brought out many of the horses and saved the life of another trooper at great peril to his own, which made him something of a hero. Lying in hospital badly burned and cut off from his family, he was bombarded with interesting, sympathetic letters from Vivienne which gave him reluctant solace. Although he could write no replies they kept coming and made the long, painful days endurable. When he returned to camp she made it clear the brand of friendship she sought was something he vowed never to give again. Females were dangerous and to be avoided. The frail rapport was firmly broken when she greeted her 'hero' with a fulsome kiss.

The reminiscences continued as Val became lost in his past, and another bottle of beer slowly emptied. South Africa. Sergeant Havelock was doing well and was popular with his men. He had friends of the same rank, and indulged his love of physical activity in a country which would give him the chance to redeem himself in his family's eyes, but Pickering had stepped up his campaign of destruction and the colonel's daughter was still with the regiment, persuing her own campaign to probe the mysterious facts which had driven an obvious gentleman to enlist as a trooper. She and her mother were besieged in Kimberley, which temporarily kept her out of his hair, yet the single letter she was allowed to send out at Christmas had been to her 'dearest friend'. It had unexpectedly touched him so that he had sent an impulsive reply. It was a mistake.

He was commissioned in the field after taking command from a dying officer and bringing victory out of defeat. At the convalescent home in a Kimberley free from siege, Vivienne had her 'wounded hero' just where she wanted him. Second-Lieutenant Havelock was of correct rank to show interest in the colonel's daughter, and Mrs Beecham approved. During those days the girl came near to discovering the truth. Entry to the Officers' Mess gave Pickering the opportunity to goad the commissioned ranker even off duty, so gaining his ambition was not the joy Havelock had anticipated. Constantly on his guard against letting slip the truth, he suffered from loneliness as he never had before. His former friends had to call him sir and hold aloof; his fellow officers lived by their own rigid set of rules which excluded those who did not obviously conform. In her determination to champion him Vivienne only increased the contempt of others for a man who took insults without murmur, and allowed a young girl to speak up for him instead.

Came the moment Havelock had constantly feared. A visiting senior officer knew the Ashleigh family well. The man even spoke of the amazing resemblance, but did not identify the moustached cavalry officer named Havelock as Valentine Ashleigh last seen as a senior schoolboy destined for the West Wiltshire Regiment. Vivienne Beecham did. In desperation, Havelock cruelly alienated the one friend he had in his bid to escape denouncement.

Drawn back from his reverie by a passing train Val felt drained by those vivid memories in which Vivienne had played such a constant role. Where were all those men now? Did they remember someone named Havelock, kicked out with dishonour? Did any of it now matter? When men were dying wholesale, when his own life expectancy was a week, a month? What had happened to that boy bearing his two middle names was surely no longer of consequence. Then why the *hell* had she turned up to resurrect it?

He opened another bottle of beer.

'I didn't expect you to come,' said Vivienne when she opened the brown door.

'I wasn't going to.'

'I'd have sought you out instead.'

'I know. That's why I'm here.'

'Come in out of the rain.'

'No, thanks. I can't stay. Your good-looking subaltern is making rounds shortly. I'll have to accompany him.'

She smiled. 'Liar! I've lived with a regiment for most of my life. I know as much about military routine as you do. Duty Officer doesn't do his rounds until much later. In any case, that handsome boy is presently in the hospital turning the heads of the baby VADs while having a small wound dressed. He slipped on the wet cobbles and gashed his temple on the door of a supply truck. The girls are spinning out the treatment as long as they can. He *is* rather cute. For goodness sake come in!'

True to her word she looked decidedly better, Val thought as he followed her down a short corridor, shaking the rain from his cap. She had on a long brown skirt and a pale knitted-silk jumper edged with broad satin ribbon, and she had done something different with her hair. It looked less severe than before, and shone in the soft lighting. Having been for most of the afternoon with recollections of a young girl, this woman seemed a stranger to him. He was not the same person, either. Whatever was he doing here?

Vivienne led the way to a room which had a resemblance of civilized living. Warm and cosy, with various armchairs, there were rugs on the floor and curtains at the windows. 'I told Mrs Rice-Bennet you're a close friend of the family, so she made no objection to your visit. Unlike the poor army nurses, we're allowed to mix with men. Make yourself comfortable. Someone will bring us tea and cake in about half an hour.'

'I'll be gone by then.'

'Why are you still afraid of me?' she asked immediately.

'Don't be bloody ridiculous!' She was no stranger. This was the same old game she was playing.

'At least take off your wet coat. It's making puddles on the rug.' She stood waiting to take it from him. 'Who's Kate?'

He glanced up from unbuttoning his sodden greatcoat. 'Eh?'

'You said she was a nurse.'

'Oh. My eldest sister's girl.'

'You have other sisters?'

'One.' He shrugged off the coat. 'Two died as infants. And a brother. I'm the youngest. That's the story of my family.'

She hung the coat on a hook in the corner and turned back to him. 'You haven't mentioned Vere, the famous war artist – the man I met in Kimberley whom you both pretended was a newsman seeking the story behind your award for gallantry. He *was* really your brother, wasn't he?'

Instantly on his guard Val said, 'Look, if you're going to pry into my life I'm going now.'

She sighed. 'I'm not prying, I'm simply putting the record straight.'

'Then don't. What's the point?'

Drawing close, she gazed up at him with a world of concern in her eyes. 'The point is that fate has given us this amazing opportunity to say all the things we couldn't then because it would have been dangerous. There's so much I want to know about you.'

'You always flaming did. *That's* what made it dangerous.'

'It didn't. I would never have betrayed you, and you know it. I've kept your secret all these years. I'll take it to my grave.'

'Don't be melodramatic.' He should never have given her his coat. He should never have come!

'All right, I'll be quiet and let *you* do the talking. What would you like to say?'

'Goodbye.'

After a brief moment of silence Vivienne burst into laughter. 'You always were the frankest person I knew. That's why I so enjoyed our vocal sparring matches.' She walked to a chair and sat, looking up at him. 'It was no fun being a colonel's daughter. The officers either had an eye to their promotion and sickened me with their insincere flattery, or were so frightened of putting a foot wrong they stiffened up in my company. You never gave a damn about my influence with father. It was so refreshing.'

'Your influence was negligible, I suspect. He was well able to judge men for what they really were.'

'All the more reason why he should have arranged for Audley to be seconded elsewhere. He was useless to the regiment. If Father had got the silly ass out of the way that awful affair would never have happened.'

'If that's part of putting the record straight I don't want to hear it,' Val said brusquely. 'I only came here to stop you from making me look a fool by prancing up and calling me *dear* Sergeant Ashleigh in front of my mates.'

'Shall I call you Valentine?'

'Not if you want to survive.'

'Val, then?' When he made no response, she smiled. 'Do you enjoy chamber music?'

'Eh?'

'How about Degas, Monet? What do you think of Oscar Wilde? Have you read *all* Shakespeare's plays? Do you agree that the chef at the Dorchester makes a better béchamel sauce than Roget at Claridges? Have you seen the latest colours for autumn?' She tipped her head sideways. 'Do *none* of those topics of conversation appeal to you?'

He shook his head in exasperation. 'You never give up, do you?'

'You never give *in*.'

'Why should I?'

'Because life's too short. Please, come and sit down for a while. Surely this is better than that terrible hovel you're living in, even if you have to put up with me. I promise not to ask anything you'd call prying.'

He gave a short laugh. 'It's second nature to you.'

'Only because you're so secretive. The more you refuse to tell, the more I want to know.'

'Exactly.'

She sighed. 'Is your past so *very* villainous?'

'Yes.' He moved across to the chair beside the fire, deciding that he would drink the tea she said was coming, then go. 'What about yours?'

'Very dull. When the 57th left South Africa we went into barracks in Northumberland for three years. Then to keeping the peace in Ireland. I grew very bored with my role. I missed you.' Before he could react, she continued. 'When Father had a bad fall during manoeuvres he had to surrender command. It broke his heart, as you might guess being someone who once also lived for the regiment. His personality changed. Poor Mother had to suffer it, but I left on the Grand Tour with a group of friends. After that I got engaged twice, indulged in charitable works, tried my hand at painting, toyed with learning to play the harp, wrote and tore up three chapters of a novel, thought about opening a flower shop – you know, all those useless things women like me do because it's expected of us. It's a dreadful thing to say to you, but this war's proving a godsend to women who've longed to really work and been prevented by convention from doing so. We'll never go back to the old ways when this ends.'

The chair was very comfortable, the fire was warm, and her voice had a lulling quality. Val relaxed. 'I can't imagine you knuckling down to mediocrity. You're too lively for that.'

'I was once. The only time I felt really happy was when I rode over the downs. Just me and Trojan. Yes, I bought your charger after . . . when they auctioned your things. He's in retirement now.'

Val remembered the gelding – a fast and furious animal with white socks. He had loved to take him out on the *veld* at dawn or dusk and give him his head. 'Too showy for the terrain in wartime. We'd have done better with whalers. I always said so.'

'I know – loud and long to everyone within earshot.'

'It was sound common sense,' he protested. 'I bought a stud farm last August. The army has been taking most of them, poor beasts. It's still the same story. They're not up to it.'

'No animal's up to mud, mire, shells and bullets. My heart bleeds for them.' She leaned forward eagerly. 'Where's your stud?'

When a girl in a brown overall came in with a pot of tea and half a date and walnut cake fifteen minutes later, Val was deep in a description of Woodlands. It made him yearn to be there.

Vivienne handed him a cup of tea and a thick slice of cake on a plate. 'You must have hated leaving. It sounds perfect.'

'Almost.' He bit into the cake. It was good. 'There's a couple of changes I'll make, if ever I see it again.'

'Of course you will.'

He glanced across at her, munching something that was reminiscent of his youth at Knightshill. 'You know damn well what the situation is. We'll have another crack at breaking through on the Somme when spring comes. The old soldiers who've survived so far are worn out, and the rest are untrained and unsuitable. We're getting nowhere against the Turks; the Russians are faltering on all fronts and their winter is upon them. This conflict will go on until there's no one left to carry on fighting. War's changed. There's no longer any honour or glory in it.'

'Is that why you've stuck at being a mere sergeant instead of *Captain* or *Major* Ashleigh, following in family footsteps?'

It came at him like a bullet out of darkness. He dropped the cake back on the plate. 'Look here, I didn't get into this for King and country. No flaming fear! On the night before I was booked to sail back to Australia I went out and got roaring drunk, then sobered up to find I'd enlisted in the very regiment I swore I'd never join. I'm only wearing three stripes because I stayed alive on Gallipoli longer than most and had no choice but to accept them.' He thrust aside the plate and got to his feet. 'Follow in family footsteps? Not bloody likely!'

Vivienne barred his way as he headed for his coat. 'I'm *so* sorry. I've touched a nerve.'

'Don't you always?' he accused, amazingly worked up. 'So much for friendship before tomorrow comes. Tea and cake and Little Miss Sweetness! And I bloody well fell for it! Right from the start you've meddled in my life and tried to take it over. You never stopped from the moment your mare threw you almost at my feet, until you sent that sword to my brother. It was because he offered it back to me with your letter that I went on a bender and ended up back in khaki. *You're* responsible – you and your interference in something that doesn't concern you.'

'Yes, it does,' she cried, as suddenly passionate as he. 'I know what's made you so bitter. You've never forgotten that dawn on the *veld. Well, neither have I*! I couldn't see what you were suffering, but I knew you so well I imagined it all too painfully. As the minutes dragged past I felt them breaking me apart as they must be breaking you.' She drew nearer, her face pale and tense. 'You abandoned honour that morning? *I* abandoned pride. I actually begged Father on my knees not to go through with it. I fought for you with tears and pleas. When it was over, and I defied him in order to watch you ride out into the wilderness, I knew I would never forgive him as long as I lived. I was very young. My parents thought I'd get over it. I didn't. I tried every way I knew to find out where you were, careless of what people thought of me. I telephoned Knightshill regularly and always received a haughty response from the butler that Mr Valentine was out of the country. I demanded to speak to Vere on one occasion. He was very charming, but firmly evasive. *Don't look at me that way*!' she cried. 'I wouldn't have made mischief. I simply wanted to know where you were. That's all. Just to know where you were,' she repeated brokenly. 'I even persuaded men friends to ask around in case you'd given instructions to put me off if I tried to find you. They had no better luck. It was as if Valentine Ashleigh did not exist.' She drew breath. 'I tried to believe that. For seventeen years

I've tried to forget you. I can't. Seeing you again tells me I never shall. I *love* you, Martin Havelock. I always did.'

As he stood completely thrown by her heated outburst she stepped forward to pull his head down and kiss him passionately, full on the mouth. When her body melted against his, an unprecedented charge of desire rushed through him dominating his senses and bringing the need for more than he was getting. Restraint was out of the question; she was as eager as he. Her room led off a quiet corridor. There, on blankets and rugs hastily thrown to the floor, they finally settled the youthful challenge each had made to the other long ago.

The rain and cold continued. Rest periods were never exactly that and Val was kept busy on unloading stores or road repairing, and with checking the equipment of the men under his command. It was a time for replenishing and taking stock, reassessing and absorbing reinforcements. New recruits straight from England had to be knocked into some sort of shape before they faced up to front-line trenches, and there was no kind way of doing it. As Val inspected them he grew angry. They were mere children who looked as though they were wearing their fathers' uniforms. Great black boots on the end of stick-like legs wrapped in khaki puttees, heavy tunics hanging on thin shoulders with the sleeves so long the hands were half hidden, and peaked caps overshadowing pale, pinched faces. The 'great adventure' had turned into a death machine, and these conscripted lads were terrified by what lay in store. A few old hands delighted in telling gruesome stories to them, but Val came down hard on the practice. The horrors would soon enough be upon them. Let them enjoy a few more days of relative peace. Who knew how many more they would have?

The battalion was also augmented by three subalterns straight from school, two captains and a major. Val reverted to a sergeant's normal duties under the command of a quiet, well-built youngster whose passion was bird watching. Val guessed Hector Milnes would have a keen eye and plenty of patience, which would help him develop the natural leadership skills he appeared to have – if he lived long enough. Val's greatest problem was how to keep the boy from addressing him as 'sir' when he was not thinking. The

Ashleigh name was almost holy to someone whose uncle had been in the West Wilts.

Throughout the military activity, Val counted the hours until he could be with Vivienne. It was not easy. Their off-duty periods did not always coincide, and they could not use her room. They had taken an enormous risk that first night and been lucky to have got away with it. Having for years sought women only when he absolutely had to, Val now revelled in the passion he shared with someone who wanted him as much as he wanted her. He felt no sense of guilt over what he was doing, only a drive to snatch what fate had offered before she played her next trick on him. Vivienne charged him with urgent life, so the shadow of death now hung more heavily over him to create a fever of longing to compensate for his past lonely years. When he had wanted no future he had survived against all odds. Now that he had so much to live for he feared the worst – and the day the battalion would return to the front line was nearing too quickly.

Whenever he could Val went to the cavalry camp and borrowed a horse. He took Vivienne one afternoon and persuaded the friendly NCO to let them have a pair of geldings which they raced across the soggy plain beneath watery sunshine. Then they returned to the room in a stone cottage on the road out of town, which Val paid for with food the old widow needed more than money.

'Shame on you, Sergeant,' Vivienne had teased on their first use of the room. 'You could lose your stripes for stealing from stores.'

'It's not stealing. I'm just collecting what the army failed to ship to me during five months on Gallipoli. I'd have given a king's ransom for some of this in that stinking hole,' he had retaliated.

Her levity vanished. 'Was it as terrible as they say?'

'Yes.'

'I'm glad I didn't know you were there. *Poor you!*'

'Poor everyone else! I was one of the lucky ones.'

She never mentioned his pilfering again.

Now Val was with someone who continued to challenge him he realized how dull his wit had become through twelve years on an isolated cattle station. He was constantly bested by her for the first few days, but he was sharpening up fast and it was as stimulating to spar with her vocally as it was to wrestle physically. They often argued about her work. While she forced him to admit that she and her team were splendid, dedicated people, he would not be shaken in his belief that women should not participate in war. She accused him of being old fashioned, of possessing an irritating sense of masculine superiority, and seeing her as no more than a soft, cuddly creature to give him pleasure when he had had a tiring day. He always agreed wholeheartedly with her assessment, which disarmed her and then ended the argument. There was nothing light-hearted about his views, however, and he worried every time she went out to the forward positions to pick up casualties. He did not trust fate.

They went riding one morning when they were both free, and stopped by an open shed covering a rusty tractor to exchange the kind of embrace denied them in public. They sat for a while on the straw-covered floor, Val leaning against a tractor wheel and Vivienne in the circle of his arms with her head against his shoulder.

She sighed with contentment. 'I feel better now. That'll keep me going until we reach the cottage. It's taken me seventeen years to wear down your resistance and now I have, you take my breath away every time.'

'Not for long,' he murmured against her temple. 'You still manage to talk all the way through it.'

She angled her face upward. 'Do your women normally keep quiet? I don't know how they can.' She then broached the subject every wise lover should ignore. 'I suppose you've had a lot.'

'Too right. In the Outback there's a woman behind every kangaroo, just waiting.'

She twisted further round. 'Be serious. It's important.'

'No, it isn't. *Now's* important, that's all.'

'Oh darling, I love you so very, *very* much,' she said with sudden desperation.

He recognized it and brushed her lips with his own. 'I know. I know. Is that why you asked that stupid question?'

'I want to be sure there's no one I should hate.'

'Only the men who engineered this war.'

Her eyes, soft with the echo of the passion they had just shared, studied his face. 'I can't hate them. In a way, they brought us together.' She touched his mouth with gentle fingertips. 'I must warn you I'm a jealous woman. I worked out years ago that a girl was definitely tied up with whatever it was that drove you to enlist as a trooper in the 57th. I want to know about her. Don't you think I deserve to be told the truth?'

'The only thing you ever deserve is to be put in your place.' He drew her closer, swamped with a longing for more time, a greater certainty of the future. She lay quiescent against him beneath his khaki greatcoat draped around her for warmth, as he gazed through the open barn door at the flat, devastated countryside beneath scudding clouds in a country alien to them both. A soldier and an ambulance driver stealing kisses and a lot more besides in any place providing privacy. Two people desperate to spend the rest of their lives together, about to be forced to part not knowing if this *was* the rest of their lives. If he went down this time all she would have to remember were these few urgent days and a past which would remain a mystery.

At Gallipoli he had suddenly yearned to leave something tangible, something which held an echo of a man called Val Ashleigh. He had bought Woodlands and had lived there for a mere week; he had finally loved a woman and been with her for so short a time. Yet there would be those two slender links with life if he departed from it within the coming few weeks. How tenuous, how fragile! She surely deserved to know why he had countered her challenge so determindly for so long, why he had been cruel to her at the end of those three turbulent years. *Of course* she deserved to know.

'I was eighteen and obsessed with joining a cavalry regiment,' he began. 'During the Christmas vacation my grandfather heard about my plan and vowed to use his influence to block any attempt by me to carry it out, and to cut off my allowance and my welcome at Knightshill unless I followed family tradition. Thwarted but determined I returned to Chartfield thinking of nothing but how to get what I wanted.'

Vivienne pulled from his arms to face him. 'You were at Chartfield? A cousin of mine married the science master there.'

Val saw Julia with his mind's eye – large nut-brown eyes, friendly smile, easy manner. The upper school boys were unaminously bowled over, but he had likened her to his sister, Margaret. For a moment he was tempted not to continue, but Vivienne was watching him in a manner which challenged him too strongly. It was not going to be easy to tell her of an episode to his discredit – an affair that started him on the downward path ending at Goonawarra. He drew her back against his chest. He was coward enough to avoid meeting her eyes.

'Julia was the new second wife of my housemaster; I was a senior prefect and captain of every school team. Girls held no interest for me. Winning the Waycliffe Cup as best all-round sportsman for the year, and finding a way to join a cavalry regiment were all I cared and thought about. She inveigled me into confiding my burning ambition, then stunned me with the news that her uncle was about to take command of the Fifty-seventh Lancers and that a word from her would get me an interview with him. She persuaded me that I could become one of his officers without Grandfather hearing about it until too late.' He sighed. 'I ignored my friend's warning about her true motives and walked into her trap.'

When Vivienne made to move he held her still. The rest must be said without interruption or it never would be. 'She told me I had to be especially nice to her in return for her intercession with Max Beecham. Like a donkey after a carrot I followed where she led, until on an evening when I was shattered by the tragic drowning of my friend, she completed her hold over me.' The barn, the view of muddy, wartorn landscapes faded as he remembered his helpless seduction by firelight in his housemaster's parlour. He continued speaking with that vision uppermost in his mind. 'Julia played a cat and mouse game from then on as I became more and more obsessed with her, and the meeting with your father was postponed. Then she invited me to the house one evening when Grieves would be away. I walked in to discover the true nature of her game and was revulsed. I then realized how I'd been duped and humiliated over the past months and I backed out in horror. Half an hour later I was accused by the Head of attempted rape and locked in a room of the sick bay.'

Val could not hold Vivienne now. She sat up filled with outrage. '*The bitch*! How could she have lied and cheated like that? Didn't you tell them the truth of it?'

'That I'd been committing adultery as often as she'd let me?' he asked harshly. 'I deserved to be kicked out for even a fraction of what I'd been up to with her. I was guilty of betraying a schoolmaster I respected, and of disgracing the family name. The latter upset me so much I jumped the train taking me home because I wouldn't face my grandfather until I'd redeemed myself.'

He wished she would not gaze at him with such fervent understanding. It made confession more difficult. 'After a week of wandering I rashly determined to get what Julia promised me. I'd never had the meeting with your father, so I knew he wouldn't recognize my face, but the name Val Ashleigh would give me away so I became Trooper Martin Havelock and told a pack of lies about my background.'

'I *never* believed them,' she said with fire.

'And made my life damned difficult!'

'If you'd told me all this at the outset, I wouldn't have.'

He gave a mirthless laugh. 'You were a precocious seventeen year old, full of self-importance, and set on imitating Julia by making me dance to your tune. Don't deny it. You'd have been outraged by the truth and ruined everything by telling all and sundry.'

'No, I wouldn't,' she contradicted hotly. 'I was so bowled over by you, I'd more likely have punched Julia in the eye.'

'That would have helped my case a lot!' He was weary of reminiscence now so he brought it to a swift end. 'After the fire your father offered to send me to Sandhurst, so I had to own up to my deception, although I lied about the reason for it. I expected to be court martialled, but he instead offered me a commission in the field at the first opportunity – a cavalry colonel's thrust at an implacable infantry general, no doubt. Only then did it dawn on me that Julia had never even mentioned me to him, so Martin Havelock need never have been created. She had had the last word in the pointless affair, and I've never trusted a woman since then.' He gave a heavy sigh. 'You know the rest.'

She put up a hand to rest against his cheek, saying softly, 'I only know I've loved and trusted you unreservedly throughout seventeen long years. I always will, *dearest* Havelock.'

Seeing the truth of that in the expression on a face which was now the dearest in the world to him, Val was swept by a new urgency that overrode all else. He stilled the hand stroking his cheek and held it in both his own. 'We have three more days. I'll go right back now and speak to the padre. He should be able to marry us either tomorrow or the next day.'

'No! No darling, *please* don't do that.'

He was severely taken aback. 'But you just said . . . what d'you mean, don't do it?'

'I don't want to get married.'

'Why? *Why* for God's sake?' He gripped her shoulders and tried to impress on her what he was indicating. 'You should be my wife. We can't go on like this. It's not fair on you.'

'I'll decide whether or not it's fair,' she retorted.

'No, you won't. *I'm* the one putting you through it so it's my decision.'

She pulled free and sat back on her heels, the determination he knew so well was evident on her pale face. '*Putting me through it*? Are you referring to what we do whenever we can at Madame Foulard's cottage? May I remind you that if I hadn't kissed you hard that first evening and dragged you to my room, you'd still be fighting me off. *I* seduced *you* . . . and don't be so damned old fashioned! I *want* you; I revel in those delicious hours together. You surely don't still believe that masculine nonsense about unwilling maidens.'

'Your cousin killed that notion stone dead,' he snapped, angered by her suggestion of seducing him, as Julia had. 'You're not on to that same bloody game, are you?'

Her expression changed dramatically. 'How could you even *think* that?'

'Then what game *are* you playing?' He got to his feet completely thrown by her reaction to his proposal. 'I've got to go up to the front line in three days' time and I don't know what's going to happen when I do.' He leaned his shoulder against an upright supporting an open hay loft above his head, and frowned at the distance into which he would soon be marching. 'I want to leave you something when I go. I haven't made my name worth much over the years, but I want to give it to you, all the same.'

She came up behind him, sliding her arms around his waist and laying her cheek against his arm. 'If I married you, I'd be sent home. I don't want that.'

'I do,' he said immediately. 'You'd be safe.'

'And *bored*.'

He twisted to face her. 'Because you couldn't get engaged twice, or consider opening a florist's shop?'

'Don't quote me,' she pleaded.

'Why not? You admitted the war's been a godsend to you.'

'Not in the way you're suggesting. You're being unfair.'

'Unfair? *I'm* not the one doing the rejecting.'

She flared up. 'I'm *not* rejecting you.'

'Then what are you doing?'

'Trying to make you see sense.' She took a deep breath. 'Despite your stubborn refusal to accept that we're playing a vital part in the war, it's an unarguable fact. I *care* about the work I'm doing. If you had ever come out with me you'd realize why.'

'I know about being wounded and about the journey to a hospital,' he interjected grimly. 'That's why I feel justified in my views on women not being involved in battle areas.'

She took his hand but he let it lie unresponsively in hers. The day had turned sour. 'Darling, having suffered and been nursed back to health, you should back those who made it possible.'

'The nurses were on ships. They didn't come within the range of guns.'

'No, they were shipwrecked by mines out at sea,' she countered. 'Why is it all right for Kate to risk danger, but not me?'

'I'm not in love with Kate.' He tried once more. 'Let me fix it with the Padre.'

'No, Val. They'd pack me off on the first train.'

'Exactly.'

'And when would I see you again? Six months, a year, whenever you were lucky enough to get home leave? I couldn't bear that. If I stay here, I'll see you every time you have a rest period.'

'If we don't move on, if *you* don't move on, if the Germans don't overrun this town. *If I'm still alive.*'

'Don't!' she cried, in distress. 'That's below the belt.'

'Sorry. It was.' He felt cold and depressed. Their parting was inevitable and he did not want to reach it with the sweetness marred. 'Come on, let's gallop the horses back and get beside the fire in Madame Foulard's cottage. I put my stripes on the line last night to get hold of a piece of bacon for her.'

Vivienne strove to strike a lighter note. 'Every time we meet I expect you to have been broken to *Private* Ashleigh.'

He shook his head as he put an arm around her shoulders to lead her out to the tethered horses. 'No, they won't do that. There's too few of us left who can tell the others what to do.' He swung into the saddle heavy-hearted, certain this issue would effect their lovemaking in the cottage where they had been so gloriously free and happy. Still, he had three days in which to persuade her to agree to his plan.

Those three days were snatched from them on the following morning when orders arrived advancing the West Wilts' departure by forty-eight hours. In the midst of hectic preparations Val went three times to the hospital, but Vivienne was out on a run and had not returned. He was eventually told that her ambulance had toppled into a shell crater and had to be hauled out. A replacement vehicle had been sent but Miss Beecham would remain with hers so that she could drive it back when it was possible. All Val could do was scribble a note to leave for her and march into the freezing dawn cursing fate with oaths that even Ash, the drover, had not used before.

Christmas Day was quiet. No one in the front-line trenches believed it was due to the Christian spirit prevailing, as it had in 1914. The troops facing each other across a stretch of bare earth, bordered each side by barbed wire, merely wanted to be left in peace on a day which made them all long to be at home with loved ones. They could not be bothered to fire at each other. What difference would one day make, anyway? The field kitchens provided hot stew which was the nearest to Christmas fare it was possible to produce under the appalling conditions, and the troops were allowed a double rum ration. Food parcels from home were still *en route*, having been bogged down along the road; the trenches were knee deep in water. Merry Christmas!

Soldiers waded through the collapsing trenches doing what was expected of them, day after day, as 1916 gave way to a new year without raising a single cheer from the men of the West Wilts. The rain hardly ever stopped. If it did it snowed. When temperatures plunged, a layer of ice formed on the miniature canals running through the front-line networks and frostbite became every man's companion. Those on lookout duty had to beware their fingers freezing on to their rifles, and bronchitis laid low more men than desultory attacks from the enemy guns. The only consolation, if any, was that the occupants of the facing front line were suffering equally.

Those first weeks of 1917 took a greater toll of Val than any since the commencement of the war. He suffered with everyone else the physical privations, but he was used to those. He coped wisely and capably with those new recruits who failed their first test of stamina, with old hands who could take no more and began showing signs of cracking, and with subalterns thrown in at the deep end straight from public school. Underneath it all he feared he was himself beginning to crack from the strain of the responsibility piling on his shoulders. It was well known that good sergeants were worth their weight in gold, but he was in no mood to appreciate the fact. Going round and around in his head was the knowledge that a new major offensive would be mounted as soon as the weather changed, and he would be a part of it. The man who had once believed soldiering was his life's blood wanted nothing more than to live in Wiltshire breeding horses, married to a woman who had made him sane again.

He missed Vivienne with a depth of loss that was almost frightening. Letters from her arrived spasmodically and seldom in the right order. She wrote of their love in uninhibited tones and told of her longing for their next meeting, but Val was beset by what he considered to be her rejection of him and found little comfort in her words. Convinced that his confession of adolescent lust for her cousin was responsible, he constantly castigated himself for telling the woman he loved of an affair she would not understand. Julia had been clever, sadistic and out to punish a boy with the physique of a man, who had made the initial mistake of not showing sexual admiration along with his schoolfellows. He had been ridiculously naïve, and dazzled by the prospect of gaining what Sir Gilliard had refused him.

Once in a mood of self-denigration it was easy to tell himself that, however one viewed the affair, he came out of it as weak, stupid or downright lecherous. Take your pick! He brooded, and it was inevitable that the second great humiliation in his life returned to the forefront of his thoughts. Vivienne knew about that and had still believed in him, but his adultery with her cousin she could not accept. Which woman would? Which woman would care to tie herself for life to someone who had been thrown out of a prestigious school *and* an élite regiment? He had been a bloody fool to tell her about Julia.

His temper grew short, he was curt and impatient with his men, he grew careless. Day after day he stared out over no man's land and willed the Germans three hundred yards away to rise up and overrun them. It would all be over then. Vivienne and his family could breathe a sigh of relief that he was finally out of their hair. Eventually, Val was tackled by John Marshall who, although he no longer commanded the battalion, or even the same company, knew him well enough to have a private word about his behaviour. They had been through the Somme offensive side by side.

'You've been a bit touchy lately,' he commented as they stood beside the emergency aid post one bitter morning in mid-February. 'Nothing wrong other than that touch of bronchitis, is there?'

'Only what we've all got. Feet like sponges, lice by the thousand, filthy clothes, itchy eyes – itchy bloody everything – and a growing urge to get out of these flaming ditches and just walk away. If you go forward the Germans'll shoot you; if you go back your mates will. It's a simple choice, and a damn sight better than staying put.'

Marshall frowned. 'You don't mean that.'

He flared up. 'Too right I do. I felt sorry for Tim, being locked up for the duration, but we'd all happily change places with him. He's so dead set on being a flaming hero, let him have a shot at being one here.'

They stood silently for a moment or two, staring at the sleety rain bombarding the landscape of mud from a mud-coloured sky. John Marshall had survived more than two years of such living, too, which was an added link between the professional officer and a maverick sergeant. They had also both just received treatment from the MO for complaints not sufficiently serious to send them to the hospital. Marshall had torn his hand on barbed wire. The dressing and bandage would not remain white for long.

'I thought I saw you in company once or twice with one of the young women of the ambulance section,' the officer commented casually. 'Vivacious, lovely bright hair. Lucky devil!'

Val said nothing. He would have walked away but was loath to leave the shelter of the awning outside the makeshift dressing station until he had to.

'I got engaged on my last leave,' Marshall continued. 'I'm not sure it was the right thing to do. It leaves us both committed to someone we can't see and prevents us from enjoying other opportunities offered because we feel guilty. A chap needs feminine company out here.' He glanced at Val. 'You two went riding occasionally, didn't you? Saw you along the road when I drove to Headquarters one day. You ride like a typical cavalryman.'

'Wrong. I was a cattle-drover. None of your fancy bloody horsemanship with swords and lances, just honest to God riding with a few thousand steers to keep you company,' said Val savagely.

'Do you miss it?'

'If I'd have left the beer alone I'd have been back there now, and I wouldn't have bloody volunteered with the rest of 'em.'

'Yes, you would,' came the quiet reply. 'You're an Ashleigh. Soldiering is in your blood. You've only to look at our regimental history to know that.' He frowned. 'Look, we've been through quite a bit together, haven't we? I've seen you hold a group of men steady under fire and in the worst conditions. You're doing what you have to now, but you no longer inspire them. When they see their sergeant morose, listless and extremely bad-tempered the men lose what little faith they had. It's not like you and I'm sorry to see it. It's also been noticed higher up. You'd better sort out what's worrying you before the big push comes, or you'll be in trouble.' He hesitated. 'Is it to do with the redhead who drives an ambulance?'

'Mind your own bloody business,' said Val.

Marshall sighed. 'I didn't hear that. I just know that when a good man goes off the rails there's nearly always a woman behind it.'

Val hunched his head further into the upturned collar of his greatcoat and softened his tone because he liked this man. 'You're all of twenty-seven and I'll be thirty-eight tomorrow. I don't need some youngster quoting me worldly wise maxims. I've seen more of life than you're likely to so keep your moralizing for boys like Hector Milnes. He's innocent enough to heed them. Yes, I'm an Ashleigh. When we go into action I won't let anyone down . . . but it won't be because of my name, it'll be for the poor buggers who don't deserve this.'

Val's birthday began like any other day – sloshing through toxic water, listening to men's complaints, checking that those reporting sick were genuine and giving a piece of his mind to those who were not, reporting to his company commander, Guy Blair, whose shattered nerves were being undermined daily by waiting for what would surely come in Spring, and eating unappetizing food distributed through the water-logged passages by cookhouse orderlies who seemed to spend all day wading back and forth. Throughout this daily routine Val's cough grew worse, but he merely joined a bronchial chorus which streched all along the front line.

He had just supervised the daily issue of rum when the post orderly arrived with a batch of letters. There was one for Val. He was disappointed to see Vere's handwriting, not Vivienne's, on the envelope, then decided he did not want one from her. He read all the family news with a sense of unreality. *Charlotte has been unwell. She is feeling John's death more acutely. Margaret and Laurence going from strength to strength. Audience with the King . . . new aircraft in prototype . . . Simon thrilled . . . Kate on her way home . . . convalescent leave . . . Tim moved to another prison camp . . . not allowed to send letters . . . all the children well . . . spent Christmas at Knightshill . . . house at Woodlands splendidly looked after by Mrs Vernon . . . lights fires and cleans every few days . . . Phil Bostock keeping the stud running smoothly . . . good man.*

Val glanced through the two pages absorbing the main points, but none of them touched him. Even details of Woodlands failed to evince any enthusiasm. He would never see the place again. It would belong to Kate by midsummer, unless bronchitis finished him off and she got it next month. He was now thirty-eight – twenty years older than that trusting fool Julia Grieves had destroyed – yet she had reached out to deprive him of the one worthwhile thing that had come his way in all that time. He screwed his brother's letter into a ball and thrust it into the slimy wall of mud beside him.

'Sarge, I got another one for you,' said the post orderly, turning from calling out the names of lucky recipients. He reached into his pocket to bring out a grubby brown envelope. 'It was brought by a bloke coming back from 'ospital. By 'and, like.'

Val took it and went into the dugout he shared with four other sergeants. The two present occupants were busy reading letters by candlelight and did not look up. Val sat on a crate and stared at Vivienne's handwriting, unwilling to open the letter. She had sent it with a returning patient to be certain it arrived, surely and quickly. She had written to tell him it was over; that she had lost all respect for him knowing what he had done to her cousin. Well, it was best to know where he stood instead of wondering. He slit the envelope.

> *My darling*, I'm so very thrilled. Dr Hapwood has just confirmed that I'm to have our child at the end of August. I think you'd better speak to the Padre after all, don't you? We want him/her to be your official heir, don't we?
>
> I love you more than ever, *dear* Sergeant Ashleigh.

Val was out of the dugout faster than if the Germans were coming over the top with fixed bayonets. The Padre was almost terrorized into interceding with the CO to gain Val forty-eight hours' compassionate leave, and permission to have a hot bath at the field hospital. He and Vivienne were married by the chaplain of a Highland regiment whose brogue was so strong they hardly understood what he asked them to promise. They were so elated they would have sworn to anything.

The day after the wedding Val was admitted to hospital with bronchial pneumonia. His wife was allowed to occupy her room until he was back on his feet, then she was signed off the books of FANY. The army arranged transport for Mrs Ashleigh as far as London. She would then no longer be their responsibility. Val wrote letters to his banker, Phil Bostock, Vere and, reluctantly, to Colonel Beecham, then gave them to Vivienne to take with her. She would move into Woodlands and their child would be born there. Neither mentioned the possibility of it growing up fatherless. Their last day together was difficult. Parting was even worse, especially for Vivienne who could not hold back her tears. Val sustained her with an assumed confidence and returned to the sodden trenches with a quieter spirit, knowing he would leave behind a little of himself when he encountered fate's final twist.

CHAPTER FIFTEEN

Christmas Eve! Tim gazed from the barred window at lights twinkling in the rooms across the courtyard. He could see the other prisoners moving about, smoking cigarettes, laughing, playing chess. His fingers tightened around the bars. He had been in solitary confinement on and off for almost a month. The room was large and furnished with basic comforts – bed, writing table with upright chair, washstand, fireplace with a small fire burning. He was allowed books, a pack of cards, and a gramophone with two records of German songs for one hour every evening. He was fed as basically as he had been before, but he was alone. He had the indignity of having to ring each time he needed the toilet, so that a soldier would unlock the door, escort him there, then take him back and lock him in again. He also had to exercise alone, after the others had gone inside. While he jogged round and around the courtyard, Tim knew he was being watched by the man he had crossed, and he burned with rage.

He had spent five days in a German field hospital after his capture, where little was done for him save the application of a dressing to his damaged eye. The medical staff naturally gave their own wounded priority, so Tim had lain on a stretcher on the ground with a dislocated shoulder and a broken jaw waiting to be moved to a general hospital for treatment. The physical pain he had suffered during those days was slight in comparison with the others around him, but it was overshadowed by the greater pain of failure. Sick at heart, he wished constantly that he had been killed. He would have died with honour like his Ashleigh ancestors, and his family could believe that heroism to match Vorne's had been within his grasp if his life had not been cut short. How would he face them all, and their legion of acquaintances? He had been so full of derring-do, so certain of his own skill and courage, so shamelessly arrogant with the women he encountered, yet all he had done in this desperate conflict was to go down with measles, work in an office well away from danger, and fall into the hands of the enemy. Had he changed his name to Ashleigh only to betray it? He should have remained a Daulton. It was surely that family's traits he had inherited, not those of a long line of heroes.

This mental self-torture intensified a fever brought on by infected wounds and lack of nourishment, so he was mercifully in the realms of delirium when he underwent the gruelling journey over pitted roads in a horse-drawn ambulance, to a French hospital behind the German lines. There, his shoulder was reset, his jaw reconstructed and his eye injury stitched up. His sight remained unimpaired, but his eyelid dragged at the corner where a scar puckered the flesh across his temple. The fractured jaw bone had given way as soon as he tried to eat solid food, so a second operation was performed. It was more successful but he suffered daily from a gnawing pain, and eating was sometimes agony. Before he was in the convalescent stage Tim had been sent to a prison camp for officers a hundred miles east of where he had been overcome and captured. He had spent the first three weeks in the camp hospital in the hands of an elderly doctor and careless orderlies. Malnutrition and fever had taken less toll of him than the inner torment that continued to beset him. He had no will to survive.

When Tim eventually joined his fellow prisoners he stayed aloof, deep in his morass of depression. There were only four other Britons, the rest being French or Belgian. Although Tim could very well have conversed with them all, he kept to himself his linguistic knowledge, especially the fact that he understood all that the German guards said among themselves. An indefinable belief that pretended ignorance might one day be useful to him strengthened his silence on the subject. Those men who had undergone trench life for two years accepted their captivity reasonably well, conditions in the camp being marginally better and drier. New arrivals were either restless and voluble, eager to make friends and to pretend nothing had changed, or moody and unpredictable. Some, in the grips of shell shock, welcomed the absence of constant fear and the thunder of heavy artillery. They remained apart, finding a corner to huddle into while they rode out their attacks of involuntary twitching. Even so, freedom was a precious commodity and being deprived of it affected them all.

The worst aspect for Tim was the open contempt of their guards. The commandant and his second-in-command were of the old school of officers who followed the code of their rank, but the conscripts who ordered the prisoners' day made no secret of their glee in being able to command enemy officers denied their pride and dignity. Tim had certainly lost all self-esteem, and the snide comments of country yokels in uniform added to that burden.

In November the five British officers had been moved to make room for some Frenchmen captured on the Somme. The new prison was an ancient French cavalry barracks on the edge of a windswept plain half circled by mountains. Drenching rain added to its aura of desolation, but they arrived to find a quite large contingent of British and Commonwealth prisoners there. This cheered the other four, but Tim was no more eager for fresh company than he had been before. They would all compare notes, and what could he say of his contribution to two years of bloody warfare? The Australian accent of some of the Light Horsemen reminded him of a man who had enlisted because he was too drunk to know what he was doing, and had come through five months of bombardment at Gallipoli with a medal to show for it. It was salt in an open, festering wound.

The commandant at Dubrais Barracks was vastly different from the correct Prussian at their former camp. Blond, aggressively handsome, stiff with Teutonic pride, Major von Model had been given the command because of a back injury which forced him to undergo heavy massage every morning. He ruled his staff with an iron hand, and seemed set on demonstrating to his enemies the civilized superiority of his race. A German aristocrat, he had a private consignment of gourmet food and Mosel wine delivered to him every month. This information was supplied by long-term prisoners, who also revealed that he frequently walked in to chat with them as if they were guests at his country seat. Yet they warned that there was a ruthless streak beneath his geniality, and he had some unpleasant habits. Tim soon discovered one of them.

As he stood in his lonely room that Christmas Eve he recalled the evening, two days after his arrival, when a guard had come for him and escorted him across the courtyard to where von Model and a pasty-faced lieutenant occupied the former Officers' Mess of the barracks, together with an extensive staff and the Major's personal masseur. Von Model had been sitting in a well-furnished room warmed by a huge log fire. He had offered Tim a chair beside it, and a glass of wine, launching into a somewhat ludicrous speech of welcome. Before long, the emphasis of his words had shifted to what war, and particularly incarceration, did to a strong, healthy young man. Tim's initial lack of response changed to wariness as the man had warmed to his theme and produced pictures of nude women in extremely provocative poses – the kind of postcards he and his fellows had found amusingly stimulating at Sandhurst. He had made no reply when von Model asked his opinion of the girls' charms, which gave the German the perfect opening for his next move.

'I see you are a man of my own preferred tastes.' The pictures of handsome young men were even more explicit. They were accompanied by the smooth suggestion that imprisonment need not be an end to a man's pleasures if he was discreet.

Tim's reaction had been instant and unmistakeable, couched in words which had earned him a week in isolation. Three days after being returned to the fortified barracks he had again been summoned. His solitary confinement had lasted ten days that time. His return to the communal games room had been met with a boisterous cheer. Everyone knew what was going on. The long-term prisoners had watched other good-looking comrades suffer similarly until von Model gave up the baiting. Only one had succumbed, and he had been ostracized. That all-male community had not condemned *what* he had done, but that he had done it with an enemy.

Released for just thirty-six hours, Tim had been woken in the middle of the night and taken across the snow-covered courtyard to where von Model was waiting in a velvet dressing gown. Tim had feared he was about to be forced into what he refused to do, but the German had too much finesse for that. He had indicated that he was confident Mr Ashleigh would decide to indulge himself when the solitary hours became too much for him. They were, especially on a night when the past was traditionally recalled and families gathered under the parental roof. But, greater than that caused by isolation, was Tim's distress over the reason for his punishment. He was now haunted by Amy's caustic suggestion that his virility might be up for auction. Was that all he was really fit for?

The sound of a key turning in the lock caused Tim to spin around expecting to see two of von Model's brawniest guards. There was only one, grinning knowingly as he eyed his prisoner from head to foot and indicated that he should bring his gear. Deeply suspicious, Tim gathered it up and followed along the red-carpeted corridor expecting his tormentor to open the door of his room and drag him in. It remained shut.

When he entered the games room another rousing cheer went up. Where other men might have given a grinning thumbs up in response, Tim felt further debased by their championship. He was being treated as a hero merely for defying a would-be sodomite. He sat in something of a daze, overcome by the noise and enthusiasm, as they brought him up to date on news of the war taken with a pinch of salt because it was reported in the German newspapers.

The senior British officer, a captain in a rifle regiment, brought Tim a letter that had arrived during his isolation, but he slid it in his pocket unread. His mother would have covered several pages with tittle-tattle which she believed would cheer him up, and end, as always, by writing of her thankfulness that he was safe and whole. She really had no understanding of her firstborn son whom she claimed to love in such a special way. The voices, the constant movement, the bright light all bewildered Tim after almost two weeks alone in a dim room, and he very soon made his way to his dormitory. To his surprise he found a stranger on his bed, reading a lurid thriller.

'That's my bunk,' he said shortly.

A face topped by dark hair appeared over the top of the book. 'Oh, are you Ashleigh?'

'That's right.'

The book was snapped shut and the man swung his legs to the floor. 'They told me I'd have to move if you came back.'

Tim sank on to the foot of the bed with a sigh. 'You can stay there if you like. I don't suppose I'll be back for long.'

'I only came in on Wednesday,' the stranger said. 'It was blasted bad luck. First day in the field after a spell in hospital in Blighty. I was sent out with a message and rode straight into the arms of a Hun mounted patrol.' His mouth twisted. 'The message I was carrying asked for more details of the latest enemy positions. Ironic, wasn't it?'

'*Blasted* bad luck,' Tim agreed listlessly. 'Welcome to Bleak House.'

'Well, it looks pretty bleak as you approach but it's not as bad as I feared. Our other ranks are having a harder time of it, I heard. The authorities and the Red Cross are protesting over their treatment.'

Tim was no longer listening. His pulse had quickened as he spotted the badges on the man's lapels – silver wreaths enclosing the figures 57. 'You're with the Fifty-seventh Lancers?'

'Yes. Piers Lassingham.' They shook hands. 'We haven't had a good war. Horses aren't up to this kind of fighting. Mud, mud and more mud. How can you pit cavalry against tanks and aircraft? Terrain like this is hopeless for weapons like the lance. You need a full-scale charge to be really effective. In South Africa we had some good fast chases trying to round up the stubborn renegades.' He sobered. 'Mounted regiments are doomed, you know. On their way out. Must be.'

Tim suddenly felt more vibrant than at any time during the past six months as he waited for Lassingham to pause for breath. In the lofty stone dormitory filled with two rows of iron beds covered in grey blankets, he might just have been presented with the perfect opportunity to discover the truth about the Ashleigh black sheep who still managed to be a hero.

'Were you in South Africa for the entire war?' he inserted swiftly, causing the man to frown because he had moved on from that brief reference to brood on his future as a mounted soldier.

'No, just the final year. I joined the Fifty-seventh straight from Sandhurst.'

'I see. Did you . . . did you ever come across a chap called Martin Havelock?'

Lassingham's frown deepened. 'Not a friend of yours, was he?'

'Wasn't there some scandal attached to him?' Tim asked, praying this man was not going to disappoint him.

'He was court martialled.' After a pause, he added, 'Funny you should bring up that name. I was thinking about him only yesterday when I tried to understand why chance had sent me straight into the arms of the enemy on my first day back in action. It seemed the most hellish bad luck, and I remembered all the incidents of similar quirks of fate throughout my career. Havelock came to mind. I'd only just joined the regiment when the case came up. Most unusual affair. No chum of yours involved, was there?'

'No . . . no.' Tim racked his brain for a plausible explanation. 'Someone once mentioned the case, but I never heard the full story. What happened to Havelock?'

'Kicked out. Cashiered. Young chap, he was. Only twenty-one or so. His men took it badly. They maintained he'd been made a scapegoat.'

'For what?' prompted Tim urgently.

'For another officer's ineptitude.' Lassingham swung his legs up and leaned back against the bedhead once more, ready to forget his miserable surroundings by telling a graphic yarn. 'Havelock was a well set up fellow, good sportsman, brilliant in the saddle – a first-class cavalryman who'd worked his way up from the ranks on merit. The ladies admired him, of course, but from the little I knew of him he wasn't interested in that direction at all. The army was his sole great passion. There was a mystery about his background, but it was pretty evident he was some toff's son who'd blotted his copybook. He conducted a feud with an officer named Pickering – an unpleasant individual with no military flair but with relatives in high places. *Very* high places. The enmity apparently dated back to when Havelock was a trooper. He *was* an insubordinate devil, so I heard, but he'd nevertheless been decorated for some pretty cool courage after his officer had been killed during a Boer ambush, and he looked all set for a distinguished career.'

'So what put an end to it?' Tim asked feeling the hair on the back of his neck starting to rise.

'I was with the bulk of the regiment stationed at divisional headquarters, but these two at loggerheads formed part of a contingent manning the outlying blockhouses. They were coming in after their spell of duty when Boers were seen riding away from a farm. The captain in charge gave chase with the greater part of the contingent, sending Pickering and Havelock, with their men, to search the farm and burn it down. What actually happened there was subsequently told in different versions by the two officers, but the facts were that when Pickering made to shoot a Boer woman and a boy hiding there, Havelock knocked the revolver from his hand, then ran off to rescue horses from the burning stables. The woman somehow got hold of the gun, forced Pickering to take off his uniform, then shot him in the chest before riding off with her son and Pickering's tunic which, unknown to her, contained sealed military orders.'

'*Good God*!' Tim was appalled. He had never imagined anything as bad as this and, in a perverse way, began to wish he had not encountered Piers Lassingham.

However, the man was caught up in his yarn now. 'Havelock brought the wounded officer in and was promptly accused by him of all the major crimes in the book. Pickering claimed Havelock had refused to obey his order to set the farmhouse alight, had vowed to take great pleasure in destroying him, then had knocked the revolver from his hand and kicked it across to the woman before running off leaving his fellow officer at the mercy of a female enemy.'

'He would *never* have done that,' said Tim forcefully, before he could stop himself.

'Only a complete blackguard would,' Lassingham conceded, seeing in Tim's outburst no more than professional defence of an officer, 'Havelock certainly hated Pickering quite intensely and wanted vengeance for things the nincompoop had done to him under the protection of his higher rank, but all save two of our officers vowed he was no traitor. The pair of abstainers were social cronies of Pickering.'

Tim was impelled to find out more, although he was experiencing a curious sensation he could not define. 'Pickering was believed?'

'It wasn't a question of that. He'd made a dangerously serious charge which could not be ignored. A court martial was convened and Havelock was accused of disobeying a direct order in time of war, of using violence against a superior officer, of disgraceful conduct and of causing sealed orders to be lost into the hands of the enemy. The poor devil couldn't deny any of it outright, but his version of the affair should have mitigated the charges.'

'And what was his version?' asked Tim, his depression and von Model's insulting punishments forgotten as the man on his bed solved a long standing mystery in such shocking detail.

Lassingham offered a cigarette and lit them both before continuing. 'I wasn't present during the trial, you understand. I was new to the Mess and pretty well knocked out by it all. I mean, one doesn't expect things like that to happen in an élite regiment like the Fifty-seventh. Dammit, we were still at war! The court martial was held under conditions of the greatest secrecy. The press would have seized on it and further undermined our position out there. We weren't the world's favourites for our conduct of the conflict. Despite the secrecy, the whole regiment was aware of what was said in court. You know how it is.'

'What *was* said?' urged Tim.

The man frowned in recollection. 'Havelock apparently claimed he had refused to set the farmhouse alight because it had not then been searched for possible residents in hiding. Pickering torched the place while Havelock was inside conducting the search. The flames drove out a woman with a boy, who let forth a string of invective. When Pickering cocked his revolver, Havelock knocked it from his hand believing he meant to shoot the unarmed woman. He kicked it a few feet away from the angry officer before walking to the woman to explain that she had been sheltering their enemies so they had no choice but to destroy her farm and take her, with her son, to a camp. At that point he noticed two troopers setting alight a barn he knew to house some ponies, and had run across to warn them and free the beasts. It was some time later that he returned to discover Pickering in his underwear with a bullet wound in his chest, and the woman gone, carrying off a British uniform – Boers often wore them to fool soldiers at outposts they attacked.'

'Did no one believe his version?'

Lassingham shrugged. 'There were no witnesses to those dramatic events. The troopers were all spread out over the farm conducting an orgy of destruction. There was indisputable evidence of the bitter feud between the two, and of Havelock's tendency to take matters into his own hands. He really hadn't much of a chance. Officers who resented commissioned rankers gave biased opinions. Others felt that a man very evidently a gentleman, who had taken refuge from justice by enlisting into the anonymity of cavalry ranks, was a bad apple liable to turn the whole barrel rotten.' He shrugged again. 'It all boiled down to the word of a gentleman officer with royal connections against that of a former trooper with insubordinate tendencies. The board members had little choice but to find Havelock guilty as charged and impose the death penalty, which was only commuted to cashiering because of his earlier gallantry and his colonel's excellent character reference.'

Tim was feeling icy cold by now and his injured jaw began to throb as he asked, 'What about Pickering?'

The other man grimaced. 'He was allowed the gentleman's way out. He resigned his commission on medical grounds.' He stubbed out his cigarette. 'That, however wasn't the end of an affair many felt had been blown out of all proportion. Disciplinary action was certainly necessary but on a far lesser charge so far as Havelock was concerned. He should have been severely reprimanded, maybe broken to the ranks again, but his career would have been saved and his honour left intact. He had none left by the time the Fifty-seventh finished with him.'

'What does *that* mean?' asked Tim, now identifying the burning sensation within his breast as that of one Ashleigh rising to the defence of another.

Lassingham's brow furrowed as he appeared lost in that scandal at the turn of the century. 'You know how regiments acquire their own peculiar traditions over the years? I'm sure the West Wilts have their own set. We all do. Well, the Fifty-seventh had their own way of dealing with officers who dishonoured the colours. I was unaware of it – the last time it had been done was twenty-five years earlier, which shows what a noble lot our officers must have been – and I have to say it seemed to me to be grossly unfair, given these particular circumstances. Colonel Beecham voted that it should be waived as it was wartime, but some of the old stalwarts insisted. He most likely gave in under pressure because he had offered Havelock every encouragement for promotion, while his wife and daughter had shown particular interest in the fellow. They had all been made to look foolish, so Beecham had to compensate with severity.'

By now Tim was so cold his body was stiff with it, and his jaw was jumping so much he was unable to prompt the man with questions. All he could do was sit perfectly still while the unwelcome solution to the mystery was unfolded by a cavalry captain who had no idea who Martin Havelock really was.

'The whole regiment formed up in squadrons on the *veld* several miles outside the town. Havelock was brought in a closed wagon by his escorting officer, and marched out to a spot facing us all. He was then divested of his helmet, sword and spurs before all badges of rank, epaulettes and buttons were ripped off his tunic.' Lassingham sighed heavily. 'I don't know what that poor devil felt, but my stomach muscles were so tight I thought they'd never relax again. You see, as the most junior subaltern, *I* had to complete the humiliating ceremony by ordering him to fall in behind my horse and then parading him the whole length of the ranks who, squadron by squadron, turned their backs as he passed.'

Tim swallowed back a lump that had formed in his throat, and his scalp rose in goose bumps as the impact of what his companion was saying fully hit him.

Lassingham sighed deeply once more. 'But here's the most unforgettable part of it. Four squadrons had executed the about turn, but when we reached the fifth – the one Havelock had served in as a trooper, then as a sergeant – the ranks disobeyed to a man. The whole business seemed to me barbaric in the extreme, and to watch these officers repeating their commands to tough troopers who defied them made me ashamed of my part in it. These rough and ready fellows showed their contempt for *us* by championing a man who had served the regiment with courage and loyalty. The atmosphere out there on that plain was so charged by then I half expected a mutiny as I led Havelock back to where his sword and helmet lay on the ground.'

'And?' prompted Tim through a parched throat.

'The parade was dismissed, and we all returned to camp leaving Havelock out there. It's something I'll always remember; him standing bare-headed, tunic flapping open in the breeze, and me suddenly sensing, without doubt, that the regiment had broken the wrong man.' He offered his cigarettes once more and, when Tim did not take one, lit his own and shook the flame from the match. 'That was the last we saw of him. I imagine he had a horse tethered somewhere nearby and just rode off.' He laid the packet on his book and blew smoke from his nostrils. 'The ritual was never carried out again. Two hundred and fifty men couldn't be punished for refusing to take part in it, but their gesture had somehow demeaned their officers. Before we returned to England a move was made by Colonel Beecham to strike the practice from the rules of the Mess. No one objected.'

Lassingham drew deeply on his cigarette then slowly exhaled. 'Can you imagine it happening today? That kind of thing should have stayed in the dark ages when military officers were all princes and noblemen jealous of their honour. How many of us now are even regular soldiers? We've schoolboys, tradesmen, farmers and a legion of commissioned rankers – a man's a trooper one day, and leading the squadron the next. Damned good at it a lot of them are proving to be. The army'll not be the same when this war's over. It'll be the men with courage and true leadership who'll be officering the regiments, not simply those who went to the right schools or come from the right families. That should do away with the Pickerings in the commissioned ranks.' He gave a short laugh. 'Just think, if that business had happened in this war they'd *both* have been summarily executed – or one would have "accidently" shot the other during an action and put an end to the feud long before it reached such a dangerous stage. I'll certainly never forget that affair.'

While Lassingham rambled on, Tim sat with his head hunched into his shoulders staring at the floor but seeing the photograph Kate had of Second-Lieutenant Martin Havelock; handsome, smiling, full of pride and wearing a DCM on his breast. Val Ashleigh had just been awarded another. Tim finally understood that courage was not only crawling across the desert to deliver a vital message from a besieged garrison, and knew it was time he began to show some of it.

The ship docked at Southampton midway through March. Kate gazed from the porthole, struck by the greyness of England. After a year in Salonika she found the cold northern light, closely packed buildings and pewter sea a stark change from the eastern Mediterranean. Yet it was *home* and the one place she wanted to be right now.

'I'd forgotten how busy England was,' she murmured, trying to imagine how it had looked to Val after twelve years in the Outback.

'Can't be any busier than the wards we've practically lived in for the past two years,' Milly replied absently, coming to stand behind her. 'I was so thankful to get away. Now I wish I was back there.'

Kate turned in quick sympathy. 'You needed a rest. We both did, even before we caught typhus.' She took her friend's hands in her own. 'Once you've got over the first day you'll manage all right. It's not as if they've just heard the news. Three months have passed – time for you all to get used to the notion of losing him.'

Milly's dark, expressive eyes still reflected her fears. 'It's Pip's family I dread facing. I'm afraid I won't show enough sadness.'

'Put them on to me. I'll let them know what you suffered when you got their letter with the news,' Kate said vigorously.

'You don't know what I suffered. That's the trouble.' Milly turned away and sat on one of the bunks where her scarlet cape lay ready to put on. 'I've got to get this off my chest to someone, Kate, and there's more chance of you understanding than them. They're too closely involved and you've been with me all this year.' She gave a wan smile. 'Except for your weeks on the boat to Gallipoli, and that argument with a German mine.'

Kate moved to sit on the facing bunk, filled with concern for her friend who looked totally drained. She knew she did, too. They had both been very ill at a time when they had also been overworked and run down. 'We're disembarking in half an hour. Didn't you trust me enough to say what you want to say before this?'

Milly began to cry. They had both done a lot of that during the voyage. Neither was certain of the reason for it but it had something to do with the harrowing things they had seen and done since the start of the war, and was somehow mixed up with their personal anxieties manifested in the young men they had tended, so many of whose last hours they had calmed. For two weeks they had lazed on board and the necessity to be strong had been removed. Kate let her friend's tears fall until she was ready to speak. When she did, words came out in jerky sentences.

'I got engaged to Pip because we were both going to war. He . . . he so much wanted to . . . well, to have something to hold on to. I did it on impulse. I told you that at the time. I thought we'd be able to meet up in France. Then I learned our detachment was going to Alexandria.' She dabbed at her red eyes. 'You know what it's been like out there. The terrible casualties from Gallipoli, then the others in our area military hospital. So many boys, Kate. So many *needing* me. Their faces. I shall always remember their faces when they first came in. After a while I forgot Pip's. I couldn't recall what he looked like. I still can't. I've watched so many die – we both have. They were carried away, we changed the sheets, and others came in.' She twisted her handkerchief in her fingers as she stared at it. 'I'm not sure what happened – whether they all became Pip, or he became just one of them – but when I got the letter saying he'd been killed in action on the Somme it . . . it didn't mean anything.'

She looked up swiftly. 'He was just another one to be carried out so that I could change the sheets ready for the next. If I suffered it was because I *couldn't* feel grief and should have done. I still don't . . . and I'm afraid I'm going to hurt his parents by my lack of it.'

'No, you won't,' Kate told her with total conviction. 'When they see how terrible you look it'll be enough. And you *do* care, Milly. I understand perfectly because I felt the same, but I can end your confusion over it. They all became Pip just as they all became Val to me. I forgot *his* face. Without that precious photograph I've forgotten a dear face I knew so very well.' Her own eyes began to fill with tears. 'I've no idea where he is now – whether he's even still alive – but every one of those boys I nursed represented *him.* I put all my skill, all my compassion, all my emotion into what I did for them as I would for him.' She reached for her friend's hands. 'We're a pair of fools. We've been told often enough that our calling should be to serve humanity, not fall in love – at least, not in wartime. We both did just that. I'm going to use this month they've given us to pull myself together, give myself a good talking to, and remember why I became a nurse. After all, I did it long before he fell flat on the carpet at my feet. I've got to get my priorities right . . . and put him out of my mind.'

Milly had regained a little of her normal composure and got to her feet with a wicked smile. 'Brave words, ducky, but if you've managed it by the end of our leave I'll eat my bonnet.' So saying she picked up the unattractive garment and jammed it on to her head. 'Love can't be switched on or off when you want, otherwise you'd have been married to Peter Reeves by now and out of the army. He was really serious over you, which had all the VADs green with jealousy.'

Kate stood up and began to fasten her cape. 'Peter's a very nice man and a clever doctor . . .'

'And terribly good-looking,' inserted Milly.

'Yes, and terribly good-looking, but he mistook his admiration for how I behaved during the shipwreck for love. I wasn't the only woman who remained calm as the *Romaine* was sinking – we all did – but he focused on me because I insisted on slapping a dressing on a deep cut in his head as he stood dripping blood on his saturated uniform. He fell into the biggest trap in the world and joined hundreds of men who think they love their nurses.'

'Rot! He's more intelligent than that.'

Kate picked up her bonnet. 'If he is he should know better than to let himself become so deeply concerned with one of his own staff that they had no choice but to transfer him to another hospital.' She paused before fastening her bonnet strings. 'I might have been tempted if things had been different. He was a very endearing person.'

'Your wicked uncle has a lot to answer for, ducky.'

Kate tied a bow firmly. 'I was referring to the war, not to Val. As I told you, I'm putting him out of my mind.'

'Hah!' exclaimed Milly expressively.

They parted at the railway station vowing to send each other a letter after a week or so with a progress report, and Kate caught a train to Romsey where she would get a connection to Dunstan St Mary. England still seemed unreal as she watched emerald-green fields, villages of thatched cottages, and narrow winding roads from the carriage window. It looked unchanged when everything else in her life was dramatically different.

Tears began to threaten again, which proved how demoralized she was, and they multiplied as she condemned her weakness after the unbelievable courage she had witnessed over the past two years. What was wrong with her? Would she never pull herself together? When Vere had cabled the ship to tell her to go direct to Knightshill rather than Ashleigh Court, because they would be there for the children's Easter vacation, she had counted the days until she could be in the comfort of her home with her family. Now all she wanted was to hide away in some anonymous room and cry until she was empty. The prospect of facing a horde of Ashleighs was daunting now it was almost upon her. Small wonder Val had resorted to drink on his return after twelve years. Maybe she should do the same. Unfortunately, there were too many military passengers on the train. A tipsy nurse would be accosted and asked to explain her behaviour. Val would tell her to do what she bloody well liked.

The thought brought a faint smile, but also a surge of longing for someone out of reach. Perhaps she would start putting him out of her mind *tomorrow*, because at the moment he was very much there.

It was almost noon when she reached Dunstan St Mary and left the train. There was Knightshill high above the village, as inviolate as ever and almost glowing in the spring sunshine. There were lambs all over the slopes, and the air smelt sweeter and fresher than any since she last left this place. A lump formed in her throat as she gazed at the house where she had spent her childhood, and wished the years away back to that time when she had been so happy and unaware of the undercurrents within the family. But even if her wishes came true, it would all happen again as it had and she would be back to the present once more.

As she stood lost in reverie she grew aware of someone approaching along the platform. His auburn hair, the owl-like marks around his eyes made by motoring goggles, and the care and concern in his face were all she really needed to open the floodgates to tears. The shock of his farewell declaration of love forgotten, Kate silently went into his arms and clung to the steadfast, loyal person she knew would never let her down. Simon held her close as he coaxed her from the station to the yard where Jessie was standing in her full shining glory. The sight of the car she had ridden in so often with him brought a fresh surge of tears. They streamed down her cheeks as he practically lifted her in to the passenger seat, and they continued unchecked as the engine started with a roar and they began to move away.

Halfway up the hill Simon pulled into a gateway and stopped. The sudden silence caused Kate to look up, and she saw that they were at the spot where they had halted on the day of Val's return – the day she had suddenly wished he would not come. She pulled off her bonnet and applied Simon's large handkerchief to her tear-stained face, saying through the last of her unsteady breaths, 'What a disgrace to my uniform! Matron would have me hung, drawn and quartered if she knew.'

'I won't tell her,' Simon said quietly. 'I won't tell anyone.'

She glanced round and took his hand. 'It was seeing you so unexpectedly, and with Jessie. It was as if nothing had changed.'

'It has, though. I thought you'd recovered from your illness and were convalescing. You don't look it.'

'I'm tired, that's all.' She released his hand and wiped her eyes once more. 'What are you doing at home, and how did you know I'd be on that train?'

He managed a grin. 'Mother told me you were coming home for a month to recover from a serious illness, so I took two weeks' leave due to me after a long spell of intensive work. I arrived at Knightshill last night. This morning I telephoned the docks and confirmed your ship's safe arrival, so I came to the station on the off chance that you'd be on that train. I'd have met them all until you turned up.'

She clasped his hand again, still emotional. 'Oh, Simon, you've no idea how wonderful it is to see a man full of life and health, and who isn't wearing a uniform. They're all so . . . so . . .'

He closed his other hand around hers that was holding his. 'We're going to forget all about that now you're here. I've worked out a plan for us. We'll have some spins in Jessie, go riding up on the Downs, take out the field glasses to look for nests with eggs in, and go for long walks so that we can catch up on those days we've lost over the last year.' He looked down at their clasped hands. 'I've missed you, Kate.'

'I'm afraid I haven't had time to miss *anyone*,' she told him quietly. 'If I'd been here I would have, but the wards are . . .'

'*Ah!*' he warned. 'We're going to forget all that, I said. For a while, anyway. Until you look a whole lot better than you do now. Promise?'

She nodded. 'I hope you're not going to order me around like Sister Bradwell.'

'*Exactly* like Sister Bradwell, except that I'll be nicer about it.'

'Oh Simon, whatever would I do without you?' she asked, emotional again.

'You don't have to do without me for the next fourteen days, so make the most of them.'

'I will . . . and I'll love doing all the things you suggested. It'll be like old times.'

He gazed at her through his owl-like eyes for a moment or two. 'I'm still in love with you.'

Strangely, the confession did not bother her this time. 'I hoped you might have found a nice girl to marry while I was away.'

A curiously indefinable expression crossed his face before he said, 'I won't make things awkward for you, but I just wanted you to know that I feel the same although I'll still be your friend whenever you need one.'

'And I'll always be yours.' She produced a smile at last. 'We're the two odd ones out, aren't we? The sole Munroe and Daulton among Ashleighs, Nicolardis and Morgans.' She broke manual contact and sat back in her seat. 'How many of them are at Knightshill?'

'All except Laurence.'

'Mother?'

'She's spending time here with the boys while he's in Lisbon talking to the Americans.'

'What about Ashleigh Court?'

Simon shrugged. 'Once your step-father was knighted the diplomatic duties left her no time. Aunt Lottie tried to step in her shoes but she prefers being at Knightshill, and Father welcomes her help with the estate. Anyway, Ashleigh Court is so well established now, family involvement is not so necessary. Mother spends less time there. You know how she and Father hate being apart.'

'I'm amazed my mother hasn't somehow pulled strings to go to Lisbon with Laurence. *They're* practically inseparable.'

'I think she tried.' He brushed absently at Jessie's brass fittings with his leather gauntlets. 'Had you heard that Tim's been moved to a different prison camp?'

'No. The letter with the news is probably out in Salonika.'

'He's not allowed to send more than one initial postcard, but your mother writes regularly to him. She's so thankful he's safe for the rest of the war.'

'*He* won't be thankful. You know Tim. He'll be eating his heart out behind bars.'

'I would, too. Any man would. But poor old Tim's had this Ashleigh tradition bred into him from an early age, and was so certain he'd make a name for himself after excelling at Sandhurst. It must be especially hard for him to know he's lost his chances in this war.'

'But he hasn't lost his legs, or his arms, or his sight,' Kate said heavily. 'There'll be another war. There always is.'

After a moment Simon said, 'You promised to forget all that for a while. Come on, let's get up to the house. It's almost time for lunch, and Father will be looking at the clock. He's *so* eager to see you.' He started the engine. 'They all are.'

Kate slipped her arm through his. 'I wish there weren't quite so many of them. I'd rather be just with you, Uncle Vere and Aunt Kitty. Wouldn't it be lovely if we four were a complete family?'

Simon moved the gear stick to put the car in motion. 'There's only one way we could be, and you've made it clear you're not interested.' He glanced at her. 'Ready? You don't want to do any fussing before we get there?'

She shook her head, sorry that she had spoken without considering his feelings. 'No amount of primping would help if you had the impression I was still ill when you saw me. Let's get there and get it over. Then you and I can start on your lovely plan for the next two weeks.'

Just before he took off the brake he said, 'If there's anything else you'd rather do at any time, we'll do it. I want to be with you for the next fortnight, whatever the situation may be. I care about you, Kate, quite apart from being in love. You can turn to me at any time and I'll be there.'

'I know that,' she murmured, pondering his sudden seriousness. Was it because he believed her to be on the verge of a serious breakdown in health because of her outburst at the station? She *must* pull herself together. Surely the peaceful pleasures he had suggested would make that possible. He really was a very special person; and she would make certain he knew it before he left Knightshill.

Vere had been watching for them and was at the main entrance when they drew up. Kate was touched by his evident delight, and by the hearty hug he gave her. 'My dear girl, it's wonderful to have you at home again. We've all been counting the days till your ship docked. So many are being sunk in the Med, and you've had that experience once so don't want it again. We breathed a sigh of relief when Simon rang the docks for confirmation this morning.' He led her inside with an arm around her shoulders. 'There's so much I want to ask you, but I'll contain my patience until you've had lunch and got your bearings again. I well remember coming home from the Sudan after a couple of years' absence. It was just before

Christmas and bitterly cold. Everything looked so grey and bleak and closely packed after the desert. I expect you find the same. Come and say hallo to everyone before you go up to your room to freshen up. Watkins lit a fire there first thing, so you'll find it warm enough.' He threw open the sitting-room door and Kate was briefly reminded of the day of Val's return as she saw nine people gathered there dressed more formally than anyone she had seen for some time. Everyone wore uniforms where she had been – mostly bloodstained. Here were women in silk and adolescent boys in tweed suits in a room with a blue and cream carpet, elegant furniture and huge Chinese vases overflowing with spring flowers. How must it have seemed to a returning exile the worse for drink?

Charlotte rose and came forward with open arms. 'Welcome home, dear. You've been away for so long doing such splendid work. I'm so proud of you.' She kissed Kate's cheek warmly. 'So are your mother and Kitty, of course. You must have a nice long rest and build up your strength with food from the estate.'

Kitty got to her feet and hesitated, looking at Margaret. Then she crossed to Kate and enfolded her in an embrace. 'You've been so splendid, my dear. The first female Ashleigh facing the enemy in uniform. The ancestors will have to look to their laurels, and your great-grandfather would have to eat his words concerning the role of women if he were alive to see you now.' She turned deliberately towards Margaret. 'I'm afraid we've upstaged your poor mother, but she'll probably go up with you while you wash and change. You'll have things to say to each other.'

Margaret left her chair, and crossed to her daughter. Kate marvelled that she looked even younger and more vital than ever, in a bronze crêpe de chine blouse and a cream heavy silk goffered skirt. She kissed Kate's cheek, wafting expensive perfume, then took her hands, saying, 'We'll talk later. You look washed out and totally exhausted. That terrible uniform doesn't help. Go and change into something comfortable and pretty, dear. Then we'll all eat lunch and relax.'

'Yes, I'll be as quick as I can,' she said, before turning to greet the younger generation. They all appeared to have become adults in her absence.

Simon cast her a sympathetic glance as she crossed the hall and he came in from garaging Jessie. 'Ordeal over?'

'Yes.' She crossed to slip her arm through his as they mounted the stairs. 'Mother puts half the female world in the shade, Aunt Kitty is as lovingly understanding as ever, but Aunt Lottie has aged quite alarmingly. I'll have to make discreet enquiries about her health.'

Simon frowned at her. 'Now then, none of that! You made me a promise.'

She smiled. 'All right. I'll wait until you go back to work.'

'I'm not going for fourteen days,' he reminded her as they reached the door of his room. 'Don't let's talk about it yet. Look, I'll hang on in my room until you're ready, then we can go down together.'

'Good. I won't be long.'

'Take your time. This is your day. Keep 'em waiting if you feel like it.'

'Aunt Lottie's dying to fatten me up, and Mother wants me to descend looking pretty. I'm not sure I can please them.'

'Don't. Please yourself instead.'

Kate washed, and dressed in a blue skirt and a pale draped silk blouse she had last worn almost three years before. She supposed it was terribly dated now. What constituted the latest fashion was a mystery to her, but her mother was almost certainly wearing it today. The familiar surroundings seemed alien, as yet. The rooms were so huge. She was used to wooden huts, or tents divided by canvas panels. On the *Romaine* she had had little more than a shelf as accommodation. The cabin she had recently shared with Milly had been necessarily small. She had once taken such opulence as this for granted. How had it appeared to a man who had lived in a red-earth wilderness for twelve years? Unwelcome enough to drive him back to it – except that he had been cheated of his intention.

All at once it occurred to her that there had been photographs in his room when she had gone in to check on him that first night of his return. Slipping along the corridor away from Simon's door, Kate negotiated the rear passage connecting the two wings and came to Val's room. It was chilly with no fire, but her shiver was due to the intense sense of his absence rather than from cold. There was the row of sporting awards bearing Chartfield School's colours, some silver-backed hairbrushes, a leather stud box bearing the initials VMHA in gold, pictures of his favourite horses, and the photograph she sought. Yet it was *not* after all what she sought. The Ashleigh brothers and sisters were hardly recognizable. Vorne was an undergraduate – dashing in his Oxford blue blazor and cap – Margaret a pretty fifteen year old, Charlotte in a striped dress and ringlets standing close to the twelve year old Vere. Ashleigh, V. M. H. was a lusty, blond child of five. As Kate stood looking at him, sick with disappointment, she remembered his face all too clearly. How could she have forgotten it? She visualized him on that hospital balcony in Alexandria as they had said goodbye. That man surely had no connection with this handsome little boy in the photograph.

Coming from the room, she was tempted to enter that of her brother next to it. It was so full of the essence of Tim it was as if he was presently occupying it. There were pictures of him galore, especially in his uniform. As Kate walked across to the dresser where they were lined up, her pulse quickened. One, taken when Tim had first entered Sandhurst, was uncannily like the photograph now at the bottom of the sea. Something about the way he was smiling, his expression, the way he held his head, the elation in his eyes made the young man in this picture the double of the one in that other lost beyond recall. As Kate picked it up it became what she most wanted, and she returned to her room to slip it into a drawer for her eyes alone.

Simon's door was open and he put aside the book he was glancing through to come to her. 'My word, what a difference! You've come to life in the space of twenty minutes. After Aunt Lottie has fattened you up you'll be back to the Kate we all know . . . and love.'

'You make me sound like a Christmas goose with all that talk of fattening up,' she said lightly. 'Tell me about what you're working on at the moment. Is the new fighter ready?'

'It's in the prototype stage. Let's wait until later when I can explain it all properly. Mmm, lunch smells good. I'm famished.'

She laughed. 'All men are permanently hungry, even when they're decidedly under the weather.'

'I suppose you've learned a lot about them,' he said as they went together down the wide staircase.

'Rather too much. Some of them get up to dreadful tricks, especially with the very young VADs. We had a Scot, a huge man with hair much redder than yours, who . . .'

'I should save your stories until an appropriate time,' he suggested as the lunch gong sounded. 'I don't think they'll be appreciated over the lunch table.'

Kate saw the wisdom of his words as she sat at a long polished table set with starched linen and glittering silver, and recalled the way she had taken her meals overseas. Conversation was lively, as always in this house. Vere told Kate of his present theatrical venture, and Kitty spoke of the new, highly successful organization of Ashleigh Court. Margaret elaborated on her meeting with the King and Queen in company with Laurence, and Charlotte went into detail about the success she was having with hothouse camellias.

'You'll be taken to see them in the morning,' said her son James. 'I think they're a splendid project.'

'Boys aren't supposed to be interested in *flowers*,' put in Holly scathingly.

'What about the ones who present them to ladies they admire?' asked Vere slyly.

'They're not boys, Papa, they're *men*. And it's not the *flowers* they're interested in.'

'That's enough, Holly,' her mother reprimanded. 'I'm sure Kate doesn't want to hear your nonsense on her first day at home.'

'I know what she will want to hear,' put in Victoria swiftly. 'Val's married an ambulance driver and she's going to have a baby.'

Into the silence Simon shouted, 'You were told not to say anything about that, you little heathen. *You were specifically told*!'

Kate got up and left the room.

CHAPTER SIXTEEN

They walked from the house in silence. Kate followed where Simon led, hardly aware of her surroundings as they entered the shrubbery at the rear of Knightshill. Azaleas and rhododendrons mingled in great banks of red, purple, apricot, yellow and white beneath the taller grove of pink and cream of magnolias. Their shoes crunched the gravel along the paths, then made no sound as they began to climb the grassy slope beyond. Simon reached for her hand. His fingers curved around hers comfortingly, but he made no attempt to discuss what had happened.

Halfway up the slope she said, 'We used to toboggan here when it snowed. All of us. Even Mother and Aunt Lottie. Only when Val was home from school. He was the one who persuaded everyone.' She could see those occasions so clearly in her mind. 'He used to career down from the very top – he was a daredevil in any active pastime. That's why he won all those sports trophies that are still in his room. He and Mother were very close in those days, and he used to take her down at breakneck speed just to hear her shriek. When he took me it was different. He was gentle and held me very tight.' She swallowed painfully. 'He was like another brother. Tim and I used to pelt him with snowballs, or push him over and roll him in the snow. He always pretended he couldn't defend himself, and we loved it when he got up and chased us, roaring like a lion.'

Simon let her talk without interruption. 'In the summer we had picnics up on the downs. Tim and I had our own ponies, but Val rode huge geldings. I'd beg him to give me a ride and, if the others weren't looking, he'd lift me on to the saddle in front of him and we'd race like the wind until I was laughing with joy. He always got a fearful telling off from Mother and Aunt

Lottie, and Uncle Vere once threatened to lock the stables and hide the key.' She looked up at the crest they were approaching. It shimmered through her unshed tears. 'When Mother took us away to live with Laurence I thought I'd never see Val again. I missed him more than Knightshill or any of the others. I suppose it was because I loved him the most.'

They reached the top and turned. Knightshill stood on a ledge surrounded by a tapestry of flowers, lawns, glasshouses, meadows and dark pines. Down in the valley the village lay beside the bright gleam of the river winding down to the Dorset coast. It was a scene which made all she had done in the past two years resemble a dark dream.

'When that photograph arrived from South Africa it seemed as though I'd got him back, and I began speaking again. With only Aunt Lottie and Great-grandfather in the house I had felt there would be no more fun and laughter.' She frowned in memory. 'It was only a picture, I know, but it was something to hold on to. It's . . . it's at the bottom of the sea now. Gone forever.'

Simon's arm went around her shoulders, drawing her against his side. 'He's in Mother's wedding pictures, taken at the same time.'

Kate had forgotten those. But she was not entitled to cherish a photograph of another woman's husband. How could he *possibly* be married after all those years alone – and with such suddenness? 'I know something awful happened not long after that wedding – something so awful Val was lost in Africa for three whole years. I can . . . I can understand that he might not have cared to come home for a while afterwards, but when he did why should he leave again after three days to live in a manner so totally out of character for twelve years? It suggests that something even *worse* happened during that brief visit to Knightshill.' She looked up at Simon in distress. 'Which of us here could have hurt him so deeply he wanted to foresake us forever?'

'But he didn't, did he? He could easily have bought that place in Australia at long distance. He didn't have to come home just to transfer his capital out there.'

'If he'd stayed, he'd still be there safe and content.'

Simon's other arm cradled her back against his chest as they continued to gaze at the scene spread at their feet. 'I think you know he wouldn't, Kate. He's an Ashleigh through and through, however hard he tried to break away. The call to arms would lure him wherever he was. He'd have joined an Australian regiment.'

They stood quietly for some time until Kate said, 'I was unprepared for what I felt when he walked in and collapsed on the carpet at my feet. I'm sure he was unaware of what had happened – then, and also when we met in Alexandria. He . . . he still sees me as the child he took tobogganing and chased around the gardens roaring like a lion. I knew that and . . . and I suppose it was acceptable all the time he . . . all the time there was no one else.'

'There was certain to be, sooner or later. He's the direct heir to all this.'

She swung round to confront him. 'Are you saying he's married some convenient woman to provide the *next* heir before he's killed in action?'

'No, Kate dear,' he said gently. 'It's not a sudden affair. Val's wife is the daughter of his former colonel. He knew her very well during his time with the Fifty-seventh Lancers. Father met her briefly in Kimberley, apparently.' He gave a tender smile. 'Another redhead in the family, he says.'

It was a further blow. She might have borne a marriage of convenience, but this smacked of a long-lost love. Was *she* the cause of whatever happened to Val in South Africa; why he left the 57th when he was on the crest of a wave? Had he loved her *so* much over all the years? No longer able to hold back her distress Kate clutched Simon while she cried her heartbreak against his shoulder. He kept her in a close embrace murmuring, 'I know, I know,' until his words made sense to her. Then her tears were also for him. If only she could love this dear man, instead.

She drew free once she felt able to compose herself. 'That's twice I've sobbed all over your smart jacket today.' He looked pale and upset. 'Oh Simon, why did I have to spoil your lovely plan right at the outset? I'm so sorry.'

'It's not spoilt. We haven't really started on it yet, but I think we should as soon as possible, don't you? How about driving to Winklesham and taking out a boat? We could tie up down the river and have dinner at the Mallard before taking the bus back to Winklesham to collect Jessie. I'll make it all right with the Elders. They'll understand. What d'you say?'

'It sounds lovely . . . and I promise there'll be no more tears.'

His smile was rather strained. 'I don't mind. It gives me an excuse to cuddle you.' He began leading her down the slope. 'I hope Victoria is locked in the cellar with only bread and water for several days.'

'I had to know.'

'Not that way. They may be my half-sisters, but I find the twins increasingly unattractive people. They've been given a great deal of leeway because my parents believe in freedom of expression and personality, but they're becoming uncontrollable. The fact that they're pretty stunning to look at enables them to get away with murder. I'm certain they'll do something utterly outrageous before long.'

Kate clung to his arm down the steep part. In truth, her legs still felt rubbery and unable to function properly. 'There's a streak of wildness in the family. Great-grandmother ran off with an Italian poet leaving her baby at Knightshill, and Uncle Vorne was reputedly a handsome fellow who could charm whatever he wanted from anyone and leave them smiling. And look at Tim. No one, even Mother, could call *him* a saint.'

They were near the shrubbery now and the slope was more gradual. Simon said, 'He might be a lot quieter when the war ends and they release him. Being caged changes people in one of two ways. They either run amok when set free, or remain mentally caged. Knowing Tim, I'd say he won't revert to type. He'll take it badly.'

'But he'll be sound in body. I've seen boys with both legs severed *and* an arm – boys of twenty. How will they live out the rest of their lives?'

Simon stopped, turned and kissed her very fleetingly on the lips. 'We're not going to speak of things like that, remember? For the next two weeks we're going to do all the lovely, happy things we used to do.'

'And pretend it's back like it was.'

'If that's what you want.'

A week passed and the pain began to dull. The photograph of Tim was returned to his room, but Kate did take surreptitious peeps at Vere and Kitty's wedding picture in their private sitting-room. She knew it was foolish but the temptation was too strong. The proud, smiling young officer alongside Vere was on friendly terms with his Vivienne even then, so the image Nurse Daulton had carried everywhere until it went down with the *Romaine* had not been smiling at her, but at his thoughts of his colonel's daughter. What had the heartless creature done to destroy Martin Havelock? Kate was certain Kitty knew, yet sensed that her aunt would not divulge the facts after keeping them secret all this time. Vere certainly would not.

She saw little of the family during the daytime. When they met at the dinner table talk was general and never concerned Val. Vere and Kitty went out of their way to be light-hearted and amusing, Charlotte had reverted to her self-imposed role of maiden aunt to such an extent it was easy to forget that James and Charles were her sons, not Kitty's. Kate's mother wrote long, daily letters to Laurence in Lisbon and to Tim in prison camp. She paid numerous visits to local families of importance, and invited to lunch wealthy acquaintances from the Shires who occasionally stayed overnight. Jon and Dick were fussed over whenever they were in her vicinity, but she appeared to have forgotten she had a daughter. Like the Morgan boys, Kate could instead be Kitty and Vere's offspring. The twins had sulked very visibly for the first two or three days, but the advent of some of Margaret's high-flown friends revived their ebullience. It was particularly evident when men were present. It was also very effective, judging by the reactions of male recipients, young or old.

Those days with Simon were exactly what Kate needed. Simple pastimes in the peace and quiet of rural Wiltshire occupied their daylight hours, each happy to please the other. Simon was in his element driving Jessie along country lanes bordered by spring flowers, but was also happy to abandon his beloved car to ride over the downs on a roan mare with Kate on Dilly, her favourite from the stables.

They found nests, and Kate climbed with him to peer in at the eggs, careless of her dignity as she hitched up her long skirts and scrambled along branches. Sometimes they just walked through the meadows deep in conversation. Kate told of her travels – omitting any mention of hospital wards – describing Alexandria, Lemnos and the immense blueness of the Aegean; speaking of Salonika, and Greek customs; giving her impressions of Malta and Gibraltar. Simon enthused about his work, revealing that he was in line for promotion because of his contribution to the design of the new fighter.

'I was allowed to fly the prototype once it had been thoroughly tested by our designer-pilot. What a privilege! I didn't tell Mother. She worries.'

'I know. She once confessed to me that she wanted to form a militant band to stop warfare in the air.'

'Good lord, did she?'

'I saw her point. Why start up there when there's enough going on on earth?'

That comment set Simon on his hobbyhorse for the rest of the walk. Three days later, when he extolled the design of German fighting aircraft, Kate got around to asking him if he still minded so much not being in uniform. He did not answer immediately, which suggested uncertainty. Then he surprised her.

'Soon after you went to Alexandria I tried to enlist in the RFC. They refused to have me.'

She halted to face him. '*Why*?'

'Said I was far more valuable to them where I was.' He took her hand, urging her to continue walking. 'I was secretly glad because I agreed with them. But I'd offered and I felt all right after that.' He helped her over a stile, then said, 'I was a bit mixed up at the time. Tim was full of Ashleigh bombast, the Elders were involved with their wounded officers, you were in uniform going to the Front . . . and Val was being stoical at Gallipoli. I suppose I thought if *I* put on a uniform you might see me in a different light. Crazy, really.'

'I'm glad they said no,' Kate told him warmly. 'I'd have worried no end about you.'

He stopped then. 'Would you?'

'What a stupid question.'

'Kate . . . you told me last week that you had always regarded Val as a brother until he fell at your feet. Do you think there's a chance that the same might happen with me, one day?' He grinned nervously. 'I can't promise anything as dramatic as that, but I might manage something unusual to take you by surprise.'

She found herself near to tears again, and seized his hands.

'You're more than a brother, you're the dearest person in the world to me.'

'Save for Val.'

She avoided his eyes. 'Perhaps *I'm* a bit mixed up at the moment. I've loved him, one way or another, since I was a little girl. It's not easy to stop.'

'You don't have to stop; just go back to the first kind of love.' He tipped her face up to his with his fingers. 'You can't have him, but I'm here for the taking when you're ready . . . or when I do my astonishing turn to make you see in a flash that you want to spend your life with me. It would be a good life, Kate,' he promised. 'Aircraft design is the thing of the future. Machines are going to be taking passengers all over the world before long. Yes, believe me, they are, and I'm in at the infancy of a new industry. I'm not an Ashleigh who'll go all over the world wherever there's a war to be fought, I'm a stay-at-home Munroe who'll want you beside me through all the thrilling stages of air travel. Will you . . . will you just bear it in mind?'

She did not know how to answer him. 'I'm a nurse. By the end of this year I could be promoted to Sister. All those years of training . . .'

He took hold of her shoulders and looked deep into her eyes. 'If Val was standing here asking you to marry him, nursing wouldn't matter a fig to you, would it?'

'Yes! I . . . I . . . perhaps not. *I don't know,*' she cried in confusion. 'He's married to someone else.'

'And he's only ever been an ideal to you. You might have known him well when you played snowballs with a schoolboy, but you have no idea what he's like now. A few chaotic days at Knightshill and an antiseptic week in a hospital ward is all you've spent in his adult company. You can't love a man on the strength of that, especially when he behaves like an uncle. Face facts, Kate, you've simply never outgrown your childish worship of someone who gave you the things you didn't get from your father. When Laurence came on the scene Val was someone to hold on to, the person who represented those happier days at Knightshill. His picture cured your inability to speak for the same reason.' He shook her shoulders gently. 'He's not merely an inspiration or the Ghost of Christmas Past, he's a mature man with a complex personality. What do you know of it, eh? Nothing! Something terrible happened to him in South Africa, you said. What? Do you know? He spent twelve years in the back of beyond. Why? Do you know that? Do you know the history behind his friendship with this woman he's married? No! How can you possibly love a man you know nothing about?'

Kate was shaken by all he was saying, and more confused than ever. 'You're shouting at me,' she said unsteadily.

'Am I? Perhaps it's time someone did!' He took her hand in his. 'You know everything about me. I've no murky past to hide from you. You've spent half your life in my company and never been hurt by anything I've done. I've protected you from the hurt of others, and I've loved you faithfully for far too long in silence. You've just said I'm the dearest person in the world. Start concentrating on reality, Kate, because that's what *I* represent.' He drew her close. 'I've waited ten days to do this and I think it's time the waiting ended.'

The kiss did not shock her the way the first had done almost eighteen months ago. Maybe they had become different people while they had been isolated from each other for so long. She had lived with pain, suffering, heartache and exhaustion; she had lived with a legion of young men who had demanded her compassion and understanding. Simon had lived with the demands of invention, an urgent need to win a race against time. He had known exhaustion and temporary defeat. He had lain sleepless racking his tired brain for answers to seemingly insurmountable problems. He had been persecuted by those whose grief sought an outlet for blame. All that time he had also loved in vain. The long, lingering embrace was a comfort to them both.

Eventually he held her away, and she saw that the bleakness in his eyes had been banished by vitality. 'I'm going to do that a great deal during the next four days, so that when I go back to work you'll be longing for the weekend before your leave ends when I'm coming to Knightshill even if I have to play truant.' A smile broke through. 'While I'm away I'll be thinking of something startling to do on arrival.'

She shook her head, finding it difficult to speak through a lump in her throat. 'There's no need for that. I know you too well.'

'Not half as well as you'll know me by the time you go back on duty,' he said, his smile broadening. 'Come on, let's make our way home for tea. I'm ravenous.' So saying, he swung around, made a half dash across the meadow, then took a giant leap in the air uttering a yell of triumph. Kate was so astonished she forgot introspection and hurried after him with skirts flying in the breeze.

Everyone was there for tea. It was the usual informal family gathering because there were no visitors today. Vere was excited because he had been asked to paint a canvas of the Camel Corps in action in Palestine. His patron was a distinguished landowner whose grandson was an officer in the exotic corps.

'I haven't done a war painting for many years. It'll be quite a challenge after so many stage sets.'

'I don't know *how* you could accept, Papa,' Victoria declared heartily, being an aspiring stage designer forever wooing Gilbert Dessinger with a view to the future. 'Stage sets are *art*. Camels carrying guns across a dreary desert isn't. As for the men who ride them, they've either gone native and are quite dulally, or they're grown up little boys living out favourite story-book adventures.'

'Where on earth did you pick up those expressions?' demanded Kitty. 'Not here, certainly.'

'From trainee officers at the camp near their college,' put in Jonathan. 'They both slip out in the evenings to meet them. Holly told me one day when she was trying to be superior.'

'You *beast*!' cried the pink-faced confessor. 'You're definitely *inferior*. I told you about that in confidence.'

'You slimy little toad,' cried Victoria, living out her own story-book adventures. 'At your age you should be past infantile blabbing. Don't you know a *man* never rats on a lady?'

'That's enough from all of you,' ruled Vere in a no-nonsense tone. 'If you can't behave and converse according to the rules of this household, we don't wish to have your company.'

'In other words, either shut up or leave,' put in Simon, who had not forgiven his half-sister for hurting Kate with the news of Val's marriage.

'I don't know what you're so cocky about,' flashed Holly. 'Just because Kate's showing you some attention at long last you think you're getting somewhere. You're wrong. Who'd want you instead of wicked, exciting, *gorgeous* Val?'

Vere got to his feet flushed with anger, but all attention was snatched away from the adolescent scene as the door opened to admit a tall, blond man in khaki – a man with an unhealthy pallor and staring blue eyes which viewed the family gathering as if it were a fantasy. Several moments of silence were broken by a strangled cry as Margaret rose from her chair with one hand to her breast. As the twins ran forward shrieking Tim's name, his mother dropped to the floor. Kate stared at her brother, seeing instead another Ashleigh who had appeared without warning, irrevocably changed.

They were in his mother's sitting-room. Vere had carried her there with Kate in attendance, but Margaret Nicolardi was far stronger than her slender build suggested and she now discarded the large, light shawl Kate had spread over her as she lay on the chaise-longue and swung her feet to the ground. Yet her lovely face still registered shock as she gazed at her son. It left him unmoved.

'Tim, this has caught us all unawares,' Vere said quietly. 'Why didn't you send a telegram?'

'Because I'd have arrived almost at the same time. There was no point.'

'Are you hungry?'

'I'd like a stiff drink.'

'Of course.' Vere walked to Laurence's decanters and poured brandy, saying, 'I'm sure you want to be alone with your mother, but perhaps you'd just tell me how it is you're here. We heard you were a prisoner of war – your single postcard confirmed the fact – but we've had no news of repatriation even from Laurence, who'd be one of the first to hear of it.' He arrived with the brandy. 'My dear fellow, you look all in. Sit down and toss this back.'

'I've been sitting for hours. It's good to stand.' Tim was very het up. Knightshill had seemed the ideal place to head for because he thought the family would be in London. He had forgotten the spring vacation, and had walked in on a noisy gathering of the whole clan – even Kate. He needed time to himself; time to get adjusted to the new Tim Ashleigh. All the way to Dunstan St Mary he had thought about wandering the large empty rooms of Knightshill, coming to terms with all that had happened; riding along the downs in solitary state thinking over past attitudes and beliefs. Now he was under presssure to explain before he was ready, and his mother was going to be difficult, damn difficult. That was already apparent. He was grateful for Vere's presence. His uncle was a good man and played his role as head of the family with sincerity.

'Where've you travelled from, Tim?' Vere asked.

'I came over on the leave train. They've given me an initial twenty-eight days, some of which I'll spend in hospital having my jaw fixed. A Hun doctor had two cracks at it without much enthusiasm, so they're going to do what they can for me before I go back.'

'Back where?' demanded his mother.

'On active service.'

'*No!*' It was a cry from the heart. 'After all you've been through?'

'Thanks to you I've been through very little, Mother.'

Vere intervened. 'Perhaps you should first tell us why the Germans released you.'

'They didn't. I broke out and made my way back to our lines. My fluent German was put to better use than at GHQ.' He took a good pull at the brandy. When he lowered the glass his mother was before him, ashen faced, her eyes full of fears.

'Why, Tim? *Why*? The terrible risk! They could have shot you down as you ran. Dear heaven, were you out of your mind?'

He stepped back from her outstretched hands. 'On the contrary. I was more *in* it than I've been for years. Mother, you're totally incomprehensible. Would you really have been happier with your son behind bars, treated with contempt by oafish guards, for as long as the war lasts – maybe for *years*? Men are being shot down in their *thousands* as they run. If you really haven't yet grasped that fact, Kate certainly has. Take one look at her face and you'll see it all written there.' He moved nearer to his sister. 'But you've never considered her to be your concern, have you? It's time you did, because by the time this is all over Kate may be the only child left to you.'

'Tim, this isn't the moment to . . .'

He cut his uncle off short. 'Yes, it is. I should have said it long ago; should have been stronger. I came here hoping to be alone for a while first, but all this might as well be tackled and the air cleared.' He drank the remaining brandy but continued to grip the glass. 'We're not winning the war, Mother. No one is. In a little over a year Jon will be in uniform, then Dick. *All* your children. You won't be able to protect them as you've done your damnedest to protect me.' He began to move about in his agitation. 'The last time we met you told me a lot of crass nonsense about my being your firstborn.'

'No, not nonsense.'

'Yes, *nonsense*,' he reiterated. 'I was special, you said. I swallowed it all because it was what I wanted to hear, but if it was true, why did you do the cruellest thing you could to me?'

'Tim, you're tired and overwrought,' said Vere, once more attempting to mediate.

'Yes, I am,' he agreed heatedly, 'and I'm going to have this out here and now unless Mother ducks out of it by pretending she can't take it. Believe me, she can. She manipulates Laurence with an iron hand in a velvet glove, and she's done the same with me until now. This is where she stops.'

Margaret appealed to Kate. 'He's exhausted. He's been through a terrible ordeal. He doesn't know what he's saying. Shouldn't he rest? Is there something you can give him?'

'I can give him the chance to sort out what's troubling him. He really needs to. I think we should all listen, Mother.'

Tim gripped Kate's shoulder by way of thanks, but he would have continued against all odds. He had bottled up his feelings for too long. 'By trapping me at GHQ you denied me what I most wanted. I was demoralized by what you had done. Can you understand what I mean by that?' He approached his mother standing in the middle of the room suddenly looking every one of her forty-seven years, despite the golden hair and elegant bronze dress. '*Can you*, Mother? It was as if you'd robbed me of my manhood by keeping me in your maternal cottonwool. I felt deeply ashamed of my comfort and security while my battalion was fighting and suffering. I began to lie, to pretend to those who didn't know the truth that I'd been through hell and back. I chased after women to compensate for my failure. A son to be proud of, by your standards.'

'That's ridiculous,' she said tautly. 'You were doing valuable work.'

'*I was going to the dogs*!' His jaw was starting to hurt, but nothing would stop him now. 'When I finally struggled free of you and got out to where I most wanted to be, we were overrun on my first day in action. I was pushed over by a German soldier and *stamped* on. Yes, Mother, he brought his great muddy boot down on my face and knocked me out. When I came to I was a prisoner. I won't describe what that entailed, but it completed what you had begun; the destruction of my pride.'

He went to the decanter and poured more brandy. He needed it. All three were staring at him when he turned back to them, and his mother looked ready to faint again. He spoke rapidly before she did. 'I didn't want to live. I wished they'd killed me instead.' He tossed back some of the fiery spirit, then walked towards her sensing a volcano inside him starting to erupt. 'All I'd cherished from early childhood had been denied me, so I simply gave up the ghost. Their insults, goads and humiliations didn't break me because I was already broken. Or so I thought.' He glanced around at the faces watching him with vastly different expressions. '*Or so I thought.*'

Kate got up from the footstool and crossed to stand beside their mother, maybe sensing that she might need support. Vere looked extremely grave. Tim drank the rest of his second brandy. It was starting to affect him, but its stimulus was all to the good because he was tiring. He had not eaten since leaving Boulogne.

'They released me from solitary on Christmas Eve and I returned to my dormitory to find a stranger sitting on my bunk. He'd been caught three days earlier. I was about to slouch off when I noticed he was wearing the badges of the Fifty-seventh Lancers.' He sensed that Vere made a forward movement, but he was more concerned with watching his mother's face and continued without pause, growing more impassioned as he spoke.

'Yes, I asked him about Martin Havelock. As luck would have it he was on the spot when it all happened.' He paused to steady himself. 'I resented Val when he turned up here resembling a vagabond. I made no secret of my contempt for an Ashleigh who could let himself sink so low. Now I know why he did. That poor devil came within a hairsbreadth of being shot as a traitor in order to protect some nincompoop with connections in high places – the kind of people *you* mix with, Mother. They commuted the sentence and instead kicked him out in a barbarous punishment ritual designed to destroy *any* man. But it didn't destroy *him*, did it?' He waved an arm with a pointing finger. 'No, he's out there winning medals and living up to his destiny as a true Ashleigh. He's doing what *I* should have been doing.'

Tim was breathing heavily and his head was starting to spin. 'You knew about the affair; that it was a case of gross injustice. Why have you kept quiet all this time, letting me believe there was a *shameful* secret in his past? Why did you allow us all to treat him as we did when he arrived from Australia? You were almost as dismissive.' When neither Margaret nor Vere spoke, the erupting volcano rose higher. 'My God, you surely didn't believe him guilty?' He confronted Vere. '*You* didn't? Not your own brother?'

'No . . . no,' Vere murmured, plainly shaken.

'Then why have I been kept in ignorance all these years? Wasn't I entitled to know? I'm a soldier; I'm an Ashleigh. I'm . . . I'm . . .' His voice was growing unsteady now. 'Was *that* part of the coddling policy, Mother? Had I to be protected from hearing anything nasty where the family is concerned?'

Vere moved a pace or two forward. 'You're not aware of all the facts.'

'I'll wager I'm not,' Tim cried. 'I wonder just how much has been withheld from me because none of you considered me man enough to be told.'

'That's unfair!' his mother declared.

He rounded on her once again. 'You accuse *me* of unfairness? That's rich!'

Kate spoke up at that point; a voice of calm in a growing storm. 'You were telling us about the man in the Fifty-seventh Lancers.'

'Yes.' Tim struggled mentally to return to that point. 'He had witnessed the punishment parade, taken a principal part in it. He said . . . he said it had made him feel ashamed. Well, I tell you, I felt *deeply* ashamed just hearing about it; of being made painfully aware of what it must have done to a twenty-one year old who'd grown up, as I did, wanting nothing but to spend his life in the army. I'd given up so easily, yet he . . .' He swallowed the thickness in his throat. 'I vowed to escape at the first opportunity – a number were succeeding all over France – and get back into action as soon as I could. Once I've been cleared by a medical board as fit I shall start again, and no one will stop me. *No one*!' he added, glaring at his mother. 'From the age of my earliest memory I told myself

I'd one day be as heroic as Uncle Vorne. I'm now wise enough to know that might not be possible, but I'm going to have a damn good try.'

'No! You're wrong about Vorne. He was a coward.'

'*Margaret!*' cried Vere.

Overwrought, she turned on her brother. 'Val said all along that Tim should be told. He was insistent . . . and he was right. He sacrificed so much trying to equal Vorne. Now Tim's going to throw away his *life* for the same mistaken belief.'

'We *agreed*,' Vere insisted.

'I've changed my mind, and Laurence will back me,' Margaret said, charged with emotion. 'Together with Val we outvote you and Lottie. He *has* to be told.'

Tim was nearing the end of his control by now and demanded harshly, 'What other secrets have been kept from me because I'm really a Daulton?'

'That has nothing to do with it,' snapped Vere, also highly worked up. 'It was done for the good of the entire family, and to protect your career with the West Wilts.'

'Yet Val thought I should know. I'd back his judgement against yours now I know the kind of man he really is. Come on, Mother, finish what you began.'

Accepting defeat with stony-faced resignation, Vere said, 'Very well, *I'll* tell you. I trust your apparent new-found wisdom will allow you to understand that it was done in your best interests.'

'*I'm* the only one who knows my best interests,' Tim said in dangerously raised tones. 'Haven't I just made that crystal clear?'

Kate came to him, her face pale and set. 'I think we should let Uncle Vere explain now that he's been left no alternative. Why don't we sit down?'

Tim jerked his arm from his sister's gentle clasp and stared at Vere with animosity. 'Let's get on with it, shall we?'

Very evidently upset, Vere said, 'When I was in the Sudan I encountered a prisoner in Omdurman's cells who had been in Khartoum when it fell. Vorne was aware that a communiqué would never bring help in time to save the garrison. He left Khartoum merely in a bid to save his own skin carrying a valuable scarab and a purse of money wrested from the man who related the story to me. I'd no reason to doubt its veracity. It bore out evidence

I'd found of my brother's villainy in other directions. The West Wiltshire Regiment's "Hero of Khartoum" was a lecher and a cheat.' He licked his dry lips. 'When we told Val the truth on his return from South Africa, he left Knightshill that same night. It was apparently the last straw.'

'My God!' mouthed Tim, feeling the foundations of his life shaking precariously. '*My God*! I've been struggling to emulate a coward while treating the real family hero with contempt. I've done to that poor devil what the Fifty-seventh did . . . and so have you by keeping your vile secrets.'

'Val said all along we should tell you,' Margaret repeated wretchedly.

'*Then why the hell didn't you*?' Tim roared. '*Why the hell not*?' On a sudden savage impulse he hurled his brandy glass at the pale silk wall covering, so that it shattered and fell to the carpet beside the chaise-longue. Then his shoulders began to heave and convulsive shaking worked right through his body as the concentration of pain, tension, humiliation and despair he had suffered since being captured became uncontrollable.

The room was in half-light when Tim opened his eyes. His body ached quite severely, but it was nothing to the pain in his jaw. Had it been broken anew? He frowned as his surroundings slowly identified themselves as the familiar features of his bedroom at Knightshill. His eyes swivelled further to encounter a girl sitting in a chair beside the window. She wore a rose-pink skirt with a matching loose silky tunic, but the warm shade did nothing to aid her pallor.

'Hallo,' said Kate softly. 'Feeling better?'

Memory was returning. 'Where are the others?'

'I told Mother I'd call her when you awoke.'

'Don't.'

'All right.' She came to sit on the side of the bed. 'Don't worry, it happens to us all sooner or later. You've had enough for the moment.' She gave a wan smile. 'I've been weeping all over Simon since I got here.'

'The last I heard you were in Greece.'

'I caught typhus. They decided I should have a spell at home to make a full recovery. I really needed a rest. I'd started blaming myself each time a man died. That's fatal. Once your professional confidence fades you become a danger to yourself and your patients.'

Tim pushed himself into a sitting position. He was still in his khaki shirt and breeches, but his tie had been removed and the waistband undone. He had no desire to come out from beneath the coverlet. It would take too much effort. Everything had come back to him now and he was unwilling to break his isolation with the one person at Knightshill who understood.

'Did you know about our family rogue?'

'Of course not,' his sister replied. 'The Elders apparently intended to die with their secret intact. Uncle Vere has just explained why to me. They felt it would put us in an awkward position, particularly you, when people mentioned him; that the knowledge would make your standing in the regiment well nigh impossible. I suppose I can appreciate that.'

'They thought I wasn't man enough to handle it, you mean.'

'No, Tim, I don't mean that. Later on you'll see everything in a different light.'

'What light do you see it in?' he challenged.

Kate shrugged her shoulders. 'Rather a cloudy one, I admit, but I think Uncle Vere had a very difficult decision to make when he first discovered the truth. He's just told me he fully intended keeping silent, until Great-grandfather heard about Martin Havelock's court martial and vowed to strip Val of the right to inherit and cut him out of the family for good. Uncle Vere was so incensed he blurted out the truth about the brother they'd all been made to revere. The old man died several hours later. The facts had to be told to everyone then present, who vowed not to pass them on to the next generation. When Val turned up, ostensibly from the dead, his brothers and sisters accepted that he must also be made aware of the fallacy regarding their older brother. The news came at a time when he had just lost everything in his drive to live up to the "hero".' She gave Tim a sympathetic look. 'Much the same time as you've heard it.'

'Oh no, I've lost little save my faith in people I trusted.'

'That's why Val stayed away for so long.' She sighed. 'Uncle Vere said he then determined never to tell another soul, because he had killed an old general and driven away his heir with the truth. The Elders respected his decision. I can understand why.'

'*You* were never expected to live up to the legendary Hero of Khartoum. It's easy for you to be on their side.'

She touched his hand with her fingertips. 'I'm not on anyone's *side*, Tim, and I'm as shocked as you. Remember the Khartoum Dinners Great-grandfather held every year? *I've* also believed the myth all of my life. But imagine if the facts were general knowledge in the family. The twins wouldn't keep it quiet, for a start. The Ashleighs would lose all credibility, and the regiment would be ridiculed for lionizing a reprobate. Would you want that?'

'Of course I wouldn't! They should have told *me* a long time ago.'

'I suppose so . . . but won't it make things difficult for you now? What will you do when fellow officers mention him?'

He sagged against his pillows. 'They won't. This war's producing unsung heroes galore. The Sudan's ancient history. Vorne Ashleigh will imperceptibly pass into the realms of victorious giants to become no more than a name, like most of our warrior ancestors. Who knows what kind of man Charles Ashleigh, seventeen forty-two to eighty-six, was? Who cares? The same will happen with Vorne, our *real* wicked uncle.'

Kate fussed with the coverlet, her hands making jerky movements which suggested tension. Tim watched her with fresh eyes. They seemed to have come together again in a curious sharing of something beyond the comprehension of everyone else in this great mansion. He was content to be in her sole company for a while.

She glanced up at him. 'Tim, *I* still don't know what happened to Val in South Africa. Will you please tell me?'

'Are you sure you want to hear it? Aren't you rather sweet on him?'

'He's married.'

'Good lord. Who to?' He wondered how many more family secrets he had not been told.

'The daughter of his former colonel. What happened in South Africa?'

He sensed that his sister was seriously upset. Had she been *that* fond of her young uncle? Was it a good thing to tell her something certain to upset her further?'

'*Please*, Tim,' she urged, as if reading his thoughts. 'His wife was mixed up in it. I'll be the only one left in the dark if you don't let me know what that man told you.'

So he told her every detail he had repeated inwardly until the day von Model had again locked him away in an attempt to break his resistance, and his new resolution had enabled him to fool the guard escorting him to the toilet to make his planned getaway under cover of darkness. The room grew shadowy, apart from the firelight, as he spoke of something he did not realize was having as deep an effect on his sister as on himself. When he finished he saw the gleam of tears on Kate's cheeks.

'Oh lord, I should have kept that to myself,' he said wearily.

She caught up his hand. 'No, you'd have been as bad as them. We've had enough secrets. It's time for us to be open with each other.'

He offered her a corner of a sheet to wipe her eyes. 'You've changed, Kate.'

'So have you. It's the war.' She dropped the damp piece of sheet and straightened to study him in the amber glow from the fire. 'I think we should keep all of this from the children though, don't you? You and I and Simon are a sort of in-between generation, aren't we?'

He nodded. 'I've certainly never considered myself on a par with the Nicolardi boys.'

'I even less so, of course, and Simon is completely out of tune with the twins.' After slight hesitation she said, 'You've often claimed that you feel a cuckoo in the Nicolardi nest. There's room in *our* nest, if you'd like to join us. We'd love to have you.'

Tim slipped away from the house early and rode up to the downs. The dawn drizzle had ceased leaving a glistening silver layer on the deep-green turf as the sun rose into a cloudless sky. He had been home three days but had not yet come to terms with the destruction of a myth. Vorne Ashleigh had been his boyhood hero; his adult inspiration. It was not easy to accept that the ideal had never existed. It was even harder to accept that he, himself, had inherited some of those less attractive qualities. Vorne had apparently been an inveterate womanizer, had run up debts and borrowed from friends, had been handsome, feckless and arrogant.

But for this war, Tim might have slid a little further down the slippery path.

He allowed his horse to canter gently, in no mood to gallop. He was still exhausted and his jaw ached constantly. Kate said it was due to tension. His sister was today going to Salisbury with Simon, who was then travelling on to his digs ready for work in the morning. They appeared to be hitting it off very well, because Simon was planning to come for a weekend before Kate returned to duty. Tim supposed he had taken up Kate's offer to join their 'nest' because he was only comfortable in their company. The Elders had been unsettled by their forced confessions, and the adolescents got on his nerves – especially the twins. Hot under the collar over his previous narcissistic response to their flattery, he now found their bees-around-a-honeypot attentions too disturbingly sexual for schoolgirl cousins.

Laurence was returning from Lisbon tonight. Tim foresaw another confrontation, for his step-father would leap to Margaret's defence. He was too weary for a further exchange of opinions, especially with an expert wordsmith. His mother wanted him to let Sir Hastings Longfellow operate on his jaw – he was one of the best surgeons in the country – and Kate advised him to clear it with the army. He supposed he should agree before Laurence arrived to take the initiative for him.

He slowed the gelding to a walk after a while, thinking of the months ahead. The weather was improving. Everyone knew there would be a fresh offensive as soon as the mud hardened. He wanted to be out there taking part in it, no longer in a bid to become the family's next hero but simply as a trained soldier doing his utmost along with his fellows. When he had gained the British lines after covering a hundred miles through German-held territory, the MO had marked him as walking wounded for home convalescence. He had protested. He wanted to find the nearest West Wilts unit, but his wound had been classed as mental and that meant a spell away from the trenches and the thunder of artillery. In retrospect he had accepted that he should get himself fit before taking on responsibility for others' lives. He owed his men that.

At the end of the long flat stretch where a bridle-path led down to the village, Tim reined in and dismounted. England was beautiful. Why had he never really noticed it before? Come to that, had he ever bothered to stand like this, in solitude, to look at scenes such as the one spread below him at the moment? Being deprived of freedom made everything so much more precious. He had seen men die, and as someone who had treated it carelessly in the past, life had now taken on a different dimension. Small wonder he needed to be alone to review these new thoughts and impressions. Knightshill was presently as noisy and as busy as a market place.

Looping the bridle over a low bush, Tim wandered the few yards to where the downs sloped away to form one side of Dunstan Valley. Over to the right he could see Knightshill rearing up from a mass of blossoms in the formal gardens, the sun glinting on the glasshouses where Charlotte's exotic flowers were grown. Dropping in a broad sweep reaching to where he stood, the rich land of the estate supported sheep and cattle, in addition to crops. The tenant farmers in the valley also worked productive soil. It was a heaven-blessed corner of Wiltshire.

His gaze travelled from the right where the Purbeck Hills rose in a distant mauve range, around to the wooded slope marking the far side of the valley, taking in the peaceful sight of grazing animals, leaping lambs, infant crops sown in straight rows, the gleam of the river high up its banks because of the late winter rains, the straggling village with the church as its hub, and the pennant of grey smoke above a train winding its way through meadowland towards the white-fenced station. Vorne Ashleigh had been heir to all this, and more besides. He had dishonoured it. Thank God his brother Vere was a vastly different manner of man, one who loved it and all family values. Now in his mid-forties, he looked set to live long enough for the next generation heir to succeed him. Val had apparently declined his heritage, so all hopes rested on his coming child being a boy. He was unlikely to survive long enough to father another if it were not.

As Tim stood dreaming about concerns that had never bothered him before, he suddenly regretted his own single state. He had been twenty-eight two days ago. Why had he not married and had a son? He was next in line if Val did not produce an heir. Once he went back into action his chances of survival were slim. He should have ensured that he would leave behind something to mark his days on earth, apart from a bevy of amoral women with vague pleasant memories of someone called Bobby. His throat tightened as he acknowledged that he had left it too late. Was that why Val had married so suddenly? If so, fate had surely been kind in ensuring that his duty as heir was done with such speed – but was it not time something went right for him?

Tim remained in the growing warmth, letting thoughts drift in and out of his mind until hunger prompted him to move. He would work his painful way through breakfast, then get in touch with the military medical authorities. They would be glad to be rid of a patient, especially one able to pay for his own treatment of a battle wound, and the patient would welcome the opportunity to escape to London. He sighed. Surely his mother would not follow and insist on supervising every aspect of his treatment.

Strolling back to his horse, Tim had one foot in the stirrup when he grew aware of another rider breasting the hill from the bridle-path. He watched over his gelding's back until the woman became fully visible, then his foot dropped to the ground almost at the same time as she saw him and reined in, as disconcerted as he. He had not thought of Amy since meeting Piers Lassingham of the 57th Lancers. She looked pale but very striking in a black habit and a hat with a turquoise plume. Her eyes were further darkened by the same brand of shocked awareness as when he had left her a year ago. How could he have let her slip from his mind?

They regarded each other in silence for a few moments, and it was clear to Tim that she was unable to ride away from the unexpected encounter. He led his horse across to her, uncertain of how to handle the situation. 'Hallo.'

'Hallo,' she replied faintly.

'What are you doing in Dunstan?' He stopped beside the flank of her mare. 'I suppose you're staying at the Stag's Head.'

'My aunt fell ill. I came to organize the catering for her.'

'Who's looking after the Regency?'

'My staff are perfectly capable of managing without me for a few days.'

There was a flash of the controlled businesswoman who had resisted his every overture. Memories of their meetings flooded back. 'I'm sure your customers aren't capable of doing without you. It's you they flock to see.'

'What nonsense!'

'It isn't, and you know it.' The silence lasted for an uncomfortably long time and Tim cast around for words to end it. 'I'm on a month's leave.'

'Uncle Lionel told me.'

'So you're not really surprised to see me.' He managed a smile. 'Is everything that happens at Knightshill known at the inn?'

She nodded, still looking wary. 'More or less.'

He put up a hand to take hold of her mare's bridle. 'We haven't a reciprocal arrangement or I'd have made a point of riding down to see you.' There was no reaction to that, so he added, 'To explain why I broke my promise to write to you every week.'

'I know why.'

'I see. Did Uncle Lionel tell you that too?'

'Everyone was very upset about it.'

'So my capture was discussed in the taproom over tankards of ale, was it? I wonder you didn't announce it at the Regency,' he said bitingly.

She hesitated before speaking, as if unsure of herself. 'Knightshill may be up on a hill but it's still part of the village. A number of men from Dunstan are in uniform, and their welfare is of great concern to us all. We . . . I know you're a rather . . . *proud* man,' she went on, choosing her words with obvious care. 'We all guessed how you might feel in captivity, and sympathized. It's nothing to be ashamed of, you know.'

He remembered his hours in solitary confinement thinking of her disparagement as she had asked if he was one of the items to be auctioned in a good cause. He was no longer so full of Ashleigh pride and managed to apologize. 'Sorry. You always read me too easily.'

'No, not always.' No longer able to meet his eyes, Amy gathered up the reins. 'I must go. I'm catching the noon train back to London.'

He was disappointed. Seeing her again had revived a spark within him; had been like a breath of freedom from the weighty atmosphere presently at Knightshill. He released his hold on her mare. 'I mustn't delay you, in that case.'

His swift acquiescence appeared to throw her, for she made no immediate sign of moving off. 'Well, goodbye then. They . . . they also spoke about your escape in the taproom and made you sound something of a hero.' The mare finally began to move off while he absorbed that last sentence, and was starting down the slope when Amy turned to call out, 'Good luck, Tim.'

They had vanished from sight before he realized she had called him by his first name. What a fool he was; how his reflexes had slowed! She was the last person he had expected to meet here, but had the events of the past year so dulled his wits he could no longer read a woman's subtle hints that her demeanour belied her inner feelings? She had sent him an optical message at the outset, telling him she had not forgotten the impact of their last parting. She had made him aware that she followed with great interest her uncle's reports on his affairs. Yet he had tamely let her go. Had she expected strong man tactics from him again? Quite possibly. He stared at the spot where she had disappeared from sight. It was too late to go after her now, but his weary brain sent him a message regarding the chance to compensate at Dunstan Station at noon.

The chance was endangered. He came upon his mother at the breakfast table and was told that a telegram had arrived in his absence. Laurence had returned a day early from Lisbon because of the crisis.

'What crisis?' Tim asked, putting eggs and bacon on his plate.

'Your jaw operation, of course,' came her astonishing reply. 'He reached London late last evening and contacted Sir Hastings without delay. As a very special concession to his dear friends, he's coming here with Laurence at eleven this morning to examine you and arrange for the operation to be performed at his private clinic two days from now.'

'Mother, I haven't cleared it with the army,' he protested.

'That's a mere formality. I'll ask Laurence to have a word with the Surgeon-General, whom he's met at conferences.'

'No!' Tim said firmly. 'I'll telephone the military hospital as soon as I've finished this . . . and Sir Hastings will have to examine me *after* lunch. I've an appointment in the village at twelve.'

Margaret frowned. 'You'll have to cancel it.'

'I can't. When a man comes here at such short notice he must expect us to have prior commitments, even when he's making a special concession for dear friends.' He forestalled any further comment. 'That's the *end* of the matter, Mother.'

Tim arrived with five minutes to spare. Common courtesy had

demanded that he meet the eminent surgeon and apologize for having to absent himself until lunchtime. Amy was standing with a travelling-bag at her feet, talking to Lionel Moorkin. Tim hesitated only momentarily, then strode up to them with determination. Amy betrayed herself by the faint colouring in her cheeks as she spotted him, but the landlord of the Stag's Head turned in surprise as an Ashleigh arrived beside them and halted with some purpose.

'Good morning, sir. Is there something I can do?'

'Morning, Moorkin.' Tim felt he should call the man Uncle Lionel. This squire-tenant interchange seemed wrong in front of Amy. 'I'd like a private word with Mrs Sturt, if you'd be so good. I'll see her safely installed in the train, I promise.'

Moorkin was flummoxed and looked to his niece for guidance. Amy turned even pinker in the face of her uncle's confusion, then kissed him on the cheek and said her goodbye messages so that he realized she accepted this extraordinary development. The man glanced at Tim, touched his forehead in a respectful gesture, then walked off across the square with several backward glances.

Tim got to the point swiftly. He could see smoke in the distance. 'I shall be in London by the end of the week. They're going to operate on my jaw again, but I'll soon be convalescent. I want to see you as often as I can before I go back.' He seized her hand. 'I was taken by surprise this morning. I kicked myself for letting you go before saying all this. I've been counting the minutes until I could ride down here and explain . . . and I'll be counting the days until we meet in London.' The train had come into view around the bend, so he pulled her into his arms and embarked on the strong-man tactics he should have employed on the downs. When he released her she was breathless, and he was in severe pain. It seemed kissing was an agonizing occupation at the moment.

They gazed at each other without words as the train arrived with a grinding of steel and great billows of smoke. Tim opened a carriage door and helped Amy up the step, following her to place her bag on the overhead rack. As the compartment was empty he bent his head and brushed her lips gently with his own.

'Set up that same little table for me,' he murmured. 'I'll be there just as soon as I escape from the clutches of the surgeon.' Stepping down to the platform he closed the door between them as the station master blew his whistle and waved the green flag.

Amy stood at the open window while the train steamed away, looking at him in a way that suddenly filled him with a sense of great responsibility. He had made Amy care deeply for him, at a time when his lifespan was likely to be very short. Yet had he not earlier this morning yearned to leave behind something of some worth, and surely the true love of a woman was just that? Sadly, the cost would be borne by her, as it was by so many of her sisters.

CHAPTER SEVENTEEN

It was Kate's last weekend before reporting for duty. Simon had arrived very early on this Saturday morning having caught the milk train to Dunstan St Mary, but the entire weekend was about to be ruined for Kate by the arrival of Vivienne Ashleigh. She had written inviting herself for a day to meet her husband's family, and Vere had replied extending the invitation to three days. He was eager to meet her. Indeed, everyone save Kate was full of avid anticipation. Even Simon said he was glad Val's wife had chosen a time when he was at home to meet her.

As he and Kate strolled through the rose garden after breakfast he challenged her mood. 'She exists, Kate. You can't pretend she doesn't, and you *have* to meet her. Perhaps it's better this way than when she's hanging on Val's arm looking at him the way I'm certain I look at you.'

She would not meet his eyes. 'I wanted to spend this weekend continuing your lovely plan for us, but we're now expected to cluster around her and do the "family" act until she leaves. Uncle Vere loses his head sometimes. He thinks we're still in the days of gracious living and social elegance. He's an intelligent man. Can't he see that things have changed? This woman has been driving an ambulance in France! She'll be overwhelmed by the Ashleigh clan on their best behaviour, in silks and satins among the best teacups.'

Simon halted and made her face him. 'Father's very proud of the family and Knightshill. Of course he knows things have changed – he works hard on his charity theatrical projects, the overall management of Ashleigh Court, meeting goverment demands for food production here on the estate and now Uncle John is dead, he has the full responsibility of the American ranch in which

Val has a double share but has never done anything to earn.' He squeezed her hands, adding gently, 'He needs to escape into the idyll he once knew, now and again. Something like this gives him the perfect opportunity. And Vivienne is not "this woman", she's the heir's wife. Father obviously wants to show off what she's inherited by marrying Val.'

'He doesn't want Knightshill.'

'Ah, that was when he intended returning to Australia. I'll wager he'll accept his heritage now he has a wife and child. That's part of Father's excitement today. Continuation of the line is very important to him.'

'Let's hope the heir's wife produces a son, in that case. I suppose she invited herself so that she could look over her future property.'

Simon took hold of her shoulders and shook her gently. 'Hey, it's not like you to be so sour. Face facts, girl. Father's only forty-five He may live another fifty years, like Sir Gilliard. Vivienne will be aware of that. She'll also be aware that she may produce a girl . . . and that Val may not survive the coming offensive. I really don't think she's coming here to assess the value of Knightshill and its contents.'

Kate had the grace to flush. 'Sorry. Putting it in those words makes me sound heartless.'

He drew her close and his voice betrayed his disappointment. 'It's because you're the reverse that you feel the way you do. You still care about him, don't you?'

She said against his jacket, 'I'd feel the same if your wife was arriving this morning.'

'I want to talk to you about that while I'm here,' he murmured, 'but let's first have a brisk walk up to that nest we found in the blackthorn at the top of the hill. The chicks should be well advanced now.'

They all dutifully gathered in the sitting-room carpeted in blue and cream, from where there was a clear view of the bridge over the former moat. Vivienne had written that she would arrive at noon and did not need to be met at the station. Vere's scrutiny of the rail timetable revealed that there was no train from Blecton Mere arriving just before noon, so they all surmized that she was not coming direct from the stud farm.

As Kate had guessed, everyone was dressed for the occasion. She wore one of her own favourite voile dresses in pearly pink which was two years out of date in style, but she had worn only uniform for that length of time – army nurses abroad were forbidden to have in their possession any civilian clothes. Milly frequently said it would perk up the patients no end if the nurses pranced through the wards in something glamorous now and again, but the authorities insisted that they were not women, they were creatures of mercy. The dress suited Kate's colouring and rather thin figure, but Margaret publically deplored her daughter's lack of style and taste.

'I despair of you, Kate,' she declared at her entry. 'You consistently fail to present yourself at your best.'

From beside Kate Simon said, 'I think she does that when nursing the sick and wounded, Aunt Margaret.'

'I thought *you'd* make *every* effort to outshine *her*,' put in Holly with heavy meaning, and Victoria added to Kate, 'After all, she's only some ambulance driver, and you're an Ashleigh. We have to let her see we're not *all* like Val.'

Simon appealed to Kitty. 'Mother, can't you threaten them with dire punishment unless they behave? They're always at their worst on occasions like these.'

Vere took over, crossing to his daughters with a wagging finger. 'Vivienne is a colonel's daughter and knew Val when he was a Lancer officer, but she's just about to meet you two. If either one of you puts a foot wrong, says one inexcusable sentence, you will leave school and finish your education incarcerated here with a strict, humourless governess. You have no reason to look down your noses at Val or his wife. Have you fought at Gallipoli and saved men's lives at risk to your own?' he demanded of Holly. Then of Victoria, 'And have you driven an ambulance under fire through the mud of France? I'm growing a little tired of your antics during this vacation. You are not women of the theatrical world yet; you are merely somewhat silly, capricious *little girls*.'

Nothing could have caused them more mortification than to be called little girls, particularly in the presence of their male cousins. Both twins blushed scarlet and looked on the verge of tears until Richard Nicolardi murmured, 'About time they were cut down to size,' and was overheard by Vere, who then turned to the four boys sitting together by the window as unofficial lookouts. 'And the same applies to all of you. One foot wrong and it'll be six of the best from me. I've overheard muttered comments about men who drink ale, and seen sneers when your uncle's name is mentioned. I've let them pass because I thought you'd gain a little more wisdom, in time. You've all been busy with your own affairs so far during this vacation, so I've been unable to assess whether or not you've acquired more mature minds. Any evidence that you haven't during Vivienne's visit will result in invitations to my study – and you'll need a piece of cardboard strategically placed in your clothing if you hope to sit down afterwards.'

The twins giggled somewhat emotionally as the boys turned pink about the ears. Their Uncle Vere did not often put on his stern, head of the family hat, so that he did so now impressed on them the importance he placed on the visit of someone they had privately named *Mrs Blacksheep*. It had been almost as titillating as anticipating Val's return three years ago, until this wigging. They now felt overwhelming resentment of this woman who, because she had married a vagabond drunkard, was now of higher status in the family than their mothers. If Uncle Vere died tomorrow, Mrs Blacksheep could come here and order them all out of the house, with legal right on her side.

Simon nudged Kate delightedly, saying under his breath, 'All that was long overdue. Father usually lets the twins wind him around their fingers.'

'And Mother does the same with Jon and Dick,' she murmured back. 'It's because they so resemble Laurence.'

'And the twins are too damned pretty.'

Kate studied Simon's half-sisters. They looked exceptionally stunning today in daring short dresses of ivory silk embellished individually, one with bronze and the other with midnight blue panne velvet. They even outshone Margaret, who had not recovered from the drama of Tim's return and his changed attitudes. She looked drawn in spite of her flattering silver-grey costume banded with beaded satin. She had returned to Knightshill yesterday for this meeting with Vivienne Ashleigh, but it was clear to Kate that her mother would rather be in London with her beloved Laurence, where she could visit Tim at Sir Hastings' clinic and continue her efforts to persuade him to accept another safe post at his step-father's instigation.

'*Gosh*!'

'Oh, I *say*!'

'Take a look at *this*!'

'What price Jessie?'

All these awed comments from the Nicolardi and Morgan boys put an end to general conversation, and the twins squealed with excitement in a manner totally unsuited to women of the theatrical world as they scrambled over their cousins' legs to get a better view from the window.

'It's . . . it's . . .' spluttered Holly.

'*Absolutely whizz-bang*,' Victoria finished, in the language of military cadets with whom they enjoyed their secret rendezvous after school.

The older members of the family, except Charlotte who viewed the visit with apprehension, moved to look out at the wide, gravelled approach to the front entrance. Kate saw, with astonishment, a very large dark-red open motorcar sweeping round from the bridge over the moat to draw up at the point where the ever watchful Thornton was already waiting to greet the new Mrs Ashleigh, who was at the wheel.

'She has her husband's knack of making an unusual entrance,' murmured Simon at Kate's shoulder. 'That's what *I* should have done to bowl you over. She's a real thoroughbred!'

Kate knew he referred to the gleaming machine, but she was more interested in the woman who had driven herself unaccompanied from Blecton Mere. Vivienne Ashleigh had stepped out and was instructing Thornton on details of her baggage on the back seat. When she turned to greet Vere, who had hurried to the front steps, Kate grew hot with a curious mixture of outrage and envy. Val's wife's pregnancy was further advanced than her marriage. He had *had* to marry the woman! She swallowed her outrage and succumbed to envy as she thought of them as lovers driven by undeniable basic longings. This woman being welcomed to Knightshill had lain with Val somewhere in France, and there surrendered herself to him. She had seen his body as Kate had seen it at Leyden's Spinney that morning. She had caressed his warm skin; had pressed herself close to him. He had held her in his arms, murmured endearments in that deep, accented voice, had given just to her his slow, sweet smile. Then they had discovered that he had also given her his child, so he had given her everything else he owned.

Kate felt sick. She had borne unrequited love all the time there had been no one else. She had managed to bear his marriage so long as it was a distant thing. Now a living woman had arrived wearing his ring and providing visual evidence that he had been as intimate with her as a man could be. It was suddenly more than she could take. No one appeared to notice as she turned in to the room and walked to the chair beside the french window which she had occupied when Val had collapsed at her feet. She felt dreadfully alone. Simon was too overwhelmed by the red car to notice her distress, and Charlotte was gathering her skirts ready to rise and greet someone new. Widowhood had taken away her confidence. She now regarded herself as an old lady.

Kitty had walked through to join Vere in welcoming the next mistress of Knightshill, and they both returned with a tall woman wearing a heavy silk skirt and loose jacket of undoubted quality. Its subtle shade of sage green complimented her hair visible beneath the stylish hat, but did nothing to dim the vivid carrot-red that looked all the more fiery against Kitty's beautiful dark auburn. Vivienne Ashleigh could not, even charitably, be called beautiful. Her narrow face was pale and scattered with freckles, but it was alive with enthusiasm as she stepped inside the door and swept them all with her gaze before saying, 'I've waited seventeen years for this moment.' She seemed considerably overcome as she added, 'If only he were here to share it with me.'

Margaret was at her most gracious. 'This is also a significant moment for us all, my dear.' She put out her hands. 'Welcome to the Ashleigh family. I guided Val from the age of five when our mother remarried, so we were especially close. I'm sure he's with us in thought today.'

The two women kissed, then Charlotte was introduced. Vivienne had a vivacious smile. 'I hope I may call you Lottie, as Val does. He said you often disapproved of things he did as a boy. I dearly hope marrying me won't fall into that category, because *I'm* really responsible even though it's taken me all these years to persuade him.' Catching sight of the group by the window, she left the Elders and crossed the carpet with quick steps. 'You must be Simon because you have your mother's colouring. An aircraft designer, I believe.'

Simon flushed with pleasure. 'That's a superb machine you have. It's the new advanced model, surely. Only ten in production.'

'Trust the enthusiast to be so knowledgable,' said Vivienne with a chuckle. 'I'm friendly with the manufacturer. His son taught me all I know about motors. Perhaps you'll show me Jessie while I'm here.'

'You heard about her?'

'Oh yes, Val brought me up to date with every member of his family when I visited him in hospital.' She swung round to address her brother and sister-in-law again. 'He succumbed to bronchial pneumonia on the day after our wedding. The honeymoon was spent in a hospital ward – he in bed with fever and me sitting beside him wiping his brow.' She turned back, immediately spotting Kate beside the french window. She went to her. 'That's something you did in Alexandria, he told me.' She took up Kate's hands and gripped them tightly. 'I only drove an ambulance, but I saw enough pain and misery to guess how difficult and demanding your work must be. *Thank you* for what you did for him. It must have been even harder to nurse someone so close to you, someone you regarded as a dear brother. He thinks very highly of you, and so do I.'

Kate's face felt so stiff she found it difficult to speak, much less return the smile of someone who appeared already to be a member of the family. Her lack of beauty was compensated for by large green eyes which faithfully reflected her emotions, and she seemed not in the least abashed by the swelling of her body which betrayed the truth. She was extremely self-possessed, undaunted by Knightshill or the Ashleigh clan in silks among the best teacups, and had undoubtedly won over everyone within a few minutes. To emphasize that, the younger element could contain themselves no longer and clustered around Vivienne begging to be allowed a ride in the machine which put Jessie well in the shade. Laughing, she agreed and fell into an animated conversation with six adolescents who had formerly been dismissive of the woman who had married their reprobate uncle.

Kate had risen to gaze from the french window as she visualized that farewell in Alexandria, when the stars had been so bright and Val had been so near yet so out of reach. He thought very highly of her! That was almost damning when she longed for so much more.

Someone arrived beside her. Warm fingers curled around hers. 'Don't be the spectre at the feast,' Simon murmured. 'She's what he wanted . . . and I can understand why. She'll give him back all he lost.' He moved round to block her view into the past. 'Let him go, darling. Please let him go and be happy for them, or my lovely plan for us won't stand a chance.'

Kate rose early the following morning and rode up to Leyden's Spinney. She needed to be alone away from Knightshill. The family would attend morning service, as usual, and Vivienne had promised to drive the younger members to Dunstan in her motor. The newest Ashleigh had endeared herself to everyone save Kate, who could not respond to her unconventional charm. Vivienne was lively, outspoken, sincere and very well informed, yet Kate could not subdue resentment of such a woman spurring an embittered, experienced man like Val to tenderness and the surrender of his body and soul. It was unacceptable. Even more unacceptable was the knowledge that if he was killed, Vivienne would be left with a vital part of him continuing in their child. All she, herself, would have was the memory of those days during which she had tended him and sponged his fevered body before that emotional farewell. Even his photograph had been taken from her by the devouring sea.

She wandered through to the pool where she had seen Val emerge naked. There she sat with her back against a tree and let the silent tears slide down her cheeks. She had been given twenty-eight days to build up her strength, yet she was still crying. It would be good to get back to work. There would then be no time to think.

It grew cold in the shady spinney, so Kate took her mare up to the downs for an invigorating gallop to warm herself up. Physically and emotionally eased, she returned to Knightshill determined to get through the day by counting the hours until she could leave in the morning. Seeing Milly again would help her to recover from this difficult weekend, and reverting to a creature of mercy instead of a woman would certainly alleviate her present pain.

Walking from the stables the pain was suddenly intensified by Vivienne, who accosted her from the direction of the rose garden. Kate was unwilling to stop, but Val's wife smiled and said, 'Please join me. We may not have the chance of a tête-a-tête later. *Please.* I want to ask you so many things.'

Kate walked across the gravel to where Vivienne waited. She looked even paler this morning, although her soft cream fine wool jumper and skirt offset her vivid hair to advantage.

'I envy you your ride,' she said as Kate drew near, and made a face. 'Ashleigh minor forbids it for a while. He also makes my mornings uncomfortable – which is why I'm out here instead of eating the delicious breakfast Kitty sent to my room.' She linked her arm through Kate's. 'Let's walk between the rosebeds. My, this is a glorious place. I can't understand all the Ashleigh ancestors who elected to become soldiers instead of living here as Vere does. He's charming.'

'Ashleigh men invariably are,' Kate replied woodenly. 'My brother could even coax a smile from a termagant.'

Vivienne glanced at her shrewdly. 'You have no time for charming men?'

'Their pain and suffering concern me, that's all.'

'You must be very lonely. One devoted, compassionate soul amongst all these gifted, colourful Ashleighs. Val saw that when he came here from Australia. Did you know he intended to leave the cattle station to you because he thought you would appreciate it more than the rest?'

Kate stayed silent, her throat too tight for words. It was a poignant reminder. Had he been on the way to loving her until this woman seduced him?

'Kate, I came to Knightshill to discover who I'm really married to.'

'Isn't that a little late?' she muttered.

Vivienne stopped and faced her. 'Far too late, but you know better than anyone else here that his chances of surviving this summer are very slim. The spring offensive has already begun and casualties are terribly high. I've had no telegram so he must be safe, but I have to be able to tell our child about his father if he's not there to do it himself.' Her eyes filled with sudden tears and her voice broke. 'From the moment I first set eyes on Val I was lost. After waiting seventeen years we had no more than a few weeks together. I'll need to know every single detail about him, so that I can hold on to them in case he never comes home.

Please tell me about the boy you regarded as your older brother. In the Fifty-seventh he invented a pack of lies about his past, and I must know the truth.' She put her hand on Kate's arm. 'You do understand why, don't you?'

Of course she did, but Kate needed information, too. 'My brother discovered by chance what the Fifty-seventh did to Val. He told me about it only last week. You were there when it happened.'

Vivienne grew calmer in the face of this near-accusation. 'I did everything I could to prevent it, including begging Father on my knees. In the light of today's splendid women I see I should have chained myself to his horse – or to Val! It went ahead, and I have never forgiven Father for allowing it. You have no notion how feeble and impotent I felt as the regiment rode out to the ritual with all its stiff-necked, absurd masculine pomp. I vowed then to be a woman of action, of total independence.' She gave a ghost of a smile. 'Then I glanced up one cold, rainy day in the middle of washing the mud from an ambulance and saw someone I'd known and loved as Havelock. I certainly acted, but my independence flew on the wind. I knew I couldn't live any longer without him.'

'You may have to,' said Kate on a gentler note.

'That's why I need you to tell me about his life up to the time he joined the Fifty-seventh. Will you?'

Kate bargained. 'If you'll tell me about Martin Havelock.'

So the two women who loved Val Ashleigh sat on a seat in morning sunshine in the gardens of his home, and drew close as they spoke of the man who had played many parts. If Vivienne did discover who she was really married to, Kate was forced to accept that Simon had been right to say she, herself, loved a boy she had once known. Young Martin Havelock who had endured the life of a trooper and worked his way to a position of rank whilst posing as an orphaned ex-stable-lad came over as a stranger. Vivienne's description of their three-year relationship made Kate realize that, but for the court martial which had ended Havelock's career, the pair would have become lovers much sooner. There had undoubtedly been an irresistible spark between them from the start.

Arriving back at the point where the regiment had disowned him, Vivienne said pensively, 'It was a blessing in tragic disguise, Kate. Sooner or later his true identity would have been betrayed.

As a trooper he could possibly retain the lie, but further promotion would have brought him greater recognition among his peers. The imposture had always been precarious. He would have been cashiered eventually, you know, but everyone would then have known him as the Ashleigh heir. The way it happened at least protected his future. It was *Martin Havelock* who was falsely convicted and punished. Val Ashleigh's record is unblemished.' She frowned at Kate. 'What I don't understand is why, after roaming the South African wilderness for three years, he should come home only to leave again in the dead of night abandoning all he was and had. Do you know?'

'You must tackle Uncle Vere. It's not my secret to divulge,' Kate told her, then asked, 'Do *you* know why Val left Chartfield so suddenly and enlisted under his middle names? I still don't understand that.'

Val's wife sighed. 'You'd have to ask Martin Havelock to explain, but I think you should just accept that he had a justifiable reason for doing it and let sleeping dogs lie. It was a very long time ago.' After a pause, she said, 'If you should see him when you get to France tell him . . . tell him . . .'

'What makes you think I'll be going to France?' Kate inserted swiftly.

'Because that's where you'll ask to be sent, isn't it?'

'I . . . yes. It's where I'm most needed.'

'Kate, if he should . . . if you should . . .' She could not finish.

'I'll do everything possible,' Kate assured her, as overcome as Vivienne. 'And I'll tell him we've become friends.'

It was a warm evening with a full moon. After dinner, Kate and Simon went on to the terrace by mutual consent. He would have to leave on the 11 p.m. train in order to be at his desk by morning. As soon as they were outside he put an arm around her shoulders, saying he would hold her wrap in place. They were both conscious of their coming parting.

'Perhaps you'll be sent to a hospital in England,' Simon said hopefully. 'We could meet at weekends, if possible.'

Kate shook her head. 'I'll volunteer for France. They need senior nurses with overseas experience, and it's where I want to be.'

'Because of Val?'

'Because of all those unknown soldiers who depend on us to be on hand. The sooner they receive treatment the more likely they are to make a complete recovery.'

He stopped and stared at the moon, saying quietly, 'You've already become Staff Nurse Daulton. My darling girl has been swallowed up by an efficient, professional woman again.'

'No, she hasn't. She's going to enjoy your lovely plan right up to the last minute.'

'In that case . . .' His kiss was restrained and indicative of his unhappiness. She no longer felt it had an incestuous quality. Her perception of him was now altogether different and it would be a wrench to part from him tonight. They stood, arms entwined, looking out over the moonwashed valley, uncertain how to end the period of metamorphosis into an unknown phase of their long relationship.

'How peaceful it is,' she murmured. 'I don't think nights are like this anywhere else on earth. You might get the stars, or that cool silvery moon; you might get the sweet smell of evening jasmine after the sun has set, or the perfume of massed roses carried on the breeze; you might get the slow dusk deepening from mauve to purple, or the sight of an owl silhouetted against the last rays of daylight, but you wouldn't get them all together as we do here. It's so beautiful, isn't it?'

'Then why leave it and go over there where the guns never stop firing and there's nothing beautiful in sight?' he demanded.

'All this won't have been lost along with so many other things when the war ends and I come back. Whatever else changes, Simon, this will always be here.'

They fell silent again, and there were only the sounds of the creatures of the night and the distant lilt of music as Charlotte played for the family safely gathered in the calmness of a rural estate.

Simon suddenly disentangled his arm from hers and faced her with an air of desperation. 'Kate, I've racked my brain for an extravagant gesture which would surprise you into seeing me in a new irresistible light, but I suppose I'm not that type of person because nothing's occurred to me. It would have made this easier if it had. Look, I know this weekend has been hard on you and somehow put a slight barrier between us, but I still believe I could make you happy if you'd let me. I know you have your work which is not only important to you, but to the war effort. Mine is, too. What I'd like is to have your promise to consider the possibility of getting married when the war ends. I'd give you a good life and you'd never have to worry about me chasing other women. I'll never love anyone else.'

He touched her cheek gently. 'I don't want you to go to France. I'll worry the whole time. But if I knew there was a real chance of us sharing a lovely plan for the rest of our lives, I'd find your absence bearable. If you couldn't ever consider it, you'll have to say so. It'll be a terrible blow, but I'll at least give up hoping for the impossible. You won't be committed to anything more than an option, but if you agree I warn you I'll do all I can to make it a certainty – by fair means or foul.'

Kate had known this would happen and already had her answer. The intimate talk with Vivienne had influenced it. Val's wife loved him passionately; he had apparently fought his attraction to her as a very young man and succumbed to it on meeting her again after seventeen years. During the course of the day Kate had taken Simon's advice and let Val go. It was a vain love, whereas this dear man beside her offered loyal devotion and happiness which was not under threat by war. Simon would be there for her when it ended.

She stood on tiptoe and kissed him lightly on the mouth. 'There's nothing I'd like more than to share a lovely plan with you when peace comes. I'm sorry you'll worry all the time I'm away, but I have to go. You must see that. It'll be all the better when we're back together again.' She put up a hand to touch *his* cheek. 'You'll never have to make extravagant gestures to arouse my interest, it's always been there and always will be. Thank you for asking me.'

This time his embrace was far more lusty and confident, but she enjoyed the evidence of the strength of his love. No one else had ever been so devoted to her, and she was definitely in the right nest now. When he reached the dangerous stage Simon reluctantly released her. Then he took a little box from his pocket and opened it with fingers that were shaking with the evidence of his passion.

'I knew you wouldn't be able to wear a ring, but I bought this as a substitute in the hope that your uniform would hide it from Sister's eyes. Will you wear it to remind you of tonight?' He held up a very small diamond pendant on a fine gold chain. 'It's nothing like the Ashleigh rubies Mother has just handed over to Vivienne as the heir's bride, but I'm a Munroe, darling, and a working man. When we're married I'll buy you something much better.'

Kate took the simple pendant, inexpressibly touched. 'This is all I'll ever need, Simon. I'm a Daulton and a working woman. We'll leave the flamboyant Ashleighs to wear rubies.'

Simon fastened the chain around her neck and they stood together in the atmosphere to be found nowhere else in the world, until darkness and its accompanying chill drove them indoors no longer dreading their farewell.

Tim was half-heartedly reading a biography Laurence had given him, but he was bored and frustrated. Sir Hastings had not become the leading man in his field without a high success rate. Not for him another patching-up job. He had broken Tim's jaw again in order to reset it correctly, which had turned what the patient had expected to be a short spell in the clinic into the prospect of several tedious weeks. It had also brought a great deal of discomfort. His entire jaw was held rigid with wires and his chin was supported in a leather sling. It meant that he could speak only with difficulty through immobile lips and had to be artificially fed. He was intelligent enough to know the outcome would put the whole thing right, but he yearned to escape the clinic and set in motion his return to action. The war was almost three years old now, and what had he to show for it? The Americans had finally entered the lists, although their troops would not be trained ready to fight in Europe until midsummer. The spring offensive had begun with an attack on the Hindenburg line in mist and heavy rain, but the objective secured and held by the Allied force had only advanced their front line by three miles. They were now bogged down once more, and the tanks used in the assault were stuck fast in liquid mud.

Tim lowered his book and gazed around the conservatory where he was spending the afternoon in a reclining chair. Potted ferns and tall plants with giant shiny leaves were placed around the lofty extension where two ornamental fountains splashed in pale marble basins supported by sculpted egrets. Biscuit-coloured walls were embellished with mock half-pillars picked out in white and gold, and the chairs were thickly cushioned and covered in white with huge rose-pink and green tropical flowers. He was surrounded by luxury while his regiment was fighting on against all odds. *Val* was fighting on. He should be out there with him. To hell with all this pampering at Sir Laurence Nicolardi's expense!

At that moment he spotted a nurse approaching along the marble-floored corridor and groaned inwardly. What was on the cards for him now? Then he realized this nurse was not one of the elegant staff of Sir Hastings' clinic because she wore the uniform of a military nurse, with scarlet cape. Good lord, it was his sister!

'Hallo!' she greeted warmly.

'Aaah!' was his anguished reply as he automatically tried to smile. 'Sorry, can't get used to keeping a straight face,' he mumbled. 'Never before realized how often one smiles in the course of a day.'

Kate sat in the padded chair beside him. 'Stop being a typical Ashleigh charming everyone in sight, including the pretty creatures of mercy all around you.'

'Mercy! They've never heard of it. I'm sure they relish my discomfort.'

She gave a light laugh. 'Poor Tim! I must say you look terrible.'

'I knew that before you came. Tell me something pleasant.'

'Uncle Vere's arranging for the soprano Madeleine Metcalfe to give a recital here.'

'Can't stand gargantuan women warbling ear-piercing notes.'

'Dear me, you *are* down in the dumps. I know how you feel, Tim, but the jaw will be done properly this time.'

'Until another German stamps on me the moment I get back.'

'But you're not going to give him a chance, are you?' she said quietly.

He had the grace to accept that he was betraying self-pity. 'No, that's right. I didn't recognize you at first. I've never seen you in your army uniform. Isn't that astonishing?'

'Not really. Our leave periods have never before coincided.'

He sighed. 'We haven't seen much of each other over the years, have we? We used to be close as children.'

Kate smiled. 'We're close again now. That's what's important.'

'Yes. I'm glad.'

'So am I.'

'What are you doing here in the middle of the afternoon? I thought your leave ended at the weekend.'

'It did. I've volunteered for overseas service and I'm on night duty at a hospital in Putney awaiting my movement orders. My friend and I hope to be sent to the same area, but there's no guarantee of it.'

Tim noticed a white-gowned blonde approaching them. 'Tea is on its way. They have a spy who notes every visitor so that tea can be brought as soon as civilities have been exchanged. This is a luxurious place, Kate. Nothing like the ones you're used to, I bet. Only trouble is the other patients are either elderly and rich as Croesus, or young and privileged. I'm the only soldier here.'

'But among the young and privileged set. Here's the perfect time to find yourself a wife. You're twenty-eight.'

'Aaah,' cried Tim as he tried to smile his thanks at the probationer who set down the tray.

'Poor Mr Ashleigh!' cooed the girl. 'You'll have to become a grump like old Sir Basil. He *never* smiles.'

As she walked away displaying very mobile hips to a young officer who was not watching them, Tim said, 'The other patients steer clear of me because they think I can't speak at all. In any case, I wouldn't consider marrying *anyone* while the war lasts. Val must have been crazy. At best he'll come through it a permanent invalid, badly mutilated, or off his head. At worst, he'll leave a widow and fatherless child.' He waved a hand at the teapot. 'Do your stuff, then. What was she like?'

'Who?' Kate began pouring tea.

'Val's wife.'

'You'll see for yourself. She's going to visit you as soon as you feel up to it. Here you are. Can you manange, or shall I help you?'

Tim took the cup with a spout for ease of drinking. 'It's only smiling I find painful. Did you have the same problem last weekend? It must have been difficult for you to accept her.'

Kate calmly sipped her tea. 'She drove herself to Knightshill in a motorcar that looked as if it could devour Jessie in one gulp. Simon was terribly impressed. We've become engaged, by the way. Unofficially, because I'm not expected to link myself with anyone, at present. Emotional relationships are prone to affect a nurse's work.'

Tim was astonished and a little worried. Kate and Simon had always been like brother and sister. Whatever had possessed them to branch off in *that* direction? 'It's a bit sudden, isn't it? Are you sure you know what you're doing?'

She put down her cup and looked at him frankly. 'I've managed without your brotherly intercession from the age of eight. There's no need for it now.'

Her words brought a curious pang of guilt. 'That's me well and truly put in my place. What do the Elders think?'

'We didn't tell them. Can't you imagine the fuss? They'd want an announcement in *The Times* and a party at Claridges. Uncle Vere would insist on giving me the emerald solitaire as an engagement ring which I'd not be allowed to wear and I would most certainly lose in the Flanders mud. You're the only person who knows so don't tell, will you?'

'Shouldn't you let on to Mother?' He did not think it a sound idea, but it was one he thought had to be put forward.

'Heavens, no! She'd count it my ultimate folly. Simon's ancestry is vague and possibly best left untraced. A nobody in Mother's eyes.'

'She'll have to know soon. When are you planning on getting married?'

'When the war's over.'

'So it's not an impulsive decision.' He was still uneasy about this curious affair. 'Well, you know he'll still be here when it's all over, which is more than Vivienne can hope for with Val. She's not even certain she'll produce a boy to replace him. When's the happy event due?'

'August.'

'But they only . . .' He broke off discreetly. So it had been a shotgun affair, had it? 'Not long to wait, then.'

Kate changed the subject. 'Mother's back with Laurence in Chelsea.'

'I know,' he said glumly. 'They both came last evening and tried to persuade me to take another post with Intelligence. Laurence really turned the screw. You know how he can.'

'No, I hardly know him. You didn't agree, did you?'

'Not likely. I'm getting back into action at the first opportunity.' He thought he should revert to Kate's surprising news. 'I'm sure you and Simon wouldn't have taken the step unless it's what you really want, so I wish you both happiness. I'll even act Best Man, if I'm . . .' he changed what he was about to say to, 'if I'm asked.'

'I'm sure you will be,' she said in the same vein.

They chatted for about an hour until Kate said she must leave to have a meal before going on duty. Tim was sorry to lose her company, but the effort of talking had made his whole face ache and he was tired. He hoped their mother would not visit that evening, although it was a vain hope.

'Goodbye, Kate,' he murmured. 'I've enjoyed your visit.'

'So have I,' she said. 'Don't smile as I leave, will you? I'll come again soon.'

She did not. Two days later she crossed the Channel to report to a hospital near Ypres.

The first thing Tim saw as he entered the Regency was a single table set near the dais, as before.

'Do you have a reservation, sir?'

He turned to a waitress he had not seen before and smiled without pain. 'Yes, that's my table over there.'

The girl looked him over with great interest. 'Are *you* Mr Ashleigh?'

'*Captain* Ashleigh,' he corrected. 'Where's Mrs Sturt?'

'With Chef, sir. There's been a little fracas!'

Although she looked at Tim as though a fracas with *him* would please her no end, he did not respond to signs which once would have led to a gratifying five minutes. 'I'll have a glass of mulled wine while Chef calms down enough for Mrs Sturt to let go of his hand and stop soothing his brow.'

The waitress giggled and went off to fetch his wine while Tim made himself comfortable on one of the banquettes in the vestibule. He had arrived early so that he could have a short while with Amy before she was swamped by a tidal wave of officers hellbent on having a good time. Damn Chef! Why must he choose tonight to be temperamental, because that was surely what the girl had meant by a fracas? She brought the wine and would have stayed to ask questions that would satisfy the speculation in her eyes, but diners began arriving in a steady stream and she had to sort out their reserved tables.

When Amy emerged from a rear door Tim once again was

impressed by her classic beauty and poise. It was hot for late May so she wore a dress in pale lavender voile which fell softly over her arms and bore a large satin waterlily at her breast. She would not look out of place at Knightshill, Tim thought, then was startled by the direction in which his mind was travelling. At that point the waitress who had greeted him spoke to her employer and nodded towards the vestibule. Amy turned quickly, saw him get to his feet, and crossed towards him. Inevitably, she was accosted on all sides by those who knew her, so Tim advanced on her instead.

'Sorry, old chaps,' he told a fresh-faced pair of subalterns. 'I have an urgent message for Mrs Sturt.' So saying he put a hand beneath her elbow and led her to the dais where he cut off all access from others by placing her in a corner and leaning on an outstretched arm which acted as a barrier.

'Did you say "there, there" to Chef and wipe away his tears? He's not creating an incomparable lemon cake, is he?'

This sly reference to their visit to the Waterfowl last year did little to ease her reaction to what he called strong-man tactics, so he smiled and softened his tone. 'Thank you for keeping the table for me.'

'I almost took it down again.'

'You didn't think I'd come?'

'I thought you were unable to; that you had been sent away.'

'Uncle Lionel would have told you if I had, no doubt. Every evening I've been here in thought. The operation was more complicated than I guessed and convalescence took a damned long time. I've looked a regular villain until now. If I'd come earlier your admirers would have thrown me out.'

'They're customers, not admirers.'

'I've got eyes, and I'm a man like them. I know why they come.'

'We're attracting attention,' she murmured, 'and I have things to do.'

He straightened. 'May we please talk after they've all gone?' As she hesitated, he added, 'I've asked very nicely, haven't I?'

That brought a hint of a smile. 'Yes, you have.'

'I'll look forward to that.'

She began to move away. 'You look much better than you did that day at Dunstan.'

'And you look very beautiful tonight.'

She walked away swiftly, but not so fast that he did not see that the sincere compliment caused the same response as his strong man tactics. Her husband must have been a totally insensitive man intent only on building up his business. The evening followed the popular format, except that the volunteers really did volunteer. A few ballads from a junior naval officer, a Chopin polonaise from his sweetheart, a near-professional performance on the piano by a pilot who was keen on ragtime, and a dramatic rendition of Kipling's *Road to Mandalay* against a background of Eastern music played by the Regency ladies. This budding Thespian leapt up again as Amy was about to end the entertainment and recited *Ode to Amy*, a poem he had written in praise of the fighting men's favourite hostess. She accepted it in a calmly gracious manner, which set Tim thinking. Public adoration was acceptable to her; mass masculine attention was permitted. It was when just one single man displayed interest she took fright. Or was it only when the single man was Tim Ashleigh?

He remained at his table until the last diners were saying their farewells, then he strolled to where Amy stood beside the door. She turned to find him right behind her and visibly jumped.

'Think how I'd have frightened you if I had come when I was hideously bruised,' he said lightly. 'Will you have a glass of wine with me? Please?'

'Are you asking nicely again?' she said, looking up into his eyes with curious uncertainty.

'I thought it was quite nicely put, but I'll try harder if you think I could do better.'

'Now you're being absurd. Shall we sit here?'

Quite safe, he thought. No doors to cut off her retreat. He fetched the wine from his table, and the two glasses he had requested from the waitress. Filling them, he handed her one and raised his own. 'I toast Amy, who inspires poets, tenors and ragtime pianists. I'll say again you are an unusual and exceptional woman.'

'What nonsense!'

He sat beside her with such suddenness she looked alarmed. 'Why do you dismiss my compliments, yet accept a public ode to your beauty and talent with disarming graciousness? *Why*, Amy?'

She shook her head. 'What goes on here during these evenings is induced by wine, good fellowship and an atmosphere of unreality. For a few hours they're in an idyllic world where every man is their brother, and every woman is true and loyal and loving. There's no "over there" for them. The past months never happened; they don't have to go back in a few days' time.'

'I have to,' he said quietly. 'Within thirty-six hours, I'm afraid. That's why I wanted to talk to you. Will you allow me to take you out tomorrow, before dinner here in the evening?'

'If that's what you'd like,' she said, looking undeniably upset. 'Isn't it rather soon after your stay in hospital to send you to France?'

'I asked for an immediate posting, but it was more immediate than I expected.'

'I see.'

'I'd like to do the things young people usually do together – take a boat on the river, feed the ducks, walk arm in arm. We'll have tea at the Waterfowl if you promise not to pay more attention to the cake than to me.'

She appeared to relax a little. 'You *were* very put out about that. I promise not to do it again.'

'Thank you. May I call for you at nine?'

'That's very early,' she protested.

'I only have one day so I want to use it to the full,' he explained, thinking how luminous her eyes looked in the low lights, and how creamy her skin was against the soft-draping voile. He longed to brush his fingers across it. 'Nine?' he repeated in a persuasive undertone.

'I suppose so,' she murmured.

'Here's to tomorrow.' He raised his glass and drank from it, his gaze fastened on her face which betrayed the truth to him in a flash. It was not *him* she was wary of, but herself. Beneath that outward assurance, the fire he had ignited a year ago still smouldered and she was unsure of how fierce it might become. She took only short sips of the wine until he put a finger beneath the stem of her glass and very gently encouraged her to finish it in one draught.

'We still have the rest of the bottle,' he explained, but she shook her head and put down the glass. 'If we're starting out at that hour, I must begin clearing up now or I'll have no sleep.'

He got to his feet. 'Let me help you.'

'Certainly not!' She took the hand he offered and stood up. Yet she made no effort to walk away to her tasks. 'I shall do it far quicker without a novice to hinder me, and you have to get back to Ashleigh Court.'

'I'm staying with my parents in Chelsea.'

'Your mother will surely want to spend time with you tomorrow.'

'I'll have breakfast with her.' He moved closer. 'Pray it doesn't rain.'

'I will.' She still made no move. 'Goodnight, then.'

He reached for her, saying softly, 'This is one of the things young people do rather a lot when they're together.'

She made no attempt to struggle or push him away, yet she did no more than grow soft in his arms. Used to girls who squealed and squirmed in delight, and some who damn nearly ate him, Tim found Amy's inexperienced surrender extremely provocative. Kissing was no longer a painful business, yet her trusting passiveness led him to be equally gentle as he touched her lips, cheeks and ears with his mouth while caressing her back through the thin material.

'Someone should have done this long, long ago,' he breathed against her temple. 'They must have all been mad.' Her arms crept experimentally to his shoulders then linked loosely around his neck as he embarked on something more worthy of his reputation. When he recognized the danger signs he lifted his head regretfully, still holding her close.

'You're far too enticing, and I've stopped asking nicely. I think you had better send me away, don't you?'

Amy seemed incapable of such an action, so he heeded the voice of wisdom and took the initiative before the situation got out of hand. Reaching for the only khaki cap left on the row of hooks, he said, 'I'll be here on the stroke of nine even if it's snowing. We'll have a day to remember.' She was still standing as if in a trance when he let himself out to the street to seek a cab.

The sun shone, the birds sang and lovers appeared in droves on the balmy May morning. Tim promised a cabbie an extravagant sum to hire him for the full day and gave him a fiver on account. Armed with the best picnic lunch the Nicolardis' chef could produce on being called from his bed and given the task just after one a.m., Tim arrived dead on time to collect the woman who affected him as no other had. She was waiting, looking fresh and very striking in a maize-coloured costume over a white blouse embroidered with cornflowers, and a straw hat trimmed with a spray of the same blossoms.

Tim did not hesitate to kiss her. This was going to be his day to remember for as long as he had to live. 'No one would believe you had spent half the night clearing up after the British Army. You look wonderfully wide awake and beautiful,' he told her with sincerity. 'I'll arouse an awful lot of envy today.'

'Even from the lemon cake?' she asked lightly.

'Even from *that*.' He took her arm. 'Come on, we've only got a few hours. Let's start enjoying them.'

They went to Richmond Park and strolled arm in arm like other couples, stopping, as they did, wherever there was an overhanging tree or secluded spot where they could stand close together and exchange a discreet kiss or two. As they walked, Tim encouraged Amy to tell him about her life which had been so very different from his own. She seemed quite willing to do this, her former challenging manner abandoned for a new eagerness to share the hours with him as fully as possible. Tim was not surprised to learn that Amy's father had been overly strict with his wife and pretty daughter, and that Sturt had regarded her as little more than a manageress for his business of which she owned the half share he thought to secure by marrying her. She described a man of parsimonious nature whose only loves in life were money and his two cats. All she told Tim confirmed his belief that young men had been first discouraged by Amy's father, then by her married status. She sheltered behind her widowhood now because intimate contact with experienced men was very deep water for someone who had never splashed in the shallows as a young girl. On the night before leaving for France last year, Tim had clearly thrown her in the depths without a lifebelt. All this was very evident to him as he talked. It was also evident that she was growing used to his amorous approaches in the seclusion of leafy branches, and gradually learning to offer some response.

The most surprising thing for Tim during that walk was that he dallied far less often than was his habit. He had such a short time with her and he wanted to learn as much as possible about the woman beneath the successful hostess. Listening to her voice, watching her expressions, seeing the glow in her eyes growing more and more luminous as she enjoyed the pleasure of that simple walk through a green park, where deer grazed and lovers expressed their happiness with clasped hands and intimate glances, Tim recalled last year when he had suddenly yearned for a day like this before it was too late.

They drank coffee in a blossom-covered teashop before rejoining the cabbie who had been reading the paper while he waited.

'Where to now, sir?' he asked cheerily. Then, when Tim gave him directions, added, 'The news from the Front ain't good. It says the Frenchies is so exhausted and demoralized there's talk of mutiny. I ask yer, where's the stuff they're made of, eh?'

'The stuff they're made of is the same stuff you're made of,' Tim replied crisply. 'Human flesh and blood. I doubt you'd be so chirpy after nearly three years out there.'

'Our rule is not to talk about the war,' put in Amy with calm authority, 'so please don't mention it again.'

The cabbie fell into a huffy silence, but neither Tim nor Amy believed it would last for long and they slid closer together on the seat as they smiled with total understanding of their mood for the day.

Tim hired a boat and acquitted himself well with the oars amid a veritable armada of craft containing girls in their springtime finery and uniformed escorts displaying a wide range of skill with oars or punt poles. There was a great deal of laughter and some rude remarks from the military when a Naval sub-lieutenant lost an oar overboard trying to free his boat which was too close to the bank from the overhanging willow branches.

'Try a battleship next time,' Tim shouted through his laughter.

'Poor man! It's the kind of accident that could happen to anyone,' scolded Amy. 'Pride comes before a fall, Tim, so keep your attention on what you're doing.'

'You're perfectly safe with me,' he boasted. 'I could have had a rowing blue at Oxford.'

'Why didn't you?'

'The colour really didn't suit me.'

He cleared the congestion of the initial stretch to head upstream where he hoped to moor and spread out the rugs on a bank with an attractive view. Not only was he ready for lunch, he was tired. He had lost some weight whilst on artificial feeding and found rowing more of an effort than he had bargained for. In any case, he wanted to talk and these were not ideal conditions for pursuing discovery of Amy, as he thought of it.

Luck continued to run their way and they soon came upon the ideal spot for a picnic. Laurence's chef had risen to the occasion to produce a selection of food the owner of the Regency Restaurant applauded as they sat back after setting it out on a tablecloth spread over the rugs.

'I'd forgotten I had an expert caterer with me,' Tim said. 'All I see is a lovely girl in yellow and white, with cornflowers in all the right places, and eyes as dark as her hair. Now you've taken off that saucy hat I'd like more than anything to pull the pins from your curls and let them fall loose.' Mention of something as intimate as letting down her hair brought faint colour to Amy's cheeks, so Tim added gently, 'I've wanted to do that since the day you asked if I was to be auctioned for charity.'

Her colour deepened. 'That was a terribly insulting thing to say to you.'

'You thought the comment apt, at the time.'

She avoided his eyes and instead studied the starched napkin on her lap. 'I'd heard gossip at the Stag, that's all. Our meeting at Dunstan Station and at Esher, where we served the troops with tea and buns, seemed to bear out all I'd overheard about your fondness for women. Then you turned up at the Regency with a girl who . . . well, she was not the kind of partner officers normally brought there, and my opinion of you dropped dramatically.' Glancing up at him, she added, 'A number of men prefer not to be seriously involved with one person when they're young, especially military officers building up a career who need permission to marry, and only if she is someone of the right class, but it seemed to me on that evening that you . . . that *any* kind of woman was chased after by you. The Ashleigh family is highly respected by the villagers, but I found I had no respect for *you* after that. When I saw you on the day of the auction being marched in by two notoriously indiscreet young women I spoke my thoughts, I suppose.'

Tim saw himself through her eyes and sighed. 'I told you at the time those girls were not *my* friends, but I was nevertheless prepared to spend . . . time with them. You might be interested to learn that I felt acutely embarrassed when I recognized you, and remained that way for the rest of the evening. So much so I took the girl home and left immediately.' He studied the classic picture of loveliness in rural sunshine she presented, then added, 'I'm sorry I prompted such a low opinion by my behaviour.'

Amy studied him in return, her cheeks now only faintly flushed. 'You've changed.'

'For the better, I hope.' He picked up the bottle he had chilled in the water. 'Let's have some wine and forget past foolishness. Today's special. We won't waste any of it with introspection. I want to remember every minute with unadulterated pleasure.' He smiled. 'I'm starving. May I please now fall upon this feast?'

She smiled back, awkwardness having flown. 'It's *your* feast, sir. You don't need my permission to enjoy it.'

Enjoy it they did. Then, relaxed by the wine and the sunshine and the peace of that backwater, he lay with his head in her lap while they told each other childhood anecdotes and laughed over similar experiences. It was a golden afternoon such as he had never known before. He would not think of tomorrow, and the only regret he had was that he had viewed her as just another possible conquest at Dunstan Station on that afternoon two months before the war began. Three years wasted!

When their laughter died and Tim gazed up into her face grown serious and soft with compassion, knowing it would be easy to love her with a lifelong devotion, she surprised him by asking why he had changed his name from Daulton.

Playing for time, he quizzed her. 'Another piece of gossip from Uncle Lionel?'

She nodded with a hint of a smile. 'I'm afraid so. Why, Tim? Why Ashleigh rather than Nicolardi?'

Remembering the recent revelation about his Uncle Vorne, he found it difficult to lie there looking up at her. What would the villagers make of the truth concerning *that* heroic myth? He sat up and concentrated on a family of waterfowl searching the bank for food. 'My mother had become a Nicolardi; my step-brothers were from birth. My sister hadn't lived with us for some years, and I suppose I felt the odd one out.'

Her hand touched his arm. 'Poor Tim.'

He twisted to face her. 'Crazy Tim! I believed taking the family name would turn me into an instant hero without further effort. Isn't *that* crazy?'

'No, it's the thinking of someone with the tremendous responsibility of having to live up to very high expectations. I know all about that, Tim. When my mother died, Father was so distressed I tried to *be* her. I devoted myself to him, did everything he told me to do in the way she had always done it. I thought that was all that was necessary, until he flew into a rage and told me to leave. I went to the Stag for a while. After two weeks he came there and told me I could never replace Mother, whatever I did, and that by trying so hard I had only succeeded in making him grieve more. When I went back to the Regency Teashop, as it was then, I was unsure who I really was. Not until he died and I went into partnership with Benjamin Sturt did I take on an identity of my own.'

Tim was immeasurably touched. He took up her hand and brushed her fingers with his mouth, murmuring before he knew it, 'You know I'm in great danger of falling in love with you?' Before she could comment, he drew her into his arms and kissed her with an amazing sense of gratitude. The embrace lengthened as her arms fastened around his neck, and her body moved against his in her growing pleasure. He lowered her very gently to the rug and, as he grew more demanding, he revelled in the responsive awakening of her senses which had been ruthlessly crushed. The raucous voices of squabbling moorhens brought recollection of who he was with, and where, so that he regretfully broke the embrace and tried to lighten the situation.

'It's only halfway through the day. I can't risk a slap around the face at this stage.'

She lay looking up at him with the glow of passion still on her. 'The girl you brought to the Regency might do that; I never could.'

'That's because I'd never treat you the way I treated girls like her,' he said. 'You're making this one of the happiest days I can remember.'

'So are you, Tim.'

On the point of returning to the rug he exercised control; something he had rarely done in past situations. 'As you're going to clear away the dinner things I feel I should do the honours now,' he said, thinking it might take his mind from temptation if he packed up the remains of the picnic.

She sat up. 'I'll do it. You have all the rowing to undertake in a minute.'

He made a comic face. 'Whatever gave you that idea? I rowed on the way here. It's your turn to take the oars now.'

'I'm perfectly willing, but I'd make a worse job of it than the budding admiral you laughed at so mercilessly,' she told him with a chuckle. 'Think what they'll all shout at *you* when I've got us stuck fast in some reeds.'

'In that case, I'll manfully volunteer, madam.'

The teasing, light-hearted mood remained as they lingered over tea at the Waterfowl. Tim even ate a slice of the famous lemon cake just to please Amy, and went into such elaborate raptures over it she laughingly begged him to stop. They parted at 6 p.m. at the door of the Regency. Amy had to prepare for the evening, so Tim returned to wash and change, then pack his belongings ready for an early start the next day. He was certain to face an awkward scene with his mother at breakfast. Thankfully, she was not in to hinder him before returning to the Regency.

The evening followed the usual pattern in all but one respect. Amy had set his table for two and dined with him openly, only leaving to make her famous request for volunteers and then announcing each of them. The evening passed too swiftly for Tim as he recognized that the danger he had mentioned that afternoon was fact. He was in love with this girl he had to leave within a few hours. He remained at his table while the other diners took their leave, and he suddenly understood the scenes he had witnessed at Victoria Station when the leave trains steamed in or out. It would be a terrible wrench to walk away and say goodbye from Amy tonight, knowing he might never come back. Had he been irresponsible to pursue this when he had nothing to offer her but one perfect day to remember?

She came across to him once the clientele had departed and her staff began clearing the tables, looking very much the assured, widowed businesswoman once more in a dress of pale chiffon over darker satin. Yet her voice was soft as she asked if he would like a nightcap in her apartment before he left. He was glad of the invitation because he had things to say which needed time without interruption.

He should not have been surprised by the elegance of her home, because the restaurant showed her flair for colour and décor, yet he was deeply impressed by the sitting-room in shades of gold. She poured brandy into a goblet and brought it across to where he stood in the corner of the room. 'Do sit down.'

'I have an early start tomorrow,' he said to excuse himself from the invitation. The way things had turned out he felt it would be unwise to prolong this tête-à-tête. They stood together while he drank the brandy rather too quickly during a somewhat forced discussion of the evenings' volunteers.

'Thank you.' He handed her the empty glass.

'The leave train departs at eight-thirty, doesn't it? I've heard them mention that time downstairs.'

'I'm not going to France. I'm catching a boat train to Southampton. They've given me lightweight uniform, so I imagine it'll be the Balkans.'

'Oh! Did you ask for that?'

He smiled. 'Not even an Ashleigh can make that kind of choice.'

'Your mother managed it when she had you sent to Headquarters.'

His smile faded. 'She's married to a very influential man. I'm a mere captain, only recently promoted.'

'There's nothing *mere* about you, Tim. You showed me that today,' she said quietly.

It was the perfect cue to bring out the little gift he had for her. Choosing it had been difficult because he was so afraid she would take offence. In the past his gifts had been what they were – payment for services rendered by a legion of girls who called him Bobby. This present was different. He hoped to God she would see it that way.

'This is to thank you for giving me all I asked of today, for showing me how wonderful life can be with the right girl.'

Amy took the velvet box and opened it to see the Regency phaeton beautifully crafted in silver and diamonds on a silver pin. It was quite small, neither opulent nor gaudy, and he believed it made no statement other than that he had put a deal of thought into its choice. He waited anxiously for her reaction. When she glanced up at him she said nothing, but he interpreted the shimmer in her eyes well enough.

He said, 'Presents are all I can offer you at the moment. Everything's so uncertain. No one knows how long this war's going to last, or what the world will be like when it's over.' He took hold of her arms. 'I'm not asking you for any promises, but if there's no one else in your life when it's all over I'll offer you much more than a jewelled pin. I want you to know that. I want you to know how much you mean to me.'

'There won't be anyone else,' she said with such sincerity he was smitten by the evidence of what he had done by encouraging her to care so deeply for him.

He drew her against him. 'Time changes people, changes situations. For now, let's remember today as a timeless span of happiness.'

His kiss evoked her most passionate response yet, and he succumbed to the instinctive urge to take what she offered. Desire overruled all else as his hands began working over her body in the overture to full intimacy. Yet a vestige of sanity remained. On the borderline between arousal and gratification Tim summoned enough resolution to hold her away and deny himself. Breathing heavily, he said, 'This isn't the way for me to say goodbye to you.'

She was trembling with reaction. 'Don't go yet.'

'I have to. You're too beautiful.'

'Please, Tim. Please stay.'

He shook her gently, torn between common sense and desire. 'Don't you realize what I'll want if I stay any longer?'

'Yes.' As he tried to accept what she was telling him, she added, 'You asked for a whole day. All I want is a little of the night to remember while you're gone.'

Self denial was abandoned. He had not been with a woman for more than a year, he was going to war in the morning, and he badly wanted this eleventh-hour sealing of true love. Breaking a virgin was a new, surprisingly erotic experience for him; introducing sexual fulfilment to an uninitiated partner who trusted him completely was an overwhelming joy. When they eventually lay back in each other's arms Amy had tears on her cheeks and Tim knew a sense of deep commitment foreign to him.

At 4 a.m. he carefully disentangled himself from her arms, dressed in his uniform and crept from her bedroom, praying she would not waken and be full of regrets.

CHAPTER EIGHTEEN

They held the court martial in the cellar of a ruined brewery. It was a very brief, offhand affair by normal standards, but these were not normal times and there were more important things to do than to make a big issue over something that was happening far too often now the offensive had begun again. The business of shooting one's own comrades for desertion had been shocking two years ago. It was now commonplace. So were the rapid trials of offenders – if they got that far. Such was the present state on the Western Front, men were often shot out of hand by their officers or NCOs if they refused to go over the top or were seen running away from the main objectives. This case was unusual, however.

There had been a night raid led by a captain who had joined the battalion at the start of April. Geoffrey Steele was a regular officer of the West Wiltshire Regiment who had spent six months in England recovering from shell shock after a disastrous raid during the Somme offensive. It was obvious to everyone that his nerves were still in a questionable state, and his heavy drinking was well known. He was an experienced and capable man who would never have been returned to trench action but for the severe shortage of officers. On the raid he had had with him a sergeant acting as subaltern, two corporals and fifty-eight men. Steel, Sergeant Price, and three men were all who returned to report failure. Two days later a corporal staggered in, badly wounded, accusing the two leaders, in his own words, of 'running like scared rabbits when they saw what they were up against and leaving their men to take the lot'.

The officer claimed that Sergeant Price had failed to link up with him at the appointed spot, which had led him to the conclusion that the right flank had not been secured as necessary. An outbreak of fierce German gunfire had supported this belief, so he had had no hesitation in calling off the raid. He ordered his men to retire and went off to search for the other half of the contingent. He lost his bearings in the darkness and found himself back in the lines without having made contact with them. Sergeant Price told the same story in reverse. The survivors then spoke up, backing the corporal's claim that they were left in a copse facing overwhelming machine-gun fire while their leaders went off supposedly to make contact with each other. None had heard an order to retreat, so they stayed until all their comrades had been killed and the options were die or run. Under intensive questioning, Geoffrey Steele had broken down and was swiftly hospitalized as suffering from recurring neurasthenia. Sergeant Price was court martialled for deserting in the face of the enemy.

As a man of equal rank and proven steadiness as well as sound judgement, Val was appointed as Charlie Price's escort throughout the trial. He might have welcomed this break from the trenches if he had not once been the prisoner in a similar trial. It revived memories of those days in a sweltering room knowing he was going to die with the greatest dishonour. His own ordeal had lasted several days. This poor devil would be given less than several hours.

Val knew Price reasonably well – a good man who had been too long at the Western Front and could take no more. Val recalled the day he, himself, had broken down and sobbed after visiting the cavalry camp. A few minutes later he had encountered Vivienne washing an ambulance. Had she saved *him* from complete nervous disintegration? He would never know, but it was a possibility. The numbers being sent home for mental disorders were growing. By the end of the year there might be hardly a sane man left. Charlie Price had crumbled under interrogation and admitted to using the excuse of looking for his officer in order to get away from the copse. Intelligence had been wrong; there had been Germans all around them and once the machine guns started, his head had begun to pound and his whole body had shaken violently. He remembered nothing more until he returned to the lines. His plea of nervous illness which had led him to act in a manner contrary to his normal behaviour was destroyed by the diagnosis of the medical officer who had interviewed him at some length.

In his guise of escort to the prisoner, and not having been on the raid, Val was unable to give evidence of Price's character as a witness but he burned with the injustice of it all. The Sergeant had been one of the first to volunteer in 1914, and had fought almost continually since then. He was married with three children – the last two having been conceived whilst on leave. His wife had never fully recovered from the last difficult birth and was finding it hard to manage on her own. Price's brother had been burned to death by a flame-thrower early in the war, and his father had very recently succumbed to a fatal heart attack leaving the Sergeant to worry over his mother as well as his wife. The two women did not hit it off, so would be unable to help each other. A request for compassionate leave had been granted, then withdrawn when all leave was suddenly cancelled with rumours of a big push in the offing. The overriding thought in Charlie Price's mind over the past two weeks had been that he must not get killed because the women at home depended on him. He was all they had left.

Amid the sparse evidence, the MO stated that he could not find signs of stress *in excess* of that suffered by every man presently engaged in active service, and Price was otherwise reasonably fit. Within a very short time sentence of death was pronounced and the trial ended. The accused sobbed on hearing the verdict, which to the overtired, unsympathetic court officers merely confirmed their opinion that he was of very weak character. Val, on the other hand, knew what it felt like to be made a scapegoat for another's failures. Fifty-six men had been slaughtered in an attack while a captain and a sergeant/acting subaltern had returned whole. Accusations had been made. Action must be seen to be taken, and it was better to put official blame on a volunteer sergeant than on a regular officer from a good family.

The stripes were removed from Price's sleeves and he was put in the wire enclosure for condemned deserters to await a firing squad in the morning. The man's remaining sanity snapped. He sat on the ground, doubled up, staring vacantly into space. His duty of escort over, Val gave full rein to the volcano of anger about to erupt from deep within his memory. He made his way to the field hospital to find Captain Frost RAMC. The MO was enjoying a cup of tea in his tented accommodation when his batman announced that Sergeant Ashleigh wished to have a private word with him on a very urgent matter.

Val heard the man say, 'Sergeant Ashleigh? I don't know him. Tell him to report for sick parade in the morning, Hopkins.'

The batman said, 'He's in the West Wilts, sir. Says it's most important he sees you.'

There was the sound of a yawn, then, 'Oh, very well, send him in – but this is my off duty period, tell him.'

Val walked in without further delay. Off duty period, be damned. This idiot had just condemned a man to death just to satisfy official records. Having deliberately removed his cap before entering, to obviate the need to salute, Val managed a reasonable tone as he thanked Frost for seeing him.

'Yes, well this is my off duty period, Sergeant – the first time I've left the wards in twenty-two hours,' said the officer through another yawn.

'Except for your attendance at the court martial, sir.'

Frost studied Val with a frown. 'Ah, you were the prisoner's escort, weren't you? What's this all about?'

'I want you to reverse your diagnosis and certify Sergeant Price as shell shocked, therefore not responsible for his actions.'

To say Captain Frost was stupified would be too mild a word. He sat with a mug of tea in mid-air staring at Val with the kind of vacant expression he had just seen on the face of the condemned prisoner. Val took advantage of the moment.

'I've served five months at Gallipoli, on the Somme for two last year and here in the Ypres sector since the end of February. I think I can tell when a bloke has cracked. I've lived amongst them for almost three years. *You* only see them when they arrive here for treatment. They don't behave like raving lunatics, they sit silently like a grenade with the pin removed, ready to explode when thrown at the enemy. That's what happened to Sergeant Price. He and Captain Steele were thrown at the same time, but you can't accuse one of cowardice and send the other home for the duration.' He pointed with a shaking arm. 'That man out there has had more than he should be expected to take. He also has family problems accentuated by the recent loss of his father. Your diagnosis was a plain and simple death sentence, which also condemned two women and three children to a future of hardship and loneliness.' Fighting to remain controlled, Val added, 'The British Army's going to lose a damned good man whatever you say, so why not send him home where he'll eventually be well enough to look after his dependants?'

The MO was now recovering his senses. Slamming the mug of tea on to a wooden crate so that the liquid jumped from it to splash all over the natural wood, he said forcefully, 'Just who the blazes do you think you are?'

'The Devil's Advocate,' Val flashed back. 'Two men commit a crime. You can't pat one on the head like an irresponsible child, and murder the other one. That's not justice – and surely a doctor's creed is to save lives, not cut them off in their prime.'

Frost got to his feet, a tall man but nevertheless several inches shorter than Val, who had rank on his side. 'Get out of here before I have *you* court martialled and broken to private. How dare you accost me like this? *Get out*, d'you hear?'

Here was yet another man who had had more than he should be expected to take speaking to a third, and reason was beyond them. 'That's always the way, isn't it?' Val stormed. 'Never give a ranker the benefit of the doubt, never believe *he* might be telling the truth. Someone had officially to pay for those fifty-six lives, which would have been lost even if their leaders had stayed with them – that copse was swarming with Huns – and so it has to be the sergeant, even though the officer was already known to be mentally unstable. It stood out a mile the moment he came back from convalescence. I'm not asking you to make Steele take the blame instead. All I want is bloody justice – something you commissioned buggers know nothing about.'

Frost turned red with rage, yelling at the top of his voice. 'Hopkins, get two brawny MP's here on the double! *On the double!*'

'That's right,' yelled Val at equal volume. 'Have *me* shot, too. We don't need Huns when we've men like you around.'

Where the affair would have ended neither would know, because at that point the drone of approaching aircraft could be heard. Their attention switched to this new almost daily threat that the Germans had initiated the moment evidence of a manpower and arms build up had been observed in the Ypres salient. Next minute, the earth shuddered as bombs began to fall all around them. Captain Frost ran from his tent towards the rows of marquees forming wards, where a criss-cross of nurses and orderlies were rushing from their rest periods to help.

Val walked outside fighting the aftermath of his inflammable temper whenever he witnessed injustice. He was soon helping in any way he could as mayhem was created amongst those already suffering wounds, and life returned to its present pattern as he helped to carry stretchers, calmed men in agonizing pain, and issued orders to anyone uncertain what to do next. When the raid ended, Charlie Price lay dead in the guarded enclosure, and Captain Frost was among the very severely wounded. Val saw it as fate playing another hand but sensed that it was still not her last.

He returned to the lines occupied by his battalion, consoled by the fact that Mrs Price would now be informed that her husband had been killed by enemy action, although official records would show him to have been found guilty of leaving the field of battle and condemned to death by firing squad. Hopefully, Price descendants would never seek out those records and think ill of the man.

As soon as he got back Val went to see John Marshall, who was now Adjutant, to request an interview with the CO, Major Salter.

'At *this* hour? Can't it wait until morning?' Marshall asked, busy with a huge pile of forms at his desk in a sandbagged dugout.

'No. Please have a word with him.'

The other man raised his eyebrows. '*Please* from you? It must be something really important. Has your wife had the baby yet, by the way?'

'No. The beginning of August. A few weeks still to go.'

Marshall grinned. 'It'd better be a boy, eh?'

'Not if he's ever going to be caught up in something like this. Better to have a girl.'

'Good lord, man, your wife was driving an ambulance until you married her. Girls will be part of any future wars.'

'I thought we were fighting this one to end them for good,' Val said pointedly.

'Do you think anyone still believes that?'

'Major Salter,' Val prompted, anxious to see the man.

Marshall sighed. 'All right, but I wouldn't do it for any other NCO. Hang on.'

The sacking curtain dividing the Adjutant's 'office' from that of their Commanding Officer enabled anyone on one side of it to hear what was being said on the other side, so Val was pleased to get aural evidence that no one but Sergeant Ashleigh would have the nerve to see him at 10.30 p.m. and as he was likely to wait there all night it might be best to give the fellow a few minutes in order to get rid of him.

Marshall reappeared and jerked his head in invitation to the presence. Val ducked through the opening and saluted. 'I *would* have waited all night, as it happens, sir.'

Major Salter nodded. 'So you also overheard that you've got just a few minutes . . . and it's only because you're named Ashleigh.'

Val let that pass, although he longed to say that everyone should be given equal consideration. His mission was too important for splitting hairs. 'I've been asked on numerous occasions to accept commissioned rank, and always refused. Captain Steele's departure has left a vacancy in the battalion. I'd like to apply to fill it.'

The CO leant back in his crude chair and smiled. 'Well, well, well, so we've finally worn down your resistance! Going to join your distinguished ancestors at last, eh?'

'That's not behind my request,' Val said shortly.

'I see. Haven't you a child on the way? Eager to make him proud of his father, that's it.'

'No, sir. There's as much pride in being a trooper as a colonel, if you're good at what you do.'

'A *trooper*?'

Realizing his slip of the tongue, Val covered it. 'A private, sir.'

'Mmm. So why this sudden change of heart an hour or so before midnight?'

'I want to be in a position of enough authority to do something when I see poor devils getting what they don't deserve.'

For almost thirty seconds the senior man studied Val through narrowed eyes, then got to his feet somewhat stiffly and said, 'I think this deserves a drink, Mr Ashleigh. I've seldom heard a better reason for wanting to be an officer in this regiment.'

Lieutenant V.M.H. Ashleigh was given seven days' home leave before taking up his new post as acting company commander – something he had done several times when a sergeant, but this time he would have greater authority and a reasonable dugout to live in, with a batman to do what little was possible for an officer living in a trench. Val begged a lift in the sidecar of a motorcycle combination to Poperinghe, where he got himself an officer's breeches and tunic with all the necessary accessories, booked a room for the night, sent a telegram to Vivienne, took a long hot bath, ate his first reasonable meal in months, then went to bed – a real bed with a mattress and sheets! – to read the rest of the mail he had picked up from the depot on arrival. The long letter from Vivienne he already knew by heart because he had torn that open outside the depot. He could not wait to see her; could not imagine the delight of being with her at Woodlands as if the war did not exist and they were free to be whoever they chose to be.

She had written about her visit to Knightshill, and gave her opinion of the members of the Ashleigh Clan, as she termed them.

> Darling, I understand Havelock so much better now. All those military portraits of be-medalled ancestors. And Vere gave such a vivid description of Sir Gilliard – surely the most formidable of them all! But I have to say that you have inherited the old man's iron will and pugnaciousness. Small wonder you risked everything to defy him.

Vivienne continued with a list of qualities Val had clearly *not* inherited from the stern, loveless general, and he was thankful the censor did not check incoming mail. What she had written increased his impatience to reach her, although her advanced stage of pregnancy would considerably limit his lovemaking. To see her, to hold her, to sharpen his wit against hers would be wonderful enough after an absence of around four months. It would be miraculous to see and hold their child, but that would have to be on his next leave. He did not dwell on the prospect of this being his last. Instead, he thought about the possible next Ashleigh in line to inherit Knightshill. If the baby was a boy, he hoped the lad would grow into a young man like Andrew Duncan. The news of Duncan's death which Val had heard by chance eight months after the event had greatly saddened him. In the midst of so many brief but close relationships, among so many deaths, that one loss had seemed particularly tragic, although inevitable.

If the child was a daughter Val knew she would be as fiery as her mother, and he would be kept on his metal. He did not yearn for a son. Unlike Vere, he was not over-concerned with the bloodline. His one great longing was for the war to be over so that he could settle at Woodlands with his small family and enjoy the happiness which had taken so long to reach him – happiness and the inner knowledge that he had, above all, been true to himself.

That theme was strangely echoed when, with letters from Vere, Charlotte and his man of business, he found a brief note from Tim.

> I know this will reach you eventually – such is the army postal system – and by then I shall be on the high seas. I need to put things straight between us. You were right. I *was* nothing but a jumped up little dingo's arse – I believe that was the expression you used.
>
> In prison camp I met Piers Lassingham of the 57th. After hearing his story I determined to get out and stop being a J.U.L.D.A. see above. When I got home the Elders also told me what *you* said all along I should know, so what I do in the coming days will be for my own conscience, not for any ancestors. I thought you'd like to know that. Good luck, and thanks.

Val lay back on the pillow ready for sleep, his mind in South Africa once more. To Piers Lassingham had fallen the 'honour' of parading the figure of disgrace before the entire regiment. So the secret was out, and by the merest chance. Fate taking a hand again? Perhaps Martin Havelock should now rest in peace. He slept dreamlessly, refreshed in mind and body. After a big breakfast he packed his valise and walked through the usual clamour of the railhead down to the station, where the train for Boulogne waited with steam billowing around the engine.

An MP sergeant stood at the gate watching Val approach, but he took one look at the pass and travel warrant and handed them back without a smile. 'Sorry, sir, all leave's been cancelled since four this morning. Everyone's to report to their units right away, and troops in Reserve is moving up to the Front. Bin doing it ever since the order came through. Must be the Big Push at last, eh?' He made a sympathetic grimace. 'Hard luck, sir. At least you've stopped before you started, so to speak. Some'll already be at Boulogne and then turned back. So near yet so far, eh, seeing Blighty across the water and not able to cross it.'

Val's disappointment was so great he remained staring at the noisy engine with his travel documents in his hand, unable to turn away. His images of himself and Vivienne in the green peace of Wiltshire, his reservoir of thoughts and ideas stored to exchange with her, his sexual need to hold and touch her refused to be denied. This red-faced man could not prevent him from going on that train. Had Sergeant Ashleigh not just acquired new rank to prevent men from getting what they did not deserve? Well, he did not deserve this. He would order the man to stand back and let him through. He would do the same at Boulogne. When he saw the white smudge of England across the Channel he would order them to take him there. He had sent Vivienne a telegram. She would be excited, start preparing for his arrival. She needed him the way he needed her. She would be mad enough to go to Victoria so they could spend the maximum time together. He had told her not to because German aircraft had begun bombing London, but she would go. He was certain she would go. And the leave train would arrive empty.

'Are you all right, sir?'

Val came from visions of his wife's body lying beneath the rubble of a railway station deserted save for the deathly still figure. He stared at a face he believed he had seen somewhere before.

'Are you all right, sir?' the face asked once more.

Val nodded lethargically. 'It's just fate playing bloody tricks again. I should have expected this.'

They all stood-to before dawn, waiting in the rain for the order to go over the top. After almost three years Val thought he had heard the greatest barrage possible, but on that morning it was as if all the guns ever manufactured opened fire on the German positions through which the West Wilts had to pass in order to capture the ridge beyond the wood clearly marked on his map. This was the time when all the men of a battalion, a company, a platoon became as one. The inveterate chatterers fell silent, the jokers stopped laughing, the broody grew alert, the brave doubted their courage. To a man they stood gripping their rifles behind a high, protective earthen wall waiting with staring eyes and thudding hearts for the moment when they had to climb up into the open, trot forward, and keep on until . . . That was the point at which each of them stopped thinking ahead. The Big Push was well underway, the ultimate effort which would have the enemy on his knees begging for an end to it all. They would be at home by Christmas.

Val commanded B Company, with young Hector Milnes as the only other officer. He was a good, steady fellow but this was his first real test in a major advance. He looked pale and tense, but Val sensed that the boy would do his utmost if he lived long enough. Fifteen minutes ago Val had been along the line checking his company. The thunderous din made it impossible to speak to the men, but he had smiled and gripped the shoulder of each one of them as a sign of his faith in their ability to do what they must. They knew him, trusted him. He had been one of them, ready to do himself what he asked of others. They would follow him anywhere. Knowing that calmed his own fear, because he *was* fearful. Now, he had so much to live for.

A glance at his watch. Thirty seconds to go. A quick look at Milnes waiting in the first glimmerings of dawn further along the trench. The boy was watching him closely, revolver in hand. Val nodded. Milnes nodded back. The nods meant: Are you all set and confident? Yes, I am. Val counted five, four, three, two, one. A long blast on his whistle and up over the mud wall which had surrounded 'home' for so long. Amazingly, it was good to be above ground; good to have a long view stretching in every direction. A kind of freedom!

He was alone in front. It did not bother him – he had done it many times before – but progress was slow. He was not trotting as fast as he used to. Well, he had not done this since the Somme last year, and he was now thirty-eight, not a senior schoolboy leading the pack in the first rugby team. Where had all the years gone? Which was the wood they must gain before taking the ridge? Everywhere he looked were large clumps of blackened stumps bearing occasional sprays of branches with leaves. Hardly *woods*!

They would get little shelter from them. The ground ahead was honeycombed with shell craters. German missiles now created more, sending heavy, rain-soaked earth flying up in spouts all around them. Bullets whistled past like the screech of gale-force winds, shrapnel flew like a deadly hail. Bodies from yesterday's aborted attack covered the ground in layers. Val trod over them; they all did. The dead felt no pain, no sense of outrage. They were at peace.

The enemy front line lay ten yards ahead. There was nothing left of it save a muddy porridge of sandbags, duckboards, the paraphernalia of trench existence, and bodies all blown into fragments by the continuous barrage. Val moved on towards the next objective as the sky lightened perceptibly. The wood rose like a mass of blackened fingers pointing at God in a grey heaven, who had surely abandoned those beneath.

A glance to his left and right showed no more than a straggle of khaki, and a subaltern holding his revolver with the left hand because the right hung useless at his side. Surely this was not all that remained of B Company.

Something hit Val's neck with a red-hot smack which momentarily halted him. It was no more than a passing blow. He went on towards the wood where yesterday's force had been annihilated. Today's was double the number. At least, it had been at the outset. They had orders to capture the ridge beyond, *at all cost*. He never liked that order. Those issuing it would be safely behind the lines while the cost was being paid. The rain became a torrent. Blood from his neck mingled with it to turn the runnels red as they coursed down his tunic. Still he struggled forward obeying orders.

The din increased as machine guns on the ridge found their range and opened fire. Bogged down in the mud as they were, they would be completely wiped out if they advanced further. Val recalled Gallipoli and that hill covered with the bodies of a West Wilts battalion. He would not sacrifice men that way again. This time he had the authority to make the decision. He glanced left and right, signalling that they should take cover wherever they could, and that Milnes should occupy the same crater as himself. Men were falling like ninepins even as they struggled to reach the relative safety of shell holes, and anyone who stopped to help them went the same way. Although they were always instructed before setting out *not* to stop for the wounded, it was instinctive for a man to help his pal to get to cover.

The nearest crater was already occupied, but these occupants were not aware of anyone joining them. They would never be aware again. Milnes and eight men arrived simultaneously; all but two had minor wounds. Their faces were ashen; they were fighting for breath. The bottom of the crater held several feet of water, so they all kicked precarious footholds in the slimy sides and clung there while the battle continued to rage.

'Are you all right?' Val asked his subaltern above the tumult.

'Got it in the arm, but it's nothing to worry about.'

'Good lad. What about the rest of you?'

The lance-corporal answered. 'Jinks and Roland need stretchers. Us others can make do with our emergency dressings, sir.'

'Good. See to it Corporal, while I do what I can for Mr Milnes and talk to him about the situation.'

They all did their best with their emergency dressings in the heavy downpour and slippery conditions, then concentrated on keeping the pair who were in a bad way from sliding down to drown in the water. Val had a look at his subaltern's arm. Shrapnel had peppered the fleshy part above his elbow but did not appear to have shattered the bone. While he applied the standard dressing and bound it in place the younger man said, 'You're bleeding rather a lot.'

'Yes, it's spoiling my brand new uniform. You can patch me up in a minute. We haven't a hope of gaining that ridge until our artillery moves forward and puts out of action their gun emplacements. We shall have to stick it out here as best we can for a while. This mud'll slow down any heavy limbers, so we're liable to still be here at the time we're supposed to rendezvous with the Fusiliers on top of the ridge.'

'They won't have got there, either,' Milnes said, 'so we shan't be holding anyone up.'

'No, too right we won't. If it rains like this all day that ridge will be an unstable slope. We'll slide down again as fast as we climb up it.'

Milnes frowned. 'It doesn't look good, sir.'

'No, it doesn't, and for God's sake stop calling me sir.'

'Sorry. It's always seemed the natural thing to do.'

'I know, son. Boys like you should be finishing your education, not standing out here knee deep in mud trying to do the impossible.'

They both ducked automatically as a shell burst very close to their cover, and fell silent for a while as they checked that the wounded men had been made as comfortable as possible.

'When the support wave gets this far, you must make your way back to our lines.' Val told them. 'By then, our artillery will have moved forward and it'll be relatively easy to cover the ground.'

They waited and waited, unaware that the guns were making heavy weather in the mud because the horses pulling them were stuck fast and could not be pulled out. Still it poured. The pool at the bottom of the crater deepened, and the sides became more liquid. The men sheltering there constantly fought for footholds as they crouched in their sodden uniforms, praying that another shell would not land right there. One of the badly wounded soldiers died an hour later. The second almost certainly would not survive until stretcher bearers could reach him. It was a thankless situation. Val risked a look over the top of the crater. It was like a scene from purgatory; a hell which allowed no escape. As if to confirm that, a thump against his tin helmet made him duck below the surface very smartly and he slithered helplessly to be submerged in the pool at the base amid the bodies. Milnes and the corporal hauled him up with difficulty, because he was a very big man. He now stank worse than before.

'That'll teach me to play safe,' he grunted. 'I'm afraid I didn't see any artillery on the way, so settle down for a little longer.'

They were hungry for they had had no breakfast, but it was out of the question to do more than open a couple of cans of bully beef and share it spread on hard biscuit. It tasted of mud, and the barrage continued around and above them, keeping them ducking each time a shell fell too near and showered them with more mud and shrapnel. The second severely wounded man died just before 11 a.m. and the support wave had still not arrived. Val began to believe the attack had been aborted and they had been left to make it back to the lines as best they could. He worried about the rest of his decimated company in other holes, but it was certain death to try and cross to them.

Just as they were convinced that the assault had been called off, they heard a curious rumbling, clanking sound, and the ground began to tremble. Next minute, above the top of the crater, they saw a monstrous vehicle bearing heavy cannon lumbering past towards the wood. It was the first time any of them had seen a tank, but they knew immediately what it was and were immensely encouraged by its presence. This was the new wonder weapon which was to win the war. They even managed to raise a cheer, because tanks would blast a way through for them and make their job easy. The cheering stopped when the side of their crater began to collapse in a great slither of mud due to the passing of the tracked vehicle.

For the next few minutes Val, his subaltern, and several others dug madly to free those buried by the miniature landslide which had widened the mouth of the crater considerably. Then Val heard an unfamiliar sound and clawed his way up to look over the rim. The tank was about twenty yards away, stuck fast in the mud and sinking ever lower as the tracks further churned up the stodgy surface. The monster had gone as far as it could. The wonder weapon had been defeated by nature. It still had life in it, however, and the six-pounder guns continued firing to bombard the enemy posts on the ridge. The other tanks across a broad front were doing the same.

Val watched with a sense of impotence. The great guns of the British Army which should have defeated the Boers had also stuck in the mud, or been too cumbersome to drag over the mountain passes. It was men who won wars – thousands upon thousands of them. Whichever side had the most men to sacrifice would emerge triumphant. He was certain of that.

The whistle of an approaching shell caused him to duck with his face a mere inch from burial in the slime. The ground shook once more as he clung to his precarious hold. Then he heard something that brought his head up again sharply. Men were screaming; not from wounds but from terror. He was experienced enough to hear the difference. The tank had been penetrated by shell splinters and was on fire, condemning the men inside to being roasted alive – a most terrible death.

The sound of those screams, the memory of burns he had once suffered, and the sight of a boy's ghastly face through a ragged hole in the tank overrode all other thoughts and gave Val the energy he believed he no longer had. Fighting the runny wall of the crater, he heaved himself from it and set off across the mire towards the blazing vehicle, heedless of anything save getting those poor devils out from an inferno.

His earlier submergence in water now aided him, for the licking flames did not easily set alight the khaki he wore. The three men still alive inside were all bleeding profusely and clearly stunned by the force of the explosion. The tank was already belching heat like a furnace.

Val obeyed instinct regardless of the pain in his hands when he touched the metal. Shouting instructions, desperately encouraging them to reach the gaping, jagged hole which was their sole escape route, he seized hold of the tunic of the first and dragged him forward with all his considerable strength through the gap until the man dropped to the earth. Then he yelled at the second, who was very young and too terrified to do anything. 'Come on, you stupid little bugger. You don't deserve this, do you?'

The boy cowered back, tears streaming down his cheeks, crying, 'Mother, save me. Oh, save me!'

'*I'm* your bloody mother,' Val roared. '*Come on!*'

He grabbed the lad as soon as he was close enough, and pulled him forward regardless of the jagged metal around the hole. Better to tear his flesh than leave him to cook in an oven. The first man was already staggering away towards the shell crater where a row of faces were watching at risk of exposure. 'Go on, follow *him*,' Val cried to the sobbing youngster, then turned back to the blazing tank where a third man, a youthful officer, was in dire straits attempting to crawl forward with a broken arm and blood obscuring half his face. 'You can make it. *You can*!' Val urged, his voice husky from the noxious fumes. 'Get here and I'll do the rest. *Come on*, man! Only a foot more.'

The subaltern's face appeared to be partially blown away, but he was making a superhuman effort to respond to encouragement. The heat was so great Val could feel his own face and hands burning, and the cuffs bearing his new rank were blackening. The man was within reach now, so Val bent forward into the hole to grasp the outstretched hands. His hefty tug brought a scream from someone who had not until then uttered a sound, but Val had him outside before he realized the officer's breeches were actually in flames. He flung himself to the ground beside the body and frantically shovelled mud over the burning legs.

Flames began to shoot from the tank to reach them, so Val got to his knees, took up the wounded man across his shoulders, then struggled upright and set off for the crater. He had covered only ten yards when he was hit in the back by a force so powerful he felt himself rise up then drop into blackness.

John Marshall stood looking down at a face he knew well even when it was covered in dirt and reddened by burns. It was uncannily like the portrait of Vorne Ashleigh in the Mess in Salisbury. It was the face of a man he respected; a man who had somehow been more than a mere friend in spite of the difference in ranks.

'What a family they are,' he commented to the doctor on the other side of the stretcher. 'Our regiment was founded by his ancestors, you know. His grandfather was the renowned old General Sir Gilliard, and his older brother distinguished himself in the Sudan. I'd say he's beaten them all, wouldn't you?'

The MO glanced up. 'Is that right he risked his life to pull three men from a burning tank?'

Marshall nodded. 'The act of a true hero.'

'Or a true fool! Is he married?'

'Earlier this year. His wife has just had a son. The news came in yesterday.'

'The poor little blighter will grow up proud of his father he never knew.'

'There's *no* hope?'

The doctor gave him a straight look. 'With wounds like his? I'm amazed they managed to bring him in alive. It seems unnecessarily cruel to send him on an ambulance journey over roads which are now little more than quagmires with planks thrown over them, but I've got to make room here by moving out patients I can do nothing more for in these abominable conditions.'

'That's that, then,' Marshall said heavily. 'I'll not easily forget him. The wild one of the family. Swore like a trooper, was a law unto himself when it came to discipline, and shrugged off his ancestry . . . but he was one of the finest soldiers I've ever come across.'

'I suppose that's why he did what he did.'

'No, I think it was because of the kind of man he was.' As he turned away, he said, 'When they put him in the ambulance, tell the nurse to let him know about his son if he regains consciousness.'

The MO glanced around at the stretchers piled for as far as he could see. 'I can't promise. I've got my hands full.'

The nurse *was* told about the arrival of a boy, and that this particular patient was a hero.

'They all are,' she said shortly, but she nevertheless watched over Lieutenant Ashleigh with particular compassion, hoping he would rally long enough to be told about his son.

Towards the end of the gruelling journey he did groan and stir beneath his blankets. Then she was struck by the very vivid blue of his eyes when they appeared to gaze at her as he gave the ghost of a smile. 'Listen to that, Andrew. It's so quiet you can hear the bloody stars twinkling,' he murmured.

The nurse was too choked to speak. The noise of the battles around Ypres was still thunderous, and it was broad daylight outside the ambulance window.

Kate and Milly spent five months at a base hospital in the Ypres Salient. They enjoyed their time together at an establishment very near to a cavalry camp, because the mounted troops were frustrated at being held so long in reserve and used their excess energy in mounting sporting events, and concerts to which the hospital staff was invited. Matron was reasonably young and reputedly much taken by a dashing major at the camp; the sisters were feeling the strain of 'all work and no play' which had been their lot for three years, so off-duty nurses were allowed to attend functions at the camp to earn a little light relief from the harrowing tasks they had to do.

Kate was sent to a ward containing shell shocked patients – the men who had been subjected to more than they could take. It was something she had not yet dealt with, wounds of the mind. Some also had physical damage, but most were reasonably able. The work on this ward was very different. A special kind of nursing was needed by men whose sanity was endangered. There were special centres for the poor victims who would never recover; they were shipped home from there to asylums under conditions which kept them from public gaze. Ward B housed those whose present instability was under observation by doctors who were unfamiliar with neurasthenia of this nature. As with mustard gas poisoning, and continuous life in earthen dug outs, medical science had scant knowledge of the symptoms these new problems produced.

Never before had soldiers suffered constant danger without adequate rest from it, nor had they been subjected to the unending thunder of guns and explosions month after month. They had never lived so long in such appalling conditions with little hope of moving on, and they had never witnessed such carnage all around them. Gas attacks brought dread; it crept silently on the breeze and there was no weapon to counter it. Flame-throwers were obscene. To hear men screaming as they became living torches affected even the strongest minds. Soldiers had gone mad before, but never in such overwhelming numbers. In Ward B were men who had suffered all those things over the past three years, and some who had been at war only a short time.

Kate was initially shocked. None of her experience had prepared her for patients who sat cross-legged on their beds staring at the wall, unnerving those facing them who grew very tense and begged for a screen to be put around the starers. They never answered when spoken to, but were otherwise amenable and allowed nurses to feed and tend them. There were others who could not stop crying – Kate was especially sympathetic to them – and some who seemed no more than unbearably weary during the day, but then entered a purgatory known only to themselves when they slept. The night staff were kept busy with these men, sponging them down and often resorting to webbing restraints to keep them from harming themselves. Many suffered involuntary attacks of violent trembling similar to severe epileptic fits which, if they occurred during meal times, resulted in food and drink being dropped over the sheets. It also made them incontinent while it lasted, so there was a great deal of bed changing to do. *Every* patient in Ward B dreaded being classified fit and sent back to the front line.

'But they must know they won't be,' Kate had declared on her first day.

'Some will,' Sister Moffatt said with a sigh. 'I know it's heartbreaking, my dear, but half our present patients merely need a long rest in bed, good food and some peace. Not that one could call it peaceful here. The Germans' bombing raids are growing ever nearer and we often hear thuds and the anti-aircraft barrage. A casualty clearing station was hit earlier this week. It sounds barbarous but I suppose the enemy airmen are aiming for the supply depots and marshalling yards behind the lines, and mistakes happen. I don't believe they would *deliberately* bomb a hospital.'

'No, they *un*deliberately sunk a hospital ship I was on. It hit a drifting mine in the Aegean. As the French are fond of saying, "*C'est la guerre*!"'

'Poor girl. Typhus on top of that. You *have* been in the wars!'

'Haven't we all,' Kate said grimly.

The patients in Ward B were accommodated in the only hutted ward, for their own safety. It was easier to guard than a marquee. Patients who had been subdued and silent from their day of admission could suddenly become hysterical and run amok. If they were caught trying to get away it was possible they would be shot out of hand. Kate dreaded that as she had once dreaded seeing amputees.

The officers were accommodated in an adjoining hut, four single rooms being set aside for higher ranking men or for those who, for some reason, needed to be kept apart from the rest. The caustic comment around the hospital was that generals never entered Ward B because none of them ever got near enough to shells to be shocked by them. The officers were even more difficult to deal with because they felt deeply ashamed, most of them having attended schools which revered honour and manliness. The nurses had their work cut out to persuade these young men that they were not displaying weakness or lack of courage, it was simply the stress of being so long under the pressures of war.

It was essential to make patients feel normal, to boost their confidence and to listen to whatever they needed to confess. Kate found the first two easy enough, but the last was often quite distressing. They would open their hearts to nurses, confiding their most private thoughts and longings then asking advice on what to do. In so many instances it was clear personal worries had added an impossible burden to what they had to endure professionally.

She spoke about this to Milly one warm evening in July as they walked along to the cavalry camp for a concert and supper in the Officers' Mess. 'Fifty percent of my boys are stricken by the disloyalty of wives or sweethearts; the lack of love and understanding in their letters. They have faced all this horror with fortitude then been defeated by the women they love. It's made me realize how careful we have to be. For all their outward show of strength, a woman can so easily break them. It's *such* a responsibilty.'

'Hey, hey,' said Milly, pulling a face, 'When the lads crowd around us tonight telling outrageous tales of derring-do while galloping about on their trusty steeds, you'll remember how shamelessly they can play on our sympathy . . . and what liars they can be.'

'Down-to-earth Milly, as usual.'

'That's me.' Then she added more soberly, 'It's the only way to get through this nightmare war.'

Kate continued to be troubled by the confessions of her patients as 1917 reached the start of autumn, with the tragedy of Passchendaele signifying the relative failure of the Big Push and the prospect of another stagnant winter in the bowels of the earth for the armies of the Western Front. It did not seem likely that she would become Mrs Munroe for some time yet. Although she longed for the end of the war, like everyone else, she wondered if being a wife and mother would be enough after all she had done over the past three years. Simon wrote of his longing for her, and of his plans for the future. When she was particularly tired or upset, Kate wanted nothing more than to be with him at Knightshill on an evening like the last they had spent together.

With the onset of autumn weather – fog, gales, unremitting rain – it was easy to feel unable to go on when such an alternative was available. Kate was in that frame of mind one day in September when something shocking happened. A patient committed suicide in front of her. One of the starers, a docile man of around twenty-three who had been diagnosed as needing no more than a good rest and plenty of nourishment, suddenly became volatile and began shouting. When Kate hurried down the ward to calm him, he pulled out a razor and sliced it across his throat, severing his windpipe.

There was an immediate meeting to discuss the case and apportion blame, but it was impossible to do so. Such was the uncertain nature of shell shock. The man was simply another casualty of war; one amid thousands. He was officially listed as having died of his wounds. The meeting broke up; the staff returned to their duties. Kate continued her day shift in her normal calm manner, but she broke down once she reached the tent she shared with Milly. She felt personally responsible for the tragedy. Surely the man had shown that, by ending his life the moment *she* had arrived beside him. Sitting in her draughty tent, with aching feet and an aching heart, while rain thundered on the flapping canvas, she resolved to marry Simon on her next leave and give up nursing without a qualm. She had had enough.

Later that evening she was summoned to Matron and she went in defeated mood. She had no defence for what had happened, yet a reprimand would not bring the man back or save his mother from grief. When Kate returned to her tent everything had changed. Marriage and Simon were forgotten. Matron had told her she was now *Sister* Daulton and was to serve on the ambulance trains plying from the railheads to the Channel ports day after day. The posting would take effect from the start of the following week. Not a word of blame had been spoken, only praise and congratulations on reaching the coveted senior rank. So, on yet another cold, grey day, Kate and Milly said farewell with heavy hearts. They had been together a long time. Milly, who had also been promoted, was due at a large base hospital the next month. Her last words to Kate were: 'Don't hit a drifting mine, ducky.'

Indeed, Kate discovered that her new life was in many ways similar to those weeks on the *Romaine*, except that she had a first class compartment to herself rather than a curtained 'shelf'. In this compartment she slept, washed, mended and laundered her clothes, wrote up her notes, combed the lice from her hair and dealt with the monthly inconveniences of being a woman. The trains carried as many as several hundred cases on each journey, some sitting up like normal passengers in the carriages if they were classed as walking wounded. There were two medical officers, three sisters beside Kate, and several dozen male orderlies, which was a vastly different arrangement from any Kate was used to.

The greatest improvement on what she had dealt with on the *Romaine* was that the patients had already been cleaned up and given treatment, so there was no question of cutting off their uniforms and washing away their filth. Here, too, were specially constructed ward cars, each containing thirty-six foldaway cots in three tiers, a pharmacy, a treatment room and even a tiny theatre for emergency operations. Kate hoped none would be necessary, for how would the doctors manage in a rocking train?

It was not a simple matter of running back and forth from the railhead to the coast, either. The *Romaine* had not encountered hold ups, as the ambulance trains did. Troop movements and supplies for the Front had priority on the railways, so the ambulance trains frequently sat for long periods on sidings until the line was clear, and sometimes they stopped because the track had been bombed or the port they were waiting to enter was under attack from German aircraft. Quite suddenly, Kate understood much that Simon had said about needing superior fighter aircraft. War had taken to the air for all time.

Kate did not always travel to the same port or over the identical route. Ambulance trains served the whole rail system presently in Allied hands, but she saw very little of the passing scene. They frequently travelled by night and, in any case, she was far too busy running her own ward car throughout a journey which could last as long as ten to twelve hours, depending on possible delays. It was a curious, unreal kind of life having a home in a railway compartment which she only left to supervise loading and unloading of patients or, if the schedule allowed it, to beg a bath on the hospital ship waiting to take the wounded home. Only occasionally did she look across the steel-grey water to the coast of England, and yearn to reach it.

Becoming a sister was the height of her ambition. Doctors treated her with even greater respect, she ruled her own small, wheeled kingdom, she knew a sense of quiet achivement. Above all, she felt she was fulfilling her destiny. Although it had never mattered as much to her as to all other Ashleighs – and she *did* have Ashleigh blood in her veins – she had done her utmost to follow family tradition and was the first female to do so. Like many other aspects of life this war had changed irrevocably, Kate knew in her heart the future women of Knightshill would make their mark in the world in grander ways than by simply producing the next generation.

Being constantly on the move meant that mail was a long time reaching her, so it was not until several weeks after it was written that Kate received a letter from Kitty with all the family news. Simon had started work on an improved fighter to outdo the one now in production, Tim had arrived in 'an area that gave him the hump', from which they deduced he was currently alongside the Camel Corps somewhere in Palestine, Vere had finished his canvas on that same subject and had recaptured his old love for military scenes, Charlotte's camellias had all suffered some dreadful blight and would have to be replaced, Laurence had to go to America and Margaret had somehow arranged to accompany him. The twins were begging to leave their school at Christmas, when they would be seventeen, but Vere would not approve their plan to devote themselves exclusively to the arts taught by a series of dilettante creatures suggested by the soprano, Madeleine Metcalfe. A family confrontation on the subject was imminent. Only right at the end did her aunt write the news that Vivienne had had a ten-pound son the previous day, and that mother and baby were both doing well.

Kate lowered the letter to her lap and stared at the wall of her tiny 'home', which was no more than four feet away. She had known deep inside the baby would be a boy. So the inheritance was secure . . . unless Val's son was killed in some future war before doing *his* duty as heir. As the train clacked over ties in the track, moving slowly because they had been warned that a raid on Calais was presently underway, Kate recalled that evening in Alexandria when she had said goodbye to a sergeant with an Australian accent. He had regretted the loss of Goonawarra, which he had willed to her 'because the boys would all get plenty'. He had also said the Ashleighs were only interested in their males, and that she was beating them at their own game. Glancing at the short scarlet cape on the bunk beside her she thought of Knightshill's ancestral portraits of men in scarlet tunics. She might not be beating them, but surely she was up there with them? Her thoughts moved to the men presently in her ward car; to all the men she had tended in the past three years. When this war eventually ended, the future would be in the hands of a legion of women all across Europe. Was it not time the insistence on *male* heirs was put aside?

During the following week Kate thought often about the infant Ashleigh, wondering if his destiny was to follow family tradition or if he might be a rebel, like his father, and go his own way. Would he grow to manhood big, blond and handsome or be slender and carrot-haired, with freckles? Would she look at him in years to come when she had her own children, and see the image of a brother, uncle, sweetheart rolled into one who once had chased her roaring like a lion, then years later collapsed at her feet on a blue and cream carpet? Would young Ashleigh one day send her a photograph of himself as a proud smiling officer, and bring a pang of regret?

At the end of the week another doctor joined the staff aboard that train. Kate was surprised to encounter once more James McIntosh, who had crossed swords with her in Alexandria. He was now a major and short tempered, but he greeted her with a warm handshake and a sly enquiry after her *uncle*. So he had never believed that truth? Looking him in the eye she replied that his wife had just given birth to a son. Only then did it dawn on her that Vivienne was, in fact, her aunt, and baby Ashleigh her cousin. Further family complications, for the other cousins were all in their teens!

The problem of kinship did not stay with Kate for long, because it was soon apparent that the senior medical officer aboard was drinking too heavily and was also paying too much attention to the sisters in charge of the four ward cars. The only women in a community of several hundred men, they began to find life difficult in the confinement of a train. The other two doctors recognized the problem, but could not see a way around it. In truth, it seemed to them minor in comparison with the work they were trying to do. The nursing sisters agreed. They were all mature women able to deal with such things, but it added to their burden of stress as they were shunted back and forth across France and Belgium in a khaki-painted train for weeks on end.

They tried to devise ways of jamming the doors of their private compartments so that they could not be opened when they were inside them, but this could not be implemented because it had to be possible for someone to enter and wake them in an emergency. Finally, the problem was solved by the male orderlies who, unasked, took it upon themselves to patrol the corridor outside the sisters' quarters. Nothing could be done about Major McIntosh's drinking. His colleagues did their best to limit it, but he kept a secret stock he topped up each time they reached a port. Everyone knew the man was suffering from his own brand of shell shock and they were experienced enough to compensate for his lapses, but they were *all* weary and under a great deal of pressure so they wished the RAMC had not tried to ease their burden by sending him to them.

Things came to a head late one evening when a patient unexpectedly collapsed and an emergency operation had to be performed. It was what Kate had dreaded, because she was on the roster as theatre sister for that night. A doctor named Barnes acted as anaesthetist, while she assisted James McIntosh. The train driver was told to slow down, which caused an argument because he had to maintain a strict schedule to fit in with troop and supply movements. Kate was very wound up. The patient was young and scared to death about what was going to be done to him. Had he been aware of McIntosh's condition he would have been further terrified.

A compromise with the engine driver reduced the swaying of the tiny operating theatre, but the surgeon was himself unsteady as he began to cut into the patient's stomach. Kate watched with her heart in her mouth, handing McIntosh the instruments he needed and exchanging speaking glances with Captain Barnes holding the cup over the boy's face and slowly dripping anaesthetic on to it. The incision was careless, but not dangerous, and the operation progressed in silence until the surgeon's hands began to shake so violently he dropped the scalpel into the gaping wound. Next minute he put his bloodied gloves to his head and cried in a strangled voice, 'I can't kill this lad! He's going to die anyway. I want no part of it.'

To Kate's horror the man who had been so strong in Egypt sank to the floor and began to mutter disjointedly about being a mass murderer. Barnes told her to take over from him, and shouted for the two orderlies waiting outside the cubicle only big enough for three people and a patient.

'Help Major McIntosh to his quarters,' he instructed tensely. 'Then fetch Captain Stride here as soon as possible.'

They went, leaving Kate facing the gaping wound as she carefully monitored the patient's pulse. Too much anaesthetic and he would die from it, Barnes took the scalpel from where it rested in a mass of blood, then glanced up at Kate.

'Are you all right, Sister?'

'Perfectly,' she replied. 'And this lad is *not* going to die, if I have anything to do with it.'

'He won't . . . and you're going to have a great deal to do with it.'

They did all they could, but lost their patient just the same. Kate returned to her quarters after seeing the boy transferred to the area behind the pharmacy where corpses were taken until they reached the docks. It had happened so many times before, yet she was still upset at losing this patient. He had been so near to reaching England and his family. She was also depressed by the collapse of James McIntosh, who would have to be put aboard the hospital ship, too. His two colleagues would diagnose instability due to prolonged stress, and the man's future as a doctor would be doubtful. John Barnes had confided to Kate as they cleared up the theatre that McIntosh had married unwisely while on leave a year ago and had received an anonymous letter soon after, cataloguing his young wife's infidelities.

'Please keep this to yourself, Sister,' he had added. 'I simply thought it would help you to understand what happened tonight.'

She had replied, 'I recently worked on a ward filled with similar cases. I understand all too well. No one can surely be out here and fail to.'

The train picked up speed and fairly raced along as the engine driver attempted to meet his given schedule. Kate tried to wash in the small folding canvas bowl, then sat on her bunk with her feet up once more feeling ready to give up all this for the delight of being with Simon at Knightshill, roaming the lanes and meadows in search of butterflies and birds' eggs. It all seemed so far away and unreal now. An orderly brought her a cup of tea and some sandwiches, breaking in to her reverie.

'We'll be coming into Boulogne in 'arf an hour, Sister. Thought you'd like to know.'

She was grateful for the tea, but could not face the sandwiches. The number of times she had chastised patients for not eating, saying they had a duty to build themselves up, yet she could not follow her own advice. On the return journey to pick up the next consignment she would get some real sleep and have a good meal, she told herself. And she would have the usual de-lousing session, because she was certain a fresh colony had set itself up in her hair and clothes.

Boulogne was more than usually busy. Several ambulance trains had come in one after the other, and more were being loaded with supplies and returning troops from ships standing in the harbour. Autumn was always the time to replenish and reinforce before snow and ice made movement difficult. Not that it was easy now, with rivers of mud everywhere. As the train slid to a halt beside the platform where teams of stretcher bearers were waiting, Kate stood looking from her window as she fastened her cape. With such chaos their return might be delayed long enough to get a bath on one of the ships. It would be bliss!

The chaos, which had been reasonably organized, turned into a chaos of a different sort as the sound of an an explosion rent the air and was swiftly followed by another. Rooted to the spot, Kate watched in disbelief as part of a platfrom and a train flew apart fifty yards away. The station began to disintegrate before her eyes as it slowly dawned on her that enemy aircraft were bombing the port where supplies and soldiers were gathered in large numbers. Troops were leaving carriages in a flood of khaki and running for the open ground beyond the station. The platforms were full of rushing people unsure where they were going and causing opposing tides which met and spilled on to the tracks. Another bomb fell in their midst as Kate watched appalled.

A voice behind her shouted, 'We're taking the train out again, Sister. Stand by.'

She must get to her patients. They would need calming. Leaving her compartment, Kate hurried along the narrow corridors towards her ward car, unable to stop herself from looking from every window at the continuing tumult outside and willing the train to start its backward journey to safety. Then she saw something which made her cry out in distress. Passing the window on a wheeled stretcher used for the very seriously wounded was a man with thick blond hair and a face she would never forget as long as she lived.

Thrusting open a door and jumping down, unaware that the train had begun to move, Kate found herself caught in a stream of stretcher bearers, nurses and orderlies hurrying forward a consignment of wounded which had already been offloaded from another train on the adjoining platform. The blond man she had seen from the window was now way ahead, swallowed up in a swamp of stretchers being taken almost at a run towards the station exits. She pushed her way through the throng, frantic to reach him. She *had* to see him, speak to him. He would know her, know someone cared. He would rally when he saw her. Little Kate, he called her. He would call her that again when he saw her. Those vivid blue eyes would recognize her, and he would give that slow, sweet smile.

The press of people was like a solid wall. They were intent on escaping the bombs still falling on ships and trains alike. The noise was deafening. Anti-aircraft fire had now begun, shattering Kate's ear-drums because of its proximity, and adding to the thunder of explosions. People were shouting and screaming; the sound in wind and limb joined the wounded, and the sick became the dead. There were tears on Kate's cheeks as she fought the impregnable block of humanity ahead of her in growing desperation. She must get to him! She had loved him all her life. She could not let him die here alone, little knowing she was so near.

There was another thunderous roar. She saw the iron roof above the platform tilt and begin to topple towards her, yet the only image in her mind as it hit her was that of a photograph of a young Lancer officer smiling just at her.

CHAPTER NINETEEN

As the troops on the Western Front prepared to face another winter in much the same positions they had held the previous year, the Russians abandoned their struggle against Germany and sued for a separate peace at the outbreak of civil revolution. With the country in ferment, the Tsar and his family deposed and under guard, and the army a law unto itself, the collapse of this huge former ally changed the emphasis of the war entirely. A mass of German troops were released from the Eastern Front to move to France and Belgium ready for a major confrontation with men who were weary, disheartened and shattered by battle.

When the situation looked extremely black in Europe, the fight against the Turks in the Middle East was starting to turn in the Allies' favour. In Palestine, where an eccentric officer named Lawrence was making a name for himself by leading Arabs in attacks on Turkish supply trains, the long drawn out attempt to drive back the Turko-German force which had begun with the tragedy of Gallipoli began to take effect. A new overall commander had been appointed and, with his installation and news of the success of numerous small onslaughts on outposts all along the line held by the enemy, came the hope of sweeping across the whole of the Holy Land.

In the latter half of that summer of 1917, the Egyptian Expeditionary Force rested and prepared for an all-out campaign against the enemy line stretching from Gaza to Beersheba, which covered difficult terrain where the soldiers' additional enemy was the scarcity of water. The battle plan took account of this, for an army could only move in these areas with the aid of thousands of animals who also needed water. Wells, then, were essential to the success of any campaign. As on the Western Front where the weather had often defeated even the most determined of troops, the forces of nature were liable to decide the outcome of the autumn battles in Palestine.

Tim joined a battalion of the West Wiltshire Regiment which consisted of men seasoned in semi-desert warfare. They were encamped in a forward base on a barren stretch between low hills, and Tim's first impression was of a yellow land beneath a yellow sun which made a man's eyes ache and his body burn. He was one of a number of reinforcements who had arrived on the same ship and were not acclimatized, so it was fortunate that a stalemate situation existed to allow them time to adjust to the tremendous heat.

The officers of the battalion were the usual mix of boys and older men; the brash, the introverted, the thinkers and the doers. There were only two other regular officers; the CO, Major Harriday, and another captain named Robert Cheshire, who had passed out of Sandhurst a year before Tim. A casual friendship had sprung up between the two captains, but both had learned not to grow too close.

After the failure of the second attempt to capture Gaza, a great deal of time was spent by the new command hierachy to review their strategy. They knew they had to contend with the very tricky problem of feeding and watering their force, in addition to fighting the enemy. The railway was the lifeline, but the Turks dominated most of it. Few routes were negotiable by wheeled transport, so animals were the only alternative. Thousands of horses, camels and mules were assembled during the summer while regiments were being reinforced by every boatload. Meanwhile, small raids on outposts, and patrols and regular bombardments of the outer defences of the coastal town of Gaza continued.

Tim took part in a couple of forays in support of REs dynamiting the railway, and once led an attack on an outpost which was soon aborted because enemy machine guns mowed down everyone within their range. Apart from that, he did no fighting and waited with as much impatience as his fellows for the big effort they knew was coming. Although he no longer burned with the compulsion to earn battle honours enough to outdo all other Ashleighs, a small flame remained and would not be extinguished until he had taken part in some major decisive action.

With time on his hands he wrote frequent long letters to Amy, describing the awe-inspiring sunsets and the way in which the terrain appeared magically transformed into another land of mystery and tranquillity during the chilly moonlit nights. *It puts a man in his proper place and shows his life as a mere blink of the eye of time*, he once wrote. Mostly, he covered the pages with recollections of his childhood at Knightshill and the subsequent years in South America. They were more like travelogues than love letters, but he maintained his policy of making no commitments he would probably never be able to honour. Even so, he ended each letter with a reference to the wonderful day they had spent together, reaffirming that he remembered every sweet moment.

Amy adopted the same line in her replies which were filled with small details of her life at the Regency, and pieces of village gossip relayed to her by her Uncle Lionel. She had known about Val's son long before the news reached Tim. He kept her letters and read them through during his quiet moments. They constituted that which he had longed for when he had reached London on leave and felt lonely amidst all the embracing couples at Victoria Station. He made no plans for the future; that would be foolish. It was enough to know that she would be there at the station if he returned and that he had something every man at war needed, no matter how wild he once might have been.

The news of Kate's death reached Tim while he was at a rest camp on the Mediterranean coast early in October. Vere's letter with the shocking facts arrived in the same batch as one from Kate herself, telling of her promotion and posting to an ambulance train. *Another new experience*, she had written. *I suppose I'm being boastful to say I've achieved all I hoped for in my profession, but when I'm married to Simon with several children at my knee I shall at least feel I did my utmost in this beastly war. Oh, when will it end?* The letter concluded with a plea for Tim to take great care of himself.

He walked alone along the sands for a long time as the sun slowly set, then returned as the moon cast its gentler light over sea and shore. He had no tears, just an icy band of regret across his chest. Ashleigh men traditionally diced with death in far flung areas of the world. It was expected of them. Their women remained safely and loyally at Knightshill. It was an unspoken fear that Val's son would never know his father; that he, himself, would not survive the war. His mother had tried to ensure that he would, yet she had done nothing to keep Kate safe. None of them had considered her loss. It was the men who were being killed. His sister had begged him to take care of himself. Had anyone ever begged *her* to do so? Perhaps Simon . . . but Kate was the last person they had expected to be taken from them by war.

As he walked, Tim thought about the early years when he and his sister were close. She had been a serious child who took everything too much to heart; intensely loyal to those around her and defensive of the underdog. Despite her size, she would champion anyone if she felt that they were being unfairly treated, although she had grown very afraid of their father and never defied *him*. She was passionately fond of Val – her other brother, she used to call him – and applauded Tim's vow to be like him when adult.

Halting to look out over the silvered sea, Tim swallowed the lump in his throat. Kate had never changed from the person she had been then. It was he who had changed. Life with Laurence in South America had been so new and exciting he had soon forgotten his small sister. Jon and Dick had arrived to create a new, very different family, and he had been wrapped up in his own predestined future to the extent of caring about little else. When they met up again years later he and Kate had been virtual strangers. He had done nothing to remedy that. The icy band tightened. He had actually thought her foolish to wish to spend her life in dreary hospitals with the sick when she could have every luxury and a riotous time with the privileged county set. What had Val called him? A jumped up little dingo's arse? Yes, he had probably been that.

He walked on towards the lights of the camp. What wasted years! On that last leave he had discovered a new kinship with Kate. Again it had been because he had changed. She was the same loyal, loving girl who took everything too much to heart – and she had still been passionately fond of Val, he was certain, despite the secret engagement. Vere had written that they were all devastated, particularly Simon, and that a cable had been sent to their mother and Laurence in America. Tim wondered how the news would affect Margaret. Would she, too, have deep regrets? Poor little Kate!

As he crossed the beach towards the flat land on which the camp was set, Tim revised that last thought. *Triumphant* little Kate might better describe her. Her letter declared that she had achieved all she had hoped for in her profession, and felt that she had done her utmost during the war years. Kate had become Sister Daulton quietly, seeking no praise or admiration. She had climbed as high as most nurses could hope to go – Matrons were few. Val had never reached the heights he had once set his sights on, and he, himself, had not yet done any of the gallant deeds he had boasted of at the outbreak of the war. Yes, Kate was the triumphant one, and she had not even changed her name to Ashleigh in order to do it. She had simply lived up to all the family stood for.

His fellow officers respected his quiet mood at dinner that evening, but when the meal was over and they formed small convivial groups, Rob Cheshire suggested to Tim a stroll before retiring. He agreed, having had enough of his sad thoughts.

'No matter how much a man curses this place he has to admit it has its charms,' murmured Rob, gazing at the dazzle of stars. 'I'll never again sing *While Shepherds Watched their Flocks* without seeing this in my mind's eye, and imagining the peace they were enjoying when the angel appeared and frightened the life out of them.'

'Nowadays, it's a Turk with a machine gun who appears,' said Tim. 'I doubt anyone will ever set that to music.'

They walked in silence for a moment or two. 'I've three sisters, as you know, but I've never said much about them, have I?'

'Not really.'

Rob gave a rueful smile. 'That's because I was younger than them, and they gave me a terrible time when we were children. Anyone who claims little girls are sweet little creatures with curls and dimples never suffered the way I did. It was three against one from the outset. If I retaliated I was chastised for being a nasty little boy to my dear sisters – who stood by looking angelic, of course.' He grimaced. 'They were all three holy terrors.'

'When did you turn the tables?'

'I never have, not entirely. I escaped to prep school and I suppose they found someone else to hound, but they could never resist verbal torment when I was at home. Remember those awful spotty years when you suddenly discover that your ears stick out like an elephant's and that you turn scarlet whenever everyone in the room turns to look your way?'

Tim had never suffered that, but he remembered the time he imagined he had been ousted by his half-brothers because his mother and Laurence began treating him as a grown man. A comparable period, perhaps.

'They're all married now,' Rob continued more soberly. 'The eldest is a naval officer's wife with three children whose ages coincide with her husband's periods in port over the last three years. Annie became a vicar's wife, but he volunteered to be an army padre and lost both legs at Gallipoli during the first month. Bella was swept off her feet by a chap in the RFC and ran off to marry him. That was eighteen months ago, and she's not seen or heard of him since he went back to Mesopotamia. My mother writes that the girl cries all the time.'

'He must be a real rotter.'

'A very handsome one, by all accounts. Bella always went for his kind.' He sighed. 'Much as I detested them when we were young, I feel fearfully sorry for them now. Margery lives in dread of Doug's ship being sunk, Annie's tied to a legless man who still insists on praising the Lord for all His goodness, and I suspect Bella cries because she can't suppress the guilty notion that Jim's death would set her free from the outcome of her own foolishness.' Rob halted to face Tim with a hint of diffidence. 'I've told you all this because I know you're cut up over your sister's death. One doesn't expect it. Brothers are being killed all over the place, but it's particularly tragic when a woman becomes the victim of war. It was when I was thinking that that it occurred to me they're *all* victims. Their men are being killed or maimed, and their lives are devastated. We've been fed up waiting for this offensive to begin. Think what it must be like for the women at home. They've been waiting around for three years, unable to depend on anything. At least we finally get to vent our frustration on Johnny Turk. They can't vent theirs, can they? They sit at home waiting, always waiting. Kate did something invaluable; she fought the enemy as surely as Annie's Fred did.' He frowned. 'I just thought it might help you to think along those lines.'

'Thanks.' Tim did find consolation in this echo of his own feeling that Kate had done a very great deal in her short life.

If she had lived as he once believed she should, she could have ended as the hapless Bella, snared by a handsome scoundrel and filled with guilt because she could not help hoping he would be killed and set her free.

When they headed for the tents they occupied, Tim was hailed by their commanding officer as they passed the large marquee serving as Head Office. Rob continued on his way as Tim ducked his head beneath the canvas to enter the area containing a couple of trestle tables, a wireless receiver, two or three canvas chairs and a large box with a heavy padlock for securing documents. The CO was presently alone, going through some papers. He smiled and offered Tim a seat on a folding stool. Tim lowered himself gingerly. They had a habit of collapsing.

'Will you have a small brandy to keep me company?' Farraday asked, taking up a bottle from the top of the dispatch box.

'Thank you, sir.' Tim wondered why he was there. His CO had expressed condolences prior to dinner, so it could not be because of Kate. He accepted the drink and waited. Gerald Farraday's older brother had served with the West Wilts in the Sudan along with Vorne Ashleigh, and this man's penchant for dropping into the conversation the link with the Hero of Khartoum irritated Tim no end, knowing what he now did of his dead uncle. It bore out the Elders' belief that revealing the truth would make regimental life awkward for him, although he usually managed to hide his feelings well enough.

'It's very good brandy, sir,' he said to break the silence.

'My godfather ships it out to me. I'm sure he imagines our Mess is in some Pasha's palace where we all don scarlet regimentals for dinner beneath swaying punkahs. Terribly civilized, and all that.' Watery green eyes surveyed him across the basic table stained with ink and bearing several fat files. 'Tim, I know you've just received some sad news concerning your sister, but I thought you should be given notice of something that came through with this evening's orders from Headquarters. I shall make a general announcement in the morning, but you deserve to be told before I do that.'

'Oh?' Tim was afraid of being informed of another posting as an interpreter with Intelligence. Surely his mother would not do it to him a second time.

'The details will be relayed to every battalion in the regiment, of course. A feather in our caps; a marvellous morale booster.' He picked up a slip of paper and read what had been written on it in thick black pencil. 'Lieutenant V. M. H. Ashleigh DCM, Two Battalion, West Wiltshire Regiment has been graciously awarded a Victoria Cross for an act of valour in which he disregarded his own safety in order to drag three men free of a burning tank under heavy bombardment, suffering very severe wounds in so doing.'

Tim stared at the long face of his CO while thoughts raced through his mind. A VC – the highest award a soldier could earn! The man humiliated by and ejected from the 57th Lancers had vindicated himself with a vengeance. News which formerly would have filled Tim with furious envy now affected him very differently. Martin Havelock could never redeem himself; could never wipe from official regimental orders the injustice he had suffered. Nor could he seize back those years in the wilderness of self-defeat. However, Val Ashleigh had reached the very highest pinnacle: he had driven the myth he had been exhorted to live up to into the ground where it belonged. The Hero of Khartoum had been completely overshadowed by the man who deserved the privilege of doing it.

'I can see you're overcome, man. That's why I chose to tell you in private,' said Farraday, breaking Tim's reverie. 'The regiment's first VC, and how fitting that an Ashleigh should be given it. In a long line of distinguished soldiers your young uncle has become the greatest of them all.' He smiled sympathetically. 'He's given you a great deal to live up to.'

'No sir, Val wouldn't want me to try to do that,' Tim said swiftly. 'He believes in every man being true to himself alone. I think that's what he's been doing in this war.'

Two weeks later it was clear to everyone that the expected offensive was imminent, but when the troops were told of the objective it was a complete surprise. A concentrated attack was to be made on Beersheba, some distance from Gaza on the Turks' main line of fortifications stretching from the coast inland. Beersheba contained many wells in addition to massed supplies for the outposts strung across to Gaza.

Tim gathered with his fellow officers to learn that Intelligence had allowed false papers to fall into enemy hands suggesting that an attack on Beersheba would be no more than a diversionary action to draw attention from a main attack on Gaza. To support this deception the numbers encamped outside Gaza were marginally increased, and a naval bombardment such as was usual before an attack would be mounted on the coastal town. To aid secrecy the advance on Beersheba would take place overnight, when air reconnaisance was not possible.

Summoning his company Tim told them the plan, saying that they should rest while they could in preparation for an all-night march. Relief spread through the ranks as they realized the waiting was over, and that they were not in for a long slog over the desert in the full glare of the sun. The men and NCOs were all keyed up for a fight. They had been involved in no more than dreary routine for too long and wanted to get on with the war so that they could go home.

There was a lot for Tim to do that day, not least of which was to prepare for the eventuality of being killed on the morrow. When the letters were written he checked his horses and equipment before going to the Mess tent for an early dinner. It was a fairly silent meal. What was there to say that had not been said a hundred times before? They were all tense, knowing this was to be a do or die affair, the outcome of which would depend on the success of the Intelligence ruse. Whatever the case, their orders were to take Beersheba *at all cost*, for their only hope of water was from the wells controlled by the enemy garrison. The entire operation could fail because they were dying of thirst. Tim thought that would be even worse than being captured a second time.

The sight of a tented camp being broken and stowed away never failed to stir Tim, and that evening it seemed particularly poignant to watch the rows of white tents collapsing almost simultaneously while fires were smothered as the sun began to sink. Within an hour or so there would be nothing but regular piles of ashes and other marks on the dry scrubland to record the passing of an army. The barren plain would soon return to its former state but, when the wind was in the right direction, some future traveller might hear the whisper of masculine voices or the hushed laughter of soldiers around a camp fire.

Before the sun finally set, the battalion formed up in marching order. Tim walked alongside the files of his company, speaking to them about the long build up to this moment which should herald the turn of the tide in the Middle East.

'Conserve your supply of water. Only drink when absolutely necessary,' he added. 'I don't need to tell you it's a fool who drains his water bottle before the end of a journey. A soldier is never sure when he has reached the end. Limit cigarettes to the minimum. Smoking dries out the mouth and throat. So does constant chatter. So you, Marks, Davies, Pointer and Pratt – to say nothing of Corporal James—' (that raised a laugh) '—will do well to remember that maxim. Right then, put your best feet forward and enjoy a moonlit walk.'

He mounted the brown gelding bearing his essential gear on its back, feeling full of confidence. He had taken steps to know his men; they respected and trusted him. How much of that was due to the fact that his name was Ashleigh he would probably never know, but they had certainly been heartened by having as their leader a close relative of the man who had just won a VC for the regiment.

They moved off beneath a sky streaked with carmine; a long, long line of men hung about with rifles, ammunition, water bottles, bayonets, rolled blankets, mess tins, field dressings and emergency rations. They had a great distance to march and a battle to fight when they arrived, but it was better than sitting around achieving nothing. If any of them thought of other armies who had crossed this holy land before them, they kept silent on the subject. They were more likely to be thinking of home and how winning this encounter would get them back there all the quicker.

Tim rode with a quiet mind, sensing that what lay ahead for him was in the lap of the gods. There was a stirring aspect about riding beneath a night sky that seemed to go on forever; one so full of stars it almost took a man's breath away. Every now and again he dismounted and led his horse to give the beast a rest, and to stretch his own legs. Several times he rode back along the column to check that his company was in good spirits and still fit. During the brief rest breaks along the route, Tim lay full length gazing at the heavens, lost in his thoughts. At one such stop it occurred to him that it no longer mattered what his name was. He was simply one of an army on the way to a fight to the death, in which each soldier would play his part to the utmost. Tim Ashleigh would do no more nor less than Tim Daulton. It had taken twenty-eight years to discover that.

They arrived as dawn was throwing pale light over the sky to their right, and they halted to await the order to advance. Each man was warned to retain some water in his bottle. When the sun came up he would need to drink, and there was a long, uncertain day ahead. One look at the town surrounded by outer fortifications, armed with heavy artillery and ringed by two lines of fortified trenches, told Tim that *at all cost* was about right. It would definitely turn into a do or die struggle. The Turks under German command in the garrison had every advantage, no matter how many attackers came at them. To reach even the outer defences it was necessary to cross an open plain offering no protection from gunfire. When the order came, they must all go without thought or hesitation. If Beersheba was not taken, the entire force would die of thirst on that plain.

The West Wilts formed part of the main assault force, while large numbers of British and Anzac cavalry, plus contingents of the Camel Corps, had taken up positions on each flank. By sheer weight of numbers they must win the day eventually. How long it took would depend on whether or not the Intelligence trick had worked. If there were massive reinforcements hidden inside the town to prevent the seizure of the wells . . . Tim would not dwell on that prospect.

They stood-to as the sun began to tint the horizon. Tim had two young subalterns who were steady and intelligent; his NCOs were all experienced in battle. He knew his company would aquit itself well today. Two minutes to go! Glancing to his left he spotted Rob Cheshire. They nodded at each other; this is it, good luck! The second hands of numerous synchronized watches reached twelve. Voices hoarse with tension and lack of water yelled the order to advance. At the same moment, the heavy guns brought up to attacking positions opened fire on a garrison taken by surprise by this major assault. The morning silence was shattered. The ancient biblical town of Beersheba became a place of unholy mayhem.

Tim started forward at a slow run. The plain was wide. Better to wait until they drew nearer before expending more energy. The ground began rising up all around the settlement as shells burst continuously, and soon return fire was creating matching destruction not far ahead of the attackers. Clouds of dust hung in the air obscuring vision of what lay ahead. Tim ran into this, revolver in hand, grenades stuffed into his pockets. The dust stung his eyes, making them water. He dashed a hand across them, but grains of grit had lodged there and continued to prick as he dodged shell holes. He heard a voice yelling encouragement. It was his own. This was what he had trained for; what he did best because it was in his blood. He was fulfilling the dream he had had since childhood, fostered by a white-haired general's vivid tales of military endeavour.

Shells were falling thick and fast. So were men. Tim ran on. Stretcher bearers would pick up the wounded and dying. They must be left where they lay. The roar of battle increased: heavy artillery, machine guns, men yelling to instill fear in the enemy, confidence in themselves. Tim quickened his pace, waving his arm to speed up those behind him. Then, through the film of fine dust, he saw he had almost reached the outer defences. The machine gun spitting bullets with unremitting ferocity must be put out of action or they would never pass through towards the town.

Signalling his subalterns to split the company into two attacking waves, Tim discovered he had only one junior officer left, and a decimated company. They all prepared to rush the outpost on his heels, and Tim left his revolver to swing on its lanyard as he took a grenade from his pocket. The gunners had spotted what was afoot and turned their fire on the advancing company.

Tim was hit in the hip, but ran on pulling the pin from the grenade and hurling it. A fusillade of rifle fire told him his men were backing him, but it would take grenades to put the post out of action. When he was then hit in the right arm, he threw the next grenade with his left – something he had perfected at Sandhurst. It blew away half the sandbagged position.

From the corner of his eye Tim saw the entire advance had been halted by the row of outer defences, which were taking great toll of the attacking infantry. As he was now closer he dropped to the ground hoping to crawl beneath the gun's line of fire. He drew out another grenade, but it slipped from his sweaty grip and rolled away. When he moved to reach it he discovered that he was not yet under the gun's trajectory. The sandy soil danced beneath a flurry of bullets, and his right hand turned into a bloody mess as it stretched for the grenade. Anger overrode pain. Heaving himself forward by digging his forearm into the loose earth he took up the weapon, pulled the pin with his teeth and flung it with all his strength. He had the satisfaction of seeing the destruction of the gun and gunners before a great roar preceded a hot rush of air, and something hit him in the back to bring blackness.

When consciousness returned, the sun was high and burning into his skin like fire. He was lying face down; his pith helmet lay several feet away. When he tried to reach it he found he could not move more than his head. He had no feeling in his arms or legs, and no control over them. He felt no pain, but he knew the sun would finish him off if he lay there for long without protection for his head. Lifting it to glance around he saw bodies lying across a wide area – bodies stilled in death. Had the stretcher bearers left him believing him also to be dead?

The battle was still fiercely underway not too far ahead. The day was not going well. Now past the outer fortifications, the infantry were having a hard time moving on the town itself. They appeared to be pinned down some distance from it.

He longed for water, but could no more reach for his water bottle than for the pith helmet. What was wrong? How long had he lain there? From the position of the sun the morning must be well advanced so, if he was so badly hurt, why was he still alive after so long? The answer drifted away into the mists of semi-awareness, and when he came from them again he knew it was because agony had overtaken him. His whole body throbbed with pain; he felt aflame with heat. With a determined effort he raised his face to stare ahead. The sun almost blinded him so that he saw nothing but a yellow shimmering blur. The noise of battle continued unabated. He tried to focus his thoughts because his eyes could tell him nothing. The sun was high overhead. Midday, and still the town had not been taken? They dare not fail. The wells were their lifeline.

Thirst tormented him on that thought. Now he could move; now he could drag from beneath his prone body the corked bottle. It increased his pain, but he must drink. Pulling the cork with his teeth he upended the bottle. Little more than a trickle touched his parched lips. His fingers felt the hole where a bullet had passed through it, although he still could see nothing but a blur. Slowly, he reached for the pale mound just ahead on the ground and pulled the pith helmet over hair that was wet and plastered to his head. The effort proved too much and he passed out again.

The sun was westering when next he grew conscious, and battle was still enjoined over in the direction of Beersheba. How could it not have already fallen to such numbers? They must capture it *at all cost*. The words rang in his head where blood pumped like the sound of thunder. *At all cost*. He moved his limbs one by one. It proved an ordeal, but each obeyed his will. That meant he could continue to play his part *at all cost*. A new thought joined that one. A man had once crawled across the desert with a vital communiqué: a man fatally wounded but driven on by duty. He had gone on for as long as life remained within him.

Tim's right arm proved useless, so he dug his left forearm into the soft, sandy soil and levered himself forward peering ahead in the hope that the blur would clear. It did not. Movement brought not only pain but terrible giddiness that heralded nausea. He retched spasmodically for an uncertain length of time. It brought an end to the dizzy sensation but left him exhausted and drenched with sweat.

Gritting his teeth he forced himself into a half-sitting position, propped up by his left arm. There appeared to be a lot of blood everywhere, but there was a communiqué to deliver. A vital message that would save the garrison. Or was there? Yes, it had to be saved *at all cost*. He inched forward dragging his legs along the sand. He would get there. He would pay whatever price was necessary.

At that point, the thunder in his head reached unbearable volume, and the giddiness returned as it increased further into the greatest magnitude of sound he had ever heard. The ground beneath him began to shake as if at the onset of an earthquake. He knew enough to distinguish it from the noise of battle. It was coming from behind him. Turning his head, his blurred vision could make out only a long dark line dancing up and down.

Tim blinked several times hoping to clear the veil from his eyes, but to no avail. The dancing line came on towards him, elongating and darkening as it did so. The earthquake gathered in ferocity beneath him until he was shaking along with the ground. Held immobile by a mixture of fear and fascination, Tim watched the sombre phenomenon grow taller and denser as it swept down on him with all the thunder of the centuries in its wake. Only when it was almost upon him did memory override his deceptive sight to tell him what it was. He had seen one several times in his life but never from the ground right in its path.

The cavalry chargers raced towards him until they were near enough for a brief vision of bronzed men holding aloft bayonets that flashed in the sun, and lathered horses with wild eyes whose hooves pounded the plain leading to Beersheba. In the split second before they reached him, Tim heard voices yelling blasphemies in the manner of the black sheep of the family. It was strangely comforting.

New Year's Day 1918. Knightshill was filled with people, as usual, but as Vere surveyed those who were sitting around the long table in the panelled dining room he could not subdue a feeling of dismay that the old house was reverting to its former style. For seventeen years he had striven to remove the military overtones by introducing guests from the worlds of music, politics, art and international culture. Tonight, there was a warlike predominance once more. The sons of those county families the Ashleighs counted among their friends were all in khaki or navy blue. Some of their fathers were, also. Most of the women, although presently dressed in silks and satins, were members of organizations engaged in the war effort. There were numerous absentees – either because they could not get leave or had become casualties of the conflict.

Vere concentrated on his own family, which increased his dismay. His twin daughters, who had celebrated their seventeeth birthday at Christmas and who tonight looked ravishingly lovely, each had a besotted young officer in tow. When had they become young women instead of pert schoolgirls? Why was he so certain it would be the subalterns' hearts which were broken, not Holly's and Victoria's?

His gaze moved to his stepson in RFC uniform, with wings on his left breast. The news of Kate's death had driven Simon to enlist despite his exemption from active service, and the RFC were so short of pilots they had accepted him gladly. Vere was deeply saddened by the loss of a niece more like a daughter to him, and even more so by Simon's need to avenge it by dropping bombs on someone else. Vere had never believed in an eye for an eye, and a young man with a brilliant engineering brain that would benefit mankind in the future was liable to be needlessly lost. Curiously, now her son had done what she most dreaded, Kitty understood and gave him her blessing.

Further down the table Jonathan Nicolardi, now a second lieutenant in Intelligence, sat beside a lovely French girl he had met on a train. He, also, could have been exempt from conscription, but he had increased his age by six months and enlisted while Margaret and Laurence were in America. His brother Richard and Charlotte's two boys were eagerly awaiting the time when they would be old enough to go to war. All the signs pointed to it lasting long enough for them to do so.

Margaret appeared to be her normal, gracious self as she chatted to those around her, but Vere knew she was broken up inside and was playing a part with a success many actresses might envy. She had not been close to the daughter who had left the family group at a young age, but Kate's death had hit her all the harder because of it. She must surely have regrets. Hot on the heels of that tragedy had come news of Tim's hospitalization with severe wounds. Laurence had discovered the true nature of these, which he kept from his wife, and for once denied her what she wanted by refusing to arrange passage for her to Alexandria. Tim was on the danger list, and the Mediterranean was hazardous for shipping. Now Jon had donned khaki behind his parents' backs and was on embarkation leave for France. Three of Margaret's children caught up in the grips of war.

With a sigh Vere thought of the other missing Ashleigh. Val was still in hospital in Southampton. He had fought a long battle and won it with the help of his wife, who loved him so passionately she refused to let him go from her and their son. In that one direction Vere found happiness and hope for the future. Val had triumphed in spite of all life had thrown at him. He had rescinded his refusal to be heir to Knightshill, even though there was every chance that Vere would outlive him, and he had produced a son to continue the bloodline.

Although he would have a restricted life there was apparently no reason why Val could not father more children, despite having only one lung and a single functioning kidney. There was a splinter of shrapnel still lodged in his skull which surgeons were loath to attempt to remove because it was too near to vital nerves. Val had to accept that it might one day shift and cause brain damage, but he had lived with the prospect of such things for long enough to cope with that. Fortunately, he wanted nothing more than to be discharged from the army and start enjoying his marriage in the serene setting of Woodlands, where he would be with his beloved horses all the time, as well as with a wife he adored and a lusty boy they had named Andrew Verity Havelock. Val had fulfilled Vere's long-ago prophecy that he would be the greatest Ashleigh of them all. Whoever came after could only surpass him by winning the VC twice.

All at once, Vere was filled with recollections of their youth here with Sir Gilliard, the inflexible old general who had mistakenly revered a lecher and coward. As he dwelt on painful memories put aside in the happiness of his marriage and years of peace in this old house, Vere was spurred to impulsive action. The meal was virtually over, and he signalled Benson to charge everyone's glass. Conversation slowly died as attention was drawn by this unusual procedure, but Kitty signalled with her eyes down the length of the table that she guessed what was about to happen.

Vere got to his feet, overcome by emotion the way his grandfather had been at those Khartoum Dinners. He knew Val would not want this, but it was something he had to do. Clearing his throat, he simply said, 'Ladies and Gentlemen, it was the custom of my grandfather to honour my late brother at an annual dinner in this room. We have a new family hero, and I wish to revive that tradition for this one night only. I ask you all to stand and raise your glasses to Lieutenant Valentine Ashleigh VC.'

Tim could see nothing of the other patients in the ward, or of the nurses who had washed him, put him in clean pyjamas and settled him comfortably in this bed last night. The voyage home had seemed endless; far longer than the outward one. He had then been eager to arrive and join his battalion. Half of them had been casualties outside Beersheba before a daring, full-scale charge by Australian Lighthorsemen had gained the advantage and stopped the destruction of the wells by the defeated Turks. Tim had a vague memory of horses thundering towards him, but it seemed part of a dream he had once had.

He had been in various hospitals in the Middle East for three months before the medical authorities deemed it safe to ship him home. He had long weeks to face yet, but at least he was in London near his family. Sister had told him his parents and brothers were coming to visit him this afternoon, and a nurse with a lilting voice had just washed his face and combed his hair in readiness. He was glad his brothers were coming. Their presence might help to ease his mother's reaction on seeing him.

The past three months had enabled Tim to know his dead sister well, for she had been one of these marvellous women whose compassion and courage offset the suffering they coped with day after day. Throughout his ordeal Tim had found comfort in knowing Kate had helped other girls' brothers withstand pain; that she had talked to them and given them hope when all seemed lost.

'Captain Ashleigh, your parents have arrived,' said a soft voice beside his ear. 'Would you like me to prop you up a little higher?'

'Yes, please.' He felt nervous, praying his mother would not make this more difficult than it was sure to be.

'There, that's better. I'll tell them they may come in for just a short while.'

He heard footsteps approaching and braced himself. A hand gripped his shoulder and Laurence's calm voice said, 'Hallo, son, it's good to see you.'

'Welcome home, darling. My goodness, you look terribly brown, yet outside it's snowing.' Icy lips kissed his cheek. 'They're cut off at Knightshill – you know how bad it can get there – but as soon as they're able they'll visit you.'

Tim relaxed. His mother was behaving admirably. 'Good, because it'll be more like midsummer before I can go there. Where are Jon and Dick? Sister said they were also coming today.'

'Jon's in France. Didn't you get my letter with the news?'

'Yes. I'd forgotten. He'll be all right, Mother, you'll see.'

'Dick's waiting outside with James,' Laurence said. 'The lads are both recovering from bouts of influenza, which is why they're not at school. Sister rules that only two at a time can enter the ward. They'll come in when we leave. Anyway, how are you, old chap?'

'I'm sure you know that better then I do, sir. Doubtless, you're on easy terms with the head of the hospital.'

'We'd like to hear your version, darling,' said his mother gently.

'Right, here goes.' Tim took a deep breath. 'I'm to have a false hand fitted sometime next month, depending on how the stump behaves itself. They swear I'll be able to do almost everything with it, including the bonus of knocking out cold anyone who gets in the way of it when fisted.' He forced a chuckle. 'Any chap who crosses me will get the surprise of his life.'

'I'll watch my step, in future,' returned Laurence in the same vein.

'I can't move my legs much, but there's a chap here who's reputed to be a marvel in that field. He saw me this morning and reckoned he'll have me walking with the aid of sticks by the time the daffodils are out in the flowerbeds beneath these windows. A bit of a crafty blighter, wouldn't you say, knowing I can't see the bally flowerbeds?'

'A *very* crafty blighter, Tim,' his step-father agreed with amusement. 'You'll have to be even craftier than he and ensure that you can see them when the daffodils bloom.'

'It's not up to me,' he said with a sudden drop of spirits. 'One eye is definitely useless. What happens with the other rests in the lap of the gods.'

'No, darling, it rests in the hands of Malcolm Richmond, the surgeon', put in Margaret. 'He has just now told us there is every chance of success providing you help yourself by keeping calm and building up your strength.'

'By that you mean not fretting about having my head held in a clamp all the time.'

'That's right, old chap. It's only for a few more weeks.'

Tim put on a smile. 'Actually, it earns me far more fuss and attention than the other chaps get from the nurses. Are they pretty, by the way?'

'Very.' Laurence chuckled. 'They'll have to watch out once you've had the operation. Sister has just told us you're a bit on the saucy side already.'

'Bally cheek,' he retorted, the bad moment fading slightly. 'Anyway, once they've done all they plan I'll be almost as good as new – a one-eyed chap with a pronounced limp and an iron fist. My career with the West Wilts will be over, so I'm thinking of asking Uncle Vere to get me a part as a villain in one of his stage plays. I wouldn't need make-up.'

There was a curious silence, then Laurence said too heartily, 'That's not a bad idea, although there are alternatives. With your command of languages you could build up quite a reputation in the Diplomatic Corps. Or, if you're still set on the army, Intelligence can always use men with your experience and skills. Think it over, Tim. You've plenty of time before reaching a decision.'

'They're just ideas, darling,' his mother added in tones that suggested she was in tears. 'You'll of course do what *you* choose to do. We accept that. Rest assured that we'll give help if asked, but we won't interfere.'

Tim was himself now rather emotional, so Sister's intervention at that moment was very welcome to him. Dick and Cousin James were allowed an even shorter time at his bedside. Tim was glad. They sounded so full of energy and enthusiasm. After three months in calm hospital wards amid invalids, their robustness was almost more than he could take. Like most boys of sixteen they had no tact, and fired eager questions at him about the battle for Beersheba and how he received his wounds.

He had a bad time that night, and had to be sedated quite heavily to keep him from growing too agitated. Sister sat with him for a while when she came on duty in the morning, and asked if he would prefer not to have visitors.

'No, oh no,' he said immediately. 'I suppose I got myself worked up about how they'd take it, that's all. It's my own fault.'

'It's always difficult for families, at first. They haven't seen what we've seen and grown used to, so when it's happened to someone they love it comes as a bit of a shock.'

Tim knew he could speak frankly to this woman. 'They went on a bit about what I could do with the rest of my life. I know they wanted to help, but it's a bit early for that. Suppose the mechanical hand doesn't do what they say it will; what if the marvel you all rave about can't make me walk, even with the aid of sticks? And suppose the operation can't save the sight of my right eye? They were talking about the Diplomatic Corps, or even transferring to Intelligence. It's ludicrous!'

'It's *optimism*, Captain Ashleigh. Your medical notes all say you've been in good spirits throughout – even during a storm in the Bay of Biscay. What have *we* done to depress you?'

He managed a smile. 'This is where I should come up with a cheeky response about cold hands and stodgy puddings. Perhaps it's because I'm back in England. It makes a chap think more seriously about his future.'

'All right, let's think about it together. Take your gloomy supposition that the hand will be useless, that you'll never be able to walk again, and that the operation fails. You'll then be a blind man with only one hand, in a wheelchair. You'll be able to hear, speak and think, you're wealthy enough to employ a servant to take you around and be your eyes, and you'll quickly learn to do everything with your left hand. You'll still be sane. Many of your colleagues won't be.'

She shifted position with a crackle of starched apron. 'If any one of your suppositions proves wrong, that'll be a bonus. Now let's consider the possibility that the staff at this hospital are the best in Britain and happen to know what they're talking about. I can see no reason why a one-eyed man who walks with a slight limp and shakes hands with an iron grip couldn't do those things your parents suggested – or anything else he has a mind to do, if he's determined.'

Tim felt remarkably more cheerful, and grinned in her direction. 'Even to wooing and marrying you, Sister?'

The bed moved as she got to her feet. 'If I had a pound for every man who's said that to me over the past three years, I'd be a very wealthy woman. You're nothing but a sham, Captain Ashleigh, lying there pretending to feel sorry for yourself! What was that you said about cold hands and stodgy puddings? I'll see what I can do for you.'

Tim laughed. 'You wouldn't dare, after telling me the staff here were the best in Britain.'

After the tricky business of being fed with his breakfast, Tim lay for a while thinking over what had been said. Even if the worst happened he could make *some* kind of life for himself. Those poor devils in asylums could not. On that thought he must have dozed, because a gentle hand on his arm brought him from sleep.

'You have a visitor, Captain Ashleigh.'

'Oh?' he murmured, still dreamy. 'Who is it?'

'It's me, Tim,' said Amy from beside him.

His earlier optimism vanished as swiftly as water down a drain. They should have warned him first. He would have refused to see her. 'I suppose Uncle Lionel told you I was here,' he said aggressively. 'Isn't it time he minded his own business instead of interfering in mine?'

There was a waft of perfume as her cool lips touched his. 'Sister warned me you were in a bit of a mood today, so I suggest you lie there quietly and let me do the talking. It's essential that you stay calm, so arguments are completely ruled out. We'll take as said all your protests about no longer being the man you were, tying myself to a one-eyed cripple, and your having nothing to offer me but a doubtful future. Let's get straight to the facts. My love for you has never been based on your undeniable physical charms. If anything, they made me dislike you, as you know all too well. So your first two protests are utterly demolished.'

'I haven't made any protests,' he protested.

'As for a doubtful future, you should know better than to say that.'

'I haven't said a word about it.'

'Please be quiet. All futures are uncertain. No one knows what lies ahead. *No one*. That leaves us where we were at the end of that unforgettable day last May when you said if there was no one else in my life when this was all over, you'd offer me more than a jewelled pin. The war *is* over for you, darling Tim, and there's no one else in my life. So go ahead and make your offer.'

Suddenly breathless, he said, 'This is ridiculous!'

'I know. When I'm longing to repeat that night we spent together, all I can do is say yes, yes, yes and start planning for the day we walk out of here arm in arm.'

'Amy, you don't know what . . .'

'Is everything all right?' asked Sister's voice.

'Very,' Amy replied in her firm businesswoman's tones Tim knew well. 'Captain Ashleigh has just asked me to marry him and I've accepted.'

'Splendid!' said the woman who had given him a talking to before breakfast. 'He asked me no more than two hours ago, but I turned him down.'

Both women laughed, and the sound of their merriment brought hope and determination bubbling up inside Tim again. He *would* damn well walk out of here arm in arm with Amy, and he would see everything around him on each step of the way. Then he would visit Uncle Lionel and shake him by the hand with an iron grip. That would be something for the man to tell them all in the bar of the Stag's Head that evening!

The investiture took place in mid-February. The sun made a brief appearance as Val, Vivienne and their son left Buckingham Palace in a cab, heading for the Nicolardis' apartment where as many members of the family as possible were gathering for a celebration lunch. Val thought it unnecessary, but Vere wanted it so much he had not the heart to put a damper on the idea. His brother had made a good job of heading the family – the heir everyone had once believed too sickly even to reach full manhood. The position had been reversed. Val did not expect ever to succeed Vere, but his son would. As he looked down at the bright blue eyes of the infant Ashleigh he saw, for a brief moment, the dark ones of a young officer on a Gallipoli beach. *I'm new at this game, Sergeant Ashleigh, so I'm going to need you over the next few weeks. You won't let me down, will you?* He wanted his son to be like that boy. He would never let him down.

The cab turned into the long street where diplomats and heads of state lived. Vivienne squeezed his arm. 'It'll soon be over, darling, and it means so much to them all.'

He grinned. 'At least I'll not collapse on the carpet in a drunken stupor this time, but I'm going to have a beer the minute I arrive no matter what you or anyone else says.'

With a wicked smile Vivenne reached beneath the baby's shawls and produced a brown bottle. 'You can have one now. They're certain to have nothing but the choicest wines on offer.'

Val laughed joyously. 'Have you got a flaming opener tucked in that lad's clothes?'

She produced one from her handbag. 'If you're quick you can drink it all before we get there.'

'Oh no, I'm going to enjoy this,' he vowed, telling the cabbie to pull up.

Sitting by the side of the road in one of the most elegant areas of England's capital, Lieutenant Valentine Martin Havelock Ashleigh, in the full dress uniform of the West Wiltshire Regiment, downed a bottle of ale with great gusto while his unconventional wife looked on.

When the bottle was empty Val gazed at her with great depth of feeling. 'I'm only here today because of your strength when I'd lost mine. You know that, don't you?'

'Yes, darling. I'd no intention of letting you go when I'd finally made you see reason and admit you'd always loved me.'

'It took me a long time.'

'Because you fought it. You've always been a fighter, dearest Havelock, and you always will be. Come on, let's get the party over and head for home. I'm dying to know how it feels to be possessed by a man wearing a VC. You will take it off before getting into bed, won't you?'

'I'll take it off now,' he retorted, removing the bronze cross on its dark red ribbon and pinning it on her coat. Then he grinned. 'You deserve it for taking me on, knowing what a liar I can be.'

She reached up to kiss him. 'Liar or not, you're all I've ever wanted. When the King shook your hand and pinned on this medal it completely obliterated the memory of that terrible morning when Father led out the Fifty-seventh to virtually crucify you.' She brushed her eyes with her hand. 'For goodness sake get me to the party before I disgrace you and burst into tears.'

The Nicolardis' large salon was filled with people, all members of the Ashleigh family. Vere came forward immediately, shaking Val's hand but apparently finding words difficult.

'Every time there's a family gathering there seem to be more of them than the last time,' said Val to ease the moment.

'You're partially responsible for that, old chap.' Vere smiled his pleasure over the fact. 'This is young Andrew's first Ashleigh celebration – the greatest in our entire family history.'

Val was watching his wife, who was surrounded by relatives eager to look at the VC she wore and to coo at the youngest member present, and he recalled the day that Ash, the drover, had crashed into their elegant tea party. He glanced back at Vere.

'Well, here I am dressed as an officer of the West Wilts, with a medal for gallantry. The old devil has won after all, hasn't he?'

'No, Val, *you* have by getting where you are in defiance of him. He'd be the first one to applaud you for that. You know he would.'